Betrayal By Serpent

JUDITH M KERRIGAN

All correspondence and inquiries regarding any written works by Judith M. Kerrigan should be directed to:
www.judithkerriganribbens.com
jkerriganwriter@yahoo.com

Published by Judith M. Ribbens
Golden Moon Studio
W2445 Main Street
Bonduel, WI 54107
ISBN: 10: 0985706600
        13: 978-0-9857066-0-9
LCCN: 2012951524

Cover design by Paul Beeley
Create-Imaginations
www.create-imaginations.com

ACKNOWLEDGEMENTS

To "The Group"—those who kindly read early versions of this
book and gave constructive and honest feedback.
And they are:
Jane Coleman, Bev Nelson, Joseph P. Ribbens, Jeannie
Kerrigan (author of *Layla*), Arica Lynn Johnson, Sarah Marie
Remmel and those who wish to remain anonymous.
Special thanks to Dawn Gray for her information on legal
firms and their procedures.
With great thanks to Cheryl I. White, author and publisher, for
valuable and honest food for thought as well as very good food
for the body.
Many thank yous to Lois Bergman whose patient proofreading
made sense of the non sequiturs, the nonsense, and the non-
existent.
To Sister Marian, SSND, who demanded I write for all the
wrong reasons.
I am finally doing it, but my way.
She would never have approved the sex scenes.

Initial comments on the book...

"...riveting. I couldn't put it down."

"...more than enough red herrings to satisfy me."

"I can't wait for the final version."

DEDICATION

To all my relations.
Most especially to my parents,
Dorothy Beno Kerrigan
and Thomas Coyle Kerrigan
and my grandmother,
Mary Ann Coyle Kerrigan,
who told me so many stories of Green Bay.

Part One

Green Bay, Wisconsin

Prologue

I woke up flailing the air, a sheet tangled around my body, fear pounding through my mind and my spirit, piercing my chest, searing my heart. I lie in the dark room, exhausted, my body shaking, waiting until my breathing slows, willing myself to a tenuous stillness.

Another nightmare. My enemies, my friends, these nightmares.

They have carried me across years of fear and loss. Sometimes I even welcome them now. They move me to action. They tell my story. When I pay attention to what they reveal, they rip me out of the denial I love so much.

As I stop shaking, I wrap myself in my quilt, leave my bed and move to my desk, turn on the small light, and begin my journal again, as I have so many nights these seven years since our world blew apart.

Writing soothes me, calms my anxieties, mitigates the horror of the pictures that will never leave my mind, no matter how hard I try to erase them. Writing appeases the ghosts who drift in and out of my consciousness.

Writing tells our story. For seven years I've made our living writing for others. This journal has been for myself, so I don't return to the pain and loss that held us all imprisoned in grief and fear for so long.

I know why the nightmare comes now. Today I must tell the whole story to the police who, after all these years, are investigating my husband's death. I must dredge up all the searing memories.

The clock light glows 2:57 a.m. The smell of a quiet September rain drifts faintly through an open window.

Is it over? Will we finally have some peace?

One

...journal, Friday, September 20...
...meeting with police and Conrad...

This morning I showered for a long time, letting warm water and lavender-scented soap dispel the sickly smell of panic. It oozes from my body all day if I don't scrub it off. It lingers in the air like the smell of uremic poisoning in the nursing homes where the old wait to die. I must be prepared, calm, in control.

~

The police arrived at the Wentworth & Foster law firm at the same time AJ and I did, walking into the lobby and eyeing us, speculation and suspicion in their eyes. There were two of them, both in suits.

My thoughts at the time: *Detectives, no uniforms. I remember Greg Klarkowski. He looks much older, more worn. He doesn't remember me. He wasn't a detective then. Dull colors surround him—tans, greys, a streak of brown.*

His suit was dark brown, shirt white, tie plain brown. His black hair was cut within an inch of its life, looking like overgrown five o'clock shadow all over his head. There was a bit of gray at his temples. Small pouches sagged at his chin, cheeks and eyes.

His eyes are sharp, alert. He is no fool. No flash. No axe to grind.

Not so the other one. He is bald, bullet-headed, bulky, and closet belligerent. He's barely controlling his macho mindset. He swaggers, using his eyes as knives, threatening, challenging the room. His color is an angry dirty orange. I see contempt when he looks at me. His face and eyes change to a dark curiosity when he looks up at AJ. AJ's height demands a form of respect. Shorter people have to look up at tall ones. I know about that. For a woman, I am tall—five feet, nine inches. But I am accustomed to looking up at men too because my Art was six feet, four. I know what that feels like. This man is my height. We stand eye to eye.

He's examining me again. He sees only female. I see his condemnation. I know condemnation intimately. I have experienced it before from others. And from myself.

They did not introduce themselves.

I wiggled my fingers in a small wave to Ardith Seacrest, Conrad's executive secretary, who was serenely typing dictation as we entered, her earpiece set over her perfectly coiffed pale blonde hair. She removed the earphones and asked us all to be seated.

I spent the waiting time wandering around the office, looking at the new collection of artwork now on the walls. I'm at home here, having worked part time for the firm for years, since Conrad offered me a job.

As usual, AJ's blue eyes, peering from under his mop of unruly curly black hair, moved from detail to detail in the room, memorizing everything, his long legs stretched out in front of him.

By use of a discreet button Ardith had already alerted Conrad we were here and he suddenly entered the room. The faint cool smell of his aftershave floated by on the air. A touch of spice, a smidgeon of mint and some fragrance that reminded me of pictures of Thailand.

What a beautiful gray suit. Thai silk. Perfectly tailored. I haven't seen that one before. It must be new. He looks like an ad for men's suits from GQ or some upscale men's magazine.

He faced the police, seated before him. Klarkowski relaxed a bit, but the other man remained tense and coiled.

"Gentlemen, I'll be with you shortly. Help yourself to coffee. It's been freshly made," he invited and he indicated a shelf where several pots were perking away, the aroma combining with the rose-scented sachets Ardith always keeps on her desk.

I love the smell of this place.

Then he turned to us. "Anna, AJ, would you come in, please?" We followed him into his office.

Conrad offered us his usual selection of teas and coffees, his "private stock" as he calls it. As I made tea for myself and got AJ some coffee, he wasted no time in getting to the point.

"Anna, given that you've been having more posttraumatic stress again, are you sure you want to go through with this? It may be very difficult, even though these memories are seven years old. They'll want details, may want to question you extensively. Keep in mind that I will be the one in control though, which is why I set the meeting here. Better here than at police headquarters. Still..."

He waited for my answer, frown lines creasing his forehead.

Seating myself at the long table that dominated his office, I shut my eyes. The night had been difficult. Preparing for this meeting has triggered gruesome memories. I was lucky Conrad was at The House when the police called two weeks ago. He was able to set the meeting here, telling them he had reasons for wanting to sit in on it.

"I had very little sleep last night. I'm nervous. I'm worried. But three deaths now are enough. I don't want any more. If this will help, I want to do it."

My mind saw the figures of Art, Andy and Sam as they had been while alive; as they had been for the many years my husband's law firm was part of our lives. The Firm, we all called it: O'Keeffe, Kinnealy, Soderberg and Moss. It was everything to all of us, the fulfillment of our portion of the American Dream of upward mobility, our livelihood and symbol of success.

"I want to contribute anything I can to finding out what's going on. If going over events from all those years ago will help, well then I'll do it. Maybe what AJ and I remember will help. Maybe this will put it all to rest."

"Did you bring your journals?"

"Yes. The shorter version and the full transcriptions. I'll be using the condensed version today, leaving out the more personal parts. Did you get the files I emailed to you?"

Conrad nodded. "Yes, and I've read enough of them to know the police don't really need your input to continue their investigation. They're fishing. That's why I offer you a way to back out."

"I can do this."

AJ, in jeans and a Packer sweatshirt, was standing at the window, watching the gulls and pelicans fly over the river. He turned to Conrad, arms folded across his chest.

"Tell me again why we have to do this. I just got in from Minnesota an hour ago and before we do this I'd like to know more about why."

AJ, at twenty-seven and just finishing his MD, has never been one to do anything without finding out all about it first.

"Absolutely." Conrad nodded emphatically. "I'll keep it brief. In the process of negotiating your mother's settlement with The Firm since your father's death, I found some suspicious discrepancies in their books, including a large influx of money just before your father was killed.

"Anna, I will discuss that with you later. You'll need to know more about that." He turned back to AJ.

"Parallel to that, the police departments of Northeast Wisconsin, especially Green Bay and Brown County, have for years battled a rising tide of drugs in the area. Because of the death of your father and two other members of The Firm, they have begun to question if there may have been a connection. This is particularly true due to the most recent death of Sam Soderberg, which is reported to have been execution style. Even though Sam left The Firm some time ago, tentacles of suspicion reach back for many years.

"They are aware, as is anyone who reads the papers and watches TV, that there's been a Mexican connection with drugs for a long time. I'm sure you realize law enforcement agencies, local through international are exploring every avenue to combat the resulting crimes.

"Since you were the family members who went to Mexico just after your father died, it's logical that the police called and asked if Anna would cooperate by telling them all she remembers of what happened back then. She agreed and volunteered your services also. I hope that's all right with you?"

He raised an eyebrow in inquiry. AJ nodded but looked none too pleased. "Is The Firm under suspicion? Is my father's reputation under suspicion? What's going on?"

I rose and walked to the window and put a hand on his arm.

"AJ, can we just do this? Conrad can bring us up to speed on his information later. You and I can talk more tonight. You know you've never been really satisfied with what you learned in Mexico. Maybe the police should know that now. If you want to back out, I'm fine with that but I have to do this."

"I don't want to back out, Mom. Like you said, I've always felt something was going on that we didn't know about or see. I'm just worried about you. It's re-traumatization. I'd feel better about it if I knew you wouldn't suffer this again."

"I have a counseling appointment with Grace this afternoon. She'll be doing her hypnosis magic to help me relax and release it. Caitlin and Caroline are coming with me as backup. It won't be anywhere near as bad as living through it the first time."

AJ remained at the window with his arms across his chest, body language that told me he was steeling himself for the worst.

For him or for me? We both are going to suffer with this. He's remembering the corpse. I can see it in his eyes.

I looked at Conrad.

"Let's get on with this."

Conrad hit his intercom and asked Ardith to send the police in. We took our chairs again.

Introductions were made. The other man's name was Thomas Rudmann.

Conrad took charge immediately, his demeanor changing, his voice deepening as if he were in court, his face set in serious lines.

"Gentlemen, as you know, I was at Anna's home when you phoned requesting an interview. Anna does research for a number of firms, ours included, and I was bringing her more work. I have represented her for seven years, since her husband, a senior partner of the firm of O'Keeffe, Kinnealy, Soderberg and Moss, died in Mexico. I attempted to negotiate a fair settlement for Anna for her husband's share of that firm. I set this meeting because my research into what is now the O'Keeffe law firm left me with suspicions about what had

9

happened back then, and what may still be going on, quite possibly illegal dealings. A few days ago, Arthur Kinnealy Sr. was officially declared dead and Anna will finally be getting the financial settlement due her from her husband's interest in that firm. With that settled, and two more violent deaths of members of that firm, I believe it's important to take a long look at what happened. I am recording this and will see that your office gets a copy. In view of my client's serious previous posttraumatic stress history, I will be stopping this interview if I deem it necessary. Mrs. Kinnealy does want to cooperate with you in every way and so does Dr. Kinnealy."

He pressed the button on the tape recorder.

"If you would state your names, employers and reason you are here...officers, will you begin, please?"

"Detective Gregory Klarkowski, Green Bay Police Department, drug investigation."

"Detective Thomas Rudmann, Brown County Sheriff's Department, also drug investigation."

Conrad nodded to me, signaling me to speak.

"Anna M. Kinnealy, widow of Arthur Kinnealy Sr., who was formerly a partner in the Green Bay law firm of O'Keeffe, Kinnealy, Soderberg, and Moss."

"Arthur J. Kinnealy Jr., MD, son of Arthur Kinnealy Sr. I'm called AJ."

Conrad then set ground rules.

"I want Anna to go through her journals in their entirety with minimal interruption. Gentlemen, you'll find paper and pens available and I ask that you write down any points you want to explore but save them for later questioning. I think this will keep us from getting off track. I want to emphasize this is entirely voluntary on the part of Anna and AJ and in a spirit of complete cooperation. I reserve the option to end this meeting at any time.

"Anna, begin please."

Two

I took a deep breath, trying for more calm. It didn't work at all well. I knew what was coming.

"This is from my journal of seven years ago when my husband was killed. I wrote this in the months after the events described, at the insistence of my counselor, to help me come out of my immobilizing shock."

~

...Merida, Yucatan, Mexico...September...

The long, mind-numbing plane trip to Mexico was a horror. Fear moved everywhere through my body and I was unable to stop it. I didn't know fear could paralyze the tips of my fingers, numb my toes, twine around my muscles, drag at my skin. Mostly it sat inside my chest, squeezing my heart, making every breath I took an effort.

Huddled on a hard bench in the airport in Miami, willing myself to breathe, I sat waiting for our flight to Merida. Airport smells made my stomach queasy. Someone nearby reeked of smoke. A woman's cheap perfume, faint but unpleasant, drifted by on the air. From another part of the airport, fast food greasiness edged its way through the halls and wedged itself in the back of my nose. These smells and the non-stop sounds felt like sandpaper rubbing against my senses, adding irritation to apprehension.

AJ, restless and impatient, moved back and forth in front of the pay phone across the wide lobby, on the phone to his brothers and sister, to MomKat and Aunt Carrie, one last call before we took off again. I watched my black-haired son, at six feet, four inches, towering over most of the passersby, trying to concentrate on anything but what was ahead, the final leg of our flight to Mexico.

I, who loved flying with my husband, dreaded entering the planes to Merida. Each plane on the flight from Green Bay became a prison carrying me through time to knowledge I didn't want and never intended to learn. Three planes. Two down, one to go.

AJ came back across the room, weaving his way through other travelers who moved swiftly past, or stood in chatting groups, or stood immobile watching the flight listings on the overhead monitor.

"Everything's as OK as it can be, Mom," he said, sitting down next to me. "Aunt Carrie is taking them all to a ceilidh tonight down in Kaukauna. Cory wants to sing. MomKat says Alex is wearing Dad's Packer jacket and won't take it off. I told her to let him. Marnie swings between clinging to Aunt Carrie and on the phone to her Girls. Was I that weird at twelve?"

I smiled a bit as I pictured Marnie, her long black hair, intense blue-green eyes, tall and awkwardly slim for her twelve years, phone glued to her ear.

"No, you were never weird. You've been Mr. Responsible since you were born, although some of your basketball buddies came close to weird. I've always thought you were too serious."

He smiled a little. "They were weird. That's why I liked them. They were my alter ego."

His smile faded. "I miss them. College has been way too serious. I miss the fun of high school."

His gaze wandered over the crowd, as if his buddies would somehow materialize to lighten the tensions he'd felt the past few days.

He'll be longing for the mere seriousness of college before this is over.

I shut out the thought of what would come.

My thoughts turned to Cory of the bright copper hair, our poet and singer and artist.

"I forgot about the ceilidh. It'll be good for Cory to sing. I hope he sings his own songs, not just the old Irish tunes. It's a good thing we're Irish. He'll get his chance to be himself there. Alex will like it too, although he's almost too, well, normal, for this family."

An eight-year-old composer-poet and a ten-year-old sports nut-accountant. A twelve-year-old wannabe princess, and a twenty-year-old who wants to know everything. What a contrast!

Normal is a relative term for this family. Alex will want to go to school and spend endless hours on the basketball court. Marnie will gather Sammi and Alicia and more of her Girls and encase themselves in the world of makeup and fashion magazines. Cory will compose poetry and songs and his little mini-plays.

Good! Let them! Better they're not here!

And AJ, our doctor-to-be, is here to help me identify a dead body—his father's body.

Thinking about the children, I forgot my own apprehension, but it returned quickly and a wave of guilt and longing twisted through me. *I want to be able to comfort all of them and here we are and there they are.*

Until the Mexican police and the consulate had said only two should come, we'd had a long family discussion about how to get us all to Mexico. Trying to decide if and how we could all go made the suspense and tension worse, nearly precipitating a family argument.

When the first call came, Cory and Alex, their imaginations on overtime, immediately went into scenarios of how they would rescue their father from the jungle. Marnie, at twelve, as Daddy's Girl, simply refused to think there was anything wrong, believing her dad, her hero, could not possibly be harmed. I wanted to be together with them so I could comfort them with hugs and touches and reassurance. I wanted to be brave for AJ's sake too.

I'm their mom. I'm supposed to be brave for everyone.

AJ caught the worry in my eyes and took my hand, trying to comfort me. All the while I saw his own face tense and lined. Our thoughts ran in the same direction.

Will the body be Art's? Am I a widow? Is AJ fatherless at twenty? And Marnie? And Alex and Cory? Oh god! It's too cruel!

I was already tired by the days leading to this trip, when we all hovered at The House waiting for news after that first call from Mexico. But I had managed. When Big John O'Keeffe came over and commandeered our library, Art's home office, to lead the search for his son, Jonny O, and for Art, I managed.

When our house was flooded with friends and neighbors and well-wishers and even, outside, the reporters, I managed. I was used to a house filled with people and dogs and cats, coming and going. I always had managed that. It's what I did as Art's wife and mother of our children. It's what I loved to do. It was all I ever wanted to do, be a wife, a mother, have a big Irish family.

This struggle is made worse by memories of the other deaths. I…

"Mom. Don't go there." AJ put his arm around my shoulders.

I nodded. I felt tears burning behind my eyelids. My mind swerved there anyway.

Such pain! This is bringing it all up again.

My father, a quiet drunk, slowly sipped himself to death when I was eleven, leaving a deep hole in his place, a deep hollow inside of me. His unfilled presence left my mother, Katherine O'Neill, MomKat, in a long gray silence that shut me out. Before that, MomKat had *not* been a silent woman. When she withdrew it was as if I lost her too. By the time she came out of it, I was emotionally gone from her as well as my father.

Drunk or not, I loved him. I missed his presence deeply. It shook my world. I know exactly what this will do to Marnie, to the boys.

In addition, my two much-older brothers, who had already left us—I never knew why—stood at the back of church and then disappeared from our lives totally. I never saw them again.

My Aunt Carrie and my best childhood friend, Caitlin Dunleavy, had taken their place. Not a little girl anymore, I grew up fast after that.

And more pain. Our little baby daughter who died in her sleep at three months, a crib death.

He's right. Don't go there! I have to shut this out or I'm not going to make it through this!

"I'm here for you, Mom. The others are too. Do you want me to call them again?"

Both his arms went around me.

14

"No. I don't think there's time. I'll be all right. It's I who should be here for you. I never wanted you to have to face anything like this. It's the waiting. It's hard to wait."

This waiting! This inaction! This helplessness! This gray of unknowing! This watching our belief in the security of our lives ripping and falling away like the shedding of skin. This is pain of a kind I could not have imagined. I never wanted any of my children to know this.

The PA system came to life with a squawked garbled message over the heads of the crowd. Passengers began to stand and gather their things.

"Mom, they're calling our flight."

AJ stood, pulled me up with one hand, grabbed our bags with the other, and we walked to find out what Death had wrought this time.

Three

We walked off the plane in Merida into a wet blast of overwhelming heat, humidity, noise, and screaming tropical colors. I felt slapped by the scene. I tried to make sense of it but sounds of strange languages assaulted my ears. Torrents of staccato Spanish, a snatch of German, a brief conversation in French, slow British English, and other languages I'd never heard rattled through my head. Confusion. Chaos.

People of all colors and sizes looked like they knew where they were going, laughing, hugging, chatting, while AJ and I stood in the midst of all this, clutching our bags, unable to decide what to do next. Abruptly, we were surrounded by four Mexican police who directed us toward a white door labeled "Securidad". I was conscious of raised eyebrows, strange fearful glances, people scurrying away with faces averted, and blatant curiosity as we were escorted through the crowd. A man in chinos and sunglasses lounged against the wall and his face followed our progress as police cleared people out of our way. I felt embarrassed, felt my face flush.

I was thirsty and had to go to the bathroom. Without listening when I requested a bathroom, they began the questions the police captain had fired at me on the phone days ago. As they spoke, that first phone call played over again in my head and I was home, standing in the kitchen, cutting up a chicken for supper. It was September, Monday of the third week after Art and Jonny O had flown out of Green Bay...

On the phone a strange male voice with a Spanish accent asked, "May I speak to Señora Anna Kinnealy, por favor?" He pronounced it "KEN' a lee".

"I'm Anna Kinnealy." I pronounced it correctly for him.

"Señora. I am Capitan Jesus Arispe Sandoval from the Merida Police. I am calling from Merida, Mexico. Is your husband Arthur Kinnealy?" Same pronunciation.

His voice was stern, brittle, the cold sharp edge of a knife blade.

I felt myself tense. *Why would a Mexican policeman be calling me? Why would anyone Mexican be calling me? Why isn't this Art calling me?*

"Yes, he is."

No call like this can be good. A quick shiver rippled up my back and down my arms.

"Why are you calling? What's wrong?"

Tiny lumps of dread formed and congealed in my chest. Why would Mexican police even know about Art? What reason could there be except something out of the ordinary? If something is wrong, why not a call from an embassy? A consulate?

"Señora, I am very sorry to inform you that there has been a serious accident. Does your husband pilot his own plane?"

"Yes, he does, but he's fishing right now." *Of course, he's fishing. Why would he even be in the plane? He's not in the plane.*

"He's fishing on a charter boat based at Cozumel but I don't have the name of the charter company right here with me." *Where is it? I think it's somewhere in Art's office.*

"Señora Kinnealy, we have information he was flying his plane and has perhaps crashed into the jungle but we have very little information at this time. A distress call was heard at the airport tower here but there was no time to obtain more knowledge because contact was broken too quickly. We would like to know if you have knowledge of his travel plans and the plane registration or identification."

"But is he alive? Where is he? Is he injured?"

Cold fear coiled inside me now. Suspicion too.

How does this man know about me? How did he get this information to call me, if not from Art?

"We do not know with certainty if he was the one flying the plane, but it's not at the airport. At this time we have not yet located the place where this plane went down. We have men out searching the area."

My mind jumped all over the place. *Why is he saying "we"? He sounds like a robot. The plane went down? Art wouldn't be using the plane right now. Why would he let someone else use the plane? He would never...*

"We need more information," he continued, "and we thought you might know more details of his plans."

"Señora! Are you listening?"

A harsh, rasping voice grated at my ears, demanding my attention. A police officer had thrust his face up into mine, his black mustache and goatee dominating his features, twitching with impatience. He was almost a head shorter than I am, with a wide body, heavy shoulders, hands on his hips, reeking of cigarettes and sweat. He looked as if I had insulted him. I couldn't remember what I had said, if I had said anything.

AJ's mouth opened as if he might protest but he shut it suddenly, lips clamped tightly together.

He's only twenty. He's even more unsophisticated than I am. We have no credibility with these men. Where is the person from the consulate?

I was so numb from the past days of tension, I couldn't feel my own face when I touched it. I couldn't push away the thought that this really had nothing to do with our family, or Big John's family, that it was all some strange dream and I would wake up sooner or later.

Abruptly, without explanation, the questioning ceased and I was escorted to a dirty bathroom by a very overweight, angry-looking female officer. The floor was gritty under my shoes. There were no stalls, just one toilet, no toilet paper. The seat was smeared with dried feces in two places, discolored, filthy. She paced impatiently, watching every move I made, while I took the few towels that remained to line the toilet seat, relieved myself, used my own tissues for toilet paper, washed my face and hands with wipes from my bag and tried to collect my thoughts.

"Agua, por favor. Yo quiero agua, por favor." I said to her twice. I was so thirsty. I knew very little Spanish but I was sure of these words. She ignored me, shrugging as if she didn't understand what I said. She did. Once outside the bathroom door, I heard her tell a male officer what I had said, catching the words agua and gringa.

He ignored both of us.

I had no energy left to protest when we were informed we must now go to identify the body. We were escorted out into the dust and heat and deposited in a police vehicle.

No offer of a visit to our hotel. Or water. Or any help.

While we were still at home in Green Bay, Big John O'Keeffe had called the consulate. They had told him someone would meet us. No one did.

The streets of Merida were a blur of people, dogs, bicycles, mopeds, carts, wagons, and numerous larger forms of transportation. I remember seeing a dusty donkey who I thought looked as tired, frightened and out of place as I felt. I watched AJ lean forward in the police car, absorbing the scenes with intense interest. I felt only dread.

It's strange how each person deals with these things. His way is to take in every detail. I only want to shut it all out.

Colors assaulted and overwhelmed me. Colors of clothing on the women, fiercely bright colors on many of the buildings, colored flags and banners, colored flowers, colored buses. I love color but these were, in the intense tropical sunlight and in the state I was in, burning and scraping my skin and eyes. I dug through my bag for sunglasses, which brought some relief.

The vehicle was air-conditioned, but dust from the streets swirled faintly through the car. I sneezed several times and finally resorted to holding a tissue over my nose and mouth. That drew a contemptuous look from the female officer, who sat in front with the driver.

We rode a seemingly endless series of streets, through a large business district, past colonial buildings and Spanish churches, through another district where wealthy homes displayed their superiority with long driveways and manicured lawns, and through a barrio of small shacks overcrowded with people who barely had clothing. That was followed by our entry into what seemed like a place of many warehouses.

We stopped at last at a windowless cement block building, whitewashed in some distant past, now stained with whatever had been flung at it or poured on it or quite possibly peed on it. Papers, cans, bottles, and miscellaneous junk had been dropped or blown or thrown against it. A cat crouched behind a large metal barrel near its walls. Three thin ragged dogs fought over some scrap, snarling at each other. The air smelled simultaneously of dry dirt, garbage, sweat from the officers with us, and a putrid stink I couldn't identify.

Capitan Arispe Sandoval arrived in a police vehicle and introduced himself to AJ. He was an inch taller than I, a thin man with a long Modigliani face. His voice held no warmth, all business. He did not make eye contact with anyone, not even with other officers. He didn't introduce himself to me.

Arrogant! He's arrogant. I have met lawyers and one obnoxious judge like that! Businessmen, too. They don't look at people; they scan them, look over them, around them, through them. He isn't even seeing me.

Without saying a word to me, he took my elbow to escort me in. His grip felt too strong and I pulled away. He reacted by taking an even firmer grip, hurting my arm. Another officer opened the door, then stationed himself inside it, as if guarding it. *From what? Why the guard?*

I looked at AJ. He mouthed, "It's OK, Mom."

It's not OK, not at all. I'll have bruises from his fingers on my arm.

I jerked my arm away and walked quickly ahead of Arispe Sandoval. A third officer scrambled to open an inner door for me. AJ followed me.

We were hurried down a straight grey corridor lined with closed doors on each side and herded directly into a bare room with a long metal table covered with a black cloth mounded by something under it. The putrid smell was now intense. I tried breathing through my mouth. It was terrible.

Lighting was dim and I wondered how we would be able to see clearly. I should have counted my blessings. Without any preliminary warning, the Capitan uncovered the lump on the table.

Oh god! Oh god! I took in a sudden breath and gagged, tasting Death.

I was not prepared for this sight at all. Somehow it had not entered my mind that I was to see a burned, decaying human body. Nor would I have been able to imagine what that might be like. I was looking at the charred remains of what may or may not have been a human. There seemed to be legs, arms, a head. There were no features where the face should have been. No hair. No separate fingers or toes, just digits stuck together. The entire body was a charred black massive cinder. Yet some greenish, grayish pus oozed out of a hole where an abdomen might have been. Flies spun dizzily, drunkenly through the air and landed on the green areas, and small maggots had begun to squirm in it.

There is no way to describe the smells. Charred flesh has a smell of its own. Rotting flesh has another. The air was reeking, dry, dusty, thick, and hot.

I was so surprised and shocked I could only stare. I tried to look away and couldn't. I couldn't move.

This is not Art! This is not human! This could not have been a living being of any kind.

I remember sensing that my mouth was open with astonishment. I closed it and was sorry I did. One breath though my nose and the full stink hit me and I gagged again. Nausea rose in my throat from deep in my stomach. I fought to keep from retching and lost the struggle. A small man in a dirty white medical coat handed me a pail and I threw up. When I looked again at the corpse, I grew faint.

I glanced at Arispe Sandoval. He seemed almost amused at my horror, one side of his mouth turned up in a small sneer.

"We think this is your husband, Señora. Is there anything you recognize?" His voice was flat, still and cold.

But he's smiling! Is he enjoying this? Is this his cruel joke? Does he enjoy cruelty?

I turned my eyes back to the corpse. More horror! I was forced to really look for something familiar. I found it.

On one blackened, clawed protruding lump jutting out from the body part nearest me, there was a ring stuck in the remains of what might have been a hand. Dirty and discolored, but with an unmistakable outline that was familiar, I saw the ring we had picked out together before we married, the ring that matched my wedding ring. We had designed it ourselves, our own Celtic design. In our entire marriage, I had never seen it off Art's hand.

In a daze, I held out my shaking hand and saw the Capitan look from one ring to the other and nod. AJ put his arms around me and I saw tears sliding silently down his face, felt his whole body trembling. There was no other way we could find to identify the body. I couldn't speak.

AJ haltingly told the Capitan the height and weight of the body seemed to match that of his father. But that was a fiction. There really was no way to tell. There were no clothing or personal effects. No luggage. Where were his clothes? His bags?

We were taken to a small office furnished with a paper-littered desk and two hard wooden chairs. The Capitan sat in one, behind the desk, I sat in the other and AJ stood next to me.

AJ read the papers Arispe Sandoval presented to us. I signed them. I didn't care what they said. I just wanted to get out of there. I asked for copies and was informed it was not necessary. That was a lie. Later we had to return to get them. We were ordered to pick up the body in two more days.

Suddenly I was furiously angry. "I want the ring!" I stood up.

"That is not possible, Señora."

"Yes it is! It's mine! I want the ring now."

I turned and ran back down the hall to the room and snatched the covering off the corpse. Reaching down, I broke off the part that had the ring. It crumbled in my hand and I shoved the loose ring on my largest finger.

Turning around, I found myself face to face with the Capitan. He was reaching for me.

I drew myself up to my full height and growled, glaring at him, rage pouring off me into the air.

"Don't you touch me! Don't you dare touch me!"

I brushed past him as he stood there and went to where AJ stood in the door with the officer who was our driver. "We're leaving now," I announced.

I walked outside. AJ followed. I heard the Capitan fume and rant inside.

After an interminable sweaty wait in the hot sun, while we both fought nausea, we were brought to our hotel in a police car.

Four

Conrad's voice startled me. "Anna, do you want to stop?"

I grabbed tissues as my eyes welled with tears at this memory. I was back in the sight and the smell. "No. I can do this." I reached for Art's ring, which I wore on a silk cord around my neck. I saw Rudmann look at the ring on my finger and pulled out Art's and held up my hand next to it.

I heard a quiet intake of breath. I didn't look to see who had made it.

I continued...

~

The lobby of our hotel was cool, air-conditioned. That coolness and my sheer determination to find a refuge in our room were the only things that kept me from fainting. There were no women in the lobby. I thought that odd. Across the lobby was the door to a bar and I saw again a man in chinos and sunglasses. I thought he might be the man I saw in the airport. Slumped over his drink at the bar, he didn't look up.

Watching us intently, a few other men, dark-haired and dark-skinned, stood or sat around. They appeared to be waiting for something or someone. A porter took our bags and stood near the elevator.

I longed for privacy.

When we were registered and finally in our adjoining rooms, we both threw up. There was fruit in a basket. I covered it up. I couldn't stand the sight of something fresh and whole and alive. A mockery, it was.

Even AJ, having begun some volunteer medical work, couldn't maintain medical detachment. After an hour immobile on the bed, he crawled into the shower, clothing and all, turned on the water and slumped down into a ball. When he finally came out, he got me up and put me on the floor of my shower where I melted into the water and my tears.

Much later, I crawled out and changed into dry clothes. Checking on AJ sprawled on his bed in his room, I began to feel a smoldering anger. *I never wanted a child of mine to see this. No child of mine should see this, ever! Why weren't we met? Why haven't we gotten help as promised? How could police do this to us?* For me, anger is good. I can move. I can act. I was pacing. I kept apologizing to AJ and wishing he had remained home.

"It's OK, Mom. I had to come. I had to be here. You know me. I have to check everything out. Even this." He got up and wandered through his room but finally retreated to his bed and lay there, wide-eyed and tense.

I became furious at the insensitivity of Arispe Sandoval and vowed I would lodge a complaint somewhere. I called the American consulate and acidly bent the ear of the man who answered, who referred me to someone else, who referred me to another. I dissolved into tears at that point and AJ got up and took over, insisting we needed someone at the hotel to help us. They promised help but it was late in the evening and no one came.

I didn't sleep all night, the sight of the body never leaving my mind, the smell still in my clothing piled on the bathroom floor. I washed Art's ring, dried it and put it on my finger again. I tried to feel something but I couldn't. I was cold and numb, encased in ice.

The next morning we got a phone call from the hotel desk. The consulate had sent someone over, they said, and could they send him up? A blond, baby-faced young man who looked like he was fifteen was soon standing in my room. He introduced himself as Sandy.

Oh my god! Another child to look after! I was wrong.

"You lie down!" he ordered after taking a quick look at me. He immediately phoned a doctor, speaking fluent Spanish, making fast notes as he listened. After he hung up he turned to AJ.

"Dude! You come with me. I'll show you how to get some help." He took AJ to a farmacía down the street. They returned, gave me two pills and I passed out. AJ did the same, after arranging for Sandy to come back in the morning.

I awoke confused about where I was, struggling out of a drug stupor, aching in every muscle, my parched mouth and throat preventing speech.

AJ was on the phone in my room. He looked up and covered the mouthpiece. "Mom, we've got a call from Jenny O. Jonny O is in a hospital here in Merida..." he broke off to write down something.

"OK, Jenny, OK. We'll be there as soon as we can get some food in us. We couldn't eat last night. It was really, really bad, Jen...I know. Thanks. I'm sorry about your brother too. Yeah, we'll see you soon."

As he was speaking all the events of the last week came flooding into my head and I almost passed out again.

Jonny O. He was in the plane too! In my grief and worry over Art, I had forgotten Jon O'Keeffe was here. How could I do such a thing?

Last week, just after the call I got from the police, Big John O'Keeffe had received the news that his son, Art's law firm partner and our friend, Jonny O, had been found by Mayan Indians wandering in the jungle a few miles from where the plane went down. His memory was gone. There was a possible concussion, perhaps even brain damage. Now I had a terrible mental picture of Jonny's handsome face burned and charred like the corpse.

This further news galvanized me into action.

I croaked "Breakfast!" pointing to the phone. My throat was so dry I could barely get sound out. AJ handed me a bottle of water and I drank it all and headed for the shower.

When I came out, room service was at the door. Still smelling the corpse, I could barely eat. After I dumped sugar into café con leche and gulped it down, my system came out of its shutdown.

I was worried about Jenny, Jonny's twin sister. She had been ordered to Merida by her father all alone, with no support, after her mother, Mary Bridget, overdosed on hearing the news about Jonny. Big John had remained at home until Mary B was stabilized.

"I can't imagine how Jenny's been coping all by herself. We have to visit them."

Sandy phoned while we were still eating and I enlisted his help. He gave me a quick verbal lesson in how to hire taxis and bargain for our fare. American to the core, I felt too embarrassed to bargain. Bargaining seemed petty. I hadn't used a taxi in years, not even in Chicago. More strangeness assaulted my mind, piling small irritations on my overburdened thoughts. Sandy assured me it was expected and the custom. "All taxi drivers expect to bargain. Most speak enough English to understand us. Don't worry." I hung up still unable to wrap my mind around it.

"I can do it, Mom. No problem." AJ looked eager, almost like he was not on such a terrible journey. I couldn't put a damper on that.

"How do you know how to do this?"

"Because I've been talking to the guys downstairs. It's early afternoon, Mom. Sandy was here this morning and he took me exploring while you were still asleep. And, yes, I slept," he stated firmly, seeing the question on my face.

"Sandy could have told me that right away." I snapped. Irritation picked at my nerves like rats' claws scraping inside walls. "You could have too."

I hurried to get ready.

Five

No sooner were we ready to go than the phone rang again. It was the Capitan. "We are prepared to escort you to the site of the plane crash. You will leave in one hour. You will need a car and driver."

His voice sounded angry. It was an order. *He's still angry about the ring. Well, I don't care.*

"We will have to have our own car and driver?"

"Yes. Have your driver call this number and obtain directions. Please do not be late." He rapped out a series of numbers in Spanish and hung up. I hurried to write them down, afraid I might not get them right.

I didn't know it then but every hotel had men who came in the morning to sell their services for touring or other help. AJ called Sandy, who told him what to do. "Dude, just go to the lobby and tell the concierge your problem."

I called Jenny, apologizing, letting her know we would be there as soon as possible. I was on the phone with her when AJ returned. "We'll call you again as soon as we're back. I'm so sorry...yes...bye."

He began to get his backpack together. "They're getting us someone, Mom. He'll be here in about fifteen minutes. He's contacting the police to make arrangements about where to meet them."

When the man arrived at our door, I had a strong suspicion the person we got was related to the concierge. They looked enough alike to be brothers. I worried about whether the man could meet our needs. We were going to need more than the usual tour guide. We got lucky.

Ramon Aguilar, Mayan and Hispanic, proved to be intelligent, well educated, and fluent in English. He was taller than the Mayan men I had seen, broad-shouldered, lean, nice-looking but not overly handsome, and clean-shaven except for a generous but carefully trimmed mustache. His manner was warm as he welcomed us to Mexico.

He smiled up at AJ and I watched as, amazingly, he and AJ seemed to bond almost instantly. *AJ has always wanted an older brother. Ramon could fit that role.*

After shaking hands and exchanging greetings with AJ, he made a slight bow to me.

AJ explained what we had to do. The smile left Ramon's face. "There will be no problem, Señor y Señora , to get you there. It is perhaps one hour east of here. I am so sorry for your loss. I will see to it you are helped in every way. I have a large family to help me and we have a small but very good business to help people such as you."

"We can pay your fee," I said quickly, not wanting to bargain.

"Mom, it's all arranged. It's ok. The concierge did it." AJ and Ramon looked at each other, smiled and nodded.

It was not ok. I remembered... *this is the week Art and I were supposed to spend alone together on Isla Mujeres, our second honeymoon, our time to be closer.* He had talked about having a room in a big luxury hotel but I begged for a small hotel on the Island of Women, wanting to have long talks and make love as freely as we had when we first married, when we first bought The House and "christened" every room in it with our passion. I wanted deep reconnection after the years of going in different directions out of necessity. He had seemed touched by this and got us a suite in a small hotel. I had anticipated such a beautiful time.

AJ read my look. "Oh, god, Mom! I'm sorry."

He explained to Ramon as I struggled to contain my tears.

"Señora, I am so sorry. Si tu quiere, if you want, I will try to arrange for another time with the policía."

"No. No."

I took a deep breath. "This must be done. I can do this. I have to do this. I will do this! Let's just go."

"Mom, do you want to call home first? We haven't called home. They don't even know we're here yet and we have to tell them..." he choked and couldn't go on.

Oh, No! We still have that to face yet! I still have to tell the others their father is dead. It was a symptom of my stress that I had completely blanked that out. *How could I forget such a thing?*

I was silent for a few minutes, picturing their faces, struggling to decide what to do. "No. Not yet. It will be a long call. We need to see the plane first. We need to find out all we can first. After we get back, after we know whether it's the plane or not, then we'll call."

The driver of our car, Miguel, was a cousin. Ramon confirmed that the concierge was also a cousin. He explained that his family paid for the right to serve guests by providing tour guides and other services at our particular hotel, that the money they made supported the extended family. He said he had taught school for a while after he left the University of Merida but it did not pay enough to provide education for the children of the family, so they began this business.

"There are many families all over Mexico who do this, depending on tourists for our income." He gave rapid instructions to Miguel and we were winding our way through the streets of Merida again.

The police station was a very clean white stucco building with flags flying outside it. Before we could even go in an officer saw us and came to tell us he was to lead our caravan. Two police cars would accompany us, one before to show the way and one behind with the Capitan.

I was startled when the officer began to ask the same questions we'd been asked before. He was polite but it was like hearing a recording, or a rehearsed act in a drama. What were Art and Jonny O doing here? Why now? What else had they planned?

He's programmed like a robot. But I have my own questions too. What were *Art and Jonny doing? Why weren't they fishing? Had they ever even gone fishing?*

I deliberately turned away to hide my own uncertainty. I had no answers.

In answer to AJ's questions as we drove to the site, Ramon kept up a running commentary about his land and

30

people. It could have been insensitive, like a rehearsed patter for tourists, but his manner and voice were soothing and he knew his country so well it was interesting, even under the stress I felt. He provided a welcome diversion for AJ at a time when it was needed.

He was older than AJ by fourteen years and when he called him hermanito, little brother, I saw a smile of satisfaction cross my son's face. It was the first genuine contentment I'd seen in days from AJ. I felt a small flow of gratitude in my heart.

I have little memory, as I write this afterword, back at home, of that ride to the site. I couldn't get my brain to function logically and I felt hollow, my insides wrenched out and left with the burned corpse. The longer we drove, the worse I felt, apprehension growing again, my muscles tense and aching again.

Driving east from Merida we followed the main highway which Ramon explained led eventually to Cancun. After about an hour we turned left and crawled along a very bad road through heavy vegetation which looked more like my idea of jungle. Finally, ahead I could see a clearing through the broad leaves of plants that grew thickly under tall trees.

As shocked as I had been with the corpse, the visit to the site became my worst moment of the entire trip. In the dim light of the morgue, the body seemed unreal. In the intense light of day, the crash site was not.

I struggled out of the car stiff with apprehension, feeling like a wooden doll. I smelled gas and oil and burning.

We walked a short way down a path through large bushes, their overhanging leaves reaching out to brush my body. The intense green energy of the plants vibrated around me. As we entered the clearing, I looked up and my heart broke. A long vine with stunning pink and wine-colored orchids had been growing on a tree. The end of the vine held an orchid slashed, bruised, and dead. The vine was torn out of the tree and dying, its flowers wilted, a symbol and a reality of Death.

Eerily, the green energy died away completely in the clearing. Taking its place was nothingness, absence. All

31

energies had been sucked out of the space. In the center was the charred hull of the plane. Every bit of vegetation around it was literally crisp, blackened, crumbling. I felt the plants around the edges of the clearing crying, mourning their terrible loss. I felt my own energy being sucked away by their despair.

It was a wonder there had been anything left of a body. The plane had come to a stop near the foot of a steep hill overgrown with vegetation. The wings were damaged from hitting trees. A path through the trees cut and slashed its way behind the plane for at least fifty yards or more. The closer trees had deep cuts, gashes, charred trunks and limbs. The nose of the plane was crushed into the cabin, the tail almost whole but soot-blackened where fire had crawled up its sides, and dented where wood and wing had hit it. Vines and pieces of metal were tangled, coiled, and twisted around each other. The clearing reeked of charred metal, wood, burned oil and gasoline.

It looks like a bomb went off! The only way a body would be left whole is if the cockpit protected it somehow. Art could never have survived this.

I saw footprints in the ashes. The Capitan explained these were from police removing the body. One set was of bare feet. *Police go barefoot down here?* A bizarre absurdity amid the unthinkable.

Wanting so badly to prepare AJ, I had said to him "This is going to be very bad" as we were on our way to the crash site. That was a completely inadequate comment. In truth, my feeble attempts to prepare him were more for me than for any help I might have been to him, and they were useless.

In the end, his seeing the body and the site turned out to be a good thing. It's been easier for him to believe. My other children are struggling, feeling abandoned, confused, hurt, and only half-believing their dad is gone.

I'll have another round of nightmares from writing this. Images and my sense of time blur. I'm having a hard time organizing my thoughts. Post-traumatic stress, traumatic grief, Grace labels it. No label comes close to describing what we've experienced. No wonder men who return from war don't want to or can't talk about what they did, what they saw.

I heard the Capitan remark that the fire must have been very hot. I agreed. There was so much blackened vegetation around us. I could imagine a ball of heat flaming out in all directions around the plane. I smelled Death. The gray nothingness left when Death sucked Life away overwhelmed me.

I couldn't understand how Jonny O had survived. Not possible! I heard AJ ask that question and the Capitan respond, saying he believed Señor O'Keeffe might have been thrown clear as the plane hit and the doors had been caught on branches and torn off.

AJ began to circle the plane, checking the smashed nose, the inside of the cockpit, the condition of the wings, and the path of the crash. He was followed every inch of the way by the Capitan, offering his "explanations" of what happened, pointing out details and interpreting what had happened to create the damage. Again I had the feeling that all the police were puppets, rehearsed, choreographed in an insane but careful pavane.

I had no doubt it was The Plane. There were all our children's names on the tail, scratched, smudged and blackened by the fire. Seeing their names in this strange and frightening place unraveled the last of my control.

I was praying Art had died quickly, immediately, but my mind kept seeing a human being burning inside the cockpit and I started hearing screams. At that moment I became frozen to the ground where I stood, my skin began crawling, my muscles jumping and twitching erratically. I couldn't stop hearing screams and my eyes wouldn't focus anywhere else but on the plane. I felt myself falling into another dimension.

The screams inside my head got louder and louder and became my screams. As I slumped to the ground, Ramon, quickly at my side, gestured to some of the people and I felt arms pick me up. Ramon and AJ brought me over to a wooden shelter. My screams became whimpers. I collapsed again onto my knees and lost track of time. I had the sensation of moving far away to another world.

When I was able to look up, there was an impossibly old brown woman, face lined with a thousand of the tiniest, finest wrinkles I'd ever seen, smiling gently at me, holding her hands on each side of my head, a few inches from my hair. She could not have been more than four and a half feet tall. As I looked at her through my tears, she became my Irish great-grandmother, who we had called the Elf Queen, a woman who, I had been told, flooded our lives with love.

I have her hair! I have her green eyes!

The Elf Queen wavered in front of me, dressed in the deep blue of the sea, the dark auburn waves of her hair framing the pale translucent skin of her oval face. Colors of blues and greens, flecked with gold, shimmered in her eyes, which were full of compassion. Somehow I knew she understood exactly what was happening to me. *She knows me! How does she know me?*

I had not known my great-grandmother. She was called "The Druidess" by my Great-Uncle Padhraig. She had died long before I was born, but I was raised on stories of her healings, her miracles, her opposition to the church, her immense love for our family. I had never seen her before. Family photographs of her were blurs of overexposure. Yet I knew her.

The Elf Queen reached out her hand and I felt her soft touch in the center of my forehead.

Ramon, now behind me, holding me up, said something to the native people in his language. The Elf Queen put a cup in my hand and mimed drinking. I drank. Two younger women knelt down on each side of me, supporting me.

I have no idea how long I knelt there and I don't know what was in the drink. After the first sip I drank slowly, deeply, with my eyes closed, still somewhere else. In tiny stages, my mind refocused and I came back. The Elf Queen was gone, the old Mayan grandmother standing there now. She smiled and nodded. I nodded to her. When my strength came back and I was able to rise, she took my hands in hers, gave them a squeeze, shook them twice, turned and left, my hands still feeling the strength and coolness of hers. *I can feel her hands now.*

I remember being puzzled by a contemptuous look on the Capitan's face as he looked at the old woman and the people around us and then at me.

Standing there, I prayed that Art had died quickly, immediately, immensely grateful that Jonny O had been thrown clear somehow.

Ramon took us back to Merida, got us food and whatever we needed.

That night we called home and told them all that we saw. It was a terrible ordeal for all of us. A terrible long phone call, that was.

~

I stopped my reading and felt the men around me stir quietly. I needed a drink badly. My mouth was so dry my voice rasped. I gulped tea.

When I could speak clearly I explained, "I never wrote that down, about the call, those details. I couldn't. And it was a long time before we all believed Art was dead. Even when we brought that heap of burned flesh back that we called his body and went through the motions of a funeral, we struggled to believe."

I was seeing again the blackened corpse that had crumbled apart more with every move, into the casket there, flying home, and finally, at the funeral home. The undertaker told us he'd never seen a burned corpse where no teeth and bones survived. We had only ashes. I was feeling tears run down my cheeks, remembering the terrible task of telling my children their dad was dead.

Conrad stopped me by raising his hand. He looked stricken.

"Anna, I had no idea this was going to be as detailed as it is, as..." he couldn't finish the sentence.

I looked at them all. AJ's eyes were shut, all the knuckles on his hands white. Both detectives looked stunned and shifted uncomfortably.

"I can go on. This was the worst part. Just let me get this done."

Six

...our visit to the hospital...

The main hospital building stood on a small hill surrounded by palms and other big-leafed tropical plants. Pink, orange, red, and yellow hibiscus bloomed our way up the curved walk. Plant-lover that I am, I had to stop and smell and touch them, taking solace in their beauty, missing my huge garden at home now going slowly to rest in the dry coolness of autumn. The building itself was low, white stucco, and cool, even without air-conditioning. I felt soothed until the picture of the corpse came back and I steeled myself for another burned victim.

I was feeling ashamed because there was a part of me that wished my own husband alive and Jonny dead. *He isn't married. He has no children. Why was it Art and not Jonny O who died? Unworthy thought. Cruel thought. Still!*

Jenny O came out and down the hall to meet us, her long brown hair stringy and uncared for, her face sagging, green eyes with dark circles around them, looking worn out, defeated. She was slumped into her jeans and T-shirt, no longer caring how she looked. I was shocked at her appearance. She had grown up as beautiful as Jonny was handsome.

She was at our house only days ago looking worried but still striking, and with energy. Now, she's drawn and hollow-eyed, her skin gray. She looks ill.

"He's sleeping now," she sighed quietly. "I'd just like to talk with you a wee bit before we go in. Just to update you on our news." We sat on some nearby chairs.

"My dad is on his way now, Anna, but he had to see that my mom won't try suicide again. She cut herself very badly. She's at Bellin under temporary sedation. She'll be transferred to Bellin Psych when they can medically clear her. They'll start a seventy-two-hour-hold then. It gives us a few days. He's going to order me back home to sit with Mom. I don't look forward to that."

She was near tears and looked so much older than her forty-six years.

"Oh, Jenny, I wish I could do something to ease this for you. I know your mom is hard to care for. Now, with two people unwell, you and Big John must feel stretched thin."

"Yes. I don't know about Dad, but I do." Abruptly she stood. "Let's go in."

Approaching Jonny's door, I thought of Jenny's mother, Mary Bridget O'Keeffe.

I believed Jenny when she said she didn't want to be with her mother. A rigid Catholic, Mary B exhausted everyone who knew her with religious platitudes, judgments, criticisms, and a whining voice. When she found out Jonny O was missing, she had overdosed and cut herself, then demanded that both Big John and Jenny O remain at her side. Big John had been at our house when he ordered Jenny to Mexico and rushed to his wife's side. Jenny would be sucked into her mother's version of hell quickly when she returned to Green Bay.

We moved into Jonny's room and I froze, stunned.

He isn't burned! He has no burns! No cuts! No injuries! How could he have escaped from that plane and not have burns? How could he have escaped from the plane at all? He looks better than Jenny.

Jon awoke when we entered and recognized me with no trouble. He didn't seem to remember AJ at first but it came to him. He said he remembered nothing of the crash.

We remained for about a half hour, telling them about the plane, in the end reduced to speaking about nothing. I was so uncomfortable, feeling angry, baffled and deeply hurt by how well he looked. *Impossible that he can look so well. Why? How?*

I wanted to ask why he wasn't burned, how he escaped. Art's charred body dominated my mind. Jon's clear skin was a brutal contrast. *What good will asking do? He doesn't remember.*

AJ barely spoke except to describe the crash site. I saw his anger, heard it is his voice. Finally Jonny said he was tired and we left. Jenny walked us out. My anger and resentment poured intensely into the air around me.

I won't take this out on Jenny. She's got enough to deal with. I willed myself into kindness.

"Jenny, if you want to use our house for a refuge, just do it. You know Aunt Carrie and MomKat will welcome you, and so will Alex, Cory and Marnie, especially Marnie. She really took to you last week. Feel free to go there when you need a break. You were such a great help when people began to show up at the house as the news got out."

Back in Green Bay, after the first phone calls, Jenny had come to our house and begged to let her help me. She greeted everyone who came, thanked them for their food and good wishes, wrote down who called and what was brought so I could send thank you cards.

"Thanks. I will. I just love your mother. She lets me call her MomKat too you know. And Aunt Carrie is so, well, someone I wish I could be like. She doesn't take the guff from anyone."

"That's an understatement if there ever was one. Well, and you just go there whenever you want. You're more than welcome. We'll call and let them know you're coming home soon."

Jenny and Aunt Carrie had spent days last week talking. Aunt Carrie is our family black sheep, being twice divorced and once widowed, or the other way around, I can never remember. She made Jenny laugh at stories of a wild young life, but when Jenny's mother overdosed and her dad ordered Jen to Mexico, even Aunt Carrie's stories couldn't lighten the air.

Riding back to the hotel I thought about the rumors surrounding her family. Gossip about "the troubles" in the O'Keeffe family had made the rounds of the West side for years among the remaining Irish families. Big John, owner of the huge O'Keeffe Construction Company, was not known for diplomacy, tact, and taking no for an answer. He'd been a great support to us for years but I definitely didn't think I'd want to spend my life with him telling me what to do and how to do it.

As we left the hospital, AJ had remarked, "I don't think I'd like Big John for a father. I don't much like Jonny O either."

"I wouldn't want Big John for a husband although, to be fair, I have to say he's been a longtime friend of Art's and that was a bit of all right."

"Why isn't Jonny burned, Mom? How did Dad get so...?" AJ couldn't finish the sentence. He was shaking from anger and I was barely containing mine.

"I don't know. I just don't know." I heard myself talking through clenched teeth. Horror at what we had seen flooded back to silence both of us.

We went to the hospital once more to see Jonny O. Big John, now in Mexico, stayed at the hospital with Jonny, whose memory of the crash remained non-existent. Jonny recognized us again and had some recall of a few of his earlier memories of times at our house. For me, it was a strange visit. I was emotionally exhausted. I saw it as if it were a scene in a movie, Big John and Jonny acting out their part, AJ and I acting out ours, none of us our real selves.

After that, there were meetings—the consulate, the police, the morgue, a funeral home, and the airport to make arrangements for the casket to be flown home. Sandy helped us fight the battle of the paperwork and "fees"—bribes, really. I believe some people profited well from my husband's death.

Ramon went with us to it all, interpreting for us, smoothing our way through red tape too. By the time we were done, we were friends. We heard about his wife and two small children, his determination to support not only his small family but his large extended familia, to have all the children educated. We didn't think we would meet again but promised to write.

At the airport, he took my hand and bent over it and kissed it. "You are a very strong woman, Señora. It has been an honor to serve you. When this is over I invite you to come back so I and mi familia can show you the famous and very interesting places of our land."

He turned to AJ. "Hermanito! I am so happy to have a little brother, even a very tall little brother! When this is over for you, come back and visit anytime."

"Oh, yeah! I will. You can be sure of it!" AJ looked so pleased.

My last sight of Merida was Ramon's smiling face.

"When this is over" echoes in my mind. It is far from over.

Seven

The funeral would have been an entirely beautiful memory. Jonny O chose to spoil it.

Big John did not attend the mass. I knew he didn't go to church so I didn't expect him to show up. Jonny O came after mass while we were still on the church steps, handed me an envelope, murmured condolences and left. I thought it was a sympathy card and just put it in my purse.

That night I opened the envelopes people had handed me, many holding money for masses and donations. When I got to Jonny's I found it was a letter demanding the return of the $5000 The Firm had given me for expenses when they heard Art had gone missing.

Aunt Carrie, still at our house, said she heard Jonny had already gone back to work the day before.

Feeling insulted and furious, I sent him a registered letter stating I was aware I was owed money from Art's share of The Firm, and I was keeping that money and told him I expected more.

~

"Conrad, I need a short break here to use the bathroom and get myself some more tea."

"Yes, of course. It's a good time to break."

He spoke to the officers. "Gentlemen, if you want to take this time to write down any questions you have for later and get some refreshments for yourselves, please feel free. AJ, do you have anything to add to your mother's story?"

"No, not right now." AJ said, then suddenly continued. "Except to say that I had my suspicions about Arispe Sandoval and I still have. I have some pretty negative feelings too about the non-actions of the consulate, mostly wondering why they didn't have someone right at the airport to meet us and see us through that terrible ordeal. Sandy was a help but wouldn't have been there if Mom hadn't called. Frankly, Ramon was more help than anyone.

"I went back eight months later to see him, to see the crash site, to see what I could learn. That resulted in pretty much nothing. Stonewalling by the police. The consulate politely regarded it as water over the dam. But I started to think then that my father and Jonny O were involved in something they couldn't handle. What it might be, well, I just didn't really know."

"Doctor Kinnealy, do you have any reason to believe your father might have been involved in making money in the drug trade?" Detective Rudmann demanded.

"Drugs? None at all, really, Detective Rudmann, except now there are two more members of The Firm dead since Dad died, Soderberg murdered recently and Moss several years ago. I wouldn't rule out drug involvement but right now, I would only be speculating on why my father is dead. Seven years ago, I thought it was an accident. Now, I'm considering the possibility that he was murdered too."

I had heard that exchange while in Conrad's little kitchen area making tea. AJ was using his "doctor's voice", authoritative, masking his anger at the implications of what Rudmann was saying.

AJ thinks that Art was murdered? I can't go there. And drugs? I don't believe it! Are we all under suspicion? I bet we are. Police are always suspicious until they rule everyone out. Is this going to be another hell just when I thought things would be settled?

I returned to the table, sat down and took up my journal, nodding to Conrad who turned on the tape recorder again.

"This part is very hard for me, as you will hear. I may have to stop briefly but I'll finish. Please don't interrupt. This is still from seven years ago, after Art's death. It was actually Jon O'Keeffe's response that began the longest nightmare of all—the fight to have Art legally declared dead and to obtain what I was owed. The Firm decided to question his death. The insurance companies, same. For a while I thought Jonny O led the opposition. In time, I learned Jonny *was* the opposition. I came to know a side of him that I had never seen.

Judith M Kerrigan

"In those first two months Jonny came several times, 'advising' I sell and leave The House, 'advising' that I really had no part of The Firm. At first, in panic, I almost listened to him and left it all. Financially, I knew we were in deep trouble. Emotionally, I was losing the iron control I had imposed on myself so I could care for my children.

"I've abbreviated much of my journals from this point to concentrate on what's most relevant."

Eight

I continued my reading...

~

Today I have to write the whole truth. I have never told this to anyone but my counselor and myself, in this journal. And God. I definitely told God. If "revenge is Mine, saith the Lord," I wanted Him to wreak it as soon as possible. He didn't then. I grew to be very angry with Him about that and many other things. He still hasn't.

Jonny O repeatedly says he has only our best interest at heart, but as time goes by his voice and manner seem to me to grow edgy and he sounds more irritated. I blamed myself first for not listening to him. Then I blamed his grief and an inability to handle it any better than we were. I finally said that to him.

"Jonny, we're all in such pain. I see you are too. I just don't have the desire or energy to tear up our lives right now. We none of us are doing well, even you." Then I saw a side of him I'd never seen. A flash of anger twisted over his face.

In a low, slow and viciously sarcastic tone, he hissed out, "Oh yes. The Kids. Always the Kids. Maybe if you hadn't had so many, this wouldn't have happened."

I could only stare at him. It was so unexpected. Then I found my voice. "You'd better back off from that, Jon. You are *way* out of line right now."

"I'm out of line?" he laughed, but his voice was scathing. "I'm not the one who puts all the pressure on Art to perform. You are a goddam baby factory. A grandiose family. A grandiose house. A grandiose life. You never think about Art and what supporting all this does to him. You never give a thought to The Firm."

He spilled out bitter invective for at least ten minutes, speaking eerily, as if Art was still here and I had to do something to fix him right now. "You take and take and take

44

and never lift a finger to help his burden." His face was contorted with hate.

I was afraid to say anything at first. I was so stunned. *Where is this coming from? He's scaring me!*

Then a small fire ignited, a flame of anger that grew into fury faster than I could maintain control of it, taking hold of me. I'd heard enough when I realized I wanted to pick up something and hit him with it. "Stop it now. Get out. Leave."

I spoke with equally deadly softness, with a vicious intensity to match his and more. I walked to the front door, jerked it open and waited in cold silence, frozen into brittle icy rage.

His look changed to what might have been horror at his behavior but he had neither apology nor any other words. He stomped down the long hall to the door, brushed past me, and just left.

I went to my room and paced for hours, his words echoing in my head, fear and rage, hurt and indignation flashing back and forth through me.

I can't fight a whole firm of lawyers alone. I don't know how. He's crazy! He has no call to say those things. Art wanted children. We loved children. We wanted more. I couldn't have more. I will, I will have what I need for my children!

The more I paced, the more furious I grew. I finally thought "Money be damned!" and called the best lawyer in town, Conrad Wentworth, and made an appointment.

Two weeks later, Jon came to my house with an apology. "I was completely out of line. I never should have said those things to you."

"No. You shouldn't have, Jon, and I just can't forget what you said."

"I know! I know! I'm so sorry. I haven't had a lot of control of myself since..."

I kept silent, unwilling to rescue him. I noticed he didn't make any attempt to take back his harsh opinions. I wanted him to admit how cruel he had been without any prompting from me. I wondered if he still held the view of our marriage he'd blurted out in his anger.

45

"I've got better control of myself now. Of course we must think of the children." His words sounded formal, as if he'd written them out ahead of time.

Where does that "we" come from? There's been no "we" in your behavior. In fact, having thought about it, I saw that there really had never been any "we" from him in his interaction with the kids. He had never made any attempt to be close to them. He made excuses, his favorite being, "I guess I'm just not a kid person."

Over time, he came to see Art, or he came to our parties when the children weren't there. He didn't seem to see me either unless I was an appendage to Art.

Now, he went on to outline his plans to draw up papers detailing Art's financial interest in The Firm and their "willingness" to acknowledge that I was owed "something" and they would "allow" me to collect that.

I kept silent.

"You're doing such a good job here," he said with a patronizing smile, "and of course you should keep the kids in the house. It's what they're familiar with."

Still I kept silent, listening and watching him put his foot farther and farther into his mouth with his condescension. He didn't wait for answers from me. He was nervous, rushing through the speech. Finally he came to it.

"You went to Wentworth. You really ought to just settle with us right now. If you don't, you know it's going to be a long battle. We aren't going to do this without a fight."

He just barely kept a civil sound in his voice.

I still said nothing

"You didn't have to do that. If you'd just waited, we were working it out. He'll cost you a lot more money. How could you have done that?" His voice became harsh.

I refused to even consider I owed him an explanation.

"No one from The Firm let me know anyone was considering anything on my behalf or that of my children." I reminded him. Then I grew silent again.

He thought I was going to go on and looked expectant. When I did not, he smiled but his eyes were cold. "Well, I suppose you'll do whatever you want. I think you will be very, very sorry."

He turned and left, his control over me nonexistent, his control over himself on a crumbling edge.

...days later...

I was on a crumbling edge too, in massive denial about my own emotional state. It was Caroline who saw it and finally insisted I go for help. I had ignored her gentler urgings.

She walked in one morning with two café mochas, handing me one. "Do you know how haggard you look?"

"Oh, thank you so much! Just what I wanted to hear."

I was finishing dishes from breakfast, planning to clean upstairs later, my hair uncombed, in old jeans and one of Art's shirts which I had been wearing in a vain attempt to comfort myself.

"How much more can you take?"

"Not much." I didn't want to admit I was suicidal, not even to myself. "I've got a lawyer though, Conrad Wentworth." I hoped that would back her off.

"That's one step. Have you found a counselor yet?"

"No."

"Well, I have. I made an appointment for you. I'll take your kids tomorrow after school. The appointment is at 4pm. The Bellin Building, Room 309. Her name is Grace."

"That's a bit presumptuous of you, isn't it?" I didn't want to talk to a counselor.

"Of course. You know me. I don't take no for an answer. By the way, your kids and mine are attending *Disney on Ice* tonight, an early Christmas present. You will rest."

Caroline had never pushed me like this before. In fact, she's laid back, has a great sense of humor and doesn't give a tinker's dam for what anyone thinks. She had taught me this lesson quickly when I was snubbed by the old money families of the East side, when Art and I were sarcastically labeled nouveau middle class.

Her exact words were, "Mellow out, Anna. Those who walk around with noses in the air will sooner or later slip on shit." This, out of the mouth of a silky-blond, athletic-figure-of-the-year, cool elegance, razor-sharp woman who moved through any economic level as if she owned the world. She sized up people in an instant and then ignored whatever negative they said and did with a fine detachment. Caroline had defied a wealthy WASP family to marry the love of her life, African-American Robinson Bradley who she once described as "the sexiest chocolate ice cream I've ever eaten."

I hadn't told her that I didn't know where next month's house payment was coming from, or about the visits from Jonny O.

His final visit that evening sent me to the appointment. Jonny showed up on the porch when I was at home alone, rang the bell, and when I got to the door, he grinned and held out a bunch of flowers and a bottle of wine.

"Pretty flowers for a pretty lady." I was puzzled, skeptical and almost gagged at his opening line, but I politely took the flowers and thanked him, inviting him in from the late November cold. I moved down the central hall into the kitchen to a cupboard where I got a vase. He followed.

"What's this about?" I asked, eyebrows raised, turning to him as I filled the vase with water at the sink.

"Well, I can be an asshole at times, and I have been toward you, so I'm just trying to make up for it. I thought maybe I could take you to dinner tonight, sort of make up for the past. The Wellington has a great menu."

He smiled his very charming smile again and leaned against the doorjamb in the door to the long hall. "You know, Art always thought you were so beautiful and I have to agree with him."

I stood there wondering if he had been drinking wine already or smoking something. I wickedly decided to see if he would go farther. He did. He began a verbal flirtation. I didn't even have to do anything more than make an occasional noise indicating I was still hearing him. I almost laughed in his face and turned back to the sink, fussing with the flowers. Finally, I asked him why he was flirting with me.

He laughed and said, "I think it's worth it." He moved further into the kitchen, leaning against the cupboards across from the sink.

Not "you're" worth it. "It's" worth it. I'm an "it"?

I decided to end his expectations immediately. I turned to face him again. "Jon, are you aware you just said 'it's' instead of 'you're'"? Are you aware that this isn't a conversation between us but a monologue delivered by you? Do you see how unresponsive I am?"

I could feel my indignation growing as I spoke. "I'm actually very suspicious. Does the fact that you've shown up at my door have something to do with Conrad's negotiations with The Firm? I do not want to go anywhere with you."

He came toward me, a leering smile on his face. "Don't be so standoffish! You can't fool me! You haven't had any sex for months. You must be plenty horny by now. Why not add a little fun in your life? I promise you I can really make your night a great one. Some good food. A little wine, well, maybe a lot of wine, and we can have a few hours in bed."

I was shocked into immobility. He moved toward me very fast, suddenly in front of me, his hands on my upper arms, grasping me. When I tried to slip sideways he pushed his body into mine and pinned me to the counter. He tried to kiss me and I turned my head sideways. His teeth scraped my neck and he tried to move his mouth lower. I twisted and struggled, finally getting my hands on his chest. He shoved one hand down the top of my blouse and tore it open, ripping it, trying to grab my breast, and rubbed his groin against mine.

I pushed as hard as I could and he didn't move. I yelled "No! Stop! No!" At my shouts, our dogs Curly and Moe, upstairs in the boy's bedroom, woke up. I heard their mad barking scramble descending the back stairs. He jumped at their sound and, slightly off-balance, moved back a little. I pushed again and he gave way, backing up.

I screamed, "Get out of my house! Get out of here!" over and over. He backed away farther toward the front hall, the dogs barking furiously at him as they followed.

"You fucking bitch! You'll be sorry! If I have anything to say about it, you'll get nothing! Nothing! I'll take it all away from you. Everything! That's a threat *and* a promise."

He turned, stomping his way down the hall, overturning the long old church pew onto the floor behind him, hitting one of the dogs, who yelped in pain.

49

BETRAYAL *by* SERPENT

After he slammed out the front door, I stood for a long time, shaking. The dogs returned and milled around, pacing from the hall to me and back. When I could move, I patted their heads and got them to quiet down. They loped up the stairs again. Still quaking inside, I crept into the hall and picked up the heavy pew and returned all the jackets and schoolbooks that had been on it, carefully straightening everything, carefully locking the door behind him, carefully walking up the stairs. I took off all my clothes and got in the shower, then remembered the back door was unlocked. I struggled into my robe and clung to the railing as I edged down the back stairs, calling the dogs to go with me. I was afraid he might have come back. He hadn't. I locked it.

Back in the shower, I scrubbed and scrubbed myself, especially my throat where his teeth had scraped my skin. I carefully dressed in clean pajamas and robe and went back downstairs to wait for my kids.

Why do I feel ashamed even now? Why do I feel I did something wrong?

I shook inside for hours. They all came home tired and happy. I only had to listen to their happy talk. Marnie, thank god, decided to sleep in her own room that night.

At midnight, I had another bout of the shakes and sat, awake and numb, in my room. I fell asleep in my chair, unable to crawl in bed. I kept seeing Jonny on top of me there. I tried to picture myself with Art, making love with him. I had lost that picture. How could I forget so soon?

In the morning, after Marnie and the boys were gone, I took my blouse and bra and burned it in the grill on our deck.

Did I call Caroline? Did I ask for support from Caitlin or Aunt Carrie? I couldn't. I was awash in shame.

It's my fault. I encouraged him. I let him go on, didn't stop him right away. I should have stopped him.

I saw Grace the next day. It was three more months before I told her of that night, before I learned that Jon's attempted rape of me is not my fault. I never told anyone else.

~

I jumped, startled as AJ exploded.

"Fucking bastard! Asshole! Son of a bitch! No! Son of a bastard!" AJ had turned rigid while I spoke but hadn't moved or interrupted me. Now he was up and pacing, anger pouring off him.

"I'll sit down in a minute," he snapped at Conrad, who was making a motion for him to calm down.

"Oh, dear god! Mom, why didn't you say something back then?" He sat down and put his arms around me.

Both detectives were sitting forward. Klarkowski couldn't keep quiet any longer. "Did you report this? He has nothing like this in his record."

"I couldn't tell anyone. I was ashamed, very traumatized, I just couldn't. I blamed myself. Besides, who would have believed me? My word against the word of a prominent lawyer? A criminal defense lawyer? No marks on me? What would you have done? Would you or anyone believe a woman now if she were to report that?"

I saw on their faces the answer to that. N and O.

AJ was up and pacing again. "AJ, sit and look at me."

He did, both anger and love in his eyes.

"Don't worry. Caitlin and Caroline are coming with me to the session with Grace. She'll be having me go back through this all again with the goal of releasing more trauma. It comes up in layers, like peeling an onion. I dealt with it back then, and I can deal with it now. I know how to help myself now. I'm stronger."

"Mom, what is this doing to your health? Trauma leaves long-term physical consequences too. We know now it can even alter DNA. I want to see you get a full medical workup."

"I won't resist you on that. At fifty-two, I feel very healthy but I still have your brothers and sister to launch into the world and I want to be around for a long time to see all of you live your lives. I want to have some more life of my own. Believe me; I know more about trauma than I ever wanted to learn. But for today, can we get on with this? The rest is really just a summary of the seven years."

I turned back to my sheaf of papers.

Nine

I noticed the detectives had made many notes and were writing down more. They were getting restless. I knew the information was more than they wanted to know and yet not what they wanted to hear. I spoke to both of them.

"I can see you're getting impatient. There's an end to this. I agreed to this meeting especially because of the murder of Sam Soderberg. I talked to Jane. I know she has to go into a witness protection program. If it has to do with The Firm, clues may be in the past. In going back through every journal I've kept all these years, four things are obvious to me.

"One, after Art's death, we all had a terrible time getting through the grief and pain. I had post-traumatic stress disorder to the point of hallucinating and being suicidal. At the same time my four children were stunned, hurt, and grieving the loss of their father. We had a rapidly dwindling bank account and I had very little paid work history and no job. I was terribly frightened by the prospect of watching us lose our house and my children starve.

"Two, I hid behind a wall, ignoring my intuition and avoiding facts. My counselor told me this is common after the kind of trauma we experienced but also I loved what I now call my 'fairy tale' life. If I hadn't had the wall, I couldn't have kept on. I still don't like trauma, but I can face it now and I want you to know that I am much stronger and willing to deal with whatever needs to be faced.

"Three, prior to the plane crash, if Art was involved in something illegal I was not aware of it. I took what he said at face value. I never saw any sign that he was suspicious of Jon O'Keeffe, never saw Big John as anything other than our friend. If there were men, my husband included, who were into illegal activities, I wouldn't have known it then. I didn't see the world that way at all. I didn't have a suspicious mind and actually I still don't operate from that perspective.

"Four, the facts are beginning to show something was and is going on with The Firm that makes me uneasy. I don't want anything more to happen to my children or to me. I need to pay attention and that's why I'm here, why I took the time to extract this information from my journals.

"I have condensed my journals as much as I am able for the above purposes. Perhaps you want to read the whole of those journals but they are private and detail our struggles to cope with the changed circumstances of our lives. I don't think my writings on that are relevant."

I paused for a breath and Klarkowski spoke.

"Actually we were hoping for as much detail as possible, Mrs. Kinnealy. It gives us a much better idea of what's happened. It answers questions we might have had to ask."

His voice sounded a bit kinder than before.

It also gives him more information, maybe leaves us open to more suspicion. He must think I'm an idiot.

I didn't want to open up that conversation so I went right on. "The following excerpts are the ones with direct relevance to The Firm. There isn't much more."

~

...two months after Art's death...

I am in shock again and rage too. Today I received a letter which I copy here.

Dear Anna,

I want you to know I'm thinking of you and the kids. I'm glad you are still in The House. Please stay there if you can. I heard AJ is working for O'Keeffe Construction. Good! Big John can keep an eye on him for me, but will you please encourage him to return to school? You know how I want them all to complete college. He'll probably have to work part time but he can do it. I'll try to see if I can get Jonny to release some funds for you. A little arm-twisting ought to do it.

All love,
Art

I am furious and hurt and sick. Who would do such a thing? Who would be so cruel as to pull such a prank? It's doubly cruel. The handwriting looks like Art's. I made the comparison with papers he'd left in his desk. Inexplicable! It has to be a forgery. I refuse to respond to such a thing. Who would do this? Is this Jonny O's nasty revenge? Why this? Why now? I have to ignore this. I won't respond. I'll give no encouragement to anyone who does something like this. I won't give Jonny O the satisfaction! It's his handiwork, I'm sure.

Weeks later the letters continue to come...

~

"Anna! Stop! That letter, other letters, what about them?"

I looked up from reading. Conrad looked surprised and somewhat angry. Klarkowski and Rudmann were on alert.

"Mom, what are you talking about? You never talked about this." AJ was up and pacing again.

"I brought them. You can read them later. As you'll see, they contained no overt or even covert threats. I thought it best to completely ignore them. Truth is, I didn't have the energy to give to them. I just couldn't deal with them. I had other priorities."

I was exasperated. I could see their judgments written all over their faces.

"I compared the handwriting to that of Art's and it seemed to be his but I was not so dumb as to think it actually was his. I knew someone could easily fake it. I believed it was probably Jonny. I also considered the possibility that someone was genuinely trying to give some comfort although I find it a clumsy attempt at best. I didn't even open them after a while. We had more than enough to deal with. The last one came over a year ago. Please just let me finish this. We can discuss the letters later. They were meaningless to me, of no importance at the time."

Klarkowski and Rudmann were writing. AJ and Conrad looked shocked. I didn't know if they were all silent because I asked them to be or if they were just so angry they couldn't speak.

I didn't care. I continued.

"Everything else related to Art's death can be condensed into a few items. I continued to get letters monthly, sometimes less. I put them in a box and placed them in the hiding space behind my closet in my room so the children wouldn't see them.

"Eight months after Art's death, AJ returned to Mexico. He had questions. I didn't want to know more. I was still in counseling and building a business. I had no desire to go to there and I still don't. He went there again two years after that and returned still dissatisfied. The police wouldn't listen. The consulate was unresponsive. The crash site was curiously intact, nothing taken by the people for salvage. He said Ramon told him the people look on it as a grave and leave it alone. They said it's haunted. The jungle was taking over. Since he's here, you can question him later about that.

"The only other brief contact I've had with anyone from The Firm was four years ago when Andy Moss was murdered. Accounts in the Press-Gazette seemed confusing to me, telling of suicide and/or murder. Possible torture. A bloody scene.

"The papers noted he was the second member of The Firm to die a violent death and they dug up the fact that Art was still to be declared dead. There was a quote from Jon about how sorry he was and how much Andy would be missed.

"A reporter called seeking a quote. She tried to dredge up Art's death. I hung up on her. My friend Cait called and told me more. I wrote down our conversation at the time.

"She said Andy was supposedly tortured because he was gay, that it was made to look like suicide. There were rumors about The Firm, that there was trouble between Andy and Jonny O, and that Andy was thinking of leaving."

~

...from my journal...

This morning Cait told me the rumors going around.

"They've lost Soderberg, you know. He's moving to Madison to join a firm there. People are thinking it's Big John's money that keeps the place going although Jon's had some really lucrative clients—lots of money and influence—corporations with big bucks, and a hint of something Mafia too."

"Andy did corporate law. If they've lost him, they lost great experience. Art always said he was very good at what he did. Jonny did mostly criminal law. Maybe that's the Mafia connection. If big corporations are his clients now, he's got the controlling power, but he may be out of his area of expertise, or not. I don't know."

Cait laughed cynically. "In my opinion, corporate law is another version of criminal law, just a different group of criminals. Have you talked to Conrad yet?"

"No, he's out of town. This will be a shock. He'll probably call soon. I'll keep you up to date."

I changed the subject. "Have you ever heard from Jenny?" If anyone had, Caitlin would have.

"Nothing. Jenny's still gone. Her mom's been in and out of mental hospitals since Jon's Mexico foray but is home right now. Drugged to the gills, I heard. Then they won't have to listen to her. She has a tongue that clips hedges and flays sinners. It's a good thing Big John has all that money."

~

I looked up. "The rest of that conversation was about family.

~

...two days later...

I went to Andy's funeral at the Methodist church with Ardith. Sadly, as far as I knew, we two and Sam were the only ones there who had ever been associated with The Firm. A young man stood far away from the few mourners at the cemetery and left before the service was over. I didn't recognize him.

...two years ago, June...

Letters continue to come addressed not only to me but to the boys and Marnie, but they're occasional, not consistent. Odd, really. Whoever does this seems to be losing interest. Good! I will not have the others disturbed more than they have already been. I meet every day's mail and hide them. Thank the powers that be that I work at home and am here every day. I can only imagine what it would do to my kids if they saw those, if they had to live in the place where I am still.

...one year ago, July...

The letters have stopped coming. I feel so relieved. Maybe I won't have migraines anymore. Even though I ignored them, they took a slow and subtle toll on me.

...three days ago...

Sam Soderberg was killed in a car crash last week, supposedly a hit and run. Aunt Carrie saw his obituary in the Madison papers. He leaves his wife, Sue, and two daughters. I got her phone number from the internet and called her this morning. Sue and I had not been close. We had been at parties, at legal functions, at obligatory meetings. On the phone her voice was cool but tinged with anger. "The best thing Sam ever did was leave The Firm and he should have done it sooner. If he'd done it sooner he might be alive."

"Why? Was he sick?"

She avoided the question. "I don't want to upset you." she said. "I know you know what this kind grief is like." Her voice was softened somewhat.

"I do. I'm sorry you have to experience this. Will you and your children be ok?"

Again she avoided my question. "I think you'd better ask Wentworth more about The Firm. I think you need to be careful. There's a lot you don't know about. I just wish I didn't know so much. I can't talk anymore."

Then she dropped a bombshell. "Anna, Sam was murdered. Details are being kept out of the papers. Police said it was done like a Mafia execution. He and Jonny O had a big fight, years ago already, over the way The Firm had been run and what they were doing. Jonny had a serious relationship with the Mafia even back then. I think Sam knew a lot more than he ever told me although I know a lot. I know Sam never stopped investigating The Firm. We've been threatened. I'm going into hiding."

Her last words were, "I hope you and your children will be safe." The phone went dead. I've tried to call her back. No answer.

Ten

I folded up my journal papers and set them on the table, looking around at the men in the room.

Rudmann was tapping impatiently on the side of his cup. Klarkowski was hunched over his pad, writing more. AJ was looking angry. Conrad looked troubled.

"That's it. That's what I've taken from my journals relevant to Art's death. There isn't much more I can add. I tried to be thorough. I don't want to do this over and over again."

Conrad stood up, walking back and forth, rubbing his chin, shaking his head.

"Anna, we should have done this long ago. Have you been listening to yourself? It's my fault. I've known since I began negotiating for you that something was not on the up and up. I put their resistance down to them maybe being in a bind after Art died and wanting to make up any losses before settling. Then I realized it was Jon O'Keeffe I was fighting. I thought maybe he was just angry because he had to fight our firm. When he finally came to me with a settlement, I thought it was over. But those letters...there's cruelty behind them, and it's behind the scenes, secret, hidden. My, god, Anna, you all could have been in grave danger."

He stopped and turned toward the officers. "Something was wrong with their books. Right now I can only say for sure there was sloppy bookkeeping. Nothing they can be charged with. I know you're already following the money, which is why I agreed to have you here. I know your departments have been digging for years. But my focus right now is on helping my client. I don't think she can add any more information. I want that clear because, in light of what happened to Soderberg and his family, I think the Kinnealys may need police protection at some point. I want your cooperation. You have questions, I'm sure. Let's get to that before we go on."

Conrad sat down again. He saw my raised eyebrows.

"Really, Anna, I'm sorry. I haven't wanted to tell you about the books until I'd found some kind of real proof and I still don't have it. Let's just let the officers find out what they want and we'll talk later."

Klarkowski took the lead. "Mrs. Kinnealy, may I call you Anna?"

At my nod, he continued.

"I'd like to let you know why we're interested in your husband's death, why we're investigating after all these years. Your account of what happened back then verifies, in a vague sort of way, an avenue that we've been pursuing. We've known for many years that there are people in this area who have been dealing drugs. That's no big revelation. It's a universal problem these days. We have long suspected, however, that there have been some men, perhaps several men, of *prominence*," he emphasized that word, "who have been involved."

He saw me sit forward and frown. I think he thought I'd protest.

"Now, we aren't making any accusations," he hastened to say. "We have no proof of who could be doing this yet, but we've been recently contacted by federal authorities and they have given us a heads up that trafficking in drugs has increased exponentially the last few months and there is a twisted path all the way from Mexico to here. We are considering the possibility that a drug cartel has been formed or infiltrated this area, even may have been operating in this area for years, *very* secretive, *very* highly connected, and *extremely* dangerous. And, we're pretty sure it's local men who are running it, or at least this branch of it.

"Our second line of investigation began years ago when we became aware that certain businesses received large influxes of money. This money seemed to have a Mafia connection, possibly through Milwaukee and Chicago. One firm in that group was your husband's law firm. Another was the O'Keeffe Construction Company. We're still trying to follow money trails, which are as twisted and entwined as the paths of the drug trade.

"Now we have three members of the firm in which your husband was partner who are dead. In addition to Mr. Moss's death, one of our cold cases, and Mr. Soderberg's murder, we are now considering that your husband might have been murdered, and involved in some other way. We don't know how. We're contacting Mexican authorities to determine what kind of investigation they conducted and get those papers up here.

"We can confirm Jane Soderberg and her children are in the witness protection program. Apparently she knows far too much of what her husband knew. Even if she didn't, given what he's turned over to law enforcement, they are all in danger. These people will assume she knew it all and will want her dead. Our department doesn't have all that information yet. Mr. Soderberg only had time to meet with the FBI before he was killed. *You* are our only connection. We've been hoping you can tell us more of what your husband was doing, where his money came from, whether he was involved in anything illegal. And even if you can't, you need to know there are those who will assume you do and want you dead too."

I didn't know what to say. Old familiar shock came back, locking my brain and tongue.

AJ was not so stunned. He looked relieved. He slapped the surface of the table to emphasize his words.

"I knew it! I knew it! When I went back the second time, I was stonewalled every which way I turned. I couldn't get anything out of the authorities. One thing I did learn. That plane exploded from the inside and not just the motor or gas tank. I'm no expert on explosions but I knew there was something fishy about the way it looked. The Mayans thought it was a bad scene, wouldn't go near it. With Ramon's help, I found some of them and got to know them and I trust their instincts. Ramon translated for me. One man, who was in a clearing on a hill about a half mile away and saw the plane coming down, said it wasn't on fire when it hit the ground and he heard the sounds of crashing stop entirely. It didn't explode until almost ten minutes later. He had gathered some of the people and he was running toward it. They had to dive for cover because it just blew. There were no screams from the cockpit. The man said the whole cockpit was burning and he doesn't remember seeing a body. They saw no one else in or around the plane.

"They searched for anyone else. They really know that area. They found no one who could have left that plane at the time. When Jon was found later he was miles away." *AJ finally is talking about his visits. He held all this back. He didn't want to make it worse for me.*

"Then there was Arispe Sandoval! What a piece of work that man was! He fits the definition of sociopath, maybe even psychopath. If he was the head of that investigation, it was covered up. You even noticed it, Mom, like they were all puppets, you said, actors in a play, rehearsed. I've now witnessed medical exams after suspicious deaths. There was no exam at all, no valid investigation at all. It was a farce! Bones and teeth always survive burning. How could there not have been some bones and teeth?"

He gave a cynical wave of his hand at the detectives.

"Good luck getting anything out of Mexico! Arispe Sandoval was on the take. He made money out of my father's death. I wondered about drug cartels back then when I was down there but at twenty, what did I know? Since then, I've been on the internet, on Interpol and other sites concerned with the cartels. Mexican police make more money from the cartels than they get paid in their jobs. I found out men buy police jobs because they can make so much money from bribes.

"Then we come to Jonny O! He wasn't even burned! That was really suspicious. I was so angry I could barely talk to him in that hospital. And then he was back here at work within days..."

Klarkowski interrupted him. "Did either of you have any inkling, any hint that drugs were involved at all?"

We both shook our heads no.

I added, "It would never have occurred to me. Art had been involved in anti-drug education when we were together and had even given talks to various organizations. We were so vigilant about drugs with our kids. I still am. I saw no hint of anything like that. The idea's absurd."

AJ added his assent to that. "That's true. My dad was very vigilant."

Klarkowski continued. "I understand you've taken in boarders for some years."

"Yes," I said, " that was the other way we made some money. It was my son, Alex, who came up with the idea when I explained to all of them how difficult it was going to be to pay for anything. We decided immediately to do that. We still have our first renter, Marthe Grimm, who needed someone to live with while she recuperated from illness. She's like a grandmother to my children now. We've had many others, mostly college students, through the years. The only other one now is Lindy Stewart, a student at UW-GB. Why do you ask?"

"Well, college students are frequent users of drugs. Do you think any have brought in drugs over the years?"

"If they did, they'd have been out on their ears. Literally. I'd have gathered up all of their belongings, put them out in the yard and refused them entrance. That was a strict rule they were given in writing in the rental agreement and they read it aloud to me before they signed."

AJ laughed. "And some refused to sign and left. You don't know my mom or you wouldn't even have asked that question."

Rudmann looked at his watch, frowning. "I have to interrupt here. We need to go. We do have more questions and you'll be hearing from us. We're going to pursue a full-scale investigation and we'll be including FBI and any other agencies that are designated to help. We want to thank you for your cooperation today. Thanks for the use of your office, Mr. Wentworth. Mrs. Kinnealy. Doctor."

He rose and headed for the door. Klarkowski looked at him oddly and I thought he might have wanted to ask more questions.

Klarkowski turned to me. "Anna, I'll be in touch with you if I think there's any way you can add to our knowledge. Don't hesitate to call if you think of anything more, even the littlest details. Thank you for your cooperation." He followed Rudmann out.

I was mystified at their sudden departure. "Well, that was odd. I expected Rudmann to fire lots of questions at me. Maybe they do have a meeting."

I got up, went to the small kitchen and poured out the last of the cold tea in my cup.

"He was really in a hurry to leave," AJ observed. "I wonder what that's about."

Conrad wasn't caring about them. He gave me a stern look. "Anna, the letters."

I took them from my briefcase and dropped them on the table. All seventy-plus of them. The two men looked horrified. AJ said through his teeth, "Mom, I don't think you should say a word, not one word! We will now read these. Just keep quiet."

I left the back way to use the bathroom off the lobby. As I came out I heard Rudmann's voice.

"...a damn fairy tale. That was the only truth she spoke. She knows more. What woman would be that dumb about what a husband does? I couldn't stand being in there with her another minute. It's a good thing I have to get back or I'd have torn her story to pieces. A fuckin' fairy tale! I'd love a good excuse to search that big house she lives in."

"Patience, Thomas, patience. All in good time," Klarkowski replied. I didn't hear the rest because the elevator door closed.

A half hour later, when he and AJ had both read each letter and put them in order, Conrad spoke.

"No, there's no overt threat. No charges could possibly be made with these. There are, however, some disturbing possibilities. Either they were, as you pointed out, Anna, a clumsy attempt to comfort you. Or, they were meant to rattle you, to keep reminding you of your loss, which is really a covert threat, possibly the work of a very disturbed individual. I see three possibilities. My first guess would be Jon O'Keeffe. Second, an unknown someone who wants to hurt you. Or third, Art was actually writing to you."

At my look of disbelief, he leaned over the table toward me.

"How do you know that was Art's body ? The ring could have been placed on someone else's hand. The court has just declared him legally dead but that doesn't mean it was so then or is now. It's my opinion it's actually what happened, that he died I mean, but the police are going to look at all possibilities and you need to be prepared. They *will* bring that up! Do you have a sample of Art's handwriting? I want an expert to go over these."

"Of course. I'll bring it to you." I was feeling very foolish. I could feel myself going into Numb again.

"Will you give me a quick rundown on your current boarder, Lindy. What's her last name?"

"Lindy Stewart. She's the daughter of an archaeologist who is on a site somewhere in Mexico. She came to us last year and in summer she goes down there to help him on his dig. She's a bright sprightly thing, all blonde and curly, with a bubbly personality. Alex grinned from ear to ear when he saw her and melts every time she opens her mouth because she's got a French accent. I think he envisions himself dating her. He's been disappointed so far.

"Her parents are divorced. Her mom lives in Paris. Lindy went to a French boarding school. She loves the house and wants to keep coming as long as she's at UW-GB. I have had no problems with her at all. In fact, she's the kind that tells me everything she's doing."

AJ grinned. "Ad infinitum."

I began to gather my things together.

"We're not done yet." Conrad was using his courtroom voice. "You mentioned to me at one time that Art kept files in your house when he had his office there. Do you know what's in them?"

"Well, not specifically. Art used to do his legal research at home whenever he could so he could be home and available to us, although he was often closeted in the library for hours. He kept copies of that research. There were also lots of files from when he was in school. He kept them as references. I never read them. Our library was mostly his home office then. The files were off limits to us all."

"Well then, I want us to go over those together just to be sure nothing's relevant to what we've done today. I can't do that now because we've got a lot of work here."

He paused, silently thinking. "No. We don't have to do that right away. Art would have been a fool to keep sensitive material there and Art was certainly no fool."

He looked at AJ. "AJ, are you going back to Minnesota right away?"

"Yes, I have to. I'm finishing my residency hours this fall. I'll be done just before Christmas. Then it's a vacation for me! After that, I have to decide what next. I'm actually considering Doctors without Borders. I was really horrified at the lack of health care for the poor in Mexico and the Central American countries. I might want to get some experience in tropical medicine."

At my surprised look, he continued, "Sorry, Mom, I haven't had a chance to talk to you about that. Perhaps" he said, looking pointedly at me, "we might want to discuss sharing more things with each other." He tapped the pile of letters.

"Well, yes. I suppose we should but I have to get to my counseling appointment now or I'll be late. I'll see you at supper tonight?"

He nodded. I stood up.

"Conrad, I'll be back to sign papers necessary for the funds transfers. I really have to go. I'm walking over to Grace's office and Caitlin and Caroline will meet me there. I have to do this whole thing again for Grace, only much more, any unfinished trauma. Just doing this has brought up more."

I picked up my briefcase. To AJ I reminded, "They'll give me a ride home."

Conrad shook his head no. "Not so fast! One more thing. Do you often see your great-grandmother?"

I looked at him in surprise. An unexpected comment.

"No. Those were the only times, but others in our family have seen her. My mother claimed to be psychic and once or twice said she did—see the Elf Queen, I mean. I thought she was crazy and so did the nuns and priests, but enough of her 'premonitions' came true so we didn't dispute it. I never wanted to be like my mother in that way. My psychic abilities

BETRAYAL by SERPENT

seem to be that I always know whenever any of my children are in trouble."

AJ looked amused. "I can attest to that! She *always* knew just where we were even when we tried to hide it from her and she *always* knew when we were in trouble."

"Why are you asking that?" I wondered. It seemed so off the subject of our meeting.

"It would be hard to defend if we ever had to go into court. Your sanity would be in question. In this situation I could defend it as a reaction to stress. It also makes you a less credible witness. I suspect the police think of you as incredibly naïve, something of a ditz. Is that the word? A trifle flaky, to put it in the vernacular. Actually I'm glad you told about it. Your report of that takes you off the hook, so to speak. They may actually believe that you didn't know anything about Art's business, that he wouldn't have trusted you. Chauvinistic of them but, right now, a good thing."

"Oh. I never thought of that." *Ditz? Flaky? Naïve? Well, I guess they would see it that way. That's not it at all!*

I decided to reframe that immediately. "We're Irish. Of course we're like that. It's not insanity. It's spiritual sensitivity." *Spiritual sensitivity sounds better than ditz.*

I wasn't about to tell him I played with the Little People as a child. Many of the kids I knew did that. We all seemed to outgrow it. The Little People told us we would grow blind to them so I wasn't surprised when I reached adolescence and lost the ability. At the crash site and Art's funeral mass were the only times in my life I'd had such experiences.

"I must go now. You might like to know Rudmann doesn't believe me. I overheard him calling this story a fairy tale."

I walked determinedly toward the door, not looking back.

"I'm not letting you off that easy, Mom."

"Neither am I, Anna."

I could feel them frowning sternly.

They discussed me for some time after I left. I felt their energies crawling all over me.

66

Eleven

...late September...journal update...

In spite of the warning from Jane, the police interest in Art's death, and concerns of AJ and Conrad, I am determined to have some semblance of normalcy for us. I checked my bank account online late last night and we now have plenty of money in reserve. I've decided not to take any new clients and I still have ample work. I was alone at the time and I cried with relief knowing we're financially comfortable. That stress is gone at last.

Today I have some time for early morning journaling, a real luxury, and the best luxury is that I can now do this on my computer. Digging out all the previous information from my handwritten pages was very slow going. This way I can keep up to date more easily. Over the last seven years, doing research and writing reports for several dozen firms, I've dragged myself into the present not only emotionally but professionally. It was high learning curve. I learned typing on a manual typewriter and thought an IBM Selectric was a miracle. Now, I scan, fax, email and Google. I adore flash drives. I do not text yet. I find it annoying to be unable to read a face and hear the inflection in a voice.

My meeting with Grace, with Caitlin and Caroline in support, went pretty well. More or less. They got angry with me for not telling them of the attempted rape and the letters. Caitlin's response was colorful. She swore at Jonny in extremely graphic terms, shocking even Grace, who has heard it all, and vowed to get him somehow. Caroline cried. She felt guilty for leaving me alone that night. In the end we all hugged and were ok. Grace did her hypnosis magic and I feel lighter, almost buoyant.

Phone interruption here. Conrad says he'll be out of town for a day or two but wants another meeting when he returns. He wants to discuss the settlement, the discrepancies in the books and what that might mean.

He'll probably preach me a sermon about the letters. AJ certainly did before he left for Minnesota. He stomped and snorted around my office like an angry buffalo.

"Why didn't you tell me, Mom? I understand why you didn't tell the others. They were too young to comprehend, but I was grown, am grown. Stop treating me or any of us like children. I'm not. I should have been told."

"AJ, I was in no shape to deal with those letters. I was not only protecting you, I was protecting myself. If I'd had to ferret out who was doing that, I'd have been even more of a basket case. As it was, I almost lost it entirely. What would have become of all of you if I'd allowed that to happen? Afterward, I was so focused on earning a living I just wanted nothing to pull me off course. They were more reminders I didn't want. Now, it's old news, old life. I don't want to discuss it. The only concession that I'll make to what you say is that I'll certainly try not to treat any of you like children anymore and you haven't any complaints on that score. I've treated you like an adult since your father died. If you can't see that, it's your faulty perception, not mine. As you saw when you read them, there was no threat involved and they stopped. I want to move on."

He stomped around a bit more but calmed down before he left.

...late night...three days later...

What terrible days these have been! They began so peacefully, so normally, and ended so painfully. What happened has affected all our lives again. That day began so well...

On the porch, Marthe sipped her tea and watched the early morning non-stop traffic flowing by on Monroe Street. She's so much a part of our family now, a grandmother to my kids as my own mother feels farther away, a possible victim of dementia. Marthe and I plan our days together.

"What are you doing today? Do you have work to do?" she asked me. At her feet, Marthe's cats, Artemis and Guinevere, wound themselves around her legs, purring loudly.

"No work. I cleared my calendar. I'm taking a day off. I have the meeting with Conrad at ten and then I'm going to the YWCA to swim, then a late lunch with Caitlin, Aunt Carrie and MomKat. Alex and Cory will be coming home late. Alex has football and Cory has debate. Lindy wants us to go to her Tae Kwan Do demonstration tonight. Have you seen her? I haven't seen her for days."

"No, but she's just getting into this semester. I think she's really busy," Marthe answered. As a retired teacher she's attuned to any school schedules. She was a godsend when she moved in and my boys' grades slipped after Art's death. An English teacher, she pulled out all the stops to re-ignite their interest in learning, even reading aloud every child's adventure book she could find after supper every night until their spirits awakened again.

She got up abruptly. "Well, I'm off upstairs to work on my book. I'll leave a grocery list in the kitchen for you."

I stood and followed. Artie trotted after Marthe. Guinnie curled up in the sun for a morning snooze. "I'm going to run upstairs too. I want to bring extra bedding down from storage before it gets cold. Today is beautiful but it won't last."

We climbed the stairs to the second floor together and I continued to a back room on the third floor where I took my time choosing and piling up blankets. I had just started down again with them when the day became a waking nightmare.

The harsh screams and yowls echoed from the front of The House through the rooms and all the floors. They went on as I dropped the extra bedding in my rush down the back stairs, stumbled, fell once, and raced through the kitchen and the long hall. By the time I got to the front door, I heard what sounded like a child crying outside. I flung open the inner door. Nothing on the sidewalk or street, not even a car.

A whimpering sound came from below. I looked down and my legs wilted in shock. The mewling pitiful sound came from Guinnie, splayed stomach-down by all four paws on the porch floor just outside the screen door. I couldn't even open it for fear of hitting her. I turned, wobbling on my legs, and bumped into Marthe, who was right behind me. Though I tried to keep her from seeing Guinnie, she did. She turned white, sucked in air and then stopped breathing and swayed.

I thought she would faint and all I could think of was *She has to help me!* and *We have to get to Guinnie!* I physically turned her around and pushed her, still holding her upright, in the direction of the side porch door. We unlocked that door and raced back over the porch to the front. Guinnie began yowling again when we came near. Marthe became even paler when she saw what had been done.

Embedded in Guinnie's paws were some pointed objects that looked like stars. I couldn't have guessed what they were, but Guinnie was struggling, which caused the embedded points to cut her feet. Blood made slow-moving paths across the porch from all four of her paws. As she struggled, they were being cut more. She must have fought whoever had done this.

I looked around. No one was in sight. Two cars zipped by on their way downtown.

Marthe kept repeating "Oh my god! Oh my god!" Her breathing became shallow. I realized we had to get the objects out fast, before she lost control, but how?

"Marthe!" I shook her. "Go get some kitchen towels and the glove hot pads! We need to get her free fast! Now!"

"Yes," she whispered, "get her free."

She turned and, still stumbling, she went back in the side door. I knelt down and looked carefully at what had been done to poor Guinnie. She couldn't move without the blades making larger cuts. I put my hand on her head and tried to make soothing noises. Although she seemed to understand I didn't intend further hurt, nevertheless, my movement brought a rippling of pain through her body and she tried harder to get free.

I reached for one of the objects but found to my dismay that the star-like projections were all sharp blades. My hands would be slashed if I grabbed one. Using my thumb and two fingers, I grasped either side of one projection and tried to pull straight up. I couldn't get it loose. My sweaty fingers slipped on the blood and metal. I was afraid to move it back and forth, knowing it would hurt Guinnie more, afraid she would struggle more. I heard a shout.

"Annie, what in the world are you doing?" Caroline was out getting her mail.

"Get over here fast. I need help!" I yelled. She left her porch and ran across the street, taking in the scene, eyes widening in horror as she moved up the steps. Not watching where she was going, she stumbled and fell onto the porch floor, crawling the rest of the way.

"Oh my god! Who the hell did something like this?"

"I don't know. I heard Guinnie's screams and I was up on the third floor and ran down and found this."

"What will we do?"

"Get her loose somehow. I sent Marthe for towels and hot pads."

Suddenly anger flashed through me. "I want the police here! I want the Humane Society! Did you see anyone? You were outside. Did you notice anything strange?"

Caroline started to answer my questions but Marthe came back, still panting hard. We decided they would hold Guinnie to keep her from squirming and I would use the padding and towels to try pulling the blades out.

"What are those things?" Caroline asked.

"I don't know," I answered as I pulled on the oven mitts, "but they're sharp and stuck deeply into the porch. If I can't do it with these mitts, then I may have to get pliers to pull them."

I reached for the first one on her right hind paw and succeeded in pulling it away but the mitt was cut wherever the blade touched it. Guinnie's foot began to bleed more as she pulled it up toward her body in reflex action. She tried to get it under her but Marthe and Caroline held her flat so she couldn't do further damage to herself out of fear or the urge to run.

"These are wickedly sharp!"

"We don't want her to get away and walk on her paws." Caroline, the least shocked of all of us, was thinking ahead.

I reached for her left hind paw and accidentally brushed something that must have been painful, which startled Guinnie and she began to struggle even more.

"Just pull quickly! Get it over with!" Caroline ordered.

I yanked on the blade and felt it go right through the mitt into my fingers as it came free. That had the effect of allowing Guinnie to get both hind feet under her and she tried to elevate her rear end and take off. We were all trying to soothe her with our voices and Marthe was bent over murmuring in her ear, sounding calm for Guinnie's sake, but I could see tears were running down her face.

I warned the others to hold firm and reached for a front paw, getting it loose. As that paw came free, Guinnie tensed even further, drawing it up under her. Using both hands, I closed them over the last blade and pulled. It didn't come loose. I pulled again and realized it was stuck more deeply than the others. We looked at each other anxiously.

"Don't let her pull on that paw," begged Marthe.

Both women held down the front leg and the cat's body tightly.

I wrapped my hands in towels over the shredded mitt and decided to move it back and forth. It came out suddenly and I jerked upward, knocking Marthe off balance. Caroline lost her grip and Guinnie escaped and ran, dripping blood, down the steps, disappearing through an opening in the grill that surrounded the underside of the porch.

We looked at each other in dismay.

"I'm going for flashlights and I'm calling police and the vet." My anger had returned and I wanted someone after whoever had done this.

"Get her treats." Marthe ordered, already on the way down the steps with Caroline right behind her. I went in and phoned for the police. It seemed to take an endless time as I gave dispatch my name and address and tried to explain what had happened.

I called to see if our vet was in. She was. Her assistant urged me to bring the cat in as quickly as possible. I got the flashlights from the pantry, more towels to wrap Guinnie in when we caught her, the treats, and a hammer and screw driver to pry away the latticework if I had to.

Outside, Caroline and Marthe together had ripped off one of the wooden grilles and were on hands and knees, half under the porch, calling to the cat. I handed them the flashlights. We couldn't see her.

I was out and walking around the porch looking for any signs of blood without success when I heard the siren coming from the north where the downtown police station was located. I met the officer at the curb.

Ben Bennett, one of AJ's classmates from high school, had been on the police force for several years. I was relieved he was someone I knew. I explained to him what had happened and he began to search with us. It was Ben who found the trail of blood coming from the back end of the porch behind the bushes.

We followed it to where the cellar doors jutted out of the side of the basement. The outer slanted doors were open and we found Guinnie hiding in a hole in the foundation just above the inner door. Marthe wrapped her hands in towels and with gentleness and murmurs of reassurance, she succeeded in getting Guinnie bundled firmly in layers.

Ben requested access to the entire house to eliminate the possibility of anyone inside. I went with him, calling to Caroline, "I'll have to stay here while he investigates."

"That's ok," Caroline said, still breathing a bit hard from the excitement. "I'll take them to the vet's. I'll call you if I need you. Marthe, let's go get my van." Marthe, with tears still running down her face, and hugging Guinnie, followed Caroline across the street. The vet's, fortunately, was only a mile away in Allouez.

I accompanied Ben on a thorough check of the house's interior, then the exterior. I was alert, hoping for any sign of intrusion, any difference, anything dropped on the ground. We found nothing. We searched beyond the trees and lilac bushes, the soft garden areas. No footprints. Nothing.

Finally, standing on the path by the river, Ben observed, "This path has more traffic than anyone realizes and not all of it is harmless. It would be easy for someone to create quick mayhem and disappear down here." No one was in sight.

"I think it's odd though that we see no one. There are always runners, and skateboarders and bikers and walkers. This is a well-used trail. Whoever did this knew this neighborhood well, knows the patterns of movement. If I were you, I'd take extra precautions. Lock those doors even in the daytime. It's too bad, but it's becoming dangerous in this town. People can't leave their houses open any more like we used to." We were climbing back up the hill to the porch.

"It's these star blades that worry me," he said. He was frowning, his lips in a thin line. "They're used in a form of martial arts." He was carefully wrapping them in what was left of the padding I had used. "Most martial arts practitioners that I know around here would never use these little toys. I'm learning Tae Kwan Do over at Walker's Academy myself and I've never seen any used. We don't fight that way. Actually, I've only seen them in some martial arts movies but I'm going to check these out thoroughly. They're called throwing stars and I can't imagine how the perpetrator got them into the paws. If the cat struggled, which a cat would do, then maybe it took two people. Someone had to hold the cat's mouth shut or you would have heard it sooner. Maybe the person or persons who did this have cuts too. We can check with the hospitals and doctors. These are very sharp."

When he mentioned Walker's I thought of Lindy. I knew she would never think of harming Guinnie, but might there be someone at the studio? I told Ben she lived here.

"Oh, I know her," he responded when I had explained about Lindy. "I'll definitely talk to her. She may know something, maybe have heard of someone who's been toying with these little devils. The martial arts schools will be the first place to start. Mistreatment of an animal like this is against the law. We'll have to investigate, although you know it's a misdemeanor. Don't expect much in the way of justice."

He would have gone on but I interrupted. "Ben, I really have to go to the vet's and see what's happened. Marthe will be a complete mess if Guinnie has to be put down."

"Uh, Mrs. K., you're going to have to go to a doctor too. Look at your hands." I'd forgotten about my hands. I looked down and my fingers were covered in fine cuts, which were oozing blood. I sighed. It would be all day before we were through mopping this up.

No meetings today. I'll have to cancel them.

The porch was still covered with blood. "Please don't wash it off yet, Mrs. K. Most of the blood is probably the cat's, but maybe my supervisor will ok some tests. I'm actually not sure if blood samples will be taken in this case, but just to be sure, you know?"

In the kitchen I washed my cuts and poured peroxide on them. He helped me bandage them loosely and then reported in to the station. I heard him request an alert for all patrol cars to do periodic ride-bys and search the area for any persons acting strangely.

"I can't figure how anyone could do that and disappear so fast." I said to him as we left. "The timing must have been perfect. Or sheer dumb luck. There are only certain hours when traffic on Monroe decreases. This early in the morning is not one of them. To my thinking, it had to be someone who knows that pattern and knows our house and its inhabitants."

Ben thought for a bit. "Well, you have that chest-high wrought iron fence and those bushes screening the street. It would be easy to be undetected. But I'm still leaning toward some sicko using the river path as access."

I called Ardith, explained briefly what happened and re-scheduled my appointment and then called Caitlin and asked her to call Aunt Carrie and MomKat.

By the time I arrived at the vet's office, Dr. Arimani, and her assistant, Nancy, had sedated Guinnie and carefully examined each paw. There would be stitches, she told us, and danger from infection, but she would not put her down. She knew the cats. She knew Marthe. I think she didn't like the possibility, a strong one, of Marthe becoming someone's patient too. I didn't either.

She insisted on looking at my hands. Caroline took charge of Marthe and Guinnie and I left them, my hands temporarily re-bandaged by the vet. She was worried I couldn't drive. I assured her I felt no pain yet and with the padding I could grip the steering wheel easily.

The ER took forever. I was not high on their triage list and waited for over an hour, listening to two screaming infants in pain, a man who was delusional and refused to remain in the room where they had placed him, and two people with broken limbs whose groans issued from the rooms where they were waiting to be taken to X-ray.

Finally, after cleaning each cut, which hurt, the nurse practitioner put on bandages which held my skin together (no stitches, thank god), gave me a tetanus shot, an antibiotic prescription and sent me home with Tylenol 3, commenting that this was the first time I had come in without my children. Ever.

Driving hurt.

Marthe was still crying when I got home. I called her doctor and he prescribed a temporary sedative. "She's been like that since we got back an hour ago," Caroline said. "I'll go get the medicine. Guinnie's still at the vet's, still sedated. Dr. Arimani wants to watch her carefully."

When she was back, Caroline made strong tea for herself and Marthe and found some ginger ale for my nausea. I get nauseous at everything upsetting, a leftover from smelling and seeing a charcoaled corpse, an image long gone but not forgotten.

My hands began to hurt more. They hurt now as I type this but I took the pain killer and it's not as bad as it was.

I've steeled myself to tell the boys. Once again, they'll have to experience another event that could damage a piece of their trust in people.

Knowing the worst of human behavior has left my trust in people damaged. What is it doing to my kids? How do I tell young people how cruel humans can be? Yes, they're older. Yes, they're resilient. But how much do they lose when something like this happens? I hate seeing innocence die. That's always been part of why I didn't tell them about the letters.

Angry! More than angry! Furious! Who did this? No answer. I want an answer!

As I expected, Alex and Cory were horrified, but spent their energy on comforting Marthe. They called Marnie in Madison and AJ in Minnesota and told them. I'm so glad they can talk about it with someone they trust.

Tonight I spent the first part of the night in Marthe's room, huddled in blankets on her couch. She slept fitfully at first but finally lapsed into a deep sleep. My hands hurt. Now the medicine isn't working. I can't sleep.

...next day...

Mid-morning I could stand it no longer, got out the hose, and sprayed down the porch, the steps, the grass, and the cellar entrance. Ben hasn't called about the blood samples, which he did take late yesterday, but I don't believe that will lead anywhere.

Lindy hasn't come home. I feel uneasy about that.

Marnie has come home for the weekend and snuggles with Marthe on the sofa in the library. She found a cute sympathy card with cats on it.

...note inserted later...

Guinnie didn't recover. Her old heart was too shocked. Dr. Arimani called just two days later and advised she be put out of her misery. More heartbreak for Marthe and a horrible decision for her to make! Another bad day.

Artie cries his way around the house, searching for her, calling for her. We buried her in the back yard under the apple tree on whose lower branch she had loved to sit to watch river and bird traffic. Caroline's twins, Jake and Jim, found a metal cat sculpture somewhere and presented it for a memorial for her grave.

The day before Guinnie died, Lindy came back. She has a boyfriend named Rick and has been staying at his apartment. The look of sheer horror on her face when I told her what happened told me she knew nothing about it. Ben hasn't seen her yet.

She explained. "I haven't been to Walker's in at least a week. I had four papers to write. After I finished and turned them in, Rick and I spent some time together," she said. I told her about Ben wanting to question her.

"I wouldn't know what to tell him about the stars. I know what they are but we never use anything like that. No one I know has ever even talked about them. They're used in

77

the very aggressive side of martial arts, which isn't the emphasis at the studio."

"That's what I thought, but he'll have to investigate."

She bought balloons to tie to Guinnie's memorial, treats for Artie, and chocolates for Marthe.

This morning, three days later, I received a call from Ben. He has spoken to the neighbors, has gone to the martial arts places. All a dead end and there'll be no more. The death of a cat is, after all, not a police priority, given what else they have to do.

"We didn't do blood work but there was a fragment of leather stuck to one of the stars. The person or persons who did it wore thick leather gloves and used some device to tap the stars into the wood."

Conrad came to the house via the river path after the cat's funeral, saw the memorial we erected under the tree, and heard all about it. He took Marthe and I out to dinner. Later, I teased her gently about having a "beau". She blushed and fluttered a bit, and declared she was too old to want a beau, but it brought a slight smile to her face. She thinks I should consider him as a replacement for Art.

"He likes you. I can tell."

I'm not ready for a "beau" either.

Twelve

More work has come in even though I'm not taking any new clients. It leaves little time to journal but I want a record of this meeting. Conrad wants me to create a paper trail of everything that could even remotely be related to The Firm and its problems.

...meeting with Conrad, 1pm...

He had his usual selection of food and drink and I took a plate of veggies and dip, a ham sandwich, and sat at the long table, gazing through the sheer curtains at the Fox River outside.

Conrad's office is beyond elegant. He has incredible artistic taste. Grey silk drapes frame sheer curtains opposite to a wall of intriguing masks from Indonesia, Native America, and Africa. His desk and the long table which dominates his room are mahogany and the chairs are upholstered in wine damask.

I could see bright purple flags flying on the West side, announcing a new art show at the Neville Museum across the way. *I must go and see that.*

"I'm grateful for the food, Conrad. I've had no lunch. I was finishing some work just before I came and counting on your hospitality."

He filled a plate for himself and sat across from me.

"Enjoy! We have more work for you. Ardith will have it ready when we're done here."

I went right to the topic we were to discuss.

"Conrad, I know you explained and I approved the final settlement but the amount it was based on is not right. It's not accurate. I remember very distinctly Art telling me several times that The Firm was making money hand over fist back then. In fact, The Firm had expanded, with satellite offices in Appleton and Milwaukee. They wanted to target high-end clients, make it a top-level firm. He bragged about it. He was very proud of that. He bought the plane because of it. They took that vacation because of it. He even talked about a lot more money coming in later."

"That's what I want to talk to you about. As I mentioned in our meeting with the police, while I was dealing with The Firm on your behalf, I discovered financial discrepancies, or at least the hint of them. Back at that point in the history of The Firm, there was indeed an enormous amount of money coming in. It was also bleeding out. At least some of the financial records indicated that."

Conrad had leaned forward and was speaking with careful deliberation.

"But strangely, not all of them. I think..." he paused, hands together in his typical prayer-like form, fingertips at his chin, "...I'm pretty sure they kept several sets of books."

"Several? That's crazy! I've never heard of a legal firm keeping several sets of books."

"Yes, it is crazy but not entirely. Legal firms always keep two sets of financial files as a matter of course. They, we, have our normal business account that shows our firm's intake and expenditures. We and they also have what is called our escrow account, where we keep monies that come in from clients, monies which have not been spent as yet. This is an oversimplification but essentially, we can't put any money into our business account until we've used it for the client.

"In The Firm's case, it was very odd. When I subpoenaed those books, I think I got mixed data which appeared to be from several sources. Someone slipped in inconsistent numbers, seemingly irrelevant pages, figures that contradicted each other, and money from the business and escrow accounts appeared mixed together. That's a *big* legal no-no. The result was that some figures indicate The Firm was barely hanging on and other figures showed very high income.

"Now, I could have challenged those figures, probably should have years ago, but you wouldn't have gotten anything if that's what they were doing. There would have been many more years of legal wrangles, lawsuits, challenges, and delays if that was the case. At the very least the IRS would have been all over them and you. I did confront Jon on sloppy bookkeeping but he blew it off. At least he did to my face."

He went on.

"It becomes even more interesting. I see two possibilities as to how I got those confusing and conflicting figures. One is that it happened by mistake, which to my mind is very unlikely. The other is that it was, on someone's part, deliberate, which calls into question why someone at The Firm would try to do that. Is this the work of a whistleblower, or...I don't know. Andy? Sam? Or someone we don't know?"

He leaned back and spread his hands apart in the air, palms up. "So you see, Anna, there has been much more to all this than I let you know about."

He was silent, obviously waiting for me to say something. I didn't know what to say. I was so taken aback I couldn't think, except for one ugly thought.

Art must have known something. He had to. He was a senior partner.

With growing horror it dawned on me that there might have been problems that began not just *since* he died but *before* Art died. Adding to that Andy's murder, and my news from Jane, I could only breathe a soft "Oh my god!"

"Yes, that's exactly what I said. Now, I have to ask this and I hope you will not take offense. Did Art ever, ever indicate to you in any way, any way at all, that there were any illegal dealings? As your lawyer, I really have to know. If there are to be any repercussions I need to know the worst. It would of course, be highly confidential. Lawyer-client privilege."

That I could answer quickly.

"No! Never! The only money I knew about was what he put in our checking account for the kids and the house. He kept a separate account for his clothing, for the cars and their maintenance, and one for home office expenses. I didn't use that but I had access to those bank statements. Once in a while, he'd mention that The Firm was doing well or, sometimes, that it wasn't, but never more than that and we'd adjust our spending accordingly. We scarcely ever disagreed because we were both very practical. You got all our personal tax files back then. You know what was in them."

"Good! That's what I've thought, what I believed all along, but I had to be sure. In complete honesty, your settlement could have been much higher had I used the larger figures. My instinct told me there was something shady and I decided to keep you and yours out of it, so I used the lesser figures and I think now that was the right thing to do. You have your money with no taint to it. I do apologize though. It was a bit cowardly of me as a lawyer. And I should have discussed it with you sooner but I decided to wait until now so there'd be no more opposition. Jonny made every effort to refuse settlement as it was, challenging every move I made. I think he finally agreed because he didn't want me to open a can of worms. I could have taken this much farther and possibly have blown everything apart back then but all of you would have gone through even more hell. You didn't need that in those terrible years. I will find a way to make it up to you somehow. I promise you that."

My mind filled with questions and they spilled out.

"What are you going to do about the irregularities you saw? Was this possibly shady money? Who do you think sent you this information? Andy or Sam? Was that why they were murdered? Was there someone else there who wanted you to find out what was going on? To challenge The Firm? To bring it down? Where *did* the money come from? Was there money laundering? What was going on?"

"Whoa! Slow down. Those are some of the questions that occurred to me. You know I have no great love for the O'Keeffe family, father and son, that is. I don't know the women. I've never trusted Jonny O or his father, when he was alive. For your and your children's sakes, I hope Art was not involved in anything shady along with them. He never seemed to me that type but then I never felt I knew Art well. He kept a quiet wall around himself in our legal world. I did see him in court. He did excellent work. Our firm should have hired him when he got out of school but we didn't. Prejudice played a part in that. Snobbish judgment. He was from the 'wrong' side of town."

Conrad became quiet but then said, almost to himself, "I believe the O'Keeffes, father and son, were and are bound up in this. I just don't know how. Yet."

"Conrad, you know there are those file cabinets of papers in our attic that I had brought up there after Art died. Do you think...?"

I stopped as he sat forward abruptly, instantly alert. "That's right. That's right. Do you know what's in those files?"

"Not really. He emphasized they were off limits. I remember once being told they weren't client files, that he'd never keep client files at home."

He remained silent for some minutes, frowning, lips pursed, thinking hard.

"Perhaps they are innocuous but if there's anything in those files, you could be sitting on a mine field." He almost whispered that.

"There could be a record of what they were doing in those cabinets. Is there any way they could be taken from your house?" His forehead wrinkled into worry lines.

"Not without keys, a truck, a dolly, and people to do it. They're very heavy wooden cabinets, four-drawer, legal-sized, packed with papers, locked and in the attic, our top floor. It would take anyone hours, days really to go through all that. Just getting them to the ground floor would take a major move. I was going to go through them and throw stuff out someday but I've put it off for years because it's intimidating. There are a lot of legal books too that I was going to send over here to your firm if you want them. I'm more than ready to let go of that part of my life.

"But now, in spite of my wanting to take a break, work is speeding up. I know I could work less but the money is going into savings. It's my insurance, my backup plan. I've gotten requests from seven clients in the last few days and, with the holidays coming up, I won't have time. I promised my kids long and wonderful holidays this year."

He sat back, drumming his fingers on the table.

"You know what? That's good. That's fine. That's safe enough. No one would think to search for them there. Let's wait until after the holidays. I have cases that need my attention here and now. I'll go over all The Firm's old papers again to refresh my memory. Then we can tackle the files in the attic together."

"I feel relieved. Going over all that's up there will take a lot of time."

Yes and you don't want to expose what was going on, Anna. You still want it all to go away. You want Art to be one of the Good Guys.

Conrad was watching me with narrowed eyes.

"I've read through your journals very thoroughly now. You are not the same woman you were then. You're out of shock and grief, and your children are too. You're a lot more confident. I admire you for how you met such a terrible event, how you helped your children and took care of them through this."

"Truth, Conrad? I don't want to know Art was not the Good Guy I think he was. I still wish I didn't have to know what might have been going on back then. At heart, I still am a devout coward, but yes, I do have the strength to do it if I have to. I am different. For instance, part of me is worried you're still angry I didn't tell you about the attempted rape and the letters, the scared part of me. The stronger part of me will bring it up to clear the air about it."

He shook his head.

"My god, Anna," he said softly. "I'm not angry with you for that. I admire you for coming through this the way you have."

Suddenly he was somewhere else, gazing out the window with the saddest look on his face, his eyes far away from the room, seeing nothing in front of him. I thought he might tell me what he was seeing.

Instead he merely said very softly, "I know something of what it takes to face that kind of pain. Yes, I do."

I thought of how little I really know of his life, while he knows so much of mine.

He came back to the present.

"However, please don't keep anything back anymore from me or your friends. You deserve all the support we can give you. There. Sermon over."

He stood up.

84

"Just a few more things. I've gone through this whole set of events checking for patterns. There are always patterns to what happens. Here's one we already know about...that someone has been watching you and your children for years. If you get more letters, don't leave them unopened. There could have been an escalation and you wouldn't have known it. You're just lucky there wasn't. Contact me and then the police. Did you bring the samples of Art's handwriting?"

"Yes, of course."

"I'll need that today. I'm having these analyzed by an expert."

I dug into my briefcase and gave him the envelope which held several examples. He put that with the letters and laid that pile aside.

"Did you ever compare dates of the letters with the information you entered into your journals?" he asked.

"No. That would never have occurred to me."

"The letters dwindled after the death of Andy Moss. The cat has been tortured right after the death of Sam Soderberg. There's no direct proof these events are related, but...who knows? They could be."

He set another pile aside and changed the subject.

"Caitlin's information needs to be investigated." He said as he tapped another page. "I want to call her. Will you let her know that's ok with you and sign a release of information for her and even for Caroline? I want to get to know Caitlin's boys too. We sometimes need street information and it pays. I might want to employ one or more of her boys. I do not have 'street cred'. Neither does Clayton, but we've developed quite a network of helpers over the years. Did you know The Firm had that too? Probably still has."

"Art never talked about that. I didn't know. And yes, I'll sign releases."

Another pile moved.

"Here's what I want you to do right now. If someone is watching you, it's important not to make any change in your regular life, to go on as you ordinarily would. However, you also need to have security discreetly installed in and around your home. Do you have cable television?"

I looked puzzled. "No. That was one of our economies. Also, some of those cable channels I can't approve of for kids."

He smiled.

"Well, it's time! You can block the channels you don't want. Of course, the 'cable' company you hire will be quite adept at adding security and not of the blocking-channels kind. I know a firm who will make sure you have a few cameras and other little gadgets."

"Seriously? Is that really necessary? Are we in so much danger?"

"I don't know. I am, however, very worried about the manner in which Sam Soderberg was murdered. Because Jane knew all about her husband's business, someone may assume you knew a lot too. Rudmann did. I don't want you and your family to be torn out of your lives, or, god forbid, dead. At most the letters were mild harassment but the cat thing, if it's related, is frightening, a definite escalation.

"I'm doing some probing, my own research of a very different nature from what you do for us. If I hit a nerve somewhere, I want to know you're safe. Give me October and November at least. If there's anything important I'll most certainly contact you."

"What do you need as a retainer for this?"

"Nothing. You've seen what I made on your case. It's enough."

He smiled, then stopped me as I began to protest.

"Anna, I'm independently wealthy. Inherited to begin with and I'm good at both earning money and investing it. I have a great deal. I don't need more."

His smile disappeared and he looked stern, almost angry.

"My motivation is to uncover what I think is some very unethical, perhaps illegal behavior by members of the law profession. I'm on the state legal ethics board. I take this very seriously."

I thanked him and left, wondering what more September would bring next besides cable TV, home repairs, and a security system.

Yesterday, on the last day of September, a letter came, supposedly from Art, this one more menacing. It sent a heightened sense of danger crawling through my mind and shivers sliding up my spine. There was a detailed account of all my movements, to the day, for the last month. It was as if a security camera had followed me everywhere I went. Still no direct threat but I feel invaded, violated. I turned it over to Conrad.

"This is escalation. Stalking behavior. We're going to be sure there's a paper trail with the police. Take it to Klarkowski." I did.

Whoever watches me for the next month will be bored to death. I'm going to have the trim on all the windows painted, and get the flowerbeds ready for winter.

I wonder about every stranger I see who even glances my way, every person who walks by, even neighbors I know. Who watches me? Where are they?

How can they watch me every hour of the day and night? Do they watch 24/7? Do they watch my sons and daughter, my mother, my friends? Anyone connected with me?

Thirteen

...October...

The windows got painted, the cable/TV security is installed, and the garden put to sleep. I wish I knew who the person watching me is. I'd insist he do yard work while he watches.

We've two weeks now of normal days. I'm almost lulled into complacency. It's a nice feeling after September's tension. Autumn is here in reds and golds and oranges. The tall elms and the maples lining the streets are singing their autumn songs to the breezes in their last performance before a well-deserved rest.

Packer fans add green to the gold. The team is doing well. Alex and Cory live in Packer jerseys, caps and jackets. Through the years I've hung on to our Packer tickets, a small miracle because they cost a fortune for us, but they're so hard to come by. I paid for them by renting them out to diehard fans who were willing to pay for individual games.

Not this year. I check my bank accounts repeatedly to make sure this dream hasn't evaporated, but the money's still there so we're using those tickets ourselves. The boys love going to the home games. Even AJ wants to come home for one. He has just two more months in Minnesota. Marnie is doing well at UW-Madison. Alex in a senior. Cory a junior. I have a sense that life is changing too quickly.

I'm relieved to see Marthe's grief for Guinnie subside. Artie, sensitive to her moods, took Guinnie's place, and follows her everywhere when she's at home. The only problem is that Marthe is now insisting she's hearing night noises. *It's her state of mind. If I ever find out who did this...! How is it possible no one heard or saw what was happening to that poor cat?*

Today, looking tired, she walked into my office with this morning's Press-Gazette and a fresh cup of tea.

"I think Cory or Alex might have been up again during the night."

"Really? They sleep like the dead usually."

"Well, I didn't actually see them. I just heard a faint sort of rustling sound. I never was wide awake and fell back to sleep very quickly." A frown deepened the wrinkles around Marthe's eyes and on her forehead.

To divert her from worry, I asked about her book.

Marthe suddenly glowed, smiling. "My book is coming along just fine! I'm going to publish it too. The research librarian is teaching me about publishing on the internet. I'll be gone all day. You're on your own. It's a great fall day and I'm walking to the library."

"Before you leave, I want to ask you, have you seen Lindy?"

"No, but then I haven't paid much attention. My head is in this book. In fact, I think I'll take off right now." She rose, folded the paper and laid it on my desk. "I'm a woman on a mission!" she laughed.

Well, that will help her heal.

Lindy Stewart has scarcely been home for almost a month. This is a big change from last year when she was in and out constantly. I've assumed she's spending most of her time either at school, at the Tae Kwon Do place or with her boyfriend, Rick. She informed me one day that Rick is expected to be UW-GB's basketball star when that season begins.

She made it very clear when she rented her room that she is a most independent young lady. Her mother divorced her father when she was ten, and the way I understood it, embarked on a European odyssey to find a newer and richer husband, preferably with a title, and to have a wonderful time looking. Lindy, educated in French boarding schools, is sophisticated beyond her years but has never been obnoxious about it. In fact, I like her independence and ability to face her life, such a total contrast to my upbringing. She's almost lost her French accent now that she's at school here. She speaks Spanish too. Alex loves it. He's got Spanish at school and would study with her if she were here. He's got a very sweet but hopeless crush on her.

89

I spoke with her father by phone just after she rented the room last year and he seemed quite nice, if a little distant and distracted. He expressed genuine care for Lindy and she verified they have a pretty good relationship, formed while she visits him in her summers off school. She's learned much from him about the Mayan culture and he told me she's spent every summer since she was ten working on his archaeology digs.

When he received big-time funding for an ongoing dig near the Mexico-Belize border and for preliminary exploration of other sites in the Yucatan, she was so proud and bragged about him. I often marvel at the difference in her descriptions of the Yucatan and my own brief trauma-distorted experience.

Still, I am slightly unsettled. She usually checks in with me at least two or three times a week, popping into my office just for quick chats. It's been too long since I've seen her.

I wonder if she's under surveillance too. Maybe I could swing by the studio on my errands. Anna! Drop it! She's not a child and she has nothing to do with our lives.

Klarkowski just called. He has more questions, wants me at the station. I've been expecting this. I called Conrad. He's concerned.

"I'll be there. It might make you look more suspicious to have your lawyer with you but there is precedent for that from our last meeting. I can let them know more about my own suspicions. Let me call them and I'll call right back with a time."

It's at one tomorrow.

Fourteen

...journal of today's meeting...

I drove down to the low freestanding building on Adams Street that is the Green Bay Police Department. A locked door separates the front desk from the lobby. I rang the bell, stated my business and was buzzed in. After a few minutes, I was shown into a room with a table and two chairs. Being there did not relax me in any way. There was a two-way mirror in one wall. I couldn't help wondering why I was shown in here and not into an office.

Conrad arrived and was shown in. Klarkowski came in with Rudmann and a stenographer. This was definitely not to be casual. "I see this is a formal interrogation, gentlemen. Is there a reason for my client to be put through this?" Conrad asked.

Klarkowski began, his manner mild and certainly not threatening. Rudmann's face projected his usual tough belligerence but he remained silent.

"Your client isn't under any suspicion at this time, counselor. We do, however, have questions about her former husband's activities. We're still looking for anything that might give us clues as to what was going on years ago and what might be still going on."

"You had that chance in my office."

"Yes, but we were called away and didn't really finish so we'd like to wrap it up now."

Conrad looked at me and I nodded to him. "I'm ok with finishing this today," I said with an emphasis on "finishing" and "today".

He nodded to Klarkowski. "Same rules apply as before, gentlemen."

Klarkowski nodded at the stenographer and began his questions.

"How long did you know your husband?"

"Since I was eleven and he was thirteen. That was forty-one years ago. I'm fifty-two now. I was forty-five when he was killed."

"How did you come to know him?"

"We grew up together on the West side of Green Bay. I lived on Chestnut Street; he lived on Oakland with an aunt and uncle. He was orphaned at age three and spent four years in St. Joseph's Orphanage. They adopted him when he was seven. We became friends when he was at my father's funeral with his aunt. We both went to St. Pat's grade school."

"And you married when?"

"When he was twenty-five and I was almost twenty-three, June, 1971."

"Where did you live then?"

"We got a small apartment in Milwaukee until he finished his studies at Marquette Law School. He had only a semester left. I worked at a store as a clerk. He worked at a law firm down there for two years, then came up here and began his own law practice. He created a partnership with Jon O'Keeffe, and not long after that, Andy Moss and Sam Soderberg. We lived in an apartment on Oakland during that time until we bought The House."

Klarkowski had asked the previous questions. Rudmann, his voice brittle, took over. "When did you move into the house on Monroe Street?"

"I'm not sure. I've been there so long and I don't think of the year any more. AJ was four so it must have been 1976."

"How did you make the down payment on such a big expensive house?"

"Well, first, it wasn't so terribly expensive. We got it because the former owners defaulted on their mortgage and it was for sale by a bank and so was a lower price. Then, Big John O'Keeffe loaned us the down payment. Art had paid his way through college in summers working for Big John's construction company and Big John liked him. We bought that house because both of us always wanted to live in that neighborhood. It was a big step up from where we'd grown up. We were delighted with it when we first saw it. We planned a large family and it was perfect for us."

"Did you work also at that time?"

"No, I stopped working when I was pregnant with AJ. I wanted to be a stay-at-home mom. I did brief work before that at an insurance company but they fired me when they learned I was pregnant. Art threatened to take them to court for discrimination but I didn't want to return to work there and we dropped it."

"Exactly what did you know about the operation of your husband's firm?"

"Well, mostly nothing. I knew when things weren't going well and I knew when they were because Art or Jonny O would mention it."

Klarkowski began again. "Jon O'Keeffe spoke to you about that?"

"Just in passing. He and Art would sometimes work together in our library, which was Art's home office. They did their law book research there."

"Was Jonny O'Keeffe at your home often?"

"Not really. Beyond their work together, he came to some of our parties but he wasn't always at all of them."

"Did they take any other trips together besides the vacation in Mexico?"

I had to think about that one. "They did do some business trips together, if they were on the same case, I think, but that was rare. At first The Firm did general law, what most firms do. Later Jon specialized in criminal law and so there weren't many cases on which they collaborated."

"Can you tell us exactly when those trips occurred?"

"No."

"You didn't even note your husband's absence in your journals?"

"In the years when the children were young I used my journals to chronicle their growth, their special occasions, and our family milestones, more like a scrapbook kind of thing. I didn't keep detailed journals until Art died. After that, I used them to relieve my pain, to keep track of what was happening, because I had a difficult time remembering due to the stress. Also, my counselor insisted on it. After a while I realized writing really helped me to pull myself together and I began to like it. I still do."

Rudmann interrupted, standing up and leaning over the table at me, his fists spread apart, his face angry. "So you can't tell us anything that your husband was involved in from back then? I find that hard to believe. Most women know exactly what their husbands are doing. To the hour! To the day! But you were 'just a housewife', a mother, just sitting around the house all day not interested in his life at all."

I was startled by his apparent hostility.

Conrad took charge immediately. "Sit down, Detective." he said calmly. "This is not going to be 'good cop, bad cop' here. You're already getting complete cooperation."

He would have continued but I stopped him. "It's OK, Conrad. I'll answer that."

I turned to Detective Rudmann, who was still standing, and addressed him. "When you sit down, Detective," I said very softly, but with total firmness.

Then I stayed silent and gave him The Look, a skill learned at my mother's knee. Mothers I knew have this skill down pat. I was obviously more practiced at it than he. He glanced away first and sat down. First lesson as a mother of four teens—*never* be easily intimidated.

"I have not been just a housewife," I continued quietly. "I have been involved deeply with my children's education, with community charities and arts organizations. I have my own interests in the art world, which was my major in college. I have not lived through my husband's life and work. If I lived through and for any others, it was my children. In addition, I want you to know that caring for a house and family is a major job. I have had to learn basic plumbing, electrical wiring, machine repair, and numerous other skills. Your view of women is skewed, Detective, especially your view of this woman."

I glanced at the stenographer, who was seated behind the two detectives. "Did you get all that?" I asked. She nodded wordlessly but kept her head down and her shoulders were shaking slightly. *I bet he's a jerk to women!*

Conrad was having a minor fit of coughing.

"My point is, I've had my own life. I didn't monitor my husband's every move."

Rudmann folded his arms over his chest and glared at me and at the room in general.

Klarkowski moved restlessly in his seat. "Just one more topic, Mrs. Kinnealy. We've heard there are hidden places in your house that have been used over the years. You spoke of using one last time we met. Would anyone but yourselves have had access to these?"

The very casualness of how he asked that put me on alert. *Why is he even bringing this up? What has this to do with anything? Don't be on the offensive or defensive here, Anna!*

Conrad stirred beside me but said nothing.

"Yes, there are space discrepancies in the house. We didn't know about them when we bought the house and not for several years after. It was AJ, when he was about eight, together with his other friends, who found some. First, while playing a game they called 'Dungeons' down in the basement, they discovered a cement block was loose in the wall of the coal bin. One of the boys got stuck trying to see into it and I had to get him out. I cemented the block in again. Just one of those skills I learned. In addition to the coal bin, there is also an old cistern that's still walled off and there's space behind that.

"In the north wall, AJ discovered a long chute-like space beginning in the attic and dropping all the way down to the basement. He and his buddies were padding the basement floor and then sending one of our cats down from the attic. He said he was experimenting to see if cats really do land on their feet if they're dropped that distance. We nailed that shut."

Conrad laughed outright. The stenographer chuckled. Klarkowski smiled, shook his head. Rudmann remained stiff and silent.

"There are others like a dumbwaiter off the kitchen, and smaller spaces as well. I asked Big John about it and he said that's often the way with older homes. As for your second question, yes, others did know—our children and some of their friends. Art and I, of course. Big John checked some out one time just out of curiosity. Friends knew because we told the story of AJ and the cat."

"Why are you asking about that?" Conrad made it clear from his expression that he wanted much more information.

Rudmann answered. "It's pretty obvious, counselor. Drug shipments. We suspect that there were big shipments and they would have to be stashed somewhere. As I'm sure you realize, we are investigating *every* possibility."

Conrad laughed again. "Are you saying you think that Art Kinnealy was running large shipments of drugs through his house without the knowledge of his wife and children, especially with boys who explored every nook and cranny?"

Conrad's eyebrows were up, face incredulous.

"I'm saying *not* without the knowledge of his wife and children." Rudmann stared coldly at Conrad.

"Do you have any evidence at all that drugs were stashed in that house?" Conrad, suddenly very serious, was using his courtroom voice.

Rudmann got a sour, but determined look on his face. "No, we don't. *At this time*," he said, his voice leaning heavily on the last three words.

I looked at Conrad, we nodded to each other and we both stood up. I picked up my purse.

"I've had enough of this. I think this was a waste of my time and my lawyer's time. My husband was not a drug runner. My house has not been a drop-off for shipments of drugs. Since Art belonged to several anti-drug organizations and even gave speeches alerting the community to this problem, I think you are going down a dead end path. If you need verification for his anti-drug activities go to the Press-Gazette morgue. They covered his speeches."

That was the end of the interview.

Outside, I looked at Conrad. "Are they just being paranoid? Are police always like that? I never want to view people with such suspicion."

"Well, you may have to before this is over, Anna. Think about it. It's a possibility. Stranger things have happened. By the way, I'm impressed by the way you handled their questions. You faced the 'good cop, bad cop' tactic with great aplomb. You answered with dignity and conviction. My investigations tell me Klarkowski is OK, but Rudmann has a reputation for sexism and bullying. You got off easy. Or, he gave up too easily, and that makes me suspicious."

"You investigate police officers? Really?"

"I always want to know who I'm dealing with. They were fishing. If they had anything, they'd be able to get a warrant to search your house and they can't. I was going to share my own suspicions with them today but given Rudmann's demeanor, I decided against that. One thing I'm sure of, there's over seven years, maybe more like ten, that need investigating. Everything, including the circumstances of Art's death."

We were walking down Adams Street to his office. The air was crisp. Heavy traffic blew car exhaust smells around us. A truck rattled by. The brakes of a bus hissed and squealed as it stopped at a corner.

"Conrad, do you think Art might be alive?" *Anna, where does that come from?*

He stopped and looked at me closely. "Do you want him to be?" he asked me softly.

I looked down, not wanting him to see my eyes, feeling guilt and even some shame.

"The truth? No. No, I don't." I said, words I didn't want to hear from myself. Then more came rushing out. "If he is, I feel terribly betrayed that he hasn't come home to me, to us. All I feel when I admit to that possibility is a furious rage, and then I really don't want to see him at all. If he isn't, I just want it all put to rest. Actually, most days I don't think of him at all anymore.

We began walking again.

Conrad was silent until we crossed Washington Street. "Thank you for being honest, Anna. I can understand your feelings. At the same time, the next truth is, it's not going away."

I stopped, looked at him and just shook my head no.

"I believe he is definitely dead, Anna, but you need to face that the circumstances around his death are odd at best, murder at worst. I hope to have papers from Mexico soon. I've made police contact there. I think AJ, and even you, had fully accurate instincts when you felt it was staged, a whitewash.

But to be honest, I'm not very hopeful those papers will answer our questions or put the matter to rest. "

"Neither am I now."

We entered his office. I left my finished work with Ardith and went home to journal today before I forget parts of it.

Fifteen

...third week, October...

The interview left me on guard, with a heightened uneasiness knowing we were being watched not only by someone unknown, but police as well, and *yes, Anna, you may be having forebodings!*

I had to chuckle to myself.

"Oh, good grief! I've become my mother!" I thought in minor horror.

When I was little, MomKat was famous, well, more like infamous, for her "Premonitions," (definitely with a capital P). That some of those events had no relationship to what portended didn't bother her in the least. We viewed her "forebodings" with tolerance and humor. She viewed them as ordinary motherly intuition.

I didn't want to be like my mother. It was embarrassing when she swooped into St. Pat's School with dire warnings. Several of the nuns referred to her as superstitious. I overheard one of the priests using the phrase "batty as a bedbug". Though I hadn't heard him connect her name to the phrase, it was right after she had left the school in an uproar. I assumed he was referring to her. I was questioned by a frowning nun about whether or not I believed I had premonitions. I was too little to know what the word meant but the nun spoke in the same disdainful tones she used for words like "pagan", "heretic", and "sinner". I could say, truthfully at the time, that I did not.

But after I had children...well, that was a different story!

With AJ's birth, something in me changed. His birth, which I expected to be like any other woman's normal birth, was not. Twenty-three hours of labor and heavy breathing, and the increasing exhaustion, changed something in my makeup. Afterward I began to experience a heightened sensitivity.

First, it was to sound, and I figured other mothers must do that too, listening as they are for the cries of their child. Then it was to color. I didn't realize for almost five years that others didn't see colors the way I did, that I sometimes heard sound in a different way.

Over the years, I discovered that I have known when my children will be sick, when they are in trouble, and where they are at all times, whether they tell me or not. While this was mostly reassuring to me, sensing trouble before it came was definitely not. The kids thought it eerie, or intrusive, depending on whether they wanted me to know what they were doing.

The most terrible thing was that when our baby died of SIDS, I heard nothing at all but I felt her leave while it happened and ignored it, not realizing what it was. Sometimes there is no reassurance or peace in knowing these things.

Curiously, although this sense extends at times to others close to me, it did not extend to Art. I told him, jokingly, that he was on his own if he got in trouble because there was no knowing what was happening to him. He laughed and said he could take care of himself, thank you, but if I said one of the kids was in trouble, he acted on it. The times I was right were too often to ignore.

Now, I feel an unknown growing. Impending. I can't identify it.

It's something in and around this house. Label it, Anna, feel it. Don't ignore it! Uneasiness, restlessness, and vague discomfort. A slight feeling of dread, some impending...what?

I discount it, put it down to paranoia because of the cat, and the police questioning, check my radar over the kids and find no reason in their lives for what I feel.

So drop it and get on with it. Journal the rest of this later. Maybe it's just that Lindy's not been here and Marthe's still hearing those bumps in the night.

She brought up the night noises again this morning. I tried to reassure her.

"It's not impossible that some small animal is living with us, being on the river like this," I told Marthe. "It

100

happened once when the kids were little. A raccoon found its way into the cellar and then, following an inner passage, made its home in the attic for some time before we found it, confused and hungry. It could be a squirrel, or, god forbid, rats. If that's the case, I need to know so I can call an exterminator and the city. Rat runs are common along the river. Bats, too, once called our attic home."

"Bats squeak," observed Marthe. "We'd hear them."

"Well, yes, but we wouldn't hear them from way downstairs, or see them unless they flew into our bedrooms at night."

"Wouldn't the boys hear them?"

"Hmm! They might. Or not. They can be pretty oblivious to things they don't want to be bothered with. I can't see them concerned with any small animals unless food disappears. Then we'd hear about it."

Marthe laughed. "Oh, yes! That we would hear about indeed!"

I shoved all premonitions aside and focused on the work that came in.

...two days later...

I can stay with uncomfortable feelings only just so long before I have to take some kind of action. Since autumn is my preferred time for total housecleaning, I decided to begin. It's still warm enough to open windows, air things out. I'm going to take three days to get a good start. I'll negotiate later deadlines for any future work and check this house for whatever might be the cause of Marthe's bumps in the night. Halloween is coming. Maybe I have a practical joker in my crew, plotting some mischief. So far no one has mentioned Halloween at all. Hmmm! And it's not just Halloween. The specter of rats creeping through the walls sends my skin crawling. I really do have to know what this is.

Besides, I need to follow Conrad's advice and live as if it's all normal. It's time to let go of my ghosts. A perfect month for that!

Cleaning is my way to soothe myself. It's a familiar, well-known series of tasks—vacuum, dust, straighten, wash, and organize. And start an inventory because that hasn't been done for years. I found my camera, a notebook, a flashlight, got my cleaning supply cart and trucked it all up the back stairs to our full, walk-in attic. Artie followed me. He loves the attic. Though mistakenly named after a female goddess, then neutered, he much prefers to think of himself as King of the Domain, especially when he's in the attic.

I ignored the files, inventoried the legal books and furniture, boxed up the murder mysteries, nailed down the loose board over the chute, and got rid of live and dead spiders and their meals. Nothing was out of the ordinary.

I moved down to the third floor.

The mid-section of the third floor was a ballroom in Victorian times. We'd occasionally used it for parties just for fun, but it had been the family playroom, where we held plays and ceilidhs, told stories and played games during the long Wisconsin winters. It holds a small stage that is a foot high and hollow underneath but very securely boarded up and our children had never successfully gotten under it. At least, I don't think so. I checked but there were no loose boards.

Now, as The Dorm, it holds all that two teenage boys can accumulate.

Clothes were all over the floor. I swept every item on the floor into a pile and left a large sign…"MOM WAS HERE AND…" They'll get that message. I refuse to pick up after adolescent boys. They know what the 'and' means. They may never find those things again.

At the rear, I checked the four small rooms and the hall to our back stairway. One of these rooms I use for storage of winter/summer clothing and bedding, it being easier to access than the attic. The other rooms are empty this year, no longer rented out to college students.

Next to the stairway, a shaft for a dumbwaiter is behind a small door. I use it for a clothes chute, having trained the boys to send down dirty clothing to the pantry, where our laundry is now installed. I used to be able to pull everything out and sort it and then send it back up clean. The dumbwaiter tray and ropes are now gone, broken by a teen too heavy for riding in it. Alex and Cory can still throw their laundry down

Judith M Kerrigan

but must get it to carry it back up. Poetic justice. Nothing was out of place there.

Well, I can tell Marthe there's nothing up here but us humans. One uneasiness put to rest.

I moved down to the second floor. Still, my feeling of apprehension nagged at me. *Why? Maybe this is about Lindy.*

No sooner had I thought that when I heard her voice.

"Mrs. K! Where are you?" Lindy shouted up the front stairs.

I could hear her coming, the stairs creaking, and I made a mental note to see if they could be nailed down tighter. Artie, who had remained in the dorm, came trotting back down when he heard Lindy, and seated himself in the door to her room, waiting for her to appear.

"Hey! Mrs. K! What are you up to?" Her head appeared above the landing.

"Lindy! I've been wondering where you were. You have mail waiting for you. What's happening with you?"

"I have so much news, Mrs. K! Have you got time to talk? Can you take a break?"

She bounded energetically up the last step, not even breathing hard, went down on her knees, slid across the smooth wood floor to Artie, scratched his head and shoulders thoroughly, and then jumped up, all of that in one move.

"You won't have to twist my arm to make me do that." I said. "I've been at this since just after seven this morning. What time is it? I need a break. I want some coffee. Let's take the back stairs to the kitchen.

"Great. It's 10:15. I've got today's mail."

She waved letters in her hand, giving me ours and keeping three for herself which she pocketed. She carried my cleaning tools down and went up for two boxes of books before I had the coffee and tea on. I got out a package of frozen lunchmeat to thaw for noontime. There were crackers, cookies, chips and some salsa. We opened these for a snack.

Lindy is an incredible combination of blond hair and dark tan skin that seems impossible in nature. She has blue-green eyes, turquoise actually, the color of the Caribbean in travel videos. The first time I saw her I had to remind myself to breathe because of my sensitivity to color. The golds, blues,

103

and greens sparkling and radiating off her leave me amazed. When she's excited, she's a rainbow.

Her figure is trim and she's small, just over five feet, like the Elf Queen. I always feel like a giant next to small women. I've never been less than a size sixteen in my adult life.

Lindy had not stopped talking, even up and down the stairs. Before we sat down to eat a bite, I'd heard about two of her classes and she was expounding on a third. She's a rabid environmentalist. She is also a great mimic of her professors, whose personality quirks amuse her no end. She's never unkind and often hilarious.

We sat down to snack.

"What else kept you away?"

"Well, there's my Tae Kwan Do. That's going really well. Mike has me teaching some of the basic moves to more new kids and adults and he thinks I'm a good teacher. You should try it, Mrs. K. You like exercise. It would take care of the pounds."

There are times when the honesty of youth is not delightful. No amount of exercise or dieting has "taken care of" my pounds. I am just large and my fat is too solid.

"You should come over there tonight. We're having another practice tournament. Some of us are ready to compete with other schools and Mike wants us to get used to the atmosphere, you know, with other people watching and all."

"Well, maybe I will," I said. "I'd like to watch you and I'd like to see Ben Bennett too, if he's there."

I stuffed my mouth with a chip and salsa.

Unexpectedly, her face turned sour.

"Oh! Yeah! Him! He's such a cop!" Her voice was instantly angry and defensive. "He's a jerk! He's suspicious of everyone. He's been asking me questions about Rick. What he does. Where he's from. Stuff like that."

Her eyes turned to blue fire. This was definitely not how she'd reacted to Ben's name before.

She hasn't reacted at all come to think of it. Has Ben been questioning her because of the blades? What has he said? Why is he asking about Rick? Tread lightly here, Anna. You know better than to go at this directly.

104

"Wait! First tell me more about Rick. You've mentioned him so often but I really don't know anything about him. Fill me in on him first."

Instantly her mood changed again.

"Oh my god, yeah! You don't. Know him, I mean. I met him the first week of school. We've been going out a lot. He is So Very Cool."

Capitalized and Underlined! Hmmm!

"He has an apartment over on University Avenue and he's very intelligent."

As she went on about him it was obvious she'd become infatuated with him. I started to feel protective, my mothering instincts in high gear. I know I've spent a lot of time educating my kids about dating, life and sex, but what does she know? Is she careful about sex? Given her life, has she been taught any of this?

I had hoped that my special intuition could kick in where Lindy was concerned as it had in my own children's lives. It hadn't. At least, not in the way it usually did. Listening to her though, I began to feel the familiar uneasy feeling I get when listening to my kids and I hear a pink flag, my term for something not bad enough to raise a red warning flag.

"Ok, so tell me more about this great basketball hero and smart guy. He sounds wonderful. Does he have a last name? A family? Does he dance? Does he sing?" I teased.

She laughed.

"Oh, Mrs. K! Does he have to be in the arts to make an impression on you? He doesn't dance or sing or paint and his name's Attenborough."

"Rick Attenborough? I think there's a British celebrity with that last name. Any relation?"

"I don't know about any British celebrity. Rick's definitely not British. He's from Mequon, just north of Milwaukee. I haven't met any of his family. You probably won't approve but I've been staying at his apartment. I love being with him and when basketball season starts we won't be seeing each other much. We have so much fun."

I am not unrealistic. I'm well aware that young people have sex but the flag just got a deeper shade of pink.

"Lindy, you know I've faced this with my own kids and I feel I just have to caution you to be careful."

I taught them to use protection, contrary to Catholic beliefs, because that was infinitely more sensible than becoming pregnant or contracting a venereal disease. I told Lindy that.

"I found it was just better to be up front with them, Lindy, and I wouldn't do any less for you. I just hope you're using protection."

"Mrs. K!" Her mouth hung open. *OK, mistake here. Backpedal, Anna. She's not as sophisticated as you think.*

"Lindy, this is what a parent does for her kids," I told her quietly. "I don't know what you've learned about sexual safety, about..."

She interrupted and her eyes flashed with anger.

"I know how to take care of myself! What makes you think you have the right to say anything to me at all? I can take care of myself just fine, thank you."

She began to rise. I knew she'd flounce out if I didn't stop her.

"Lindy," I leaned toward her, "this isn't criticism or meant to harm you. I say this because I really care. I said the same thing to my own children."

I kept my voice quiet and tried to let her see the caring I really felt.

To my astonishment, I watched her face and body crumple as she burst into tears.

"I'm sorry. I just don't want to talk anymore."

She left the kitchen and stomped upstairs.

Oh dear! I've hit on something, but what? What is this about? Leave her alone for a while. Let it be. This is not just a developmental change. She dated several boys last year with no imbalance in her moods. Why this tension now? Is it Rick? He's the only new factor in her life. At least the only one I know about.

After putting away the food, I took a cup of tea back to the second floor with me.

If she hears me working, maybe she'll decide to continue our conversation. She's twenty now. She's capable of working through these things for herself. You are not her parent, Anna.

On the second floor there was little to do. I saw no sign of any animal droppings, any flies and spiders. *We clean here regularly.* I ran the sweeper in my room, straightening my drawers and closet. I tackled the contents of the computer room, originally the dressing room for the master bedroom. The desks needed serious re-organizing and I was about halfway through when I heard her crying.

I listened as Lindy's quiet sobs filtered through her closed door and stood there trying to decide what to do. Had she been my child, I'd have known, but with Lindy...*well, I don't know. Hold off, Anna. Give her time.*

There was no sign of any disturbance. I checked the Hidey Holes. Nothing. I checked closets. Nothing. Well, not exactly. In the linen closet on the second shelf from the bottom, where I kept piles of sheets, I found a strange, shallow, roughly circular indentation on all four piles, as if something had rested there, spread out over the tops of them. *What made that? Is someone storing something in here I don't know about?* I smoothed the sheets and checked the other shelves in each room, preparing to move downstairs. Nothing.

Suddenly, Lindy's door opened and she emerged, her eyes still red from tears and her face worried.

"Mrs. K., I've got to talk to you."

I prepared myself for more revelations about her relationship with Rick. That wasn't it at all.

"I've been getting the weirdest letters from my father. They make no sense to me. He's writing about leaving the site! That's crazy! Last month he wrote me he just got money from CCAI, the Cross-Cultural Archaeology Institute, supporting further excavation. He would never abandon this dig! It sounds like he's mad at me because I didn't write him back right away after his last letter and that's the only thing I can think of he might be mad at."

Tears rolled out of her eyes and down her cheeks as she thrust two letters into my hand.

"Here! Read these!" she demanded.

As I took them from her, she turned and went back into her room and curled herself up in the small chair next to her bed.

I followed, sat at her desk and withdrew them from their envelopes, which were postmarked from Mexico. They were dated two weeks ago and one week ago respectively. The letters were extremely short. Reading them didn't take long. In fact, I prolonged my attention to the letters before looking up at Lindy because I was so surprised at their tone. I couldn't believe her father would write this way to his daughter.

This is how he communicates? These are awful! Rigid, abrupt, cold, unemotional. He typed his first name for a signature, not even "Dad". The second letter was almost like the first.

"Lindy, does this make any sense to you? What do his usual letters sound like? Are they all like this?"

"Well, he's not really a lengthy writer. Not a lot of time, you know. But his letters are always much more interesting. He loves to tell me what he's working on and no, they don't make sense because he's just gotten more money and I can't see why he'd be closing the dig like he wrote in that second letter. There's so much more to excavate. If something happened to slow him up or put off work on it, he'd say so. Look, I'll get you one of his usual letters and you'll see."

She went to her closet, drew out a shoebox full of letters, rummaged through and handed me one.

"Are those all from your father?"

"No, most are from my mother. Her letters are like journals. I never even have to call her because she writes everything in her head so I always know about her life, and she's not interested in mine, but Dad and I talk on the phone at least once a month because he really doesn't have time to write about all he does. That's another thing. I called him last month and he was his usual self and he didn't say anything about closing down the dig.

"There's more. There's no cenote on that dig." She pointed to a line in the first letter.

"What's a cenote?" I imitated her pronunciation—suh-*no*-tay—accent on the *no*.

"It's a well." She stopped and frowned, then continued. "The cenotes lead down to underground rivers and caves with water in them, but not in the area where he is. He's in jungle lowland. The northern Yucatan peninsula rests on pitted sandstone with underground rivers but he's in the south. There is no cenote on this dig and he talks about a village and there's no village on this dig to clear! Unless he discovered one since I was there."

I interrupted her. "Lindy, just let me read this and compare his letters." I took an older one she held out and read it.

Not only did he write by hand, but it was so much friendlier, warmer, full of detailed news of the dig, and four pages long. *That's a journal length in my mind! Her mother's letters must be books. He enjoys writing to her, almost like she's a colleague.*

What are the possibilities? Has anything happened? What? Is he ill? Is there trouble of some kind? Would he tell her if there is? Yes, I think this man would. He's very open here about the delays, the difficulties. True, none of them are serious, but still.

"Might there be something happening that he wouldn't tell you about to prevent you from worrying?"

She moved to the edge of the chair, her hands twisting around each other in her lap.

"He's always told me before. He had one year when there were Mayan rebels, when they were in danger, and he kept me up-to-date. In fact, I didn't go to the dig that summer. I met him in Merida and we had a few weeks together up on the coast and he did research at the University of Merida. See, he works with a professor from the University of Mexico, and he could leave then because Professor Menendez took charge. That was before the increased funding. In the end, nothing really happened. The rebels didn't come to the camp or anything. It was just that it was a possibility and he didn't want me in danger."

"Might he be ill and not telling you?"

"Now that would be more likely. He pooh-poohs illness all the time and he's picked up some strange bugs in his travels. It could be he's having a round of sickness—malaria or dysentery, although he's pretty good about taking preventive measure for those. He wouldn't tell me until it's over. He thinks of illness as just part of the job and, well, a weakness. As far as parasites and other tropical diseases are concerned, he just thinks that's normal. Otherwise, he's always been healthy as a horse."

"Even horses can get sick. Do you want to call him? You can do that using our phone, you know." I became curious. "How do you get hold of him on a dig?"

"Well, it's a little difficult. He has a cell phone but he's not always near it. He leaves it in his quarters because he has to go to higher ground to use it. He doesn't always answer it if he's busy or preoccupied. I just leave a message and he calls when he gets around to it."

She sat up straighter, more tense, her face scrunched with worry.

"I've *never* worried about my dad before. He's been so good at taking care of himself."

"I can relate to that. Art was like that."

"Then you know what I mean." She paused, frowning. "But I'll feel a lot better if I know he's ok."

"Here's what I think. I think he's probably very busy, but he could be sick and trying not to alarm you, although he's obviously not very good at that, is he? There's no use sitting here guessing at what's happening. Why don't you call, leave a message if he doesn't answer right away, and wait to see what's up? Then you'll be able to concentrate on your Tae Kwon Do tonight.

She jumped up, her expression changing from worry to one of thoughtfulness.

"You're right! I don't know enough. Going there is months away. Or, maybe I can go down during January break. I can be there for almost a month's time including Christmas holidays. I'll write. I'll try to call too. I will! I'll put my call in now. Will you be going with me tonight? I'd love to show you what I can do."

"I'd love to see it."

I rose and moved out of her room to the back stairs landing.

"Well, my own "dig" is this house and while there's still daylight, I'm determined to excavate one more floor, checking for Marthe's bumps in the night."

Lindy laughed, her usual bounciness returning.

"I haven't heard anything at all. I think she's imagining it." She started to leave the room and then turned back.

"Thanks for the other advice. I am taking precautions. I definitely do not want to get pregnant." She all but danced out of the room.

Thank god for all my years with teens or I'd have botched that one.

I went down to the kitchen and made myself a sandwich, thinking I'd faced today's drama pretty well.

The cleaning's gone well too. I'm going to skip the main floor and do the basement. I can open the windows and doors and really air it out today. Then we won't have our usual spider migration from basement to upstairs when the weather turns cold. In fact, I'm going to hose that place down.

The only way to thoroughly clean our unfinished old basement is to spray it down from top to bottom using a hose with a good spray nozzle. The accumulation of dust, cobwebs, and dirt can then be swept into the sewer in the floor. It's a once a year job that goes fast. I'll get this done today.

Sixteen

...journal, evening...

It's at this point that my day became totally bizarre. In my wildest dreams I couldn't have imagined what was to come.

Getting the hose from the garage, I pulled it down the basement stairs after me and attached it to the faucet in the rear of the basement. I left the outside door open to allow warm air to get sucked through and opened the screened basement windows.

Beginning at the rear of our long and wide basement, I alternated spraying and sweeping down the water to the drain. I was about half way through the when I turned to the front and thought I was hallucinating. Literally.

Emerging at the front end of the basement, from a hole behind the old coal bin was at least two feet of a large snake, a very large green snake. With a body as thick as a fencepost, it was cautiously slithering out of the hole, pausing every few seconds to test the air with its tongue. Astonishment froze me to the spot.

I watched as the snake grew to six feet and was still emerging, coiling its body up in a pile.

Where the hell has that come from? I want to run. Dare I run? Will it come after me if I run? If I spray it, will that stop it? What if it gets out of the house through the cellar door? This is the kind of snake that squeezes people to death!

I edged toward the back stairs slowly and reached the bottom step as the snake began to uncoil and come toward me, the end of it finally emerging from the hole. *That thing is humungous!*

It began to come at me faster, uncoiling with a swishing sound as it slid over the floor. *Panic!* I quickly backed up the lower flight of stairs, then turned and climbed two steps at a time as the snake moved toward me faster. At the top I slammed the door shut and leaned against the wall, breathing fast. I heard a soft slithering noise on the other side.

Hunting! He's hunting!

Totally irrationally, I shut and locked the back door, then took the back hall stairs two at a time and slammed the upper door too. I put a chair under the door handle even as I realized it was a ridiculous action. *Anna, snakes can't turn doorknobs. Where's everyone? Where's Artie? That snake will eat the cat!*

Then I heard a car at the back and, racing to the dining room window, I saw that Marnie, home unannounced and unexpected, was just getting out of her Honda. Caroline was across the street getting out of her van, coming home with the twins, who bolted into their house.

"Don't go in that door!" I ordered Marnie through the open window. She looked at me like I was crazy. "There's a snake in the basement!"

Caroline heard me and looked at me like I was crazier.

"I just discovered it and you can't go in that way."

Marnie laughed. "Mom, you're not afraid of snakes. What is this?"

"I am of this one. I just discovered it coming out of the old coal bin. Oh, my god! The cellar door! Come on! We can't let it get out! It will hurt someone!"

Not waiting for them, I raced out the front door and around the house to the cellar door. It was still open. I could see no sign that the snake had come out. Reluctantly, I made myself inch down the steps to see if it was still there. Marnie and Caroline were now breathing heavily behind me.

There it was, head and main body draped partially up the stairs, the long tail end s-curving across the floor. I heard Marnie gasp and turned. Both women stared past me, mouths open, eyes wide.

"Where did that come from? Is that an anaconda?" Marnie gasped.

"Get out! We have to shut these doors!" Shoving them up the cellar steps, I pulled the inner door closed though I knew I couldn't bar it. Marnie helped me shut the outer cellar doors.

"That will keep it for a while, I hope."

"How did that get in there?" We all three exclaimed this at the same time.

"We have to find Artie! He could get eaten. If that snake gets Artie, Marthe will be...Lindy's home. The last I saw, Artie was in Marthe's room and so is Lindy...in her own room I mean."

Marnie turned and ran to the front porch steps, took them two at a time, dashing in the front door.

We followed Marnie inside.

She found Artie in the library, in a window looking down on the cellar doors. He'd been listening and watching us. She grabbed him, ran up the stairs and put him in my room, shutting the door. He let out loud meows of protest. I remembered with relief that Marthe was gone.

Lindy came out of the library with the phone in her hand.

"What's going on? Why is Marnie home?"

"I need the phone right now. There's a huge snake, an anaconda, in the basement!" I took the phone out of her hands.

"A what?"

She wouldn't believe us. Caroline grabbed Lindy. "Come on! You have to see this!" She propelled her outside to the south side of the house to the basement window nearest the stairs.

I called the police. They politely informed me that I should call the Humane Society. I politely informed them that a hungry sixteen-foot anaconda is a threat to all small creatures and to children as well. They said they would send someone and would probably have to shoot it. I told them I'd try the Humane Society first, or the Wildlife Sanctuary.

Caroline and Lindy came back.

"It's a Green Anaconda, Mrs. K." Lindy said calmly, "and it's very hungry. You're right. It would eat Artie. Whole."

"Whole? A whole cat at once?" Marnie asked.

"Oh yeah! A whole pig, a whole child. When it's hungry it's very active. This one is hungry."

I called the Wildlife Sanctuary, who provided a bit more help. They did not rescue snakes, the woman said, but "there's a snake rescue team out of Milwaukee that we call when we find some non-indigenous snake like this. Can you bring it in to us?"

"No way! It's very active and at least fifteen or sixteen feet long. We have no way to capture it. What am I to do in the meantime?"

She suggested I feed it a large quantity of meat, preferably organic "so it won't have problems with chemicals." *Chemicals? Organic?*

"I can't leave here," she said, " but I'll find another volunteer to check it out. I'll call the snake rescue people for you too. I need your address and phone number."

And that was the start of a long parade of sightseers. I hosted the visits of police, of course. Ben was off duty at the station, heard the call and came with another officer. Two Wildlife Sanctuary volunteers were delighted to see such a "great specimen". The Humane Society representative, Candy, held a class in Anaconda 101 for Lindy, my boys and Martha, Rob and Caroline and her boys. The staff from Hazelwood Historic House, which is down the block, along with several other neighbors "just dropped in to see what's going on".

The Green Anaconda got fed an enormous chunk of meat, a gagging procedure to watch, photographed by Rob in detail, and it went more or less quiet afterward.

I treated our family and the visitors to pizza and went to watch Lindy and Ben at the martial arts demo.

Candy, (yes, Candy, and tiny and cute) remains with us tonight until the snake rescue people come tomorrow to get our green visitor. He/she/it (?) truly is a beautiful shade of green.

Just before I fell asleep I remembered the indentation in the pile of sheets. I sat bolt upright and knew that the creature had found its way somehow into that cupboard and back down to the basement.

How many times has it gone up and down? How long has it been here? Did it get out? Whose pets or children might it have eaten in the neighborhood if it got out?

We had all been in danger for who knows how long.

I got up, made sure the linen closet door was secure, and passed out at about 3:30am from sheer exhaustion.

...next day...

This morning the team from Snake Rescue arrived and took less than fifteen minutes to cage the snake. The boys loved it. They, Candy, and Ben assisted in gathering up the coils and pushing it into the cage. Rob stayed home from work and got pictures of that too.

Before he left, Ben told us about the police department's calls regarding snakes.

"You'd be surprised how many people keep these and how many lose them. This is probably our seventeenth call this year. Actually the large ones are the easiest. We can find them faster. It's hard for one of these to hide. The biggest danger is when they're hungry and might grab a child or pet for food. It's the skinny poisonous ones I hate. A lot of this kind of pet ownership is strictly illegal. People think they're getting something that's legitimate and the animals have been smuggled in."

I'll never find out who did this. It's probably one who got away from its owner. I don't want to face any other explanation such as—did someone put it here deliberately? Actually, that seems too outlandish.

Marnie had come home for no particular reason. She left this morning.

Lindy talked to her dad and he assured her everything was under control and he would call her in late December, when he had to make a decision about the dig. There was no trouble, just some questions about ownership of the land, jurisdiction and such. He told her he had just been short on time, had little time to write.

"He didn't sound worried at all, Mrs. K, so I'm not either."

I finished the basement.

...last week, October...

I called Conrad today, extremely upset.

"Conrad, I've just gotten another letter. This one is all about Marnie. Everything she's done for the last two months. I'm feeling more than a little sick. I can't protect her in Madison. Who could be following her? Why?"

He was not pleased.

"I don't like it, not at all. That snake might have been a stray, but with the cat incident and now this, I'm worried. Keep those doors locked now. Please make Marthe and the boys use that security system. Whoever it is wants to scare you."

"They're succeeding."

"Bring the letter to Klarkowski and a copy to me. By the way, the handwriting is not Art's on those early letters. It's a very good forgery though. I'll speak to someone I know about Marnie. I'll have him watch the watcher. He's a pro. Be sure to let me know if anything, even the littlest thing is strange or off or odd.

"I want to tell Marnie, to warn her."

"Can you hold off on that until I get someone in place? If she gets nervous and changes her pattern of behavior, the person might disappear before we have a chance to find out who he or she is. I'll call to let you know what my man finds."

"OK, I can do that knowing she's watched by someone on our side."

Halloween night has come and gone, crisp and cold. Except for all the children who were trick or treating, it's the quietest we've had in years, anticlimactic after the episode of the snake.

I've drilled the boys in the need for security. The locks are changed and we all have new keys. I found a loose board down at the bottom in the back of the linen closet. It's now firmly nailed shut. I didn't tell anyone, especially Marthe.

Now I feel helpless. There's nothing more I can think of to do.

No news from Conrad yet about who watches Marnie.

Tonight it feels like this month lasted forever. Two bizarre episodes now. What will be next?

Seventeen

...November...

I'm determined to lighten the mood for all of us, although I seem to be the only one needing that. The boys loved the episode of the snake and are oblivious to any threats, deep into the fall semester of football, band, chorus, a play rehearsal, and now and then, actual schoolwork.

Marthe is positively euphoric.

"I have wonderful news! My book is to be on Amazon in just a few weeks." She waltzed herself down the hall.

"That's incredible news! Do we get to read a sample, a chapter or two, before this happens?"

"Oh, yes! I'm having copies made for a few people to read. I want feedback. I'll need to have one of the boys take me to Kinko's and back. I can hardly wait to see it all printed up! There's so much I have to do too. The librarian told me to think about art for a cover, and I still have to decide on the title. I have a page-long list of possible titles. The right title is very important, you know. It's what sells the book. She says if we put it on the internet, I have to use Facebook and Twitter. Now if I only knew what those are." A puzzled frown creased her forehead. "She tried to explain but I don't quite understand how they fit in."

I hadn't seen Marthe this excited ever.

"This is so great! Why don't you have the boys show you Facebook and Twitter? They know how."

"Oh, I could, couldn't I? They'll love teaching a teacher. What fun!"

"It's a good thing the boys know what they're doing. I don't. Oh for the days when birds were the only thing that tweeted!"

Marthe has her own special request for a Christmas holiday.

"I want to go to Chicago to a performance of *The Nutcracker Ballet*. It's something I've wanted all my life. Well, actually I've wanted to see a Russian ballet company do it but I'll be very happy with Milwaukee or Chicago."

So we began a search for a performance and tickets on the internet. A surprise awaited us. There is actually a Russian troop giving holiday performances in Chicago. Marthe is ecstatic. She called Marnie to invite her to go along.

I went with Lindy to Walker's Academy several nights ago. I've watched her twice since the Day of the Snake. So have Alex and Cory. If I had ever worried about Lindy's ability to take care of herself she's dispelled any possibility of that during these exhibitions. My martial arts knowledge is still the Bruce Lee movie kind, but I can tell she's good. Mike Walker has high praise for her. In fact, his whole group acquitted themselves very well. Alex and Cory decided they would never challenge her to anything and they wanted to join and learn. I thought of the letters and my uneasiness, which still nags at me. Before we left, the boys were enrolled. I wish I could have given them self-defense lessons long ago. I wonder if someone might be following them. And Marnie. Conrad hasn't called. I phoned but Ardith said he's been out of town.

...later...

I'm determined to finish housecleaning but I got sidetracked again. This morning brought another delay. I'd just finished my morning coffee when the phone rang. It was Ben Bennett.

"Mrs. K, can you come down to the station? We need to talk to you. We have some questions we'd like to ask you."

The tone of his voice was calm and quiet yet I had the impression my remaining home was not optional. I felt myself tense up.

"Now what? Is this about the cat or the snake?" I asked him.

"No, no. I don't want to discuss this over the phone. It won't take long. Can you come?"

"Yes, fine, no problem. It will take me about fifteen minutes to get there."

I was to ask for him at the desk.

Should I call Conrad? There's little time but maybe he can get it reset or handle it.

I called and he was gone from the office. I decided not to put this off.

Half an hour later I left the police station angry. The whole interview had taken less than the time to drive there and back. He asked the same questions others had. They've used Ben to try to get more out of me.

I walked out on him, telling him that the interview had wasted my time and his. I left a message for Klarkowski that if he wants to question me again, he should make arrangements with Conrad first.

The semester will end just before Christmas and Lindy's immersed in her classes. If she's gotten in touch with her father lately, I don't know. She hasn't come to me again. I assume she made further contact and is satisfied he's ok.

...second week notes...

Last night calls came from AJ and Marnie about our holiday plans. Marnie was enthusiastically lobbying for the ballet in Chicago and lots of shopping. AJ was more interested in a hockey game with Alex and Cory.

No more cleaning to do. The House is ready now.

It's after 9pm. Conrad has called and asked if I can meet with him tomorrow.

"You're working late. You're the last person I expected to call."

"Yes, I have papers I still have to look over tonight. Can you come in about your will tomorrow?"

I've decided to update my will, so I'm glad he called. He said he has some papers he'd like me to see too. I also want to tell him about my visit to the police station. He set out two hours for us to talk.

Two hours? That's a lot of a lawyer's time. I wonder what this is about.

I'm too tired to ask.

Conrad's office looked wonderful this morning with huge pink and red poinsettias in the waiting room, and an enormous white poinsettia sitting on the table in his office. Smaller pots of red anthuriums lined the windowsill between the gray sheer curtains, now held back by wide golden ribbons revealing the river below. He had Ardith's homemade sugar cookies topped with cinnamon to eat and hot cider and chocolate to drink. The cinnamon smell mingled in the air with Ardith's cranberry scented candle.

Clayton Foster stuck his head in the door to wish a happy Thanksgiving. I had to chuckle. His tie was askew, shirttail out of his pants, and he had on dark blue pants and a brown suit coat. I have never been in his office but I suspect it's the polar opposite of Conrad's.

He certainly is. He's a small man, balding, with thinning mouse-gray hair plastered into a comb-over. His eyes are a watery grey, his face narrow, and his ears stick out a bit. He seems unimposing but sometimes he gets a shrewd look on his face and I think he's someone to be reckoned with if he has to be. He grinned, toasted us with his cookie and left us to our business.

We read over my will, made some changes to it and worked quickly through the details.

"I'll have Ardith type up the final copy. I recommend you keep a copy here, one in your desk at home and one in your safe deposit box. Since most of your children are adults, it might be a good idea if you sat down with them and discussed it too. You may run into opposition to that. Children, even grown children, don't like to discuss a parent's death. I think your children will be even more sensitive than most. If you want me to do it, I will. What do you think?"

"I think you're right, especially having lost their father the way they did. Actually I've already talked about what I want with AJ, but it would be good to make the others aware of what would happen. Is it set up so they won't have to go through probate?"

"Yes. It goes into a trust, and they all receive their share from the trust. In effect, they are members of the trust. Does this make sense to you?"

121

"Mostly. I found some information about it on the internet and that helped. Do you have a booklet on it too? I could have them read it."

"Absolutely."

He leaned back and looked at me very closely. I grew a bit uncomfortable under his gaze. I thought about Marthe's remark months ago about Conrad being interested in me. I still have no interest in him or any man. He smiled, and nodded, more to himself than to me. I felt measured and found acceptable.

The police questioning had been uppermost on my mind since I walked in because a small lump of fear was sitting in my stomach.

"I have to talk to you about what happened the other day." I rushed to get this out before he went onto something else. "I was called into the police station and questioned again."

I gave him a nearly verbatim account.

Conrad didn't seem surprised but he too was annoyed, his voice irritated as he replied.

"It sounds to me too as though they had Ben fish for information from you because he knows you. Since you know they can't search without a warrant and can't get a warrant without due cause, and they know you know that, just refuse them if they call again. Then you call here at once. I'll leave instructions with Ardith to contact me wherever I am. My advice? Invite Ben and me to your Christmas party. I am invited, aren't I?"

His eyes were twinkling.

"You know you are. The invitation's there on your desk and yes, he's invited too."

"Good. That should be fun! Any more letters?"

"No, but my nerves don't do well if I think about it. I have to keep very busy. I'm almost paranoid about Marnie, alone there in Madison. The younger boys are safer, I think, at school where they're under watchful eyes and I know AJ can take care of himself. He's read the letters. The others haven't yet."

"That's the next matter I wanted to talk about. Marnie is ok so far. My tracker hasn't seen anyone suspicious. He or they may have stopped after that letter. Can you hold off telling her for a few days? He'll end his surveillance the end of this week if all seems normal."

"None of our lives seem normal anymore. The closest I came was in September, before the cat was killed."

"Anna. I want you to seriously consider, seriously consider," he emphasized, "that Art was definitely involved in something illegal, something big. I still have no proof yet, but I'm pretty sure it was drugs. However, I may end up finding that proof because of my investigations and where they're leading. You need to prepare yourself for that eventuality."

I couldn't even reply at first. The implications were too much. I felt a wave of shame and I know I blushed from embarrassment. Had I been married to a drug dealer? Was my husband lying to me all those years?

"I'll think about it, Conrad, but it's really hard to believe."

"I want you to think how you'll protect your children from a lot of negative publicity if there is proof somewhere and it comes out. How will you handle having your house searched if police do find what they think is proof of involvement of someone in your house? I know it seems absurd, but it could happen."

"I'll think about it very carefully." I promised.

I picked up a small research project from Ardith and left. Instead of going to my car in the parking lot, I walked through a bitterly cold icy wind to St. Willebrord's Church on Adams Street. A long V-shaped line of migrating geese honked overhead, aiming for less inhospitable lands. Part of me wished I could go with them, out of danger. *They face danger too, Anna. Two thousand miles of danger.*

Does everyone have to face danger sooner or later? Or is it just some people? I have never let myself even think about people who face threat before except for a few seconds of sympathy after hearing about or reading about someone's troubles. Not even much empathy until Art died. Empathy is a whole different matter. It exacts a price before we can feel it. The price is our own pain, our own troubles.

Sitting in the shadow-filled church, I couldn't help but run all the old memories of our life together through my mind. I felt sick. What if I had been married to a crook? I prayed that Art had not been involved. I didn't want to know that my husband of all those years was deceiving me, all of us. *There is no comfort here, or anywhere.* I left and the shadows followed me home.

When I got home, I kept what I had learned to myself. I've gone up to the attic and made sure the files are locked, that there are no loose papers or notebooks among the legal books. I closed and locked the door to the attic, putting the key on a small ring, carrying it with me as I continued my preparations for the holidays.

How would a legal firm make lots of money under the table? I can't imagine and really don't want to know. I just want a nice holiday season. I'll immerse myself in the coming activities, create wonderful holidays for myself and the others and face it afterward.

...end of November...

We had a sumptuous Thanksgiving dinner complete with early Christmas trees. I'm a stickler for real Christmas trees but I compromised this year and we got an artificial one so we could have at least one tree up as long as we wanted. I insisted on a fresh one for the upstairs hall, a white pine that keeps its needles longer than the others. The pine smell floats through the house and sends me into fits of nostalgia but it's nostalgia tainted by suspicion and fear. What was going on all those years ago?

The next letter detailed AJ's activities for the last three months. I showed it to him. He verified it was accurate to the finest detail. Someone even watched him in the ER while he was working there. We brought it to Conrad. AJ refused to have anyone investigate.

"Then I'll have two people tailing me. It'll be a damn parade!"

Conrad is keeping his watchdog tracking Marnie. I feel she's safe enough for now. I didn't tell her. She has several girl friends who are with her almost constantly. I think now whoever it is will pick Alex or Cory to follow.

I sent a copy to Klarkowski.

November has ended with a major blizzard.

Eighteen

...December...

I've been busy. I've been wrapping up my business. I'm ending it, winding down slowly. By the end of the year, I'll be free to explore other avenues, perhaps to pursue something in the art field. I'll continue to work for Conrad but no one else.

It's clear now, crisp, and achingly cold. We've shoveled ourselves out of very deep snow much earlier than usual. Blizzards like this last one usually come later in the winter, in the thick wet snowfalls of February and March. I love snow. I love winter. My favorite scenes are when huge flakes float very gently down for hours, or when the sun lights a thousand diamonds covering every surface, or when I wake in the morning to find every single twig on every bush and tree covered with hoarfrost. White magic!

This year the magic is dulled. Even with security, I'm hyper-vigilant. With the episode of the snake and another letter, uneasiness nags at me. No denial on this score. Someone or something threatening and unwelcome is in our lives.

I worry about who's watching Alex or Cory or both and when that letter will come. I spoke to the vice-principal and principal at school. They promised to be alert for anyone unknown.

I force my attention on the preparations for Christmas with effort, willing us to have a very special holiday season. The boys wanted a third tree to put up in The Dorm and went out to a tree farm to cut it themselves. Cory spent hours going from store to store and finding unusual ornaments to hang on it. It's breathtaking—blue, gold, and white tiny lights, wide gold ribbon twined in the branches, thick with icicles, mirrored glass balls and crystal.

The party is scheduled for the second Saturday with everyone, family and friends, invited, with presents for all. Conrad is to be our guest of honor. He's done so much for us.

Lindy will stay with us for Christmas even though the semester will be over. Her mother wrote to invite her to Paris for the holidays but Lindy refused. "She has yet another man in her life and I just don't want to face that again. I won't go there." She will definitely go down to Merida on her January break to surprise her dad.

Ben called and, off duty, came over to question me yet again about the "drug" traffic. Same questions. I told him there's nothing more to say.

What else is there to say? I've noticed nothing suspicious, though I've spent time watching and trying to sense anything out of place in the neighborhood. I let Conrad know Ben came but he didn't think it harmful.

"You're cooperating. The police can have no complaints with your behavior. I'll see you and him at the party! I'm looking forward to it."

A light snow came last Saturday, the end of the first week of this month, just a dusting.

Ben says the police are investigating in the whole Astor neighborhood. That must be going down really well with some of our neighbors!

We girls had our ballet in Chicago—Marnie, myself, Aunt Carrie, Caroline, and MomKat, who we now know has the beginning of Alzheimer's. Despite some confusion and failing memory, she was enchanted by the music, the dancing, the whole production and the Christmas lights. Her dementia is coming on too fast for me, although her doctor says it's about average. It won't be long before she doesn't remember us, may not even remember who she is. I spend as much time as I can with her. Next Christmas she won't know us. I can't imagine that. I don't want to imagine that.

We had three days with long shopping trips, lunches filled with laughter, and nights on the town. I'm greedy for time with her while she can enjoy it, while I can connect with her.

Marthe is floating on memories of the ballet. The publication of her book is delayed while she has someone do the cover art and she still can't make up her mind about the title.

I took Caitlin for a massage and to have her hair done, sent a huge box of food from Figi's and a box from Beerntsen's Candies for the boys. She didn't want to go to Chicago with us, saying the boys need her at home but I know Caitlin feels out of place when she doesn't have money. I didn't press her to go.

Now that we're back, wrapped presents are piling up under the trees. The House sparkles and glows. We have candles in every window and lights on all the bushes in the yard, with spotlights on The House itself. Smells of cinnamon, chocolate, nutmeg and mint float around with every baking session. Young people come and go continually. Delightful chaos.

Rob Bradley, the twins and my guys got to their hockey game. So did Marthe and Lindy! Marthe told them she'd be writing another mystery and has to do research on hockey because it'll be part of the mystery. Lindy just loves the sport. To my great surprise, the men took to the idea of taking Marthe along. They came home impressed.

"Marthe's a tiger, Mom. She can yell right along with the rest of us. It was kind of embarrassing that she took notes though." Cory gave me a blow-by-blow report.

...second week...

Two days before the party and Conrad has called to say he can't make it. I'm so very disappointed. He apologized profusely, saying he's embarrassed to back out. He sounds tired and said he's been working on a very difficult case involving lots of research and investigation. He said he'll share details when he gets back but he's going to be in Milwaukee and then Chicago. Before I could ask him anything more, he said a strange thing.

"I hate to ask you this, Anna, because I know it brings up a painful past, but tell me again what was it that made you think it was Art's body you saw?"

My breath left my lungs. For many moments I couldn't speak.

"Anna? Are you there?"

"I'm here." I breathed in. "I just didn't expect that. Why are you asking about that?"

"I don't want to discuss why I need to know on this phone but I'm going to need to have as many details as possible that you and AJ can give me. It seems to have a bearing on what we discussed in my office a few weeks ago. I promise to tell you when I get back, which will be Tuesday after Christmas. Are you ok with telling me what you remember now or would it be better to wait?"

"I can tell you now. There isn't much to tell. You already know about the rings. The one on the corpse was a match to mine. You know that."

"That was all?"

"Big John got dental records for both men and faxed them down but we were told there was too much damage to Art's body. Maybe a match could have been made with newer techniques available now but back then, and in Mexico, it just didn't happen. I'm not even sure Mexican police gave it much attention. I'm not sure they even told us the truth. My vague impression, through my pain at the time, was that they just wanted it all to go away. One thing—when we got the body home there were no teeth and the bones were totally charred. Our funeral director was astonished and said that he'd never seen that before. There was nothing else. As for the plane, you know that the children's names were on it. I saw that myself. I don't think AJ will remember much more either but I'll tell him. I know he paid closer attention to details than I did. Call him though, and question him. He may recall more than I do, some little details. I was so out of it, so in shock."

I was feeling upset and my voice told him that.

"OK, I just needed to ask one more time. I'm sorry."

He sounded contrite and even sad.

"I'll call you as soon as I get back. Have a wonderful Christmas and my love to everyone."

"Thanks, Conrad. You too."

I hung up wondering now what? Is Art's death the case he's working on? Why couldn't he talk on that phone? Where did he call from? Is he going to Mexico to see about Art's death?

I checked caller ID and looked up the area code. Miami. *Miami? It could be he's going to Mexico. What is he going to do there?*

Was that Art's body? Is Art really dead? I refuse to go there right now.

I plunged into the holidays again immediately after that call. I volunteered a morning at St. John's preparing meals for the homeless. We went to St. Pat's the Sunday before Christmas for mass, and spent that afternoon at my mom's listening to gossip about everyone in the Irish Patch, including that it was no longer exclusively Irish, (as if it has ever really been), with Hmong, Hispanic and African Americans moving in all the time.

For the most part, my family was happy about new faces. We were fully aware that not too many years past the signs in the businesses had said "No Irish Need Apply". But my cousin, Conan, was not so enthusiastic.

"There's drugs here now, and they've brought 'em. I can see them on the corners, making their deals."

"How would you know what a drug deal looks like anyway?" challenged Uncle Pat.

"You can see that from TV!" Conan's face and eyes, red and swollen from alcohol, glared out a challenge to one and all.

"TV! That's yer school of learnin' is it?" Uncle Pat grinned. "More like the bars ya been visitin'!"

The topic died in the swift flow of the conversation in other directions. I was grateful. I didn't want to have to explain even the little I knew, nor did I want a family argument. I wanted peace.

The party was a great success.

Christmas was so much fun. We ate too much, sang too little, and laughed a lot.

Nineteen

...last week of December...

I can barely write this but I must. Our world has fallen apart. I don't know where to turn.

Tuesday after Christmas came and went and Conrad didn't call. Finally, Friday, while I was in the kitchen making soup from the last of a turkey carcass, the phone rang. I thought it was for one of the kids and called to Marnie to get it.

"Mom, it's for you!" It was Conrad and he asked if he could come over immediately.

"I'm taking the river path. I have something I must show you immediately."

"OK. I'll put all the backyard lights on. Be careful. That's an icy walk right now."

When a half hour came, and he hadn't arrived from his home upriver, I sent Marnie out to meet him. She was the only one home at the time.

"He's probably being really careful walking. Just meet him and pretend I didn't send you."

"No problem, Mom." She got into her parka and boots and took a flashlight. It was the early dark of winter and only 4:45pm.

She was back within fifteen minutes, white and shaking, breathless from running, calling out even before she got through the door and up the back stairs.

"Call 911! Conrad is hurt! Call 911!"

I did and then raced to get on my clothing, handing her the phone. "Talk to them, show them where he is. I'm going there with blankets. How far is he from here?"

"By the little park, St Francis Park. Mom, he's really hurt! I didn't want to leave him but there was no one to help. I didn't have my cell phone!"

"Guide them there." *Oh god, that's a long way from here.* I grabbed two blankets and a small pillow and raced out. In the dark I found my way along. I don't know how.

The lights from our yard didn't illuminate the way for very far, nor did the lights from anyone else's yards or the businesses along the way. Far past the city limits and into Allouez, I nearly stumbled on him, a dark large lump lying half on, half off the path, coat open, dark blood splashed black against the snow, face cut and bruised. Around him were papers scattered all over, an open briefcase a few feet away. My fingers sought his neck. No pulse. I covered him with blankets and pillowed his battered head. I called his name again and again even as I knew he was gone. I knew. I just knew.

It seemed an eternity before anyone came.

With strange irrationality I thought that somehow, if I could pick up his papers it would make it all right, but I abandoned the task after I realized they were all over, even down on the ice of the river where they shone pale grey in the lights from the half moon. It looked like someone had shaken the briefcase out, or it was torn from his hands and broke open. I kept putting those I could reach into my pockets, stuffing them in.

Do blankets keep dead people warm? I knelt down beside him and cradled his head, calling his name. Far away, I heard the clarion siren of the rescue squad, a second police siren echoing behind it.

Alex and Jake came running along the trail, calling my name. When they found me, they made me move aside and they began CPR. I didn't have the heart to tell them he was dead. I wanted to believe maybe he wasn't.

It seemed so long before Marnie led rescuers down the hill and along the path to where I knelt. Rescue squad and police took over. Jake and Alex lifted me up out of the way.

I still had this crazy idea that we needed to pick up Conrad's papers. I had the boys try to find them all in the dark. The police stopped them, saying they would do that. I dissolved into sobs. We watched as they worked over him. They wouldn't declare him dead at that moment before they tried to revive him. I had a quick spike of hope but it didn't last. I knew.

The police asked us to return home, after obtaining our basic information. Klarkowski arrived as we were leaving and asked us to remain available for questioning. We made a slow, sad procession back to the house in the cold night.

Hearing the siren of the ambulance go by, I insisted on going to the hospital. I couldn't bear the idea of Conrad being alone there with no relatives or friends.

At the hospital he was finally declared dead. AJ got the medical information from the doctors. Conrad had been beaten severely and stabbed to death. I began crying and couldn't stop. What a terrible death!

We returned home and waited. Marnie, Cory, Jake and Alex huddled together on the living room couches. Jake was on his cell to Jim, who was at the Ashwaubenon Mall with Caroline and Rob.

"They're on the way," he said to us. I looked at him. A streak of blood still smeared his face even though a nurse at the ER had cleaned up the blood on the boys' hands and mouths.

I went to Jake and hugged him. Wide-eyed with fear, he looked defeated, pale, near tears. "You did your best for him but he was gone. There was no more you could do." I pulled him into the kitchen and washed his face as those tears slowly fell.

I had given the hospital Clayton's name as the person to be notified but didn't know his phone number, nor if Conrad had any next of kin. When we got home I tried to find Clayton's number in the phone book but apparently his phone is unlisted or he lives out of the metropolitan area. I called the now-closed office and left a message.

Ardith will be just devastated! I don't know Conrad. I don't know anything about his life. Who are his family? Where are they?

Marthe, quietly sobbing, sat immobile at the dining room table, Marnie's arm around her shoulders. The boys still sat silent in the living room.

Makings for the soup were still on the kitchen shelf. No one had eaten. I tried to pick up where I left off but couldn't do it. My hands shook so much I couldn't hold a knife much less cut with one. No one wanted food anyway. I threw it away.

AJ went down to the crime scene. He came back to report. "Its crawling with police. Allouez PD, Klarkowski and Rudmann are all at the scene. Klarkowski wants to come up to question us when they're finished. That will be soon. The crime scene is badly compromised—footprints all over. It will be a miracle if they find any uncontaminated evidence, but I can't see how that could be helped. Rudmann's fuming."

Caroline, Rob, and Jim arrived. I made us all coffee and tea for the long night ahead.

Just before midnight, Klarkowski and Ben arrived. The questions began. Klarkowski, irritable and appearing tired, was not pleased we had gone to the hospital. I, just as irritably, told him I didn't care, and that human decency demanded it.

I told him everything I remembered about Conrad's call and unloaded my pockets of the papers, giving them to Ben.

"He was very carefully guarded about what he was working on. It was related to my husband's death, but how, I don't know. I wish I knew more. I'm very scared. Two of my children and myself have been stalked, our lives chronicled in detail without our knowing who's doing this. In two different states. In three different cities. For more than three months. Conrad had someone trying to find out who was doing this."

"So you have no idea what he wanted to tell you, or was bringing to you or what he discovered? Can you be sure his death is even related to the papers he was carrying?"

"No. Not at all. He wouldn't discuss it on the phone. I got the impression he wanted me to examine the papers but he didn't say that exactly, just that he had something he wanted to show me."

Ben questioned AJ and Marnie. Because they were minors, Klarkowski stated I would have to be present when Alex and Cory were questioned. It didn't take long. It felt like forever.

After Jake was questioned, Caroline and Rob took their boys and left.

I was exhausted, devastated and frightened. *He was my friend, my support, the person I've trusted most next to my family. Who can I trust now?*

Klarkowski called later and said he would most likely be back with more questions tomorrow and this case was being investigated as a homicide.

I looked at the clock. Almost two a.m. It's already tomorrow.

The murder hit the news the next morning. Media tried to call us repeatedly. We unplugged our landline and used our cell phones.

"Mom, there are creepy people in our yard." Cory was standing behind the sheer curtains in the living room. People lingered on the walks and the river path and even in the snow in the yard. AJ called Ben and the spectators disappeared from the yard when police drove by. They've thinned out now. The temperature has dropped to a frigid below zero. It's too cold for curiosity.

I'm an emotional wreck. I can't imagine that dignified, elegant man as a dead murder victim and yet the picture of his battered face never leaves me. Questions whip through my mind, flailing me. I have periods of shaking and tears run down my face. Sometimes I don't feel them or know I'm crying. I just know I've cried when I see my shirt is wet.

Klarkowski phoned again and said he wants me to see something. He came and took me down to the crime scene. It's cleaned up except for the blood around the place where Conrad lay. Small drifts of snow have begun to cover the blood. Klarkowski pointed to some letters in the snow. Faintly the letters A, K, and N, almost unreadable now, show through a covering of flakes. One of the letters is flattened by a footprint, another smeared.

"Do you know what this might mean?"

"No. I have no idea."

"We think Conrad wrote these before he died. They have very small amounts of his blood in them."

135

Was he alive when Marnie reached him? She didn't think so but he must have lain there for a while. Oh, god. Poor man. He knew he was dying. Alone and cold and dying. What was he trying to tell us?

The mail came today with another letter. Alex and Cory are the targets. Four months of activities listed. AJ called and left voicemail messages for Klarkowski. There has been no response. There is no Conrad to inform. I don't even know the name of the person who watches Marnie.

New Year's Eve doesn't matter, and matters terribly. Conrad will not be part of our new year, never again part of our lives.

Twenty

... January, week one...

Now that he's gone, I hold little hope of finding out what Conrad knew so the questions never cease. If he was in danger and murdered, will the murderer be after us? Beyond any doubt, I'm sure his murder has to do with whoever or whatever he found. I would love to get hold of all those papers. I even sent the boys to look for any that might have been blown down or up river. They found nothing. The police have been thorough. With their suspicion of me, without Conrad's influence, I'll never get to see the papers. The crime scene tape is down. The boys say blood is still in the snow. Whatever Conrad wanted me to see is gone—taken away or blown away or buried in snow somewhere.

My attempts to contact Clayton have been futile. He must be gone for the holidays. I've left messages on the office phone but no one has returned my calls.

It's four days after New Year's. Ardith just called, emotionally a mess. She heard it on the news. I invited her over.

"I'm at the airport, here in Green Bay," she said. "I've been down in Arizona visiting my daughter."

"Do you need a ride? I can come and get you."

"No. I left my car here in the parking lot. I'll come to your house as soon as I can thaw it out."

When she finally arrived, it was in a thin cloth coat and she was freezing cold. I got out a little electric heater and had her sit close to it.

Her blonde hair was, for once, not perfectly done, stray hairs escaping down the side of her face and at the back of her neck. Holding a hot cup of tea in her hands to warm them, she spoke, her voice thick with emotion.

"I am so terribly upset, but in a strange way I'm not at all surprised. He's been nearly obsessed with this investigation, working night and day at it. I was afraid he would be hurt. He was quite secretive about it. That was unusual. He's always been open with me about what he does...was doing. Oh! I can't think of him in past tense!"

She fought tears, her eyes becoming red-rimmed, and had to take a deep breath before she could go on.

"I think he's dug deeply into something that's more than he can...could handle. And that's saying something because I've seen him handle some very frightening cases."

"Ardith, I'm so sorry you had to hear it from the news. I called the office and left voicemail but there's been no answer."

"I know. We closed the office for two weeks so people could take a long holiday. I thought he'd be back before we closed. When he didn't show up, I could only just leave. I think he may have even gone down to Mexico to follow his leads."

"I think so too." I said and told her about the call. "If I'd thought this would lead to his death I'd have urged him to stop."

"It wouldn't have done a bit of good. Once he set his mind to anything, all the gods in the universe couldn't have stopped him. Frankly, I don't think his death will stop this now either. If I know him, he's left a trail, with enough information to make sure that trail can be followed, will be followed."

I brought her up to date on what I knew.

"Do you know of any files at the office that might give us clues to what was in those papers?"

"None. You have a file with us, of course, in fact, two. There's your case against The Firm, and then there's your will. There's a computer he uses at the office connected into our network and our research data, and I can check that but I don't think he'd keep this kind of information where there was any chance someone could see it, even at the office. He's investigated other dangerous cases now and then and kept the data on his computer at home until it was needed. I think that's what he would have done in this case."

"Ardith, one of the terrible things about this is that I know nearly nothing about him. I feel so badly that I never even asked. Where do we send condolences, offers of help?"

"There's not a soul that I know of. He never spoke of relatives."

She left promising to search at the office for any information she could find.

"I'll get hold of Clayton too."

Later Ardith called to say she received the official autopsy results. Conrad died of damage from stab wounds to his liver and heart. He was officially declared a murder victim.

She'd gotten to Clayton. "He's waiting on another line and I'll put you through to him."

Clayton was horrified. "I'm still out of town, on the way back from a ski trip. We'll be home later today. I'm sorry, Anna, for you and for us. He was our mainstay, our..."

His voice broke. I heard him take a deep breath before he continued.

"Conrad had no relatives and I know he named you in his will to execute his wishes for his funeral. He changed his will just recently and told me that. He's left instructions and money for his funeral. It's mostly all arranged. When the police release his body, Ardith can help you with the arrangements. They're very simple. I know it's one more thing on you but if you wouldn't mind? I'll call you as soon as I get back, after I see the office staff. They're all in shock."

"It's the least I can do for him. I'll call her right away."

The funeral was the exact opposite of the Irish wakes I was used to attending, somber and quiet, yet I felt at home with the Episcopal ceremony, so like the Catholic one I knew. Conrad, practical and thorough, had simply wanted a memorial service at Schauer & Schumacher Funeral Home followed by an Episcopal mass next morning. Ardith and I had very little to do. He wanted no open casket and requested cremation.

To my great surprise he wanted his ashes scattered in the Caribbean. He had left money to cover it all, including plane fare there and back for me and another of my choice.

That was the first of many surprises from Conrad.

Twenty-one

Dream

I step carefully along the river path from white paper to white paper, careful to avoid the deep blood-red snow. I hear nothing. The trees are bending back and forth in a soundless wind. Snow crystals hang in the air, excruciatingly bright, piercing my eyes with needles of light. On the ice at the edge of the river, parallel to me, a black-robed Conrad walks slowly, solemnly, his white hair glistening, his hands dripping red. In the center of the river, swimming parallel to us is a long golden streak. Though I can't see its head, I know it, my familiar enemy, Anaconda. I look down and long grey strips of cloth trail from my arms, waist, and body—the remains of my own shroud.

We walk for a long time, farther and farther upriver until we come to the locks at De Pere. I feel Anaconda grow angry, writhe and thrash in the river. The locks are frozen shut and its path is blocked. It turns toward us and seizes Conrad, twisting around him, dragging him under the dark water in the center of the river.

The scene changes swiftly and I am racing over the De Pere bridge to the western side where the paper mill sucks water from the river into its turbines. I see Anaconda swimming below me around and around, creating a whirlpool. It reaches out of the water and slithers up a pylon and comes swiftly, reaching for me.

Sound shatters around me as Conrad screams, the only sound I hear. I am slowly sucked into the whirlpool.

The water changes from icy blue to clear red as my blood begins to ooze out of my skin. I see my children below me, tiny babies, their hands lifted up to me pleading to be rescued. A ghostlike Art drifts beside me. Wanting his help, I try to wake him up, shaking him.

Wake up! Wake up! My screams make no sound.

He floats, expressionless, cold and ice blue, dead.

I swim down to the children and we cling together as we slowly drift to the surface. The whirlpool's power pulls us toward the mill's undertow. I can't swim and hold them at the same time. We are a few feet from the mill's jaws, and going deep into...

I awaken suddenly feeling a sick despair in the pit of my stomach, gagging on it. Another nightmare. I move out of bed to my bathroom, stomach cramping with diarrhea, stumbling over my shoes in the dark. I sit in pain on the toilet until my body is empty of all matter left from what little I've been able to eat.

At my desk, the small light on, I write it down to empty the dream from my mind. They come almost every night now. Diarrhea of the psyche. I have trouble concentrating, trouble even thinking.

It's nearly morning. I force myself to stay awake because my mind wants to go back to finish the dream. I try to envision a happy ending. My mind refuses to follow my will and I can feel us being sucked ever so slowly down and down into a maelstrom.

... January, week two...

Clayton called to notify me that I have to be present at the reading of the will. The official letter is in the mail. I can't imagine why I should be there.

Today, the day of the reading, has been cold and nasty, with a wind chill of fifteen below. My eyes watered and my nose burned with every breath. Breathing through my mouth was like inhaling icicles. An acrid smell from one of the mills cut its way through the cold.

I went to the office with AJ, Marnie, and Marthe. The atmosphere was subdued and sad. I could see he would be sorely missed by members of his firm. They made a point of coming up to offer condolences and I got and gave hugs as they filed by.

For the actual reading, only a few members of the firm were there. Ardith, of course. Two junior partners I scarcely knew. Clayton read the will. He had barred all news reporters, but didn't ban the two detectives, Rudmann and Klarkowski. I thought it odd but since I'd never been to a reading of a will, what would I know?

Ardith was stunned, breaking down as she learned he had willed her a retirement fund of $750,000. She got up and rushed out in tears. I was utterly astonished. When he'd told me he was wealthy, I'd never imagined that much. To the junior partners and other members of the firm he also left very generous sums. As expected, Conrad's share of the firm went to Clayton. I kept wondering why I had been asked to be present.

Clayton then came to the personal property. A cash sum went to a charity for people with AIDS.

Then, to my and everyone's enormous astonishment, I became the recipient of all his personal possessions as well as the bulk of his estate. This included two homes—in Green Bay and Cancun, Mexico—investments in stocks and bonds, his art collections, and bank accounts in the United States, Mexico and another account and property in Switzerland.

Switzerland? He has a Swiss bank account? Swiss property?

There was a collective gasp at each announcement. If I had expected anything, it was certainly not this. My mouth hung open. I burst into tears.

Clayton took off his bifocals.

"Yes. I did read that right." His voice sounded a bit annoyed. He was watching my astonished tear-streaked face.

"It seems he felt he had made some mistakes in negotiating your settlement from The Firm. He wouldn't tell me what that was but he said he wanted to be sure he made amends for that error in judgment. He had, of course, discussed a few of the changes with me some months ago when he updated it, but not this part. I assume you know what that error was."

I think Clayton thought I was going to enlighten him. I wasn't. I couldn't speak. I was completely overcome.

The others were dismissed and AJ, Marthe, and Marnie were asked to wait in the outer office while Clayton took me into his own office. It was definitely the exact opposite of Conrad's. I tried to find a box of tissues in the chaos but couldn't. My nose was running and I had only the remnants of a paper napkin in my purse. I stood there trying to make that do as he searched through piles of papers, found and gave me the keys to Conrad's home in Green Bay, the home in Cancun as well as to several safe deposit boxes and a sealed envelope containing what Clayton said was a summary of Conrad's financial holdings. He had not read them, he said. They had been in a file that Ardith had found. I was in tears still. He finally found me some tissues.

"I can see this is a shock to you, Anna, but you must know that Conrad held you in high regard."

He paused to clean his glasses on his tie. After taking piles of papers off a chair so I could sit down, he continued.

"As you see by that bequest to the AIDS foundation, it may also be something of a shock to you that he was gay. He certainly didn't reveal that to most people, a wise move when we first began the firm in this town. I knew it, of course. Ardith, too. I've always thought that even though he was gay, she had a crush on him. Silly woman. He and I had few secrets from each other because, friendship aside, we never wanted our firm to be subject to any forms of blackmail and we never were," he added with pride in his voice.

"Conrad did, however, have something he did not confide in me, and that was whatever he was working on when he died."

I heard annoyance discolor his voice.

"He only told me it had something to do with your old case against your husband's firm. He had found some new information, but what that was is unclear. He hadn't finished compiling his facts about it and Conrad never ever revealed conclusions without thorough research and being very sure of his facts.

"I want to offer you any resources of mine and our firm's that you need if you wish to pursue this," he said. "Do you have any idea what he had discovered?"

I shook my head no. then found my voice.

"He didn't explain on the phone when he called. The police have all the papers that were scattered on the ground around him that night. I picked up some, those that were near him. I handed them to an officer. There were others all over.

The wind blew them around or maybe they were thrown around. Do you think he might have kept copies somewhere?" I had finally stopped crying as I spoke. "I think what he was working on were problems having to do with my settlement from The Firm."

Clayton shook his head and sounded irritated. "Well, we searched but we haven't found anything yet."

I thought that odd but didn't say so.

Wouldn't this concern this firm too? How is it Conrad didn't share more of this with Clayton?

I thought of one thing.

"Last September, after I read through the papers about the settlement, we discussed the financial state of The Firm when Art died. Something wasn't right about what they reported as their profit. Art had told me way back then that The Firm was making a lot of money. Conrad told me later he thought Art's firm was keeping either poor or misleading financial records. I assumed Conrad was working on that when he called the evening of his death. Can you look for duplicate papers, or computer files, or ...?"

My voice trailed off, and I struggled to keep from crying again.

I couldn't even imagine what might be in the papers. I couldn't think straight. Conrad's death is unreal. The bequest is even more unreal.

I don't know how to be rich! This is frightening! How do I handle all this?

"I don't think the police will give me access to the papers." I said. *I can't take this much longer. I wish he'd finish this. I have to get out of here.*

Clayton looked thoughtful.

"I'll see what I can do about that. I'm becoming very interested in this, not only for myself but for our firm. I'll have to update myself on what he was doing. Is it alright with you if I begin my own investigation? At this point there would be no charge. I'll regard it as an internal matter. I respected Conrad very highly and if he thought this was so very important, it is. I'd like to know what intrigued him so much after all these years."

He was silent for some moments.

"Do you realize you are a very wealthy woman now?" he said.

I shook my head no.

"Truly, Clayton, I can't imagine it. This feels so unreal. His death feels so unreal."

There was a long silence. He appeared to be thinking. I just couldn't speak at all.

Finally he spoke again.

"There have been rumors all along in our little legal world in town about the financial status of The Firm. We all knew they had ambition, that they wanted to be a very large firm and were expanding. Mostly, I put the rumors down to jealousy. The Firm did land some big legal cases and well-off clients and that, among the Old Guard, is enough to set off all kinds of gossip. But rumors have persisted, even up until your final settlement and beyond. I think Conrad was attempting to run some of these rumors to their sources, to find out the truth. He had a passion for truth and couldn't stand hearing people bad-mouthed. Anna, I have to tell you that there are people in this town who have bad-mouthed you and Art for years. I'm not talking about all the usual gossip here, the petty stuff. Have you known about this or did Art shield you from it?"

"Well, I knew about the petty stuff because it came back to me over time. Green Bay is a big small town. We grew up here and knew lots of people. Art, I think, tried to shield all of us, the children and me, and even my family. I knew we were snubbed by quite a few because of being from the West Side and we were actually once called 'nouveau middle class' but I didn't think it was all that vicious."

I stopped there, thinking of Guinnie. That was certainly vicious. But those rumors were long ago. Surely they've died out. Was that what harming the cat was about? Even now? That thought hadn't occurred to me. Not petty! And certainly vicious! Are there people I know who are that cruel? Who? Why?

Clayton went on while I was remembering.

"I think you must have ignored a lot of it. At least, that's my take on your behavior. Art was not so quiet about it in the law world. He was furious at times, and raked a few over the coals for their snobbery. It seemed to me that's what fueled his ambition. And he did seem to be protecting you. That's why I brought this up. In any case, I will certainly act on your behalf to see what I can find out about Conrad's recent investigation."

He sat back, his pencil made a rat-a-tat-tat on the desk.

"Yes! I will!"

His determination showed in the pulsing muscles in his lower jaw.

Then he relaxed a bit and smiled.

"By the way, did Conrad tell you he was gay?"

"No. That thought never occurred to me. Are you his partner?"

Too tired to censor what I said, I blurted this out and then, embarrassed, covered my mouth with my hand.

He laughed.

"No, not that kind of partner, just the law firm kind. As far as I know, he never took a partner. This town, in my own opinion, would have been too intolerant of that. When it comes to being gay, this town, traditionally, has been pretty much like the military—don't ask, don't tell. I don't know what he did in Mexico, or in Europe, where he often traveled.

"Conrad's education and culture far outstripped most of the population of Green Bay. He could have taught classes in many subjects at doctoral level. He had near total recall. He was a first class pianist. Sadly, I only heard him play once. I never knew why he hadn't pursued a career in music. His love of art was great. You'll find he has a collection of paintings somewhere. He spoke vaguely of acquiring a collection. He has some beautiful ceramics too. But again, I never saw most of it, other than the masks on his office wall. He kept his private life very, very private. I've never even been to his home. It was his sanctuary, I believe."

He became silent again and lost in thought. I was thinking he might have been remembering his partner and their times together. I felt it was time to leave. Anything else could be finished later.

I'm feeling so tired, so depressed. I have to leave.

"Clayton, I have to go. I've left AJ, Marnie and Marthe waiting and I don't want them to face reporters alone."

Clayton came instantly out of his reverie and picked up his phone and punched in a number.

"Ardith, tell the reporters waiting that I'll be giving a press conference in fifteen, no, make that thirty minutes. Show them into the large conference room and give them coffee, yesterday's coffee, if there's any left over." He smiled maliciously. "That ought to soothe their nosy souls for a while. I'll have someone show Anna and her family out the back way. Can you have Jim get their car and bring it to the alley door, please? I'll bring their key out in a moment."

He called in AJ, Marthe, and Marnie, and made sure they were ready to go. He, like Conrad, had a back door to his office. We were ushered to a rear elevator and when we got down to the first floor, an aide brought us to the alley, where the car was waiting. We went home, where I gave them all my account of the meeting.

At home, I couldn't shake off my depression and it didn't help that AJ was wired. He was determined to find out what was going on. I lay on the living room couch with a headache pounding behind my eyes. He paced.

"I'm going to pursue this, Mom. I have so many more questions now. The rumor is Jonny throws money around like it's going out of style. If The Firm isn't making money, where is he getting it? His dad's money? How could that be? His dad went missing three or four years back on that hunting trip to Montana and he wouldn't be officially declared dead yet, just like dad. O'Keeffe Construction seems to be doing ok, but somehow I can't see Jon as the head of that construction company nor as an investment wizard.

I want to get into Conrad's home and see if he left any clues there. I suppose the police will have been there because of his murder, looking for clues too, but who knows? I want to trace where he went, see if I can find out who he saw, who does his investigation for him. All law firms employ investigators, their own or contractors. I bet Conrad had great sources."

I shook my head. *I want this to stop. I can't lose him too.*

"I don't want you in any harm's way. There's been too much death already. You have your practice, your medical career. How will you do something like this? No! Please don't! AJ, I don't want you murdered too. Leave it to the police."

"Mom, I have to." He paused and took a deep breath, watching me. "After this murder, now I'm thinking Dad was definitely murdered too. I have to."

His statement brought my mind out of my fog of grief. In my emotional state I'd been only half-listening. His words set off something.

Murdered? Art murdered? Wait. Who said that before? Someone suggested that before. Conrad? Back in September I asked him about it when we were walking back from the police station. No, I asked him if he thought Art was alive. But he said I should prepare us for Art being murdered, didn't he? Did he? Or was that prepare for a scandal. Or was that AJ? I must have blocked it out of my mind. I did block it out. I can barely think straight.

I looked at my son and slowly, agonizingly, came to the realization once again that nothing was over.

I have waited for years for this to be over. I've shoved it away or let this slip from my mind again and again while there has been stalking and murder after murder. Denial again and again.

AJ waited, watching my face as I absorbed what he was saying.

I let the tears drip down my cheeks, not even bothering to wipe them away, as I realized that perhaps my life, all our lives might have been based on secrets and lies and my own stubborn denial. That is frightening!

AJ came over, sat down next to me, and put his arm around my shoulders.

"Mom, I'm so sorry to bring this up to you again but yes, I believe Dad was murdered and I believe we have to face that as a possibility, that his death is an unsolved crime, that he may have been involved in something illegal, either as an adversary or a participant. I've been ignoring it for so long, but Conrad's murder makes it imperative I stop avoiding it all. This complicates life unbelievably badly but I have to know."

"AJ, I'm fighting my own denial, my intense wish that this would all be over. I've been fighting this for months to the point where I don't even remember what people say to me. Conrad brought that up. You brought that up. I even asked Conrad if he thought Art was alive and then forgot I said it. He asked me how I felt about that and I'm ashamed to say I don't want your father alive any more. There's been so much sadness and pain. Seeing Conrad dead in the snow, knowing the others were murdered, I just wish I could erase it all. But you're right. We have to know. We have to find out what's been going on no matter where it leads."

A great lump of sickening fear sits in my stomach. I know he's right, not only for his reasons but also because I have a serious reason of my own. It has just dawned on me that, from the police point of view, I am the person who has benefited most from the death of Conrad. I am their primary suspect. We have to get to the bottom of this.

"We'll go to Conrad's house tomorrow."

I went to bed and cried myself to sleep.

Twenty-two

I had never been to Conrad's home though I've always known where it is. In a row of similar homes, it faces the Fox River on Riverside Drive in Allouez, set into the hillside. From the street they all look like simple one story houses but they're not. Built into the hill going down to the river, they all have three floors, with balconies off the second floor. They're middle-class homes but modest for a person of wealth. Conrad definitely didn't flaunt his money.

Marthe came with AJ and me. After what Clayton had said, we wondered what we would find there and speculated on the beautiful objets d'art we would see. I expected another place of tasteful elegance.

Instead, when we opened the front door and walked in, we were stopped in our tracks. We saw only complete devastation. My headache of last night began its dull internal pounding again.

It was trashed. Furniture overturned. Pillows and cushions ripped. Broken glass everywhere. Cold. The living room picture window was smashed and letting in the winter air. Through the arch to the kitchen, the refrigerator was open, food tossed across the floor, water puddled on it, ice around the edges.

We gaped at the destruction. My stomach clenched. AJ, instantly alert, was the only one of us to move cautiously out of the foyer into the living room. Crunching sounds came from under his feet.

"Someone could still be here." He said softly. "Damn! I can't walk silently on this glass!"

From what I could see, the destruction was brutally done; sculptures targeted for smashing, paintings ripped off the walls and thrown on the floors, their canvases cut and torn, their frames cracked. It seemed to me that everything and anything of value was a target.

I reached for my cell phone and didn't have it. Tiptoeing my way through the mess to a closed slant-top desk, my eyes followed a cord from the wall and found a phone inside. I was relieved when I heard the dial tone.

In a very quiet voice, I called 911 and gave the dispatcher our location, afraid to talk louder in case anyone was still in the house, afraid to walk anywhere for fear I would make it worse, if that was possible, and afraid to call to AJ in case that might give him away.

Marthe remained standing silent just inside the door, her hands to her face in horror.

I could hear AJ as he continued his way carefully through the upper floor, checking it out. He finally came back and reported there was no one up here with us.

"Mom, the person who did this was enraged. It looks like the work of a psycho! This is scary! I know the police will declare it a crime scene but I'd sure like to do my own investigation first."

"I wish you'd said that before I called them. Be careful! Someone could still be on the two lower floors," I whispered as he left the foyer again.

Do you suppose the police did this? They must have been here searching. A mushroom cloud of anger began gathering over me. *How could they leave something like this?*

AJ had little time to make his examination before the Allouez officers were at the door. Green Bay police detectives were with them. Klarkowski and company, out of their jurisdiction. That told me volumes about how they viewed me. All departments were cooperating when it came to my movements.

My mushroom cloud blew apart and I lost total control of my temper.

"Did your officers do this?" I demanded. I swept my arm around the area.

"If you wanted to search this place, why didn't you do it legally? You never notified me you were going to do this. What gave you the right to destroy this man's property? At the very least, this place should have been guarded! You should have been watching this place if you suspected murder. Look at this!" I was hissing mad and part of me knew I was making little sense but all my angry grief was pouring out.

I could read on their faces they were surprised by the state of the place. It didn't change my mood.

Klarkowski's face was wooden, his body rigid, his voice cold.

"Mrs. Kinnealy, we didn't do this. We did come here immediately after his murder but there was nothing we found that indicated any crime had been committed in this house. It wasn't like this. And because his death was murder, we had ample probable cause. You hadn't inherited the property at that time. We searched before the reading of the will, so this could be a simple case of vandalism of an unoccupied house."

"It *was* my property at the time. I know law well enough to know that it was my property from the moment of his death and you needed a warrant, even though the will hadn't been read. You never checked with Clayton Foster. You didn't want to check. You did whatever you pleased. That's a violation of the law." I had a fleeting thought I could be wrong on that but I was beyond caring.

"Did you find it locked?" he demanded to know, ignoring my comments.

"Yes, of course, and I am the person with the keys which I got directly from Clayton. How did you enter this house when you searched it if you never got the keys from Clayton or from me? I'm calling Clayton."

My anger had taken over my mind and my tongue. I felt myself falling into the maelstrom I'd dreamed about.

In desperation I turned away, focusing on calling Clayton for help. As I hoped, his number was programmed in and I pushed speed dial.

Calm yourself down, Anna, or you'll make this worse! I was on the verge of losing it entirely. This destruction was the last straw. I knew I had to gain control or I'd be in more trouble. I was shaking with rage.

The receptionist answered and I gave her the details, asking that she notify Clayton and Ardith right away. She said she would. I turned back to Klarkowski, who hadn't moved. He continued.

"As I said, we did search, right after he died and before we knew it was yours, but we certainly didn't leave it like this. Perhaps someone else came. Perhaps your son AJ came and left it open."

I didn't dare speak. Fortunately I didn't have to.

AJ walked into the living room. If he'd heard what Klarkowski said, he didn't bother to address the personal accusation.

"Every room is like this," he said, his voice hard, words clipped. "Even the statuary, bushes and trees in the back yard are destroyed. There are footprints in the snow. The lower door to the yard was open, the lock destroyed. There are no other doors or windows open and unlocked except the smashed picture window. This was a job done very thoroughly and with premeditation. Everything of value I've seen was targeted for destruction. Whoever did this knew his way around, knew what he wanted to do, and did it as an act of revenge. There's some evidence of a search as well but that is not primary."

Klarkowski looked skeptical but didn't respond.

It was too much. Conrad had been the target of a terrible hate and rage he didn't deserve, that destroyed him and everything here he had possessed, just because he was trying to help us. My emotions swung between guilt and rage and I felt my control dissolve totally.

"You get out. This isn't your jurisdiction," I hissed.

AJ saw my face crumple and came over to me and hugged me.

"I'm sorry, Mom. You've hardly had time to grieve his death and now this. I know how much you want to preserve his memory."

He gathered Marthe into his embrace as well and placed himself with his back toward the officers. I broke apart completely, sobbing, no control left.

The police went outside until the crime scene crew arrived.

Twenty-three

It's been a terribly long day.

By the time the crime scene people arrived and the police came back in, Ardith had called back. She connected me to Clayton and he had me go on speaker phone. He sent Klarkowski and his cohort packing in no uncertain terms.

"Detective, it's not your jurisdiction and there is no probable cause for you. You leave. APD stays. If I have to come over there in person, I'll raise a lot more hell that this. We still have no copies of Conrad's papers. Cooperation works both ways."

He continued. "Anna, Ardith will be there as soon as possible with the insurance people. I want you to get photos of everything from every angle and from top to bottom. Document everything including every move you and anyone else makes. Let me know if there's anything more I can do."

Klarkowski left. I know he'll get any information he wants from APD but for now it's a standoff.

It took hours for police to finish as they carefully documented everything and as AJ followed in their footsteps photographing everything. They didn't like it much but they all had heard our lawyer's dictum and went along with it.

They took casts of the footprints in the snow and found fingerprints. Ours were taken for "purposes of elimination". Point to Klarkowski. He'll have them now.

When I finally walked through the house, I was horrified anew. Destruction was everywhere. I became angry again at the brutality of it all. I became more frightened too.

In the bedrooms, mattresses and springs were ripped, some drawers and closets emptied onto the floor, others not even opened. Some of his clothing had been torn and cut, some of it untouched. It was so random, so senseless, so strange. I saw holes in the walls where someone had smashed through to empty spaces behind, usually where wires or plumbing snaked down to the basement or upstairs.

The two lower floors were not quite as bad. It seemed to AJ that the person began in the basement and became angrier as he went along. I sensed jealousy, revenge, rage, all of that.

The person who did this was writing Conrad's epitaph in destruction. His death is so much more a violation with this terrible chaos added.

Conrad had an art studio on the second floor where every one of his paintings were slashed and broken. However, we discovered a climate controlled room which was locked. There was damage to the lock but it was intact. When I used my key to open it, I found he had more of his art collection there, and he had stored some of his own finished work. He was an accomplished painter. No surprise. Was there any talent he didn't have?

My emotions were dissolving into numbness—a relief.

AJ interrupted me. "Where is Ardith? I need to go home and get these photos on computer. I've done all I can."

"Go. Take Marthe with you—she's exhausted—and bring back help and cleaning stuff. Go in my top right-hand desk drawer and bring my folder marked 'Conrad's House'." He left.

Minutes later, the doorbell rang and Ardith had ignited a fire under the insurance company because the agent and the adjuster walked in with her. I recognized the agent as one of the parishioners at St. John's, Denny Carstensen. A small man with thick glasses and a buzz cut, he took one look and went pale. For a minute I thought he looked like he would faint, but when he spoke his deep voice boomed out.

"Oh, lord! This is terrible! This is sad! I can't believe this!"

I had never ever seen Ardith angry. She has always been beyond calm and cool. Until now. She was furious. "Appalling. I can't believe this either!" she echoed. "Someone went completely out of control here. Totally unacceptable. We should have hired someone to watch the house. I never thought of that. I'm so sorry. This won't happen again." I thought *Woe to whoever has done this if she finds him before police do.*

The adjuster, whose name was Ed Woodruff, stood with laptop and camera, mouth open. "It's as bad as any hurricane Ah've ever seen," he drawled in a thick southern accent. "And Ah've seen a few."

We were interrupted by the doorbell again and it was men to take care of the window. I called a restaurant and ordered hot food and coffee for all. It was long past our lunchtime. Denny ordered the delivery of a large dumpster for the next day.

And so the day went. The late afternoon dragged into evening, all slow, nit-picking work. Alex and Cory came to help. I sent them home at nine p.m. They have school.

Finally, AJ and I were alone. I was in the main bedroom, sorting and folding the clothing tossed about. One of the dresser drawers was jammed.

"Can you see if you can free this drawer?" I asked him.

"Finally we've got some privacy!" he said. "Mom, if Conrad's computer is anywhere, it's well hidden. I've been searching and haven't had one bit of luck yet."

He tried dislodging the drawer but had no luck with that either.

"I forgot to even look for a computer," I replied.

"There's something in stuck in here. I'll have to take some boards off the back I think."

He left to get our tools and I continued in another dresser. I wasn't paying any attention to him when I heard him exclaim, "And here it is!"

I looked up to see a big grin on his face.

"What's that?" I asked, puzzled. In his hand he had a slim metal case, silver, about four by five inches.

"It's the next best thing to a computer, an external hard drive! Conrad was smart. I know he wouldn't have left evidence in only one place and in only one form. I figured he had a computer and that's what I was looking for but this is every bit as good, even better! I bet he put everything he was doing onto this and hid it deliberately. We can still look for a computer but this is a great find."

He was triumphant, gloating.

"AJ, how could the police have searched and not found that? Surely they checked the drawers."

"This was very cleverly hidden. If the tape holding it hadn't come loose, we wouldn't have found it either. It was probably the cold that loosened it and anyway, I suspect they weren't looking for this little baby. The house wasn't trashed back then. There would have been no reason for them to look for something like this. They had all his papers from his briefcase."

I almost felt like smiling. *Thank you Conrad!*

"It's probably protected with Conrad's password but I'll find a way to get in. Maybe this will have the originals of the papers he was bringing to you. I have my work cut out for me tonight."

He was nearly drooling at the prospect and decided to stay at the house.

"We need to have someone here and if I go home and the guys see this, they'll be at me all night. I want some peace and quiet."

"You won't get any sleep, will you?"

"I'm wired, Mom, so no, I won't. I've just finished becoming a doctor. We weren't allowed sleep. I'm used to it. Will you call me when you get home with Conrad's date of birth? I'm going to use that as a start to finding his password. See you in the morning."

I went home hoping for quiet too but my day wasn't over yet. I phoned AJ with Conrad's DOB. Then, as I was preparing for bed, our house phone rang. I thought it might be AJ again. It was a woman and I didn't recognize her voice at first.

"I hear you're a rich woman! Aren't you lucky!" High-pitched, tense and tinny, her voice was like glass breaking on cement.

Who is this? How does she know I'm rich? That news has traveled fast and far! In the time it took my mind to think this, she went on.

"I want to talk to you."

It was a demand.

"Who is this?"

157

"Ahhh! You don't remember, but then why would you? This is Jenny O'Keeffe. We need to talk." *What? Jenny? Not the Jenny I remember.*

"Why?" I blurted out, too tired to be polite. *What could she want from me?*

I had heard via the grapevine that she was cut out of Big John's will, which may or may not have been true.

I felt wary. *Why here and why now?*

I really don't want to talk to any sister of Jonny O, even if she was so helpful back then. I already have too much on my plate.

"Well, darlin', I think you and I should talk about my wonderful family. And The Wonderful Firm! There's a lot you never knew. Now that you have money of your own, my insolent brother can't destroy you as he'd like to, so I think it's safe to reveal a few family secrets."

Sarcasm, anger, hurt. All were in her voice.

I inhaled a long slow breath and let it out just as slowly. We've all heard rumors from the Irish Patch for years, especially from Caitlin, that hinted at a very dark secret in the O'Keeffe family, that there was a good reason Big John's wife was either in church praying like crazy, or in a home for mentally ill.

Are the rumors true? Is Jenny O willing to talk about them? What does she mean about Jonny wanting to destroy me? Can he possibly be still angry that I hadn't responded to his coming on to me? Absurd! No, probably more like still angry at the settlement. He'll never let that go. He isn't the letting-go kind. Is he responsible for Conrad's death? Could he be the one who damaged Conrad's house? I have to talk with her. If she has any information at all, I want to know what it is. What's happened to her since she disappeared? Would she know if or how Big John and Jonny were involved in what The Firm was doing? I have to know what she knows.

"I'm in the midst of the task of going through Conrad's things right now, but by the day after tomorrow, I'll want a break. I'd like to have lunch somewhere, my treat. Will that work for you?" I offered.

"I don't come to Green Bay anymore. Can we meet in Neenah? There's a small restaurant there on the river. Say, noon? Look for me at a back table."

She named the place and street and the line went dead.

The phone rang again. It was AJ.

"I just wanted you to know, I'm in some of the files on the external drive." Before I could tell him my news, he rang off.

I had one more important task. My inner radar had been nagging me all day about Marnie. Something was wrong. I called. She denied any problems.

"I'm fine, Mom. Sammi and Alicia are visiting me this week and we're having a great time. This is a first. Your radar's not working right. You're totally stressed out. You need some R&R. Get some rest."

She's shutting me out again.

Twenty-four

...next day...

AJ was sprawled sound asleep in the guest room, still in his clothes, when I unlocked the front door of the house. I let him sleep.

Wandering quietly through the place, I felt like I was violating Conrad's privacy by even being there. A bleak gray day made it worse, a reminder of the cold brutality of his death. The living room light was dim with the big picture window boarded up.

Unwilling to face it, I left to get us some coffee, bagels and cream cheese so AJ would have something to eat.

Anna, you have to do this. Just finish whatever you can.

So I went back and began cleaning, tackling the two lower floors. While I worked, I remembered Jenny's voice, brittle and rough, no emotion.

Jenny. What about Jenny? What do I know about her?

Recalling bits and pieces from the past brought up my childhood memories of the twins. Two siblings couldn't have been more opposite. Where Jonny O could be brash, arrogant, devious, outgoing, and sports minded, I remembered Jenny as quiet, shy, almost completely silent, to the point of disappearing from anyone's consciousness. Sister Mary Andrew, the fourth grade teacher, once locked her into the classroom for hours, forgetting she was there. It was easy to forget she was there.

She got spectacular grades but I couldn't remember a single shared confidence with other girls, a single time when she went anywhere with us. If she hadn't been included in class pictures, no one would have remembered she went to school with us. Like a ghost presence, she was. She graduated high school with high honors and Big John and the newspapers made much of the fact she was accepted to Bryn Mawr, one of the elite Seven Sisters schools.

When she came back, she tried to fit in but it couldn't work. She had never really been one of us. There were rumors of her mom's mental illness and how it hurt the family, even how mental illness was "the vengeance of the Divil" on Big John for his harsh treatment of his workers. But then Irish are always good at bringing in the Saints, the Divil, and Jaysus as participants, willing or un-, in human affairs. Big John, always in control, worked hard at impression management in the community, making sure all knew what a benevolent man he was.

What did Jenny do with her life all these years?

My musings were interrupted by AJ, awake and at the computer.

"Mom, I think you'd better see this," he called down the stairs.

I went up and bent over his shoulder, looking at the screen. The letterhead was The Firm's. The form was a brief memo. The subject was "O'Keeffe matter."

"We need to stop Big J" was written at the top.

The recipients were five, one of whose names I recognized from old newspaper headlines, Anthony Andrietti, alleged mob boss in Milwaukee. It was written by Art.

Stop Big J from what? Why would my husband have written that to a mob boss? But that wasn't the shocking part. The shock was the date—eight years and six months *before* Art's death.

What? So long ago? How can that be?

"Mom, who is Andrietti? Who are these men?"

"Andrietti was an alleged Mafia boss from Milwaukee. I remember his name from stories in the Milwaukee Journal. Why was Art sending a memo to a mob boss? I have no idea. I would never have thought Art *knew* a mob boss. I don't know these other men at all. These aren't Green Bay names."

"I know you don't like hearing this, Mom, but I'm not so surprised at the idea Dad might have been involved in dirty dealings. I know Big John was into illegal stuff, although he wouldn't see it that way. The construction business is a tough one at best and involves lots of political maneuvering and some really nasty under-the-table stuff."

I started to speak.

"Wait! Just listen to me. When I worked construction for that company back then, I heard the men talk. There were more than just rumors he bought his contracts with favors, built sub-standard structures, and who knows what else?

"Think about this. When Dad died, Big John managed our whole response to that in every way he could, rushing to our house, taking the calls, making calls, telling us what to do. Remember the whole turmoil about who was going to go down to Mexico? Big John fixed that by choosing me to accompany you and buying my ticket. If it hadn't been for his wife's attempted suicide, he'd have been with us every step of the way.

"Now I believe the whole thing, the death and the plane and all of it, was staged. You've always said that I accepted Dad was dead more easily because I went down and saw the corpse and the plane. That's not true. It wasn't easy at all. Everyone was seeing an isolated great tragedy, but I saw this as part of a pattern. The pattern was that Dad had withdrawn over the years from all of us, even you. I think he was a good man when I was very young but he changed slowly, became more remote, more disengaged from us. You know he did. You had to persuade him often to join us in our fun, in our family life. He lived right here and yet he left us."

His words suddenly shattered something in my mind. Memories, puzzle parts of a pattern which hadn't fit into my world then, which my mind and heart ignored. Memories of a man who had slowly closed down over ten years, bit by bit, who changed from an open, enthusiastic, fun-loving man to a...what? What did he become?

I don't even know. He certainly grew more cynical, less trusting of human nature. With the exception of Jonny O, he eliminated most of his earlier male friends. He began to shun the gatherings of the Irish clan of relatives. He spent more money than ever before, the plane being one example. He withdrew into his library more often, even avoiding his own children. He began to criticize Caroline and family members and our friends.

I put it down to the pressures of work and a cynicism that comes with knowledge of human flaws. The truth was, I hadn't wanted to see what was happening.

"Mom?" AJ looked wary, expecting, I think, that I would mount a protest. I couldn't. My mind was fragmenting, breaking, and if I told him what I remembered, I knew I'd have to admit my marriage had been decaying, all my bright fairy tale tarnished. I wanted this story to be something else, so I thought of something else. I know why I love denial. It's so much easier than truth.

"There's another possibility. Maybe Art was actually investigating something illegal. You didn't trust Jonny O or Big John. I've not trusted Jonny O these last years. Maybe your dad didn't trust them either. Maybe he was trying to discover what they were up to."

It now sounded a bit far-fetched to me but maybe Art was, could still be, a "good guy". I wanted to know my husband was a good guy. *I don't want to admit I lived with the man I'm now seeing.*

The relief on AJ's face was touching. I could see he too wanted to believe his father was honest, not involved in anything illegal. My heart went out to him.

"How did you bear this all these years? Alone. Grief is a messy process at best and then this on top of it. How did you manage? School. No money. Having to work and..." My voice trailed off as I saw the enormous pressures and stresses he lived with.

"Whatever your father did or didn't do, I never wanted this for you, for any of you. I love you."

"I know, Mom. We all know. You're our glue. I saw it through your eyes, even when I doubted the story. I wanted to see it as you did, to believe it was all good. The others did too, especially Marnie." He reached for my hand and held it.

I smiled a bit. He got that right. I realized he got a lot right. He was a grown man and I was suddenly proud of the man he had become because he'd had the courage to face these most unpleasant truths.

Be honest, Anna. You still want this to go away. You don't want to know any more.

I told him I was proud of him. "...and you know, your father was a lot like you when we first met, when we were married. Whatever we find out, I want you to know that he was a good man at one time."

I said that in a firm voice but I was shaking inside.

Was he? Did my husband become a stranger? Did I really know the man I married?

"I believe you, Mom." He grew quiet. "What are we going to do?"

"We're going to mop up this job and go from here.

When in denial, change the subject!

"How did you find this file anyway?"

"I don't know for sure. I was playing with possible password combinations using Conrad's birth date. People always use their birth date and I just got in using his email address and a lucky combination. I'm going to have to try to remember it. It was a reversal of some of the numbers. The file doesn't have a name, only a number. There are other numbered files and it looks like Conrad numbered those he wanted to disguise. I'm working on those first. As for the document itself, it's been scanned in. I'll show you how when we're back home."

"AJ, I can scan a document. What else have you found?"

"Not much more, but this can't be the only device here. I still think there has to be a computer here somewhere."

He looked at me with speculation.

"Mom, are you really willing to take this all the way? It could end up messy, even a scandal."

I rolled my eyes.

"Honey, according to Aunt Carrie and the neighbors, we're already a scandal! Why not make it good!"

He laughed.

"OK, then I have a mini-plan here. I'm going to include Ben. He's been helping me anyway, and I know he's been told to keep his connection with us. That's a good thing for us. The more open we can be, the more we include him, the less suspicion we're under. He also thinks there might have been some very powerful men involved, that this is bigger than even the police think right now. Actually, he's pretty worried. He told me he's afraid there might even be someone in the department who's dirty. What if he's right? We need Ben. He needs us. I think we have to trust Klarkowski too. What do you think?"

Yes, we'll need the police on our side.

"My gut feeling tells me Klarkowski is ok," I conceded with some effort. "Yes, we need to trust Ben too. I hadn't thought of it before, but if this really runs as deep as it might, I wouldn't be surprised at all if we find an officer or two are in on it. We can't know how far this reaches, how many people are involved. We need to be careful. This is very dangerous information. So, you work with Ben, share with him, and this is what I'm going to do next."

I told him about Jenny O's phone call.

"Maybe Jenny O can shed some light on Jonny's actions and what Big John might have been up to back then."

I stood up as I said that and looked around.

"Come on. Let's keep looking for a computer."

We went over every possible place, dressers, drawers, tables, chairs, on top, underneath, behind...and then went through all of it again. Nothing.

AJ looked discouraged.

"Maybe I'll have to start looking for Hidey Holes, like at our house."

"It looks like someone already tried that," I said pointing to the smashed walls.

I plopped myself down at the kitchen table, looking around.

"I don't know. We've checked everything in sight."

I happened to look down at the floor. A dirty mess was oozing from under the refrigerator. "Eeeew! I missed a mess. AJ, help me move this refrigerator out. If I leave this, we'll have an awful smell in here."

It made sticky sucking sounds as we rolled it out, mired into whatever had congealed under it. The grill over the coils on the back was furry with dust, not unusual. What was unusual was the Christmas-paper-wrapped, rectangular shape duct-taped inside the grill. When we got it out and unwrapped it, there was Conrad's ultra-slim computer.

AJ did a break dance around the kitchen, then helped me clean up. I laughed for the first time since Conrad's death. And then I stopped. If he had done that at Christmas time or before, he left us a hidden Christmas present. Had he known he might die?

How terrible! He did. He really did.

An Allouez police officer stopped by as I was preparing to leave and said he would do drive-bys. He suggested we might want to hire someone to housesit for a while. He told us that off-duty police sometimes take part time guard work and gave me a his card.

AJ called Ben and hired him.

Twenty-five

...journal...bedtime...

I hoped that was the end of this day. It definitely wasn't. Marthe was in a dither.

"Lindy called just fifteen minutes ago in tears, nearly hysterical. Her father is missing. She'll call again in another hour. Here's her cell phone number and the number of the bed and breakfast where she stays in Merida."

"Did she say any more, give any more details?"

"No. She's driving back from the dig to Merida and will call when she gets back. She just said that she can't find him and needs help. I'm really worried, a young girl alone like that in Mexico."

"Don't worry about her on that score, Marthe. She's accustomed to being there and knows her way around. She'll be all right. We'll just wait for her call."

Lindy had left us Christmas afternoon for Milwaukee to be with Rick, then flew out of Milwaukee on to the Yucatan, intending to surprise her father. I haven't spoken to her since then and she knows nothing about Conrad's death.

AJ, home to pick up clean clothing before returning to Conrad's house, called Ramon and we arranged for him to phone her in Merida. I guessed what was coming.

"She'll want me to go to Mexico. In fact, she asked even before Christmas. I know she sees us as more her family than her mother. If she can't find her father, she'll want one of us there."

I have to see about Conrad's house in Cancun. Can I do this right now? What will it do to me? I've been shaken to my core for days and days now. Everyone tells me Cancun isn't like Merida and that I'll love it there, but it's still the Yucatan. Can I go without all the memories overwhelming me?

Right after the reading of the will, AJ called Ramon and gave him the address, asking him to check on who takes care of it and what kind of shape it's in. Ramon called back to say it's a very beautiful house and that he's spoken with his cousin, who is the caretaker.

"He said there are household staff to care for us should we want to come down. He's having them get the house ready. Apparently Conrad left a bank account with Ramon's cousin for the care of the house."

Then, two days ago, just after the disaster we found in the house here, we called Ramon and reported it to him. AJ, on the other line, explained the necessity of having someone guard the house carefully. He let Ramon know we would probably be coming down in the near future and would phone him with details later.

Ramon was delighted.

"I look forward to seeing you, my friends. Actually, I think I have met Conrad two years ago when I went to visit at that house. I am much saddened by his death. He was a very nice man, very distinguished and intelligent. I am so sorry this is such a sad journey for you and will do all I can to help you, to make this a pleasant time. Please call me at any time if you need more help. I am in Merida now but will go personally to check the house before you come."

He assured us he would take care of everything and hung up to make arrangements.

Now AJ is in favor of the trip.

"Mom, I think we should go. I know we're busy up here but Lindy is family and we can use a short vacation. You're stressed. I finished an internship and walked right into this with no real break. Why don't you hire Caitlin to oversee the cleanup of the Allouez house? She knows how to get things done and will be very thorough.

"I don't think Lindy's dad is in any real danger. From what she's said, he's a top man in his field and very accomplished at living in tough situations but since she's so worried, it would be nice to do that for her. I have my own agenda. I want to see what I can find out about Dad's so-called accident, though after seven years it's going to be very iffy. But I was a kid then and not a doctor. Now the police might cooperate more with me. I'd like to see what's in their files if I can.

"You have Conrad's...your...house to check out. I can't get used to you as owner of three houses." He shook his head. "Things sure have happened fast lately."

"Oh yeah! I can't remember what day it is today. Christmas feels like the distant past."

The phone rang and it was Marnie. I told her about Jenny and Lindy.

"You have to go, Mom, not only for Lindy but for yourself. Cancun is a big resort area. It's not Merida at all. Nothing like it. It would be fun. Relaxing. The whole peninsula is an archaeological treasure trove of buildings and art. You'd love it. Ask Caitlin or Caroline to take over the cleanup of the other house. If I could get some time off, I'd go too but I took my vacation days at Christmas and now I don't have any left."

"I wish you did. I'd like you to come. Your brother made the same suggestion—to hire Caitlin, and you don't have to convince me. Lindy's like one of you to me. I know I have to support her. She's as much a part of this family as Marthe has become. I also have Conrad's ashes to take to the Caribbean. First, though, I want to meet with Jenny O. I have the gut feeling she's ready to talk more about her early life."

"Call me back and tell me what happens. Love you, Mom."

I could really use some R&R. Cancun, in the middle of winter. What a blessing that would be! What awful reasons for having to go.

"AJ, what about Conrad's computer? About the files? I want to know what's there."

"I'll work on finding any other passwords and opening as many files as possible tonight and tomorrow. Then I'll bring it all back here, make copies, and hide it in one of our Hidey Holes if I have to. It can all wait for a bit. Actually, maybe I can put the files on a flash drive and take my small computer with me and work on it there. Let me see what I can find first."

He went online and made our flight reservations for two days after my meeting with Jenny O, then called Ramon again to let him know our arrival time.

Cait agreed to oversee the house cleanup. "I know just the firm to do that. They're called C. Fitzgerald & Sons. I just got laid off for a few weeks and I can use the work."

169

When Lindy called we were able to give her reassurance that she would have help.

"I want to let you know how it stands here, Mrs. K. I went to Dad's office in Merida and talked to everyone I could and no one's seen him for weeks. The number I called at Christmas isn't in service. A professor at the University of Merida said he heard the dig was shut down. So I went there and found a skeleton staff and they said he's off surveying another site but they couldn't or wouldn't tell me where. The guy was lying. The site is close to the Guatemalan border, the roads are awful, and the car I'm driving won't make it there again. I'm running low on money and I still want to visit some of the other sites to see what others in the field have heard."

"Lindy, just wait. Ramon is getting us a good car. I'll have him get one for you. Wait at your B&B until he contacts you."

"Mrs. K, I know you can't afford a lot either."

"I can. I have so much to tell you." I gave her the news.

"Oh, no! I'm so sorry! Oh, that's horrible! His death, I mean. You've had a terrible time! And here I'm asking all this of you. I'm so very sorry."

"It's all right, Lindy. We need a change from here. It's been so difficult and we could use a break. I can hire help now instead of doing it all myself."

It took a while to reassure her we could help her. "We can stay at Conrad's house. I have to check it out anyway and scatter his ashes in the Caribbean. Conrad paid for airline tickets for two to take his ashes down there. This will work out fine."

I gave her Ramon's phone number and let her know he'd be in touch with her.

"I'm wiring money to you as soon as I can. Then you can stay at the house after we arrive. Don't worry. We'll find your dad."

I spent the next half hour making the arrangements. Ramon said he'd find her in Merida and get her a car. He had me send the money to the account Conrad left in his cousin's name and he would bring her that too.

What a relief it is to know someone down there we can trust. I'm so glad we know him.

AJ returned to Conrad's house.

It's not my house. It's really still his.

After all that had happened in the last few days, and especially today, I dropped into bed thinking I would be unable to sleep but I did. I dreamed police were chasing me along a tropical river by canoe and I was more scared of the piranhas in the river than of the police.

Twenty-six

Today I don't have time to dwell on dreams. Life is moving faster. I'm making myself write in my journal each night so I don't get too far behind.

We moved into a round of planning, packing, errands, and I hoped for a meeting with Clayton. He was gone again. I finally connected with him and he was anxious to know what we'd been doing. More about that later.

Meanwhile, I have two rebellious teens on my hands.

"Mom, it's January break! We could write reports on Mexico, on the archeology sites. Our teachers would love it!" Teen "persuasion", not unlike mafia persuasion but not as violent, unless one counts being talked to death, went on for some time.

Finally I'd had enough.

"I'm not saying you can't come down but first you *will* finish your interim commitments. You have almost a week after your current classes before the spring semester begins. I'll think about letting you, maybe, possibly, come down at that time. Not now! Note, I said I'll consider it. Let me just get through today. I'll give you an answer in two days."

I thought I said that firmly enough.

They high-fived each other and left, planning what to wear to fly down there.

AJ, entering my office, heard the exchange and rolled his eyes.

"Personally, Mom, I'd like to use them as bait for ice-fishing on Lake Winnebago. I'm going back to Conrad's, to the other house. It's more peaceful. I'll meet you later at Clayton's office."

When we met he'd found several passwords and had opened a few more files. I thought he'd share this with Clayton but he told me just before we walked into the office not to mention the computer and files at all.

"I don't know why, Mom," he said when I questioned him. "I just have this feeling we have to keep this quiet for a while. Let's just wait. I want to open every file and both of us read them all before we share. And I'm a long way from getting through all the files."

He would say no more.

We filled Clayton in on the mess at the house and what we had done. AJ did mention that I had found a few papers, receipts for purchases. Clayton seemed surprised and wondered where Conrad's personal papers might be.

"There must be more. Maybe we should search again."

"We won't have time, Clayton." I said.

I told him about Lindy's plea for help.

"I'll have to go down there eventually anyway so I'll check out the house down there. That's where we'll be staying. I'm taking the ashes too. In the meantime, I've got someone to oversee the cleanup of the Allouez house and a guard there round the clock, just in case."

"Anna, I've initiated a subpoena for the papers police found at the death site. I'm also digging out all the old background on your case against The Firm. I'm even considering reopening the case again on your behalf so I can get access to their books. It won't harm you financially anymore. Conrad saw to that. I think he would have wanted to pursue this. Of course, we'll never know for sure."

He became silent, then remarked, "You know, I sure miss him. We all do here."

He seemed lost in a reverie for several minutes and I didn't want to interrupt. I could imagine all too keenly the loss they felt.

Then he came out of it abruptly, sitting forward.

"I just want you to be careful. Be sure you have someone at the house to watch your boys and Marthe."

"Oh, we do. We've hired Ben for the Allouez house and to check on the boys too."

I told Clayton about the coming meeting with Jenny.

173

He nodded. "I've heard rumors about that family for years too. I wouldn't be surprised at anything. Big John was quite a character. Maybe he was more than that."

AJ informed Clayton he was going to begin digging into the accident down in Mexico.

"You be careful, Annie. You too, AJ. I'll keep an eye on Marthe and the others. As a lawyer I'd advise leaving power of attorney for health care of the kids and a good sum of money for the house, maybe even financial power of attorney, to Marthe."

"That was the other thing, Clayton. I want to be sure there's enough money available for them. I just set up the account for her, but I will leave the health PoA. I hadn't thought of that."

"Just what we lawyers are for. I'll see to it money is easily available for them. You have a good time now! Don't make it all business! It's a beautiful place, or so I've heard. I've never been there myself."

We have all our errands done, our clothing packed. We're taking our passports just in case we might have to go over the border into Guatemala or Belize.

I told the boys they can come for five days after January Interim ends and before spring semester. They're ecstatic. AJ made them get their papers together and showed them how to make their online reservations. They took off for Barnes & Noble to get maps and travel books. Once again our library is the planning station for a trip. I become nervous watching them, remembering. I pray for a happier outcome to this trip.

"There's one very serious item we must talk about right now, AJ."

I was having a last cup of Sleepytime Tea before bed and AJ was about to leave for the other house.

"You realize police regard me as the prime suspect in Conrad's murder because of the inheritance I received. If we leave town, their suspicion will increase big time. I don't think they can arrest me. There's no evidence against me. I was with Marnie and Marthe when he was killed, but it sure won't help."

"Oh my god, Mom, I forgot."

He slapped himself upside the head.

"We *have* to go. In one of my calls to Ramon recently he said there'd been a man who showed up at the house in Cancun who told the caretakers he was Conrad's friend and he wanted to stay overnight. They refused, of course. The man got ugly, impolite and disrespectful to Ramon's cousin but she stood firm. That was just after Conrad's murder. I didn't tell you at first because you were so upset. It didn't actually seem connected to anything here at the time. Then it slipped my mind with all we've had to do here. Now, I think it might be definitely related. I think if no one had been there, we might have had another trashed house."

"I'm glad you didn't tell me then. I couldn't have taken more bad news. That settles it though. We have to go no matter what that does to police perception of me. If there's a connection down there with what went on up here, I bet Conrad found it. Maybe going there will lead to more information about why he was killed."

That leaves my meeting with Jenny O.

Twenty-seven

I drove down to Neenah early because it had begun to snow and I wanted to be there on time. I found the restaurant, a little teahouse surrounded by boutique shops. Killing time, I saw a light cotton blouse in one window and went in to try it on. *I love this. It'll be perfect in Mexico.* I paid for it and started out of the store, reaching deep into my pocket for my car keys so I could throw the bag in the car. Feeling crumpled paper, I pulled it out.

I knew immediately it was one of the papers from the night of Conrad's death. Smoothing it out I found it had some kind of chart on it, hand-drawn boxes with names in them and lines connecting them. An organizational chart? The words "FOLLOW THE MONEY" were penciled in at the bottom, faint and worn, but legible.

The names were clear. Art, Jonny O, Big John, a police sergeant...not Klarkowski. More names...two prominent local Green Bay politicians, a state senator, Angelo Arrietti, and several others I didn't know.

Conrad knew everyone involved! Wait! Is it everyone? Involved in what? Have I just found the reason Conrad was killed? Had he put this together himself or had he gotten help? If so, whose help? Whose money? Money for what? Money from what? Will the police think I've withheld evidence if I turn this in? I want to see the rest of those papers from his briefcase. Yes, I do.

I had no time to deal with it and put it back in my pocket.

Jenny O was sitting at the very last booth in the restaurant, her back to the wall, watching me all the way in. *My god! She looks like hell.* She had dark circles around her eyes. Her hair, a glossy brown years ago, was now lifeless, dyed badly in a humdrum light brown, uncared for. *Is she on drugs?*

176

Her mouth curled up on one side in a cynical smirk and she let out a mirthless laugh as I sat down. "Well, well! Don't you look good! Money becomes you!"

I decided to lay some ground rules right away. "Jenny, don't go there. I won't tolerate it. Either we talk as reasonable acquaintances, if not friends, or I leave. I didn't come here for sarcasm and I won't do that to you either."

I looked her directly in the eyes and held her gaze. She looked away quickly.

Good! I can hold my own with her.

I continued to look at her. She knew what I was seeing.

"I don't want your pity."

"It's not pity, Jenny. It's concern. You don't look well."

She was silent for several moments. "I'm not well. I've become a version of my mother, different diagnosis, same field."

Again I decided not to talk around anything. "What is your mother's diagnosis? Where is she now?"

"A-a-ah!"

It was half-groan, half-sigh. "Right now she's labeled with major depressive disorder, chronic, no remission expected. I don't believe it. I think we could have the same diagnosis. Mine is post-traumatic stress disorder."

"From trauma," I said. "I do know about trauma. What kind of trauma?"

A waitress came and we ordered coffee. Jenny took the break to pull something together inside. She sat up a little straighter and squared her shoulders. When the waitress left, she began.

"My father managed the PR for our family well, didn't he? You must have noticed. We all tried to look good, but my mother didn't do it so well and, although I tried to look good, I didn't do so well either. Only Jonny O, Golden Boy, could hold it together. Of course, he didn't get it as bad as we got it. At least, I don't think he did. You don't beat around the bush. Well, I won't either. My father sexually and verbally abused all of us."

I felt my eyes open wide and my jaw drop, both at the news and the timing of its delivery.

177

"You look shocked. That isn't what you expected to me to say, is it?" The muscles in her face were tight and her jaw barely moved when she spoke.

"I'm numb right now or I wouldn't have been able to tell you. This is a funny, as in funny peculiar, disorder. I go from completely numb to emotional mess in seconds, like a yo-yo. I thought for years I had Mom's kind of depression. Then I thought I was bipolar. Now I find out I was fucked by my dad and brother and so was my mom."

"And your brother! Jonny abused you too?"

She watched me.

I didn't try to hide my facial expression. My mind was running scenarios from years of knowing her dad and brother.

"You're seeing them at your house, aren't you? How charming my father could be. How charming and fun my brother could be. You're remembering them. You find it hard to believe. Well, shit! Sometimes, so do I. Denial is so...so comforting."

I nodded my head yes, still finding it hard to talk. "I am remembering."

The waitress brought our coffee. I curved my hands around the warm cup, my fingers cold, my hands shaking because I was remembering, but not the charm. I was remembering Jonny O's visit to me after Art's death.

"Oh, my god! You saw something, didn't you? You know about this, don't you?" Anger rose in her voice. "You knew? You knew!" She leaned forward, her face contorted with rage.

"No! Not the way you think! I didn't know! I'm remembering Jonny, after Art died, how he came over, how he came on to me, how he was enraged, how he tried to rape me. That's what I'm remembering right now, and there's something more. I can't bring it into my mind right now."

I rubbed my temples, as if that would clear away this waking nightmare. I was seeing her as a child. Silent Jenny. She was being abused then, abused into silence.

I felt a slight throbbing in my head, my skin crawling. *A vague memory? What is this?*

Her eyes narrowed. "He tried to rape you? Of course! When he couldn't get what he wanted and you stood up to him by hiring Conrad, yes, he did. Well, that doesn't surprise me. And my father. Did he hit on you too?"

Her mouth returned into the cynical lip curled up.

"No, he never did. I don't remember any time when we were ever alone. Nor was I ever alone with Jonny until after Art died. He actually didn't seem interested in me at all before that. Not even in high school. I think I wasn't Jon's type."

She laughed this time, still cynical but genuinely amused.

"No. You are definitely not his 'type'. My brother is a closet homosexual and a pedophile. He used me to 'practice' being hetero rather than admit it to himself. I think he thought if he could do it with me, it would cure him somehow. Between the Catholic Church and my father, Jonny was a terrified and ashamed little boy.

"My mother tried to protect him when he was little because my father insisted on throwing him into ultra-male, super macho situations to 'make a man' of him. She was never successful. Big John would cut her down at every turn and it destroyed her to see him demand of Jonny what wasn't there. Jonny still won't admit he's gay. I don't think he even admits it to himself. No one in my family ever faced the truth. Including me, back then."

I could see in her eyes that her mind had gone back to "then". The tragedy of it was enormous—how they had lived like that for years, how Big John kept a lid on it all, how Mary Bridget went to suicide and back again and again. *No wonder she spent so much time in church.* Then my own denial began to creep in. *Maybe Jenny is creating a story here. Maybe this isn't true.* My mind felt tangled in some kind of waking nightmare.

It got worse. Somewhere deep inside I knew that my husband was in this too. It was clear to me, from my own experience, that he was not gay. His enthusiasm for sex with me had been total for many years. But the last few years of our marriage he was different. Something went on between Jonny O and my husband that pulled him away from me and the kids. Was there some kind of sick seduction there? Or was it that Art knew what was going on? Again something tugged at me from the recesses of my mind but I couldn't get my brain to zero in on it.

I looked at Jenny. She was spent, slumped into the booth, not even trying to maintain a façade. No. She was telling me, if not the whole truth, then at least her truth.

"Is there more? What else? How did you survive all these years?"

"I blackmailed Big John." Her voice was flat, emotionless again.

"Above all he wanted to look good to everyone outside the family. He paid me monthly to keep my mouth shut. He threatened me a few times but I knew he wouldn't carry out the threats. I had my insurance. I wrote out an account of what I remembered. There are several copies deposited where he couldn't find them, one with my own lawyer, in case of my death. He must have gone to great lengths to be sure I wouldn't talk because when he died, the payments continued for two years, like he had it set up."

She looked up. "I heard of Conrad's murder and had to see you. I heard you're involved. He was my lawyer too. He had a copy of the account I wrote. At first he didn't know what was in it but later, I can't remember when, about two years ago, I had him read it. He was shocked but he had to keep my secret. Attorney-client privilege. I was in no shape to take it to court. Now I don't trust Clayton Foster. I don't know what to do."

Was that what triggered Conrad's investigation? No, it was more, but that fueled it. I'm positive about that.

Jenny interrupted these thoughts. "I've had a drug problem, prescription drugs at first, then anything I could get my hands on. I finally went away to a treatment center and I've been straight for quite a while, but then the nightmares began and the shakes and the memories and...well, I'm still in counseling. Doing better but a long way from ok."

I reached for her hand. "I'm so glad you came to me and told me. I believe you."

Tears began sliding from her eyes down her face. I don't think she even felt them. "I thought you wouldn't believe me. Hardly anyone has, even my own mother. She won't admit that anyone does these things. In her world, these are sins that are never committed by anyone she knows, only by evil crazy people somewhere out there."

She waved her hand in the air.

Unfortunately the waitress thought she was signaling and came right over. Her bright smile disappeared when she saw Jenny's tear-streaked face.

"More coffee, please and could we have menus?" I said quickly. She almost ran away.

"Jenny, there's more you don't know. There's an investigation into the whole operation of The Firm, and lots of unanswered questions about Jonny O's behavior and Art's death, and that crash years ago, about how Jonny could have walked away from it, about where it happened, and even if it was Art at all. Art's body was burned beyond recognition. I believed it was him, the ring on the body matched mine and it was embedded in the body's hand. It was definitely his plane, but there's enough uncertainty to make some people wonder, including AJ, including me too now. Did you know Andy Moss and Sam Soderberg were both murdered?"

I had her attention but both of us put on masks while the waitress poured coffee and left our menus.

"Do you want to hear what I know?" She nodded but wanted food first so we took time to order. After our food came I began the story from the time of the accident to the present. I left nothing out. She deserved the truth as I could see it.

"Most of it is news to me. I haven't seen my father or brother since back then. I never went home even when I heard Big John died. I was glad, relieved. I communicated with him before that on the phone or by email if I had to, but mostly not at all.

"I visit my mother only now and then. It's so painful to see what she's like. Someone told me she was never like that before she married my father. I have more empathy for her now than I used to."

She shut her eyes for a time, then spoke again.

"I think there must have been, maybe still is, a lot going on no one knows about. I don't have the courage for a court trial for abuse. Not against a lawyer. Jon would destroy me in court. I don't know if I'll ever have enough courage, and it's my word against theirs. I never had any hope that either of them would admit what they've done."

"Jenny, you talk as if your father was still alive."

She looked stricken. "It's the PTSD. Sometimes I really feel he is. I feel haunted, you know? I didn't even know he died for months after. An old high school classmate saw me and offered condolences. She had read it in the papers. That's how I learned he was dead.

"I never went home again after we came back from Mexico. I was so relieved to be up here. Jonny came on to me in the hospital while we were there, and I knew Mom wouldn't believe me and Dad would make it worse, so I just left."

"What do you live on? Is it enough, for counseling and living expenses? I can set up something for you. I believe Conrad left me this money to help us, to help anyone who has been a victim in this."

"No, Anna, I'm ok. I have enough. I have a small trust from my grandmother, and I do part-time work as an editor for a textbook publishing company here. It gives me spending money, when I can work. I work as much as I want, when I want, and this posttraumatic stress stuff...well, I need that flexibility. Sometimes it's overwhelming. My counselor says I'm close to being through the worst of it. So..." her voice trailed off.

I let her know I had to leave for Mexico but gave her my cell phone number and I took hers. I told her about Clayton's support.

"Maybe you can get his support too."

"Thanks. I'll remember that, but surprise, surprise, I don't much trust lawyers."

When we parted it was late afternoon. We planned to meet as soon as I got back.

I just saw Caroline to update her and Rob on everything. They promised to look after Cory and Alex. I called Caitlin and updated her too. She promised to keep her ears open.

I almost forgot the paper in my coat pocket. When I found it again tonight I put it in my closet Hidey Hole with everything from Conrad's house.

When we get back, I'm going to get all these papers together somehow and see what I can find.

Another January day over.

Twenty-eight

...journal...last night in Green Bay...

Marnie came home unexpectedly, saying she had gotten some time off. It was a good thing, given what I knew I had to do. I was worried and angry. The nagging memory surfaced. I remembered a time when there had been some question of Jonny's treatment of our boys. Art had handled it. I remembered something about Art remarking that Jon was not very good with kids, and I had taken it to mean he was too impatient, only that. Now I'm sure he was hiding something from me.

I almost had AJ cancel our tickets for Mexico. This was more important. Jonny O had been in our house too many times over the years. I wanted to find out if he had done anything to my kids. I hadn't said anything to Jenny but if he had harmed my children, lawyer or no, he was going down.

Last night I first filled in AJ almost word for word on my meeting with Jenny and told him what I planned. He agreed. He was furious, pacing back and forth in the library where we were having our dessert.

"Mom, in my studies I saw what sexual abuse did to children. I'm a mandated reporter now. I want to know too. If anything happened to them, we'll need to get them help. You don't know this but after Dad died, sometimes I called family meetings so I could be sure they were ok and to give them a chance to talk. I mean, these were beyond the meetings you had with us. They never talked about anything like this. I wouldn't have even thought to bring this up, but now we have to know. This is damned serious!"

We had Marthe sit in too.

They were all shocked, but Cory, to my surprise, said he had always felt uncomfortable around Jonny O.

Alex echoed, "Me too, but more because he didn't like kids. We all knew that, Mom." He looked at Marnie for confirmation but got no response. She remained silent for a while, as the boys gave examples of Jon's indifference and irritation toward them. Then she spoke.

"I think he tried to do something to me once." She was blushing. "The thing is, I didn't feel like doing what he wanted me to and I blew him off. He tried to get me to sit on his lap and stroke his arm while he stroked mine because he loved me, he said. I just wanted to play with my dolls. I thought that he must be tired or something and told him to go to sleep."

She laughed. "It's kind of funny when I think of it."

I wasn't smiling. Neither was AJ. His eyes shot fire but he kept quiet, not wanting to interrupt her.

A chorus of "what did he do then?" echoed around the room, serious faces turned toward her.

"He got up and left as Dad came in and Dad looked angry and I thought he was angry with me but he was angry at Jonny and they went into the library to talk and Dad shut the door really hard. I heard Dad yelling at him. It never happened again. I remember thinking Jonny O got a really bad scolding and being glad it wasn't me."

AJ and I looked at each other. We both knew immediately what happened. The others saw our look and wanted an explanation. AJ explained about "grooming" that pedophiles do to children and they grew quiet.

"Did any of you have similar experiences?" I dreaded the answer.

There was a pause as they all seemed to be checking their memories. They shook their heads no.

"It sounds to me like your father stopped Jonny right then and there. I want you to know that if you have any memories at all, you come and tell us. Even when we're down in Mexico, you call us, you hear me?"

I got solemn nods from all.

Marthe assured us she would be available for all of them and they should know they had her backing too. She told us all that while she was still teaching she'd had to report suspected abuse numerous times and knew the process well.

We discussed a lot last night. I'm still having a minor debate with myself about the wisdom of opening this can of worms when I'm leaving so soon. Then again I have more than enough reason to believe that what we don't know really does hurt us. Confronting it is the right thing to do. I learned a lesson listening to them. Like a typical mom concerned with the practicalities of rearing children, I didn't give my children enough credit for their awareness of the deeper undercurrents among the adults surrounding them. Or for their own innate wisdom.

We settled the details of their care, making sure all our cell phones were programmed for each other. They all wanted a trip to Cancun and I decided then and there that they should all plan on it. I wanted everyone to apply for passports right away too, even though they didn't need them for Cancun. Travel was now a very real possibility for us all, thanks to Conrad. I thought of Conrad's request that I think of how I'd protect my children if this became a notorious case. *Now I have the money to get them away if I have to. Thank you again, Conrad.*

"Go down to the post office just past the cathedral here on Monroe. They can give you all the information and work you through the passport process. Do it asap, while we're gone. Pay the extra money to have them done faster if you can. You too, Marthe.

"But just remember I'm not promising anything about Cancun until we find out what the situation is down there."

Marnie volunteered to coordinate the passports and then dropped her bombshell. "Mom, I don't want to go back to Madison right now. I'm being followed and I'm scared."

"Damn!" AJ exploded. "I was afraid of that. Maybe we shouldn't go, Mom. That worries me a lot. The letters. Get the letters and let's deal with this now."

In chorus, they all asked, "What letters?"

It was a long meeting. They each read the letters, the early ones and the last few. After, there were long minutes of silence. Cory broke it. "Well, shit, damn, and hell! I wish I'd known this sooner. I could have watched for it!"

In chorus, "Cory!!!"

"Mom, we all use those words, just not in front to you. Respect for age and all that. But these," he waved a pile of the letters around, "are an occasion for swearing. I'm really angry that you didn't let us know about these! We're not babies. We need to know about this stuff! Geez, Mom, I'm seventeen now."

Alex was standing in front of me, feet spread apart, arms crossed. "It's scary to think this was happening and we didn't even know it. If someone had decided to take it further and hurt us, we would have had no warning, no...no... I can see you not telling us when we were little kids but now we're older. We should have been told!"

"Same here, Mom!" Marnie got up and stood next to her brothers.

"In Mom's defense..." AJ began.

I held up both hands toward them all.

"No, AJ. Alex is partly right. I wouldn't and shouldn't have told you long ago. That's too much of a burden for kids that young. I feel very right about that decision, but I was wrong to keep it from you now. I'm sorry.

"AJ, it's time for it all, even if we're leaving tomorrow, even if it takes all night to do this. And Marnie, one of the persons following you is protecting you."

A chorus of "What?"

"Conrad had someone follow the follower to be sure you're ok. In fact, the person following you may just be the guard he hired."

AJ rubbed the stubble on his face, ran his fingers through his hair. "Ok. Ok. Mom, they have to know what we suspect."

He looked at me for long silent minutes. Three faces turned from one of us to the other, back and forth. "Mom. You have to tell it all. All you had to endure." His eyes were asking. I knew what they asked.

We sat them all down at the long table where I worked and I told them all that I knew, all that had happened, including Jon's sexual assault. This was the hardest time of all. Marnie came and put her arms around me.

"I never knew what you were going through and I was such a little bitch to you. I'm so sorry."

187

Then AJ summarized all the questions we had and why we had them and what he hoped to learn in Mexico. Questions were asked and answered. We told them about the investigations going on. In the end I saw there were only adults left in our family. Alex and Cory grew up all the way.

We told them who they could rely on if threatened. Cait and the boys. The Bradleys. Aunt Carrie. Clayton for legal help. Ben as AJ's friend and as a police officer.

Marnie chose not to return to Madison to get her things unless someone went with her. "I don't have to go right away anyway. I have clothing here and can buy anything I need."

"What about school and your job?"

"Mom, I have some other ideas I'll talk about when you get back. I think I might want to change direction but I'll wait. We can all come down to Cancun. With a house there, even if it's small and crowded, it will be fun. You remember fun, Mom? You need some fun! Things have been pretty grim lately."

"Fine with me but remember, I'm not promising anything until I find out what's going on down there. First priority is to support Lindy in her search to find her father. Second, is to find out about the house. Third, bringing Conrad's ashes to the Caribbean."

I looked at Cory and Alex. "Your first priorities are schooling.

"You're still sounding like such a 'mother'!" This from Cory, accompanied by an exaggerated sigh.

"I AM such a mother!"

Later AJ and I discussed what we could do legally.

"It's not enough, Mom. The DA would never consider prosecuting that. I sure want to confront him though! Let's wait to see if Marnie remembers more. I can't believe he'd try only once unless Dad caught him the first time and scared him, threatened him. I wonder how long Dad knew what he was. Is. I wonder if he approached any other children."

In my room, I called Caitlin. She was still up although it was after eleven. I filled her on everything.

188

"Ok! Best thing you could have done! There's one more thing to do tonight though. I'm sending three of my boys over. Something for your boys and Marnie. You know."

"I do. I'll wait for them." Half an hour later, Sean, Mike, and Liam were at the back door. I called everyone down. Her boys laid seven rocks on the dining room table.

"One for each of you. You too, Ms. Grimm." They endured hugs from Marthe and I, handshakes from my boys, and loved the hug from Marnie.

In bed, I sat up thinking about all the times Jonny had been at The House.

I hope I can get some sleep on the plane tomorrow. It's not a good night for that right now.

Part Two

Yucatan

Twenty-nine

...January...

My stomach was fluttering before I left home. I couldn't eat and dropped an apple in my bag for later. Marthe handed me coffee to go. Marnie drove us to the airport.

"How many stopovers?" she asked.

"Just one this time. Miami. Are you going to feel safe here at home?"

"Yeah, Mom. I'm ok. Don't worry. You have a good time now. Don't make it all about Lindy's dad."

"No. I won't. That won't take long. I'll see all of you in two weeks at the most. I'll call you when we get to Cancun."

"Love you, Mom. You too AJ, sometimes."

"Twerp!"

"AJ, no one has used that word for years. It's dork."

Miami. Déjà vu.

AJ is on the phone as he was all those years ago, only this time it's his cell phone. He called Ramon again, then friends in Minnesota about his apartment and work there. Now he's talking to Alex. I write or watch passengers amble or hurry by, talking and laughing. I envy them. I wish I could make this trip just once without Death standing at my shoulder.

In spite of my efforts to shut out old memories, they insinuate themselves into my thoughts at every turn, so now that I'm on the way, I dread this trip. Apprehension wraps itself around me like the anaconda now in my dreams—grief over Conrad's death, entwined with concern for the safety of those at home, entangled with all the questions about Art and the Firm, twisted into worry about what effect Mexico will have on me, and tied up with my concern for Lindy.

AJ snapped his phone shut and looked at my face.

"That was then, Mom. This is now. Stay in now."

They called our flight and we boarded.

193

BETRAYAL by SERPENT

Tired from the long night we'd had and the intense activity of the last few weeks, I dozed during the long hours from Miami to Cancun but another nightmare attempted to form itself, this time a snake coming out of the sky flying alongside the plane. I gave it up and wrote in this journal for a while. I need my writing. It soothes me.

...arrival, early afternoon...

Cancun's heat and humidity dripped over my body, which is, of course, in winter mode. I felt sticky and smothered as soon as the tropical atmosphere surrounded me. Airport memories washed over me, but thankfully, there were no Mexican police officers to take control.

Instead, a huge bouquet of flowers and a smiling Ramon greeted us, and Mexico was suddenly bearable.

"Señora." He handed me the bouquet and then took my outstretched hand in both of his, delight shining from his eyes.

"Señora, su seguro servidor," he said, using old formal Spanish with a flourishing bow over my hand, laughing, exaggerating the gesture. "Welcome to Mexico! I am so delighted to meet you again after all these years, after so many cards and letters, and after so much life has gone by. I hope this visit will help to ease the pain of the last journey and your loss now, and I will do all I can to make it so."

His greeting, delivered with kindness and the sweet-spicy scent of flowers, drove away all the apprehension I had endured for the last few days. I was flooded with relief and delight.

"Ramon, I just want to hug you!" So I did. That made it even better.

I stood back to look at him. He had seemed like a young boy years ago. Now he has aged into a more mature man, face weathered by exposure to sun, even slight wrinkles around his eyes. Confidence. I see that in him. Age becomes him, makes him more handsome. He has grown into himself. But there's something else. Sadness maybe? Haunted by something? I have no label for what I see.

He and AJ shook hands and thumped each other on the back.

194

"¡Hermanito! Congratulatiónes! Tu es El Hombre, ahora. ¿El medico, sí?

They stood looking at each other with obvious delight and then Ramon turned back to me.

I laughed. "¡Sí! He is The Man now! And look at you! You have become more of the man too, with a thriving business. I want to meet your wife, your children, see where you work, and...

"Con perdón, Señora, for interrupting you. Most certainly we will have time for those things, but the young señorita is coming from Merida this afternoon and I would like to get you to the house of Señor Wentworth...I am sorry...your house. It is a long way from here up the coast to the north. We must leave here quickly."

"Of course. This is our first priority." I said. "I think of it as Conrad's house too. He became a good friend over the years and I miss him so much."

"I am so sorry for your loss. I hope that I can ease your way through this visit and make as much of it as pleasant as possible."

He took my hand again and held it but I had stopped listening. I had a deep and intense feeling Conrad was standing beside me and I sucked in my breath and held it, waiting for...what? Mentally I thanked him and told him how grateful I feel for his house and his legacy. I pictured a small cozy home and I hoped it would be adequate. At that moment, I had the feeling he was laughing.

"I do not want to be rude," Ramon's voice slid gently into my thoughts, "but we have to get you through customs. They are checking everything at this time. It is unusual. I do not know why. I have a car and driver waiting. AJ, we have errands to do, people to see." A look passed between them that told me they had already been discussing something. I raised an eyebrow and faced AJ.

"We'll fill you in, Mom. We have some news, but this isn't the place. Let's get to Conrad's house first." AJ grabbed the smaller bags we had carried with us and Ramon indicated the direction of the baggage area.

"Sí, Señora. It is fortunate you have a private home where you can stay. We can feel safe there. We can make that our base of operations." Ramon held my elbow and guided me through the crowd.

"You make this sound like an expedition, an investigation. Are we in danger?" I thought he and AJ might be overdoing it a bit.

"Mom, this may be more complicated than we first thought." AJ's face took on a very serious look.

Ramon shook his head. "We do not speak here."

We arrived at the baggage area. Tourists were all around us. Guides held signs with the names of travel groups on them. Elderly couples headed for tour buses, their baggage already collected by the touring companies. Families gathered children around them, attempting to keep everyone together in the crowded space. Bright colored shirts, skirts, shorts and dresses created a shifting rainbow and my color sensitivity went on overload, almost overwhelming me. *Cancun is certainly not Merida. There is a holiday atmosphere.* I waited, people-watching.

We picked up our bags and moved into the line for customs. I couldn't help but think again of the police at the airport years ago who insistently took charge of our lives as we stepped off the plane.

Thank heaven we don't have to do that again.

Except, it *was* happening again. When AJ moved to the head of the line and handed the man his passport, we were rapidly escorted to another room and the door slammed behind us. Wordlessly, with cold looks and exaggerated slowness, they examined every inch of our luggage. My stomach got tighter, then shaky with the rise of fear.

"Why are we being treated this way? Why..." AJ stepped closer to me and put a warning hand on my arm, shaking his head no in a very slight movement. I heard his soft "ssshh". His face was devoid of all emotion, empty, controlled. He turned back to the officials and said, in Spanish, "I am Dr. Arthur Kinnealy and am here to bring my mother to her home."

That made no change in their attitude and actions.

Ramon, who had been watching them carefully, finally spoke. I didn't understand what he said in his rapid Spanish but he did not smile and his voice was stern. He produced his own card, handing one to each of the three inspectors. They all looked at it solemnly, then nodded to him and carefully repacked everything they had taken out.

He signaled for AJ and me to move toward the exit, asking us to wait outside. He remained behind. When he came out he looked grim and moved us quickly toward the car. He made a quick sign to AJ rubbing his thumb and fingers together. I knew that sign. They wanted bribes.

In the car, I looked at him, my eyebrows raised in question. He shook his head. "En la casa, por favor, Señora," he spoke softly into my ear. "We speak only where it will be safe. I know this driver but not well enough yet to fully trust him."

What is so dangerous that we can't even speak in front of someone he knows?

Ramon began a series of "tour guide" descriptions of the sights as he had done so many years ago. It was a good diversion for me. Being a tourist felt better, until the odor of something burning came through the open windows.

I can smell the plane. See the plane. Blank this out! Now!

I made myself focus on Ramon's voice and the scenery passing by.

Because the boys had brought home a map of the Yucatan and I had examined it quickly before we left, I had some idea of where we were going. The ride north took over an hour, first through the Zona Hotelera, filled with huge hotels, painted in golds, pinks, blues, and oranges backed by the turquoise sea shimmering with sunlight just beyond.

Oh how I wish I could go for a swim in that water.

Cancun was clogged with traffic, and we were forced to drive slowly. I loved the sights. The colorful buildings and the diversity of people strolling the streets created a moving picture of the tourist photos I'd seen in the brochures the boys brought home. A huge open-air market left me wishing we could stop and just wander through it.

"That's on my list of things to do here. It looks so intriguing, so exciting." I told the others.

"We will, Mom. Soon."

BETRAYAL by SERPENT

Then we drove through Puerto Juarez, a shocking contrast. The poverty, the immense difference between rich and poor, was extreme. Ramon explained that this town and outlying villages are where most of the workers in the hotels live, that they make as little two dollars per day in wages for long hours, "twenty-five cents an hour or less. There is no minimum wage here. Large hotels take advantage of this. Some people are trying to get the government to set a good wage but the rich owners do not want to pay more. They prefer to bribe government officials to keep it this way."

There were unpaved streets lined with tiny houses, aging walls, tin roofs, and hot, sweltering sun.

No air-conditioning here. Tourist brochures never show this.

Ramon's face looked suddenly older, more lines wrinkling the corners of his dark eyes, a grim sadness in them, his mouth a tight line. I heard a carefully controlled anger in his voice as well.

"Even with all the tourism, there is much poverty here. Sometimes very rich men demand that the women who serve in the hotels provide sex. For the poor, tourism is like a knife with a smooth blade edge and a rough blade edge. Both sides cut. The only difference is that one leaves a little less pain. My family works very hard to stay away from the knives of the rich. We now can choose where we work. It took a long time to get this far."

Even when I was a little girl I was "rich" in comparison to this! Now I'm even richer, one of those rich Americans. I'll have to think long and hard about this wealth. I don't know what to feel. I'm in two worlds, the one I was brought up into and the one into which I've been thrown. I'm going to need help. A new lawyer? Clayton will do for now but...will I need someone with more experience? An accountant? An investment firm? So many decisions to make.

But not the decision of whether or not I can eat today. I think people here must make that decision often.

We drove past Punta Sam, which I knew was the port for the ferry to Isla Mujeres.

Will I ever get there? How different our lives would have been if Art's plane had not gone down.

198

On the road north, we passed a series of very expensive homes set far off the road behind large ironwork gates. Landscaped gardens were visible through breaks in huge oleander and hibiscus hedges. The flowers were glorious, riots of pinks, oranges, golds, reds, peaches and yellows amid the deep greens. Palm trees were everywhere. *Look at those palm trunks. They have colors in them. They're not just brown.* I couldn't get enough of the beauty. My own gardens at home are so pale by comparison. My sensitivity to color was in high gear. For a while, I let myself enjoy drowning in this rainbow.

"It's a good thing you're not driving, Mom, or we'd be in the bushes," AJ teased, and then explained to Ramon about my reaction to color. I got teased some more.

I was intensely conscious that this was the ride Conrad took to his home. I felt him sitting with us. *You must have enjoyed this, relaxing into this beautiful setting as you rode home, Conrad.*

"Both north and south of Cancun are being developed. The eastern coast, to the south of Cancun, is now called the Riviera Maya. It is more for tourists. These are private properties. My family staffs a few of these homes when the owners are here. As I told you, we are staff for Señor Wentworth's home also. That is why I was able to so easily find help for you. I met him once two or three years ago but I did not know him well. I work the hotels only and not in homes."

"Well, I feel relieved and pleased at that." I smiled at Ramon. "Just let me know what you and your family need or want and I'll provide it."

"And we will provide all the comforts of your home for you, without snow," he laughed, his eyes a warm brown and his smile generous.

"Actually, I am missing the beauty of the snow, but not the extreme cold and the ice."

He laughed. "¿Es mucho frío ahora?" he asked.

"Oh, yes. It's been a very cold and snowy winter so far."

"Someday I would like to see snow as you see it. You can be my tour guide then." He laughed as he said this.

"Yes. I can do that. You will come up to see us someday."

Small talk prevailed for the rest of the journey.

199

BETRAYAL by SERPENT

The tenseness in my body began to drain away little by little.

Maybe I'll be able to relax, to let go of so much of the stress of the last few weeks. This feels like it was a good decision, coming here.

Thirty

Finally, just past the small town of Boca Iglesia, we turned onto a lane landscaped with lush big-leafed flowering plants and tall palms, and paved with packed red gravel. The shore of the cobalt blue sea lay on the far horizon as we drove the long path. The sea disappeared as we curved around to the front of a stunning adobe home, three stories tall. On the second floor, long high windows overlooked the drive. Flower boxes under the windows held blooms in shades of deep reds and wines. A portico covered the burnt sienna stonework of a large patio shaded by heliotrope vines which dripped with purple flowers that twined overhead. Heavy, thick smells where rich earth had been turned over drifted up where the heat of the sun warmed it. Flower perfumes, some sweet, some spicy, floated by on the air.

I was in total awe.

"Oh, my! The picture I had in my head is *nothing* like this."

Conrad's house is so-o-o much more than adequate.

AJ stood open-mouthed too. "My god! Look at this! I thought it would be smaller. This is fantastic!"

A tall heavily carved wooden door opened as we exited the car, and a very short, somewhat portly older woman came out smiling. She wore a long black skirt and a light cotton blouse hand-embroidered in a floral pattern. Her blue-black hair was pulled back from her brown face into a bun. She welcomed us in Spanish. Standing next to her, I felt like a giant again. AJ responded with his own Spanish greeting and Ramon formally introduced me to Adelina Sálazar Díaz. He explained that she is our main housekeeper and cook, in charge of others who she hires in as needed. The others included two young women who cleaned, a gardener, and a chauffeur if necessary. He hastened to assure me that Conrad had been accustomed to hiring them, that they were

BETRAYAL by SERPENT

completely loyal to him and that there was a bank account in Mexico with money for their salaries.

"As I said on the ride here, Señora, they are all members of mí familia."

He had told us there was deep concern in the family when they heard of Conrad's death because they were afraid they would lose much-needed income.

"Of course we feel badly just because he has been killed, but also we were worried a new owner might not be as kind as he was. That you have it now is a great blessing for our family. If, for some reason, owners do not come, then much income is lost. Children are then not able to remain in school; sometimes even eating is a problem. I was very happy to learn you are the owner."

"I had no idea. I want your family to know I will be sure they have this work," I reassured him again. "I know something of what it is to live on that edge. If I have anything to say about it, your family will eat and the children will be clothed and have schooling."

The staff took our bags as we followed Adelina into the house.

"Adelina is our matriarch of mí familia although we have a very old abuela in a village in the country."

"Wait! She is the matriarch of your family? Is she your mother? Grandmother?"

He laughed. "No, No! I call her mí Tía. She is the daughter of the oldest sister of my father so she is my cousin but I like to tease her because she is the *very oldest* of my cousins." Adelina made a face at him.

"Adelina is very proud of the service of our family, Señora. Long ago she was given special training by a wealthy family at a large hacienda in the mountains where we are from. Now she trains all our younger family members."

I asked him to be sure to tell me if I overstepped her bounds. "I am certainly not used to servants."

He laughed. "AJ has told me that."

AJ had a large grin on his face. I could only imagine how my son had described the way I ran my own household.

"Did he tell you I scrub floors, hose down basements, discover snakes...?" I was about to add a long list to that.

AJ, with a much-exaggerated, sad and resigned look on his face, heaved a long sigh. "I told them we, your children, are the servants." He feinted away from me. "I'm kidding!"

I had given him The Look.

"Señora Adelina," I asked, "comprende Inglés?"

She held her thumb and forefinger about a half inch apart, saying, "Poquito."

I responded, laughing, "Mí Espanol es muy poquito también."

"I will translate for both of you," Ramon repeated in English and Spanish.

It was immediately clear that as the new owner of the hacienda, I was to be given the grand tour.

Adelina began, "Señora, I will show you everything now, before I must begin to prepare the food for today so you will know what is available to you."

"You don't have to do that..." I began to say but was interrupted by Ramon.

"Señora, you must do this. It is part of her expectation of you. You are the new owner. You *must* be given the tour."

Oh! I have a lot to learn about having servants.

I had much to learn about Conrad a well. I was and still am so totally astonished at the picture of Conrad this house revealed. Here was a Conrad no one up north has ever known.

Up north I had only seen him in elegant but carefully restrained settings. Here is a house that reveals a setting that is lush, colorful, sensuous, even erotic. A Chihuly glass chandelier in rich pinks and reds; a mosaic of Botticelli's Venus rising from the sea with Adonis next to her—both nude, he aroused. *Oh my!*

Immense silver candlesticks stood on the mantle underneath that. Walls are painted in peaches, turquoise, golds. There are exquisite linens in huge carved chests, and the kitchen is stocked with everything the gourmet cook could want. It is nothing short of amazing.

This is not the Conrad I've known The man who lived here is anything but reserved...is a lover of rich color and sensual textures and...

I stood in the kitchen breathless with surprise at the difference between the two settings.

"Did Conrad entertain people here?" I asked. "When he was at parties he could always hold his own with any gourmet cooks, but I don't ever recall him inviting anyone to his home for a meal. His kitchen there is strictly for a single man."

"Sí, Señora," Adelina said. "He did cooking himself when he had guests here, but that was before I was here. *I* was his cook in the last year." She emphasized "I" very firmly.

Ramon said, "You need to know, Señora Anna, that the power can go off frequently and that the house has its own independent generator which is set to turn on automatically if that should happen. Most of the energy used in the house is solar, which I will show you later."

The kitchen is connected by a short corridor to a small office, sitting room, and bedroom, where Adelina lives when she plans to remain. The others come and go as needed. I wondered what their homes are like.

Ramon went on explaining, "There are also some small bedrooms in a separate wing, off to the left of the living room where employees sleep if they must remain too late to go home."

I can't believe this! Conrad has…had…all this? Because Conrad's dead, I have all this now. Why? I feel ashamed, guilty. This feels all wrong.

My eyes began to tear up and Adelina became concerned and said something to Ramon.

"She is wondering if there is something wrong, Señora Anna."

"No. No. I'm just thinking of Conrad, missing him, wishing he was with us. It's fine. I'm fine." *Why did he will this to me?*

She nodded understanding as he explained to her. I regained my composure.

Behind the house, with access from the kitchen and dining room, is a huge open-air courtyard partially enclosed with walls about ten feet high. It too is beautifully landscaped, with a pool, hot tub, and furnished cabanas for guests to change in, each cabana as big, maybe bigger, than some of the houses in Puerto Juarez.

In the distance, past an expanse of green jungle below the hill on which we stood, the Caribbean shone deep blue. A large cruise ship, looking like a child's toy, moved slowly along the horizon.

I turned to Adelina. "Muy excelente! Muy hermosa. Muchas gracias por your care, Señora Adelina." My poor Spanish failed me.

AJ and Ramon attempted to hide their amusement at my linguistic tangles and failed.

"Just let Ramon translate, Mom."

Thirty-one

Adelina remained in the kitchen to begin preparing food for us as we continued our tour. From the patio, Ramon led us down three small flights of stairs that began by leading away from the house, then curved and returned down three more flights to doors leading into the lower level under the house. Ramon and AJ said nothing about what was here. I thought we were going to a basement to see the generator. In my wildest dreams I could not have imagined what is actually there.

Another carved wooden door opened into a long cool dry room that ran the length of the home, its walls illuminated by indirect lighting, small spotlights throwing soft pools of light over work after work of framed art and freestanding sculptures.

"Oh! This is a gallery!" I immediately recognized a Gauguin on the wall to my left. I was drawn in, transported, and walked slowly along one wall, recognizing works again and again from famous artists.

Conrad kept his best collection here!

I was halfway down the wall when I realized they were all nudes or semi-nudes, male and female. *Astonishing! Nothing in his collections in Green Bay hinted at this. These are beautiful, voluptuous, sensual, and alive. Renoir...a painting of Aline, his mistress. Gauguin...the women of Tahiti. Two of Helga, the secret model of Andrew Wyeth, and so many more.*

These must be copies. They can't be the real thing. I don't care if they are. I love them. I don't ever want to leave here. I have died and gone to heaven. I've loved all and any art since I was a child. Now I was totally thrilled.

AJ and Ramon waited as I walked slowly down one side and back along the other wall, as I wandered from sculpture to sculpture, touching, circling each, marveling, my eyes drinking up the colors and forms. Conrad's passions, for beauty and human sensuality, were clearly on display here.

It's like he was two people. Not once when he was alive did I ever see him show this side of himself. I'll never really know it now. My tears came sliding down my cheeks. At his loss. At this incredible beauty. I heard his ghost sigh with regret.

When I got back to AJ, he said, "I didn't know how you'd take this, Mom. Ramon told me about it. Are you ok with this?"

"These are so beautiful. I'm missing Conrad so much!" I just let my tears fall. Then his meaning dawned on me.

"AJ, these are masterworks! These are beautiful! Why would I not be ok with this? I am more than ok with this. It's so incredible!"

"I meant the nudes. You always were so careful about what we saw."

"AJ, give me some credit! This is not the porn of adolescent boys! I have no objections to art that celebrates the human form and senses!" My tears stopped. I was exasperated.

"Well, I didn't know for sure." He looked a bit sheepish and turned away, a little grin on his face, and walked back through the door, pausing in the outdoor light.

Oh, for heaven's sake! A grown man and he's reacting as if he's in his teens. Exasperating.

I glanced at Ramon as I turned back and stopped. No young boy stood there. His expression was alive with interest, with delight. He was seeing not just my assessment of Conrad's passion, but my own sensuous appreciation of the paintings and sculptures. He was reading every thought and feeling I was having and loving it. *I have never seen a man look at me like that!*

His eyes were telling me I was one of the masterworks on the wall. I was not dressed. I was woman, female, appreciated, almost adored. More astonishing to me, I loved his look.

Even though I had truly enjoyed sex and sensuality with Art, I have hated it when men undress me with their eyes, seeing the lust and greed in them. I had shut it all out after Jon O'Keeffe's assault.

But even Art never looked at me the way Ramon is. His look isn't greedy at all. If he wasn't so much younger and married, I know I would encourage this look to become much more.

This thought awakened me with a shock that hit so fast I became weak. *I have been dead! I have been walking with ghosts!*

My breath caught. Fire lit deep and low in my belly. *I haven't felt this for years! This is unmanageable! Not now!*

My breath came faster, my legs began trembling. *What am I thinking? I'd better get out of here or I'll embarrass myself.*

AJ, still outside the entrance, called to me. "Mom, Adelina has food for us and we need to freshen up. The car we sent to pick up Lindy should be on its way back already."

Ramon smiled softly, inclined his head slightly to me, and turned also, leaving me to calm my body. *Thank god! This is so embarrassing!*

After a few minutes the fire dimmed, but not by much. It was more minutes before I moved. I was left with an aching longing to be touched, stroked, and...

...for the first time in years I want to make love with a man. Memories of making love with Art poured through my mind. It has been far too long! What have I done to myself? What have I lost?

I took one long look at the gallery and vowed I would come back and spend time alone here.

Thirty-two

On the second floor I was met and shown to my room by a young woman who introduced herself as Tomasita, "but please call me Tomi" she said in English. The bed was set in an alcove that extended out over the back garden. A subtle scent of flowers mingled with the fainter scent of the sea. I looked up and saw a large glass skylight.

I'll see the stars at night.

The bedroom and sitting room were enchanting, filled with young hibiscus, begonia, and orchid plants. Pale yellow walls with accents of pink tiles were hung with ferns of all kinds on small shelves in alcoves tiled right into the walls. It was like living in some elf or fairy's room. As I was examining the ferns I caught sight of a tiny lizard, iridescent green, hiding near the bottom of the fronds.

Magic! This is magic! I love this place.

A large lavender tiled shower, an old fashioned bathtub on claw feet with thick white towels hanging on the side, a lovely cinnamon-hued carved wood dressing table with an old-fashioned crocheted runner, blue bottles of lotions and a floral perfume set in trays on its top, were all part of the bath. On the bed simple white linens were covered with a real American quilt, a garden of flowers being the motif, of course. I looked at the stitching. Not machine-quilted, completely sewn by hand. A thousand hours of work or more.

My clothing had been laid out on the bed and I chose a loose summer shift and clean underwear. The rest was whisked into drawers by Tomi, who made sure I knew where she placed everything.

"Muchas gracias, Tomi. I'm going to take a shower right away," I said. She made sure I had bath linens and left.

I really need this shower to calm my body and my mind. What an overwhelming day and isn't done yet! There's still Lindy, and whatever AJ and Ramon couldn't talk about, that whole thing at the airport. Get back down to earth, Anna.

Before my shower, I had heard sounds of AJ and Ramon talking. Now, afterward, as I dressed, it was quiet except for subdued sounds from the kitchen and patio where Adelina was working. I smelled food. Spices.

Something with tomatoes. Fruits and cinnamon. I bet she's an incredibly good cook. Dare I expect anything less after all this?

I decided I wanted to see the rest of the upstairs before supper and walked into the corridor. I could hear AJ in a room to my left singing to himself. I turned right and went to the end of the long corridor, intending to work my way back room by room.

When I opened the door at the end of the hall Conrad's presence came leaping into life again.

What I saw was the most sensual room I could imagine. Two walls of deep mauve served as a backdrop for a king-sized bed, covered with a rose silk quilt. The bed's headboard was a tree with the most intricate bare branches that ascended to the high ceiling. There was no footboard. The rest of the room held softly cushioned sofas and chairs and two chaise longues upholstered in print in pale mauve, burnt siennas, deep rusts, ivory and sandstone colors accented with black. Eight wide horizontal mirrors in carved black wood frames hung on the walls around the room. Two walls were washed in paler shades of sienna and rust. The long casement windows overlooked the front patio where we came in. A yard full of flowering trees and bushes stretched out below them.

On the wall opposite the windows, a set of double leaded-glass doors, in intricate patterns of beveled glass leaves and flowers, could be opened to a small private patio, with another bed outside. The bathroom door was closed.

I can only imagine what that's like!

I never got there. My attention was totally taken by something else.

On the wall next to the bed there was an intimate portrait of three young people, two men and a very young woman, barely clothed. The woman seated on the lap of the central figure had long red hair and a saucy, insouciant look. Her voluptuous figure was wrapped only in a sarong around her hips. She seemed familiar somehow but I couldn't think why. The other man, standing, held close to that main figure by an arm around the waist, was dark-haired and dark-skinned, African, and completely nude. The seated main figure, in a pair of shorts, was a young Conrad!

No, his real life was definitely not in Green Bay. Whew! I think I've learned enough about the Conrad I didn't know for one day!

I turned and left, quietly closing the door. Clayton said Conrad was gay but maybe he was bisexual. Did he really intend me to see this side of him? It became very clear to me he had valued privacy, at the cost of creating a retreat thousands of miles from the place he called home.

Where was his real home? Where was he born? Where did he grow up? Who were the two others in the portrait? What had they meant to him? One does not have a portrait done with casual acquaintances. Conrad is a mystery in his life and in his death.

I hadn't thought to look for the artist's signature and would have returned but I heard Lindy's tense voice downstairs and AJ's door opened and he came out, looking fresh in chinos and a white shirt, no shoes.

We went downstairs

Thirty-three

Lindy flew out of the living room and into my arms, her eyes red-rimmed, worried, frightened. I had never seen her so unnerved.

"I'm so relieved you're here! I don't know what to do. Something is terribly wrong. I can't get any answers, not from anyone. I've always thought it was a good thing my father was so independent and now..." she broke off and began tearing up. "I'm just so scared for him. Did they tell you? About the cartel?" She glanced from Ramon to AJ, who both shook their heads no.

"Why didn't you tell her?" Lightening flashed out of her eyes at them. "He may have been kidnapped!" She was about to go on but I stopped her.

"Lindy! Wait! There hasn't been time." I flashed my own look at AJ. There had been plenty of time on the plane, in the car, no need for such secrecy, such cloak-and-dagger behavior. He and Ramon got the message and looked away.

I hope they feel really guilty!

AJ tried explaining. "We aren't sure about anything, Mom. And we don't know who to trust. Until I could talk to Ramon and the authorities and, well, everyone..." his voice trailed off lamely. He could have filled me in and knew it.

"Let me make it clear that I will not be shut out of any knowledge that comes to any of you. Whatever we have to do to resolve this, I will have totally open communication at all times. I won't tolerate secrets, information held back. Is that clear?"

Mom has spoken, dammit!

I was still hugging her and felt rather than saw Ramon and AJ look at each other.

Good! They'd both better get this message.

I didn't wait for their answers. I took Lindy's arm and led her out to the patio.

"Tell me everything that's happened from the time you got here. You men will fill us in on anything you know when she's done. Then, we will have supper. After that, we will plan."

I heard Ramon inform Adelina. Lindy and I settled ourselves on chairs next to each other. AJ and Ramon pulled up their own chairs across a low table from us.

Ramon, taking his life in his hands, interrupted, "Señora, may I order drinks for us all?"

I looked at them both. Solemn faces, laughing eyes. "Yes. Gracias! That would be a good thing." He did.

Lindy was impatient to begin but I touched her arm. "Just wait until the drinks come. I don't want interruptions. I want to hear everything that's happened since you left our house. The whole story." She nodded acceptance of that.

Tomi brought out delicious iced fruit drinks. I introduced her to Lindy and AJ. She smiled and shook hands and then left.

Lindy began. She had flown into Merida from Milwaukee, leaving earlier than she planned.

"I am so over Rick, Mrs. K! The visit to Milwaukee was awful. He got so possessive and well, I'm just not into all the partying he wanted to do so I told him it's over and left. He's still texting me but I'm not answering back. Anyway, he can't connect with me here. That's my good news. The bad news is here."

Thanks to generous Christmas money from both parents, she began with plenty to live on. First she went to her father's apartment in Merida, but when he wasn't there, she rented a room on her own. This was not unusual. What was unusual was that he had not left a key to the apartment at his office at the University of Merida. It had always been his custom to do that. She thought maybe he had just forgotten, or maybe changed habits.

"After all, he didn't know I'd be here. When I didn't find it, I started getting worried, especially remembering his letters. You know what they were like."

Tears welled up again and she became silent, remembering. We waited for her to go on and slowly she came back to the present.

BETRAYAL by SERPENT

"I've kind of lost track, where was I? Oh, yes. So I went to his office, you know, to get the key, and he wasn't there and I couldn't find it in the usual place. I talked to Professor Menendez and he said Dad was at the dig, that he hadn't been at the office since early December. Well, that wasn't right! He always kept in close contact with Prof. Menendez before but the professor had no explanation, and hadn't done anything to connect with Dad. Menendez said he had been busy due to the end of the semester. That made sense but also sounded kind of lame to me, like an excuse, but I couldn't get any more information out of him. So my trust in him wasn't very high at that point and still isn't because he treats me like a child.

"Then, something was so not right with Dad's office either. It was neat, clean! Dad's office was never neat and clean. He had piles of papers all over, work in progress, stuff like that. He's organized, knows just where everything is, but no one else ever did and he'd never let me or anyone touch it.

"I looked for things, papers, anything. Nothing. Many files, naturally, of archaeology papers, but they were old ones, in the cabinets. Nothing on what he's doing now. There wasn't a trace of what he was working on. It's almost like he removed everything about the dig from his office, but why would he do that? Then I thought maybe, like, it might all be at the dig.

"Professor Menendez was there while I looked and he got sort of worried too. I tried to call Dad on my cell and there was no reply, not even a voice mail service, just nothing. The professor decided to phone colleagues and went to do that. I really searched the office then. I even looked under rugs and behind pictures and everything. Nothing! When the professor came back, he said no one had seen Dad. He had phoned someone, a man who recruited workers for Dad, who told him the dig was closed down, that Dad had told him to lay the workers off until he returned and that was two weeks before Christmas and he hadn't heard anything since.

"So now Professor Menendez finally got worried. He called some students who he thought had been working on the dig and the ones he got hold of reported that they had been sent home at that time, you know, like back in December, and didn't even have their grades from Dad. He was supposed to grade them and send it to their major professors."

214

"Did you make any report of this to authorities?" AJ broke in.

"Yes, of course. I went to the police, to the U.S. Consulate, called Billings University, where Dad teaches between digs, called the Cross-Cultural Archaeology Institute. He's just missing. That's not the worst. You remember, Mrs. K, I called Dad from Green Bay after his weird letters? Well, I was talking to him after anyone had seen him and he didn't mention any of this! He would have! He always told me this stuff. Where was he then? What was going on? It had to be really serious if he didn't say anything to me."

"Maybe, if his work was being threatened he removed it to save it. I can see him doing that, but then of course, where is he?" I said.

"Another professor said there might have been some cartel activity in the area, that there's a rumor a new drug cartel is operating in the Yucatan, but no one really will say for sure. Dad would never have left a dig unguarded! Never! He hated to see archaeological sites looted or damaged.

"So I took Dad's old beater car—I found those keys— and went down to the dig. It's way down near the Belize-Mexican border.

"It was weird. There were four men there who said they had orders from my father to guard the dig, but they hadn't seen him for a month. I didn't even know them and I know lots of the workers. They said he'd gone off to check out another possible site but he left papers there and his things, and that is so odd too because why would he clear out his office and then leave stuff at the dig unattended? When I saw the open trench along the edge of the pyramid he's excavating, I really knew something was wrong. No archaeologist leaves an open trench and just goes off like that. I asked the men about any cartel activity but they blew me off. They see me as a gringa, and young, and well, before I could check everything out, I got scared and left. I didn't like the men at all." Lindy sounded as discouraged and dejected as she looked.

Ramon interrupted. "This is part of my news. I have heard rumors of new cartel activity. I have distant relatives there and I asked them about it and they have said no, that is not happening. But if it is true, I know they may be very frightened to speak. My relatives only say they believe there has been an increase of drug activity from South America through Belize.

"The situation is not clear. I can get no information yet on any police investigation of such a thing. However, my relatives said there seems to be activity in the remote jungle areas and traffic on the Río Hondo, the river that is a border between Belize and Mexico. There is even talk that a cartel is using construction near Tulum to disguise their activity. What is one more boat, one more truck? Much can be disguised with such activity. There are many other places along the coast where smugglers can have a place of operation." He sighed. "Too many!"

"Would your father close a site if he hears about drug activity?" AJ asked.

"Well, he might, but he was very good at working under adverse conditions, usually negotiating some arrangement with local people. It would be a kind of 'you do your thing and I'll do mine' setup. He did that once years ago when he worked in Turkey and there was unrest that involved the opium trade. But if he thought any activity might endanger the site, he would try to stop it or get authorities to do that. He has the backing of CCAI and they have a lot of influence but when I called, they said they hadn't heard from him asking for any help with any problems. He would resist any closing if at all possible." She shrugged, looking dejected. "I'm just guessing really."

I had been listening and wondering. *Could all this have anything to do with us? With Conrad's death? Who would even know that Lindy's father would be connected with us? Conrad has owned this house here for how long? Years? I don't know. Might he have been aware of or even caught up in this? Involved somehow? There's too much we don't know.*

"Lindy," I began carefully, not wanting her to become even more upset. "Might there be any connection to Green Bay? Any possible connection to UW-GB? Or even to your living with us? I know that sounds absurd but I don't want to rule out anything at this point that might give us a clue as to where to look, or why."

"Well, of course, my father knew I roomed at your house. He could have mentioned it to someone. I know he told people that I'm a student at UW-GB. When he first researched literature about archaeology down here he ran across a book on ChiChen Itza that had been translated from Spanish by students from UW-GB who worked on a dig for a professor from Merida, but that was long ago. I don't know any other connection."

"Mom, I think there is." AJ spoke. I looked at him with surprise.

"You do?"

"Ben told me two days ago that way back when Dad died, the Mexican police did consider Dad's being involved in the drug trade. They contacted Green Bay police to make inquiries. Sorry, another thing I forgot to tell you. I know"...he held up his hand at my attempt to speak. "I forgot in the rush and yes, it sounds improbable, but it's not all that impossible. Think about it. There could have been a corridor of trade back then. If not Dad, what about Jonny O? Or the Mafia? What about all that money coming into The Firm? Or even someone else we don't know about? Right now authorities are doing all they can to shut down the Mexican border trade and if I were running an operation, I'd look for another route, try to develop another way to go. Tourists with small planes might be a way to run drugs, maybe."

He saw my skeptical look. "I'm just trying to think like a drug dealer."

Ramon grinned. "You are not ruthless enough, hermanito."

Then Ramon grew serious. "There is another possibility that we who live here know for certain is happening. Human trafficking. This is a fact."

We all stared at him. I was completely taken aback. This was the last possibility I could have imagined. AJ sat back in his chair and I could see his mind racing. Lindy looked angry.

"My father would never have been involved in that! He would have tried to stop it! He wouldn't have made any agreement with anyone doing that!" She grew furious and would have gone on but Ramon interrupted.

"That is not what I am saying, Señorita." His voice became quiet but determined. "I am saying your father may have discovered this and is in grave danger *because* he opposed it, because he did try to do something about it."

"I'm so sorry. I..." she was unable to go on, her eyes wide, a frightened look on her face. She was seeing the full possibility of what might have happened, that her father may even be dead.

"I am sorry, Lindy. I did not want to tell you this, but you need to know what we could be facing here. We all need to know, is that not right, Señora?" My demand for full communication was thrown back at me. Well, I would not back down.

"Yes, we do. We need to know exactly what we are facing. Ramon, tell us all you know about this." I looked him directly in the eyes and saw...*admiration? Did I read that right?*

He began with AJ's call from Green Bay. He looked at AJ and then back to me.

"When you call and tell me about the murder of Señor Wentworth, I begin to think back to when your husband was killed. I think about AJ and his search for answers that no one would give him. I begin to think about what the police did and did not say and do. We have a problem here. Sometimes the police are honest. Sometimes they are not. It becomes hard to know who to trust, even, I am sad to say, en mí familia."

He looked at AJ. "You tell me this man, Conrad, was investigating the death of your father or something do to with his law firm. I decide to see if I can find out what might have been going on. I have relatives with the police also. I remember the circumstances of the death of your father. A very strange set of circumstances.

"One relative has told me that even then the police knew of human trafficking, but he has tried and he cannot gain access to the most important papers. Perhaps they no longer exist. Those many years ago, after several months, your father's case was quietly put to rest, with no one following up on it. This tells me that someone paid well to have it die, for the man who investigated it was known as ambitious and tenacious. He would have continued the case. He would have contacted your police. Someone else buried it deeply. The man who investigated your case died in an 'accidental' shooting within months of the plane crash. There is a rumor he was shot by one of his own men in a drug raid. My relative will continue to look for any papers but he must be very careful."

"Are you talking of Arispe-Sandoval?" I remembered the man's arrogance.

"No, Señora. He was muy malo. I think he has long ago gone back to the north where he is from. Perhaps even now he is dead. No. The man who tried to carry out the investigation was higher up in rank.

"There is more. The American Consulate also let the case become quiet. They did have reason to think the death of your husband was accidental," he looked at me, "but they had equal reason to suspect it was not. They did nothing. That is suspicious. More, I think you were stopped at the airport today because someone is still alert to your name, most especially because AJ bears his father's name. I believe someone was watching for you and AJ. This is why I waited until now to tell you this. I have taken steps to be sure this house is secure for you."

I looked around and Adelina was hovering inside in the door to the kitchen. I had a feeling she had been listening and wondered how much of this she understood. Ramon looked around and she nodded to him.

I looked at Lindy. She was exhausted. *It will take hours to talk this over. She needs a break.*

"I think Adelina's more than ready to feed us and I need time to absorb all this. We must speak more of this later. For now, can we eat?"

Everyone nodded.

I took Lindy to the bathroom in my suite to freshen up. We didn't speak at first but just looked at each other, both of us trying to take it all in. When she came out of the bathroom, drying her hands, she was looking even more tired and worried.

"Let's just not try, right now, to even think what might be happening," I said. "It's all speculation and rumors. Let's wait. You're not alone anymore. Now there are three more to help you. We'll get to the bottom of this."

"I have to go back there, to the dig. I just have to," she whispered.

I put my arms around her and hugged her.

"I know." *And I need to find out who waits for AJ and me. And how this is connected to what happened to Art. And...and...and there is no end to the possibilities, to the questions whirling in my brain.*

Thirty-four

Adelina is an excellent cook. We had a pork dish with many vegetables, sweet potatoes and a chocolate dessert. She beamed as she saw us devour it all. I was so hungry. I had eaten only my apple and some airport snacks all day. She had made an iced chocolate and coffee drink for after, also delicious, and cooling. I went to the kitchen to thank her personally.

My less than perfect Spanish…"Muchas gracias. ¡Delicioso! Increíble!" …and a huge smile got my message across to her.

Her response surprised me. She took my hands, an act of familiarity I suspected was not usual, and said solemnly, "Señora, I take care of you muy bien. I help you many ways."

I had the feeling she meant more than cooking and I made a mental note to spend more time alone with her and my Spanish-English dictionary.

"Sí. Esta es muy bien. We will talk." I assured her.

On the patio we drank our drinks, enjoying the cooling evening air for a while, putting off the inevitable. Finally, AJ could stand it no longer. "Whatever is or is not going on, we need a plan now as to what to do."

Lindy stated bluntly, "I'm going back to the dig. I have to. I have to see what I can find there, from the workers, from the dig itself. Mrs. K, I wish you'd come with me. I can't make you but…" her voice trailed off wistfully.

"I wouldn't let you go alone! Of course I'll come with you." AJ erupted into a flurry of objections. I waited. When he ran out of steam I restated my intentions to go.

"I've also decided to make a return visit to the crash site of the plane." He looked horrified.

"I am not in shock anymore, AJ. I'm not grieving Art anymore. You said it yourself this morning. That was then. This is now. I think there's much I can gain by facing this. I want to know what the people who lived in that area saw and heard and know. I'm convinced they know more than they let on. I know you went back there but that was years ago, and you were a young boy to them, and they probably wouldn't have given you any credence. Maybe they'll talk to me as his widow. Arispe-Sandoval had only contempt for them. I remember seeing it in his eyes and body language. So I know they wouldn't have told him all they knew and they might have thought I felt contempt too. Who knows?

"Besides, I owe a grandmother a debt of gratitude. I don't know if she's alive still, but if she is, I want to thank her in some way. She saved my sanity, maybe even my life." I saw Ramon nod.

"I know who it is you are remembering, Señora. She is alive. She remembers you."

"I can go with her, AJ," he said. "I will be the translator for her and for Lindy. People will trust them more if I am with them."

"So, what am I supposed to do? Sit around and wait? Just follow you around? You know what I want to do." He stood and began pacing, irritated.

"No!" I said. "Of course not. Now you can deal with the Americans at the consulate in Merida. I want to know just as much as you," I ticked off items on my fingers, "why they dropped the ball here, what was really done back then, who is involved in investigating this human trafficking, what they are doing, who they think is involved, whether they think there are drugs involved. You're a doctor now. They'll listen to you now more than they did to us back then, more than they have to Lindy, more than they would to me. You're the logical one to deal with CCAI on Lindy's behalf here while she's at the dig. They have to be informed what's happening, or not happening, if they haven't already been.

"We need you to find out how the system works here. And we may need someone up here while we're down there. I don't want to be out there without someone I can trust as backup. I'm not ignoring what you want. I'm being very practical, and careful. Perhaps you can persuade them to come to the dig and do something."

AJ seemed mollified. "What about this house? Conrad's affairs? What has to be done about this?" He waved his arm to take in the surrounding land and house.

"Nothing right now. I'll have to do an inventory and have all the art catalogued and photographed, probably even appraised, but I bet Conrad has that somewhere here, maybe even on his computer, a file we didn't open yet. I don't have to sell the house. I think it's paid for and there's money to keep it open and staffed."

Ramon had more information. "Señora, in Mexico foreigners usually cannot own land, but they can lease it for 100 years. There are papers on record of this. If Señor Wentworth did this or succeeded in buying the land, I can have someone find those papers for you and begin the process of the transfer to your name." Ramon grinned again. "Another cousin."

"Hermanito," he said to AJ. "I can ease this way for you here and su madre is correct. There must be a contact here, at least for a while. Insurance. Good insurance." Again a look passed between them.

Do they still have some information they aren't speaking about or are they just on the same wavelength?

At any rate, I saw AJ relax and nod.

"Our last task, scattering Conrad's ashes in the sea, can be set aside until this is done. Ramon, we'll need to rent a bigger car, perhaps even have a driver, something that can take us on back roads. What do you think? What supplies should we take?" I was feeling tired and, if there was more planning, just wanted to get it done.

Lindy looked like she would melt into the ground from fatigue.

"No problem, Señora! I have another cousin, well, actually, my brother. He is a tour guide. He will be glad to help us." I couldn't help but laugh.

He smiled too. "Here in Mexico family is muy importante, Señora Anna."

"It is to me too, Ramon."

We ended our evening by setting up plans for the next day: contacts with the consulate, the police, Cross-Cultural

Archaeology Institute, and an excursion for equipment and supplies.

I showed Lindy to her room where Tomi had turned down the bed.

"Do you think my father is alive?" Her voice broke as she slumped into a chair. "Mrs. K, the cartels are torturing, beheading, hanging people up north and dumping bodies in the cities and countryside. What if my father's in their hands, being tortured, or is dead? I can't bear this."

"Lindy! Stop! Don't go there. You said yourself he's very good at survival. If anyone can get out of a dangerous situation, he can. I think his calls and letters to you, and the strangeness of them were to put you off, keep you out of it by giving you no details of what was happening. He knew you'd want to come to his rescue. Think of him as Indiana Jones." I suggested. That brought out a small smile.

"I used to kid him about being Indiana Jones, although he's not afraid of snakes. Not the nature kind. He said he didn't ever trust human snakes though. There are human snakes involved here, aren't there, Mrs. K?"

"Yes, Lindy, I think we have to face the fact that there are human snakes of a poisonous kind involved in this whole thing. Our task is to discover who they are."

"And then do we kill them?" Her voice sounded like a slash in the air.

I looked at her, startled by the knives in her voice, and saw the anger she couldn't control any more. *Woe to the person who crosses her right now.*

"I sincerely hope we don't have to do that."

I left her and sought out Ramon. I had one more question for him. I found him in the kitchen with Adelina.

"Ramon, I would like a description of the man who was so rude. Will you ask Adelina to describe him for me. Was he American?"

"Sí, Señora." He translated for us.

"He was shorter than you by about four inches, had brown hair, and was older, perhaps in his fifties. He was American. He was well-dressed in a white suit and wide-brimmed hat. She did not see the color of his eyes because he wore sunglasses."

"Was there anything unusual about him? Anything that stood out?"

"No. I wish I had been here to see him. I would have remembered more. She does not."

"OK. Thank you, Señora Adelina. One more thing, Ramon. Do you think Arispe Sandoval is still with the police or involved in some other way in this?"

"No. I know he is not. He is not mentioned at all anymore. We think he is long gone. Why do you ask?"

"Arispe Sandoval was a cruel man. Sadistic. I saw it in his face. I can easily see him involved in human trafficking. I now believe everything we had to endure was staged, manipulated. He was the person who did that, I'm sure. You don't know where he is now? Have heard nothing of him?"

"No, Señora Not since then."

I thanked him and went to my room.

I believed him then but now, as I write this, I'm not so sure. Ramon has secrets, I think. And Arispe Sandoval was greedy, controlling and enjoyed cruelty. He would have loved to sell other humans for money.

Thirty-five

Sometime in the night I awoke. Above me, through the window in the ceiling, were a thousand stars. I lay enchanted. The warm night around me was darker than any night in Green Bay, even in the north woods of Wisconsin. Blackness of this kind feels comforting to me. I drifted in it, losing even the feeling of the bed under me. There were windows open and I could hear sounds of night creatures unfamiliar to my ears. *There are iguanas, lizards, tree frogs, bats, what else? What sounds do they make? There are no familiar sounds here.*

I could have floated in the black forever but I heard a slight scraping sound through the windows. Getting up slowly, I went to Conrad's room to the patio and sat on the bed out there. Nothing but blackness, stars, and the small puddles from solar lights below marking the path through the garden.

El jardín. Mí jardín. I have a garden here now too. A beautiful tropical garden.

The smooth waters of the pool were a dark mirror of the stars. I began to feel a sense of deep peace, drifting in the stillness, the stresses of the last weeks slowly dissolving into the night.

This is what Conrad loved here. The deep peace of the night. The ability to be, just be, without fear of exposure. Did he fear exposure up North? He must have. No fear. I actually have no fear right now. Relief!

I suddenly wanted to see the gallery again and hoped it was unlocked. *Wait! I have the keys. I still can't see this as my house. Unreal.* Returning to my room, I threw on a light cotton robe over my loose nightgown and took it off again. *It's so warm, such a soft liquid night. I don't need that.*

I found my ring of keys and made my way, barefoot, down the main staircase, my night vision growing acute. Following the glow of the path lights into the patio garden and down the cool stone stairs to the gallery, I made my way through the night.

The door wasn't locked. I walked in and turned on the soft spotlights above the paintings. Time stood still as I slowly moved from one to another, pausing to savor each. Most of these were not the well-known masterpieces I had seen in expensive art books. I thought they were mostly lesser-known works, but I know the styles of many artists. I have spent hours and days and months in galleries, museums and books.

I can hardly wait to find out more about all these works, know their stories. Most of these are European, some American, and a few of these are Mexican artists. That's a Frieda Kahlo and who was the muralist, her husband? Yes, Diego Rivera. Funny how I remember her work more than his. All her pain was in her work. Maybe that's why.

Part of me thought they might be very good copies and I wanted to find Conrad's inventory and provenance, if it existed. *I so much hope these are the real thing. These are mine now. I love them so much!*

I stood before each one, taking them all in, thinking about my own body, large by modern American standards. Here, in the silence, I came face-to-face with how I had covered over my tainted self-image for years, refusing until now to acknowledge how I had flayed myself with the constant comparisons my mind made of my body versus the "ideal" and of the shame I'd been taught in Catholic schools about being female.

These are full-bodied women like me. Every time I meet a smaller woman I make that comparison. If I'd lived in the time of Renoir, I'd have been thought glorious! These are Women, painted Large and Luscious. I feel so sad that I've done that to myself!

I put my hands to my face and found that I was crying. The thought of being considered beautiful was hard to believe. The thought of how I had seen myself all my life was heartbreaking.

My hands moved over my breasts and down my stomach and hips. I looked down and wondered if I could even repair that mental damage. I was so ingrained with the American image of rail thin and tiny as the way to be.

I had a sudden whimsical thought. *I might have been Renoir's mistress. I might be a famous nude. In ancient Celtic*

227

BETRAYAL by SERPENT

times, warrior women fought nude, fearlessly. I put my hands on my hips and struck a warrior pose. That brought a smile to my face. I laughed out loud and then froze when another soft laugh echoed mine. I turned, startled, the peace of the night shattered. To both my relief and embarrassment, it was Ramon, leaning against the doorjamb.

What is he doing here? How much did he see? He saw everything on my face. I felt myself blush. The look on his face was desire. Tender and fierce. *For me? No, I think I'm reading that wrong.*

"I am so sorry to startle you, Señora. I saw the lights and decided to investigate." His voice was soft, husky. He cleared his throat and drew a deep breath, as if coming to a decision. A sly smile came to his face.

"In the spirit of honest communication, which you prize so much, I have to tell you I have guards around the house."

"Why? What for?" I took an unsteady breath, trying not to stammer. I felt myself blush even more. *Thank God for low light!*

"Señora, I am taking every precaution. My knowledge of what is happening in my country tells me that any connection you have made with what is going on puts you in danger and puts everyone in danger." He gestured toward the upper floors as he came further into the room. "Everyone."

"In the spirit of honest communication, just what do you think is really going on? I think you have much more information than you have told me so far. Es verdad?" I regained some composure.

"Sí y no." He gestured toward a loveseat close by, inviting me to sit. I thought he would pull up a chair but he sat down next to me. I felt the heat of his body. The memory of his earlier look and my feelings in response came back, but I kept my face as blank as possible. I was very conscious of the thinness of my nightgown, of the swelling of my breasts, the hardness of my nipples.

"Then tell me what you know." I commanded. "I hate insufficient information"

"So do I, Señora, so do I." He drew a deep breath and seemed almost reluctant to speak. "Here in the Yucatan we have always had illegal activities. Most of the time, we

228

continue our business by avoiding any interaction with dangerous people or we pay bribes to have them ignore us. If illegal activities are occurring sufficient to shut down an important archaeological dig, then someone high up does not have enough influence to overrule the power of those responsible for these illegal activities, or that higher up person is taking bribes too. This has been happening for a long time. Before the death of your husband. Many years. Today the police at the airport wanted bribes. And they knew your name. They were waiting for you and AJ. I don't know why. Yet."

My face now registered my own nagging worry. *Why us? Why this name? I can't even imagine why. What's going on?*

"I must pay you for the bribes. You mustn't use your money for that, for us."

"AJ has paid me already. Do not worry."

I continued. "I read long ago about the Colombian cartel but that's not Mexico. How can this be? Why can't your police stop it? Just what is 'it'?"

"It is smuggling, and not only Colombia and Mexico. It involves Venezuela, Ecuador, Costa Rica, Guatemala, Belize, and other countries, and all aimed at the United States and Canada because that is where the money is.

"As to what is happening now, I know that at this time it involves both drugs and human trafficking, the selling of women and children, young boys and girls, slavery, prostitution, baby adoption, any of these or all of these. Even the sale of black market gems. Anything illegal that makes money that is what the cartels will do. I am most interested in this human slavery."

His eyes turned to obsidian. He looked away, far away, silent for a while. I thought he wasn't going to continue. Then he leaned forward, his arms resting on his knees, his head hanging down and when he spoke his voice carried the weight of guilt and sadness.

"I have a cousin who is one of the desaparecidos. He disappeared when he was nine, eight years ago. My family has been looking for him since then. We believe he was sold to a man from the Far East but we hope that he is still here in Mexico. Some of my family have hope. I have no hope any more. I have spent much time learning what I can about the evil men who do this and I think he has been used and is dead."

He straightened up and turned toward me. Our eyes met, mine horrified, his hard and angry. I laid my hand on his arm.

"I'm so sorry." I was imagining my own boys and Marnie being sold. I remembered the loss of my baby girl. "Losing a child for any reason is hard, but this is just terrible, frightening!"

"I have many cousins, but we are not influential, we do not have much money to bribe officials, even if we wanted to. Even if we could bribe them, we are sick of the bribes, the dishonesty, the disregard for human life that is what goes on in our country. Many horrors lie behind the 'luxurious' resorts, and the colonial 'picturesque' and 'rich' vistas described in the travel brochures. The men who buy sex slaves have the money to stay at the wonderful resorts and to cruise the streets until they see the child they want. They have the connections to others, even men from my own country, I am ashamed to say, who will then kidnap and sell the children. Or worse, because of poverty and need, some families sell their older children to feed the younger ones."

Disgust and passionate anger made his voice harsh, and he turned his face away for many minutes. I knew I should not speak. When he turned back to me, he had himself under control again.

"I am sorry you are now involved in this but I think you have been involved in this unknowingly for a long time. Not you, yourself, Señora," he hastened to assure me, reading my face, "but someone you know."

Sí." He softened his voice, "even possibly your former husband, or an associate. Someone from El Norte such as this other man who was with your husband, the man you call Jonny O." A speculative look crossed his face. "Perhaps many someones!"

I grew sick at the thought of anyone, especially Art, being involved in human trafficking and wondered who in El Norte might be hiding a terrible secret vice such as this.

He laid his hand on mine, eyes softening, but his voice still held pain. "I am so very sorry I told all this to you. I should not have been so hasty and foolish. I see this causes you pain. But you see, it was after your husband's plane crash that I began to hear more and more of this, from the Mayan people you saw at the crash. There were other white men, gringos, who came through there searching the wreck and questioning, even torturing the people, wanting answers to questions about the affairs of white men from El Norte which no Mayan could answer.

"I stayed with AJ and you, to help you in your pain, but also to see what more I could learn. It was clear that you and AJ knew nothing. It was not clear that Jonny O and your husband were innocent of anything illegal.

"I did not reveal all this to AJ at the time, except to tell him that my family was interested in this matter, that there may be a connection. He has been eager to help, but I have not said too much because I have been afraid he would act without knowing what could happen to him here or en el Norte."

"And he would," I agreed. "He's always wanted to know everything about everything and never rests until he finds answers. He's always wanted to know more about his father's death, about the-police investigations. He's always had his suspicions there was something 'else', something more. You know this. It's why he came back down here afterward."

Ramon relaxed completely.

"Sí. Sí. I feel relief, Señora! I have needed someone to trust with this, and wanted to believe I could tell you this and you would not condemn me and turn me away. We have both known loss. I had hoped there could be a bond between us." His eyes as he looked at me were old beyond his years.

I was brought into the present by the movement of Ramon's hand on mine. He was gently running his fingers over the back of my hand, and then he lifted it and brushed his lips over my skin. I breathed in quickly and he looked up. His eyes were again as they had been last night, riveting intensely into mine.

With a small smile, he breathed softly, "In the interests of open communication, may I please call you by your first name?"

BETRAYAL by SERPENT

I laughed a little, my breath quick in and out. "Sí. Soy Anna."

"¿Habla tu Español?"

"No. Poquito. Muy poquito. I wish I did, but there's no one to speak it with en el Norte. I do pick it up quickly when I hear it and have someone with whom I can speak it." I did not withdraw my hand from his. Without conscious decision I was stroking his palm with my fingers.

"Then I must teach you. I will love to teach you. For us here, when you try to use our language, it is a sign of respect and good will. Yes, I will help you."

He gestured, indicating the paintings in the room. "To me, you are the women on these walls. I love women. Young women. Old women. Todas las mujeres. You know mujeres?" I nodded. "You are all so beautiful because you sacrifice your bodies, your blood, to give us our lives. To me, you are all goddesses."

"I wish more men felt that way!" My body was pulsing from within with a sensuality and sexuality made extremely intense by the celibate existence I have lived for over seven years. I could barely control my voice. Yet my past also flooded through me, a whirlwind of ghosts swirling and twisting around me. I could feel my upbringing, my religion, my marriage, all pulling at me. I felt confused at the intensity of my feelings. Above all, my embarrassment at my size loomed large.

I don't know how, but he saw it. He acknowledged it by leaning over and gently kissing me on my forehead. "Diosa! Goddess! I would like to show you something. Would you come with me?"

He rose, pulling me up, still holding my hands.

With the movement, I felt some relief flow through me, not erasing the sensual sensations but easing them to manageable levels. "Where are we going?"

He didn't answer.

Thirty-six

We left the gallery, turning off the lights, moving with care along the now-faint solar lights of the path. Far out over the water in the distant east, I saw a dim glow. Dawn would be coming soon, but it was still dark in the garden, in the house, and up the stairs as Ramon gently led the way to the door of the far room, Conrad's bedroom. When I pulled away, he held firmly to my hand.

"You must see this, so you can be free."

"Free?"

"You will see." We entered the room and he closed the door. He went to one wall and pressed a button and drapes opened to reveal the front windows. The moon glowed low on the horizon and starlight flashes dotted the sky.

"I would like to show you who you are, if you will let me. Will you? I will not hurt you. I will never hurt you. I only want you to really see yourself. You are very beautiful."

He came back and took my hand and led me to stand in front of one of the long slim mirrors. Standing behind me, hands on my shoulders, he whispered, "Now watch! Look first at your face and hair in this light."

I saw myself, partly in shadow but lit softly by the starlight and the waning moon's silvery glow. His fingers traced the contours of my face.

"Do not speak, only just watch yourself," He said softly. I gazed at my face but tensed as I felt Ramon's hands circle my waist. "Wait, Diosa, and trust just a bit longer, so you will see all your beauty."

I felt his warm soft breath on the back of my neck. "I do not intend to hurt you in any way," he whispered again in my ear, his breath warm on my earlobe.

I looked at myself in the mirror and felt a wave of embarrassment, then a flush of sexuality so strong I nearly sank to the floor. Years of deprivation sent my system into overload.

233

BETRAYAL by SERPENT

Years. All these years! How did I live all these years without this? Without a man's touch? Without affection? Without closeness? What have I lost? How many might-have-beens? How many never-weres?

His hands gently lifted the straps of my nightgown and he slowly lowered first one side and then the other down my arms. His hands slid under the top and moved the gown down over my breasts. I was quivering from his touch, and hunger for more overwhelmed me. I swayed and he pulled me to him as he moved the gown down lower.

"Look at what I see!" he breathed in my ear. "Look!"

Suddenly, instead of seeing myself with my own eyes, I saw my body through his eyes. I had never seen any woman's body through the eyes of a man, had never even thought it possible. Now my own body was rich in beauty, full breasts, nipples hard from excitement, a waistline curved inward, a belly swelling slightly forward, wide hips rounded outward, and as he dropped my gown to the floor, legs long and muscular and smooth and...

Beautiful, I am. This is Goddess! I am the paintings!

Ramon's hands and fingers softly traced over my shoulders and down my arms, then slid up under my breasts and moved like a feather around them, around my nipples. Waves of pleasure rippled through me. "Did you nurse your children?"

I nodded, unable to speak.

"Yes, you would. Your breasts show it but not your nipples. Many women who nurse have darkened nipples. Yours are still pink. Very pretty. Very sweet!"

His hands continued down my belly. My body ached with desire. "How many children came from here?"

"Five."

"Yes." His fingers became feathers brushing my thighs and hips. I felt a wave of wetness inside me. He whispered into my ear. "You opened your body many times to accept the desires of a man, and you returned his gift a thousand-fold, with his children. You are a miracle and you helped that man make miracles. No man can grow a miracle like a child inside as a woman does. For this, above all, I love women."

He stopped talking and stroking my body, then stepped back. I thought "More!" but when I tried to speak my voice had gone silent. He turned me slowly around and moved behind me. In every mirror in the room, one after another, I saw myself, my naked body, from every angle, reflected many times over. I caught my breath.

"You are a work of art. You are desire. You are Goddess!" And so I was.

He moved me against his body, breathing into my hair until my breathing began to synchronize with his. My nipples and breasts slowly rose and fell as we breathed. I was filled with the sight of my own body as he saw it. My eyes caressed my body in the mirrors. I never wanted to stop looking. I felt the desire men feel toward women, knew why they so often can't keep themselves from looking with hunger at us. Had men seen me like this before? Was it only Ramon who saw me in this way?

I breathed it all in, sensing, not even thinking. After a long time, I had the thought, as I had earlier, that Art had never looked at me like this.

*No. That is not quite true. At first, for a while after we were married, he came close, very close. But he never...*Ramon pulled me closer. "Now you are seeing what you missed these many years. You have not been adored, Goddess. He desired you. He enjoyed you. He loved you as best he could but he did not adore you. I adore you."

He waited as that sunk in to my mind, to my heart. Tears hovered in my eyes as feelings of loss overcame me. We stood for some time until he saw desire coloring my face again as I became conscious of his arousal.

"Diosa, I will not enter you now but know this. There will be a time when I will, when we have can talk out ghosts away, when you are not ashamed of your sensuality, as you have been taught, when you can adore my body as I adore yours, when our spirits join together totally."

Ramon's penis was hard, pressed against me. I reached back searching to hold it. He took both my hands and pressed his hardness into them.

"I have ghosts too. I must find a way to leave them behind. I would have nothing between us. Nothing." He pulled away and swiftly left the room.

I stood, naked and longing, looking at the closed door as the ghosts of my past swirled through the room, bringing memories of all that had happened, and desire for all that had not.

I don't know how it was that I got to my room. Dawn was just breaking. I felt that time had stopped for an age of darkness. I went into my shower and let water run down over me until I could see Dawn bring full morning light into the room. I had always passed mirrors quickly, but now I lingered, looking at myself, trying to recapture myself through Ramon's eyes. Gone. Aching disappointment. I began to cry, burying my face in my pillow so no one would hear me. I didn't stop for a long time.

He's right. I'll have to dispel the ghosts before I see myself again as he sees me. Religious ghosts of Shame and Guilt. Ghosts of Grief and Loss. Ghosts of a marriage without...without what? I have filled everyone else's wants and needs. I have ignored all I did not get. What do I want and need?

One answer came.

I want Ramon. I want my body and my spirit filled with him. I have not wanted a man for too, too many years.

Thirty-seven

When I went downstairs it was mid-morning. I had bathed my tired red eyes in cold water until they looked nearly normal, then dressed for the day in white cotton pants and my new blouse. AJ, gulping coffee, oblivious to any change in me, brought me up to date.

"Ramon left right after he woke us up. He's gone to Cancun to arrange for cars, one for me to use and one for your trip to the dig. I called the consulate and they've been in touch with Cross-Cultural Archaeology Institute. There's a representative on his way down. Apparently he's newly assigned or they would have had someone here sooner. Lindy and I have an appointment for 1:00pm with a consulate representative who's coming to Cancun."

Lindy came down, hair wet from her shower. She and AJ ended up rehashing the plans from last night, weighing pros and cons of each planned action.

I stayed out of it. I was in another world, feeling intense sexual desire, yet wary at how quickly I was caught up in desire for a man I scarcely knew. I struggled to bring myself into this day and this hour.

At the same time, to my relief, I felt the grief and tension of the last few weeks ease a bit. Winter stiffness was draining from my body and a craving for sunlight took its place. Coming here was a good decision, a good change.

Their conversation ended when a call came that both a consulate representative and the person from CCAI would helicopter into Cancun together.

Adelina called us for our late breakfast on the patio. She fed us more than I could get down. Huevos rancheros, soft rolls and butter, some kind of sausages, tortilla-like flat bread rolled up with creamy custard inside and cinnamon sugar on the outside. She made the best coffee I had ever tasted.

BETRAYAL by SERPENT

The car was delivered by the rental agency so she and AJ left for the appointment, to get the things stored in the locker and to arrange for care of her father's car.

While I waited for Ramon, Adelina took me by the arm and we went into her office. She sat me down and brought out a tray of what looked like salves and medicines, which is what they proved to be. She pantomimed insect repellent, stomach cramp medicine, disinfectant, mouthwash, and other substances she had prepared. She even had a vaginal cream. I wasn't sure what it was for until she grabbed a banana and graphically showed me. I never did find out if it was a lubricant or a preventive of pregnancy or disease. We both had a good laugh at her show and tell. It smelled good but I didn't figure on using it.

I pantomimed labeling the jars and we found tape and a pen so I would know what each was for.

"Muchas gracias, Señora Adelina. Muy bueno. Yo quiero que a visitar a la farmacía pero..."

She interrupted me. "No, no, Señora. Estas son excelentes. No farmacía!" She made a sour face, making sure I understood pharmacy products were not as good as hers.

Oops! Wrong thing to say!

She labeled everything in Spanish. I added my own label under hers. I knew Ramon would translate for me if necessary.

Ramon. How will it be to see him today? Thoughts of him don't leave my mind, sensations simmer in my body.

I shook them aside and, using my dictionary, asked Adelina if we would have food to take with us. Again, wrong thing to say. I need not have asked. She showed me the large basket of fresh fruits and vegetables cut and ready in the refrigerator, spiced meat that didn't need refrigeration if we ate it soon, breads sliced and ready to eat, spreads for the bread, and bottled juices. A large container of water sat in the freezer partially frozen. It would be completely frozen by tomorrow and, melting slowly in the heat, we would have cool water to drink as we drove.

Ramon told me there are many and very good restaurants on the way but Adelina certainly did not think them adequate. We could have eaten for a week and we had planned to be there for just three, maybe four days at the most.

As we finished a late lunch, Lindy came in with good news from the meeting. The consul and the archaeology representative had organized intense inquiries in Merida, covering that scene, since she had already been there with little success. The archaeologist, named Simoneska, would meet us at the dig tomorrow about noon, by helicopter. Knowing she had worked with her father for years, he asked her to go over the camp thoroughly, looking for any clues to what happened.

"AJ's going with them and will stay in a hotel in Cancun, then helicopter in with them. I found someone to care for Dad's car and the consulate provided me with a taxi back. They seem to be cooperating better now. Ramon is bringing a large van for us to travel to the dig."

"A helicopter ride! Oh, AJ will love that! I wish I could ride in one too. I've always wanted to do that. I'm adding that to my bucket list." The promise of help lightened my mood considerably and I felt hopeful, almost lighthearted.

Ramon came into the kitchen and Adelina began to get out the food she'd been putting away so he could eat. He launched into the list of what had been done and what we still needed to do. He had been able to get us tents and other gear, with extras in case any had been looted from the dig.

No sign in his face of what had happened between us. A feeling of unreality crept over me. *Did I dream last night? I should definitely have more dreams like that. It's better than all the nightmares.*

He continued to address me as "Señora" in front of the others until I decided I'd had enough of that, that it was silly from any point of view.

"Ramon, will you stop calling me Señora and call me Anna, please?" He agreed with a smile.

Adelina nodded several times too, smiling broadly, with a look that made me wonder if she knew what had happened.

I feel like a schoolgirl. I wonder if Ramon has a "reputation". Another ghost to be put to rest. What do I really know about him? And a further ghost. I am a schoolgirl when it comes to relating to men romantically. No experience with

BETRAYAL by SERPENT
*anyone but Art. And Jonny O. Get your head out of this,
Anna. Focus.*

"I need to buy some clothing more suitable for a dig.
When can we do that?"

"We should go right away," Ramon said as he drank the
last of his coffee. "There is an outfitter in Cancun. We have an
important matter to take care of later, when we return. I have
brought maps that we will be studying. It is important to know
the territory."

Lindy nodded enthusiastically. "I agree with that,
Ramon. After we come back I can start educating you about
the dig, Mrs. K."

Adelina urged him to eat more first but he said he had
been home and had been fed at mid-morning. I thought of his
wife and children and felt guilty. *Ghost.*

The "car" turned out to be a huge, beat-up four-wheel-
drive whatever-one-calls-it van which I thought could have
housed six people in Puerto Juarez.

"Does that thing run? It's old."

"Do not worry, Anna. In Mexico, as in Cuba, we have
the best auto mechanics in the world and can make anything
run. This is the correct vehicle to use. It is especially adapted
for this kind of expedition. I myself am not the greatest
mechanic but Jorge can fix anything. This can take us
anywhere," he explained. "We carry our own spare parts."

"We may have to sleep in here in an emergency," Lindy
said when I wondered at the size of it. "There are wild animals
out there, Mrs. K! Jaguars, boa constrictors, crocodiles." She
grinned. "You'll love it!"

"Jaguars, boa constrictors, and crocs. Stranger even
than Oz. I'm so-o-o not in Wisconsin anymore and will you
please call me Anna too? And I'm more worried about the
human predators."

"I can't call you Anna. You feel like a mother to me. I
can call my real mother by her first name, Therese. She doesn't
feel like a mother to me. But you're actually not my mother so
I can't call you Mom, so my compromise is Mrs. K. That
sounds weird, but, well, humor me!" She grinned again, then
added, unsmiling. "The human predators, yes, they *are* far
more dangerous."

240

Ramon had brought our driver, Jorge, and introduced him to us. Jorge and Lindy went inside to bring the last of the bags.

Brother or cousin?

"We are brothers," Ramon said with a smile, reading my face. "Do you know your eyebrows go up very high when you want to ask a question?" He added as we waited for them to return.

"Sí. And when I'm skeptical, and when I'm surprised, and possibly for other reasons as well."

"I enjoy watching your face. It is so expressive. Whatever you feel is there. I do not think you are very good at lying. I like that. I see that you are attracted to me still, and I feel the same for you. When there is time, we will talk. I have much to tell you about me and much I want to know about you."

Whatever more he wanted to say was interrupted by Lindy's arrival.

In Cancun, I bought khaki pants, T-shirts, a hat, light cotton socks, and some stout boots. I didn't want my feet to touch anything poisonous. Lindy laughed at that. She was in sandals.

Ramon and Jorge, who had gone to find more café con leche, returned to find us waiting outside the store with our packages. I was on my cell phone to Marthe and my boys. They were excited. Was I really going into jungle? Would I get pictures of a jaguar?

They wanted to be with us "like, now, Mom" and I promised them the trip when we were finished but insisted they and their sister would all have to agree on where they wanted to go, so I left them with their plan to comb the maps and travel books for the best sights to see. Marthe promised to give them all hugs.

Back at the house Ramon and Jorge laid out all our gear and repacked our vehicle. AJ called to update us.

"If we find any evidence of foul play, there are plans for an all-out search in place, ready to be executed, including helicopters and police." I stood in the living room with Ramon, relaying to him AJ's words.

I felt suspicious that, after what Ramon had told me, the police themselves, at least some of them, might be involved in whatever was going on. I said this to AJ.

"Well, Mom, we just have to trust in these plans for now. I'll keep in touch by voice or text."

"AJ, I don't know how to text."

"Have Lindy show you how. You need to know that. It's a useful skill."

Ramon's gaze changed as he kept his eyes on me, desire filling his face. We were alone and he quickly crossed to me and kissed me on my eyes, then backed away and left the room.

My body went into sensual overload again.

Adelina fed us our evening meal, announcing she would be going home for tonight. She showed me the food for our ample breakfast and again reviewed the food to take with us. After she was sure I knew just what to do, Jorge drove her home.

Ramon and Lindy steered me into the dining room.

"You are not yet ready, Anna, to make this journey," Ramon said as he flattened out a large map on the table. "Lindy knows where we will be but you do not. It is time for a lesson in geografía. It is fortunate for you that this is one of the subjects I teach."

He looked delighted at this prospect and proved to be a very good teacher. Before we were through, between the two of them, I had a working knowledge of the area of the Yucatan to which we were going.

Then Lindy took over for a lesson in archaeology.

She finished her lesson with the future possibilities. "There's more to this, Mrs. K. Because of recent discoveries, we now know that the whole of the Yucatan, Southern Mexico, Guatemala, Belize and Costa Rica are full of unexcavated Mayan cities, towns, and villages. All of this area has the potential to be a World Heritage site, perhaps the largest on the planet. It is also a place of great ecological importance and undiscovered medicinal potential. My father is aware of this

Judith M Kerrigan

and could actually be somewhere in the jungle identifying more sites. I'm so anxious to find out where he is and what's happened."

"We will. Don't worry. For tonight, I love being your willing audience but information overload has set in. Can we take a break? The rest will have to wait for tomorrow."

"That sounds like a good idea, Mrs. K. I'm done here and we'll have the whole ride to teach you more."

Lindy raced up the stairs and Ramon and I were left alone. We stood looking at each other for a long time, communicating much by face and body only.

"Perhaps it is time to talk of our ghosts," he said quietly.

We moved into the living room and sat at opposite ends of one of the long couches.

He began. "I will tell you my story. When I was a boy, I lived in a high mountain village with not many people. As a little boy I fell in love with a girl in my town. Her name is Maria Angelina. I never even looked at anyone else. When I was seventeen and she was sixteen we had made love many times. We were married because she was already pregnant. This is not so uncommon here in Mexico. To marry young, to be pregnant so young. When she was nineteen we had our second child and that was the year something terrible began to happen."

In a voice heavy with sadness, he told me of her illness. I learned how she slowly became dangerous to their two children when paranoia and hallucinations got worse and worse, how no curandero could help her, how he had to leave her in a mental institution and turn the care of his children over to his mother so he could make money for his family. He spoke of his children, of his hopes and dreams, of years of working his way through college and slowly building his family's business, and how he had never had time to love another, often not even the relief of sex, and never another love until he saw me step off the plane.

"I do not know why I feel this toward you, only that I do. Except for Maria, this has never happened to me before." I could feel his energy reaching out for me, drawing me to him. He changed the subject back to his children.

243

BETRAYAL by SERPENT

"My children are in the mountains now, guarded from the dangers of the cartels, and I see them only when I can take time out from this work. They want to come to the city but I am afraid to have them here. I have opposed certain members of one cartel. They would use my children to force me to do what they want. My children would be in very grave danger here." He paused and shuddered, looking grim, then continued. "But now, I want to know about you."

So I spoke of my own life, my ghosts—the death of my father, my mother's emotional disconnection and her impending dementia, my loss of my baby girl, my aborted marriage, the trauma and depression after Art's death, the struggles to support my children, and my Irish Catholic background, which had been a good belief system while all was fine, but had served me less and less as trauma unraveled my life. I spoke of the religious guilt and fear that lashed at me, of the shame I felt. And while I spoke, I felt something release me. My ghosts dissolved into the realization I have a choice.

I can choose my beliefs, my ghosts, or I can choose loving, and if it is one or the other, love will be my choice. I don't want to be alone anymore.

I told him this too.

"No. I do not want to be alone either," he said softly.

"Ramon, I am much older than you. That is another factor."

"Anna, I do not care. I do not see the age of a woman but the light around her, the feeling I have when I am with her. I have the same feeling again with you that I had with Maria. I say again I have never felt that for another woman in all this time and I have met many younger women."

He took my hand and said, "You have not seen all of your house. Come with me."

He led me to the third floor and we walked out into the stars shining around us on an open rooftop looking out over now-dark sea in the distance, where lights twinkled from boats on the ebony waters. The front wall of the house extended into a high wall on the west side. A large bed, an open air shower, and an ancient wooden cupboard surrounded by potted plants were in its shadow.

244

The night begged for nakedness, for melting into the hot liquid darkness perfumed with flower scents, the earth's loamy erotic odor rising from below.

He stood at the door, waiting as I walked to the edge of the patio and stood gazing at the far sea.

"If you do not want to do this, it will be all right. I understand. For me, I want to make love with you," he said in a quiet voice.

Here is your choice, Anna. Love or loneliness. And I chose.

With starlight dripping down on us, we undressed each other slowly and showered together, our hands memorizing each other's body, playing with each other until we were both intensely aroused.

"Wait," he said as he walked to the cupboard, where he searched among jars and bottles, finally drawing out a small jar. "I want you to have much pleasure." When he opened it I knew what it was by the smell of cool ice. Adelina's mixture. I told him how she had shown me what to do with it and he threw back his head and laughed.

"I never told her I am attracted to you, but she always reads me as if I am a book. She has read you too. She approves or she never would have left us alone. She went away tonight so we could make love."

He drew me close to him, kissing me again and again as he spoke.

"She has many love potions. This is the one I prefer. You will love it too. It feels like champagne."

He knelt in front of me and slid two fingers full of the mixture inside me. A warm tingling began and my insides lit on fire. I laughed and moaned at the same time.

"It is like champagne inside me! It's cool and hot and bubbly all at the same time."

"My turn." He stood in front of me, naked, fully aroused. I took the mixture on my fingers and massaged the long hardness of him. Closing his eyes, he leaned into my hands, groaning with pleasure.

I pulled him to the bed, lay down and opened my body to him and so we joined our bodies and spirits again and again until we both fell asleep from deep satisfaction.

BETRAYAL by SERPENT

We woke during the night and went to my room and made love again until I fell asleep.

I awoke to his pounding on my door.

"Anna! Wake up! It's time to go."

Oh, god! What did I do? Anna, that may be the dumbest thing you've ever done in your life.

Dumb feels so-o-o good!

Thirty-eight

We ate a quick breakfast and put things away. While Lindy ran to her room for some last minute items, Ramon went to the bathroom and I went outside with my backpack.

"Buenas días, Señora," Jorge said as he opened the door of the car for me. I looked at him and knew instantly he was aware of what had happened during the night. His face was one very large knowing grin. He added, in Spanish, "I hope you had a beautiful night"...long pause..."of rest." He turned away before I could reply and went for the last of our supplies in the house.

I feel wonderful, if you must know. A little sore, but I haven't felt this good in years! I didn't tell him that.

The vehicle was not air-conditioned. Given its apparent age, that didn't surprise me. In the cool of the morning it didn't matter but I was not accustomed yet to the heat of the day. I can't imagine what I would do in this climate in summer. I ordered myself to just deal with it.

Our trip was long and uneventful.

We travelled south back through Cancun but instead of riding through the Zona Hotelera, we continued south on Highway 307. I got out the map again to follow our progress.

"Here is where you went to the plane crash." Ramon leaned over and showed me a point on the map in the opposite direction, between Merida and Cancun and north of a main highway. The nearest village was Izamal and a site called Itza Mna.

"So that was where we went. I never knew that. I was so disoriented by it all. I don't understand why Art and Jonny O were even flying over that part of the country."

I spent some time discussing all that had happened so far with Ramon and Lindy. Neither one could make any clear connections between the murders in Green Bay and here in the Yucatan.

After a while, we became tired of talking about the unsolvable and from then on our conversation was about Mayan sites and beliefs, archaeological techniques, Lindy's French upbringing, and small talk.

But one piece of information caught my intense interest. Ramon was speaking of the sites.

"Farther south we will be near two areas of preserved jungle, the Calakmul Biosphere Reserve and the Sian Kaan Reserve. Kaan or Chan is a word for serpent. We have many kinds of snakes here."

I was instantly alert. "What is that word, the one for serpent?"

"Kaan. Here, I will draw it for you and show you." He drew a simple glyph of a serpent and another that was more complicated, the head of a snake. He then wrote the letters Ka'KAN. "The accent is on the last syllable. It is also written Cha'CHAN and it can be written Kan or Chan. It can also mean 'sky' and 'captor' and the number 'four' and is associated with lightning. You see how our languages are complicated.

"What is it? What is wrong?" He saw my sudden heightened interest.

"Conrad wrote those letters in the snow as he was dying. K, and A, and N. I saw them. Conrad was trying to tell us something. What does this mean? Tell me."

"Anna, I do not know what it would mean to him, but I have been suspicious that the glyph *KAN* is used by one of the cartels. I do not know yet if that is true. It is a rumor only. I do not know what Señor Wentworth might have had in mind but it sounds to me like perhaps he had information about a group called Los Serpientos. This is supposed to be a new cartel running black market merchandise through here. I have thought it is only a rumor but now you tell me this and I think perhaps it is more. This is not good news." His face took on a cold hard look.

Watching him, my intuition sent up a warning flag. *He knows more than he's saying now. He looks worried and angry. He's holding something back. I can't pursue this right now. Now it's about Lindy's dad. But I'll remember this. Change the subject for now, Anna.*

"Well! Another unanswerable question. There are too many to pursue right now. Now we have to find out about Dr. Stewart." I watched as some of the tenseness left his body.

"Would you go back to teaching me again for now? I like it."

He did.

After that, we were silent for a long while. Finally Lindy said wistfully, "I wish you could tell me if my father is safe," and lapsed into a silent reverie, finally curling up on the seat and going to sleep.

Ramon and I were silent too.

When I was sure she was asleep, in a very quiet voice, I asked him, "Do you think her father is alive?"

He did not reply and I thought he didn't hear me. Then I heard a very soft, "No. It would be un gran milagro, a great miracle, if he is. The men of the cartel do not leave people alive to tell tales."

"I don't want to think what will happen if we find her father dead, what she will have to go through."

Ramon reached over and took my hand.

I was about to ask him what more he knew about the cartels but Jorge said something in rapid Spanish. I heard the words Felipe Carrillo Puerto and knew we were near that town. We took a break for food, gas, and water. I wished again that I was a tourist and could explore this place.

When we were finished, Ramon climbed in the front seat with Jorge and we were on our way again.

Thirty-nine

At the village of Xulha we turned west and passed two more tiny settlements, each with a few small huts, before we turned onto a narrow dirt road going south again. No people were in sight at those places.

We're in jungle now! The vegetation became thick and relentlessly green, a green so intense I felt it vibrate. Occasionally I saw flashes of red, orange or blue through the branches of the trees, a relief to my eyes. Bird sounds reverberated through the green walls. I couldn't identify any of them.

"There are Wisconsin birds like the oriole here, Mrs. K. They migrate down to this area for the winter. I hope we'll see the quetzal. It's native here and a beautiful and sacred bird. If you see one it's a good omen. Not long now!" Lindy was sitting forward on the edge of her seat. "I hear a helicopter."

Seconds later I heard it too, flying low. The road was now a dirt path and bumpy, pitted and sometimes rocky. Jorge slowed to a crawl, easing us over some places slowly to evade bad potholes and twisted roots.

This would be impassible if it was raining. Now I see why we have this vehicle.

Lindy looked eager, giving directions when needed. Ramon was alert. He said something in Spanish and Jorge nodded, focused on getting us to our hidden destination. Occasionally Ramon had to get out and direct us over difficult spots.

"How did you get that old car of your father's over this, Lindy?

"I didn't. There's another way in and I left the car at the beginning of that trail and hiked in."

It took longer than I thought it would. AJ and the others must have waited for us for at least a half hour. Finally, after a winding road up a steep grade, we came out on the flat top of a large hill, almost like a plateau. Although the top was cleared of vegetation down to dirt, brush and trees still covered the sides. The green vibration eased a bit. I saw two tent tops far down below through a break in the treetops at the edge of a large rectangular clearing.

"My father thinks there may be a smaller Mayan structure under this hill. Here's where the helicopter landed. He hated that idea. The sites are so sacred to him, whether excavated or not. See that tall hill over there," she pointed off to our right. "That's what he wants to excavate, the whole thing. The long trench I showed you in my drawing is on the other side and it looks very promising. There's another road around this hill going into that part of the site, the one I used last time, but it's much more difficult to travel, just a wide walking path really. This is the easier route."

Jorge drove us slowly in low gear down a long switchback path.

As we descended, the jungle came closer and I felt it physically beating like a heartbeat. The green pulse pulled and pushed at me. The heat increased too, radiating from the vegetation and from the earth itself. I forced myself to take deep breaths. *It feels as if hands are pressing my chest and back, pushing into each other.*

As we reached the bottom, the clearing appeared almost immediately through the trees and Jorge eased our vehicle to a stop at the edge of the jungle where it began.

Good! I can breathe better in clearings. It's worse when the trees close in around me. What a strange reaction I'm having to this place!

AJ and three other men headed toward our vehicle as Jorge brought it to a halt. AJ came to offer his hand to me as I slowly stretched my legs out. Lindy hopped out quickly, looking around.

"You came the hard way, Mom. It's much more fun in a helicopter."

He began introductions.

Walton Herder, from the consulate, was tall and slim, looking mid-thirties in age, distinguished by a shock of thick brown slightly curly and carefully trimmed hair. He was dressed in impeccable khaki pants and a tailored blue shirt and fit the word "Patrician" to a P.

251

BETRAYAL by SERPENT

He definitely doesn't shop for clothing at WalMart. How can he look so perfectly cool in this heat? I'm already wilting. Pull it together, Anna. Don't faint.

He greeted Lindy first, expressing his concern and reassuring her he was doing everything possible to locate her father. It sounded like a formal declaration.

Oh my word! Pampered patrician politician. I'm going to laugh. Stop it, Anna! I focused on my breathing. *This place is making me crazy.*

Matthew Simoneska, from the Cross-Cultural Archaeology Institute, was older, Arican-American, perhaps in his early fifties, almost as tall as AJ. His skin was a dark chocolate color, his hands rough. A large man, he looked weathered by much time spent outside, his tightly curled salt and pepper hair adding to that look. Lindy had heard of him and informed us he was known for his archaeological expertise. She looked very pleased to have him with us.

"Lindy, I'm so sorry we meet under these conditions," he said in a deep liquid voice as he shook hands with her. "I hope you'll help me here. I've just been assigned to this project. My previous assignments have been to Africa, where my first interests were. I've not caught up on everything yet. I've got your father's previous work on my computer and want to read that and also find out from you what you know about this dig." His smile was warm, sincere, and I liked him instantly.

The third man stood at parade rest with a military straightness about him. His clothing was camouflage greens, much worn and a bit scruffy. He was deeply tanned, slightly shorter than I am, and grim of face. His age was hard to guess, perhaps forties. Long straight black hair was held at the back of his neck by a leather tie. When Herder introduced him as a member of the staff at the embassy, he seemed a bit startled but said nothing. I thought at once that he was CIA or DEA or some law enforcement person. His name was Kevin MacPherson, "but everyone calls me Mac." He turned to Lindy and opened his mouth to speak but she looked around, a frown on her face. He waited, watching her intently.

"Where are the other men, the ones I left here to guard the place? We'll need to find them." Lindy was looking toward the tent.

"There were no others here when we arrived, Lindy," AJ informed her. "Everything seems undisturbed though. The tents are still here. Nothing seems trashed or..." he stopped, seeing her worried look.

"They should have been here." She turned to Simoneska. "You know, I felt uneasy with them. They weren't men I met in the summers I worked here. I wonder if they really were employed by Dad. That makes me even more determined to get to work, to discover what's been going on here."

She wasted no time and took charge immediately.

"I've given a lot of thought to what needs to be done since I spoke to you. I want to thank you for coming. We'll need all the help we can get."

She let us know she planned to go through everything in the tents only after treating the entire site as a dig, setting up a grid over the area, photographing and combing each section of the grid for anything that might be found.

"If my father has been kidnapped, there could be evidence anywhere. I've thought this out very carefully and want to be sure we miss nothing. After we can walk freely in this area, then we can go through the tents, and the sheds.

When this immediate area is clear," she swept her hand around the place where we and the tents stood, "we can move to the dig itself. I don't want to waste any time. I looked for papers relative to this site in my father's office and there were none so they have to be here somewhere. If there was a threat, he would hide everything if he could."

Herder looked miffed, Simoneska seemed impressed, and Mac was amused. I could almost hear him say "Yes, ma'am!" to himself. AJ stood off to the side and grinned.

"Mrs. K, you're our camera person. I want you to photograph each area as it's marked off. We'll catalogue anything we find and bag it."

MacPherson nodded approval. Simoneska agreed.

BETRAYAL by SERPENT

Herder appears to think he should be in charge. Or perhaps he's resenting a young girl ordering him around. Or both.

Mac finally spoke up, extending his hand to shake hers. "I'm glad to meet you, Lindy. I've known your father for many years and I'm sorry we've never met. He's mentioned you many times. I'm trained in tracking and I can be of help. I can read the ground for footprints and other signs and we can document that. Later, when you don't need me here, I plan to see what I can find along the jungle paths."

Lindy was again pleased. "Just what I wanted! I knew there would be tracks and signs. I was a little worried I wouldn't know how to deal with that and I'm so glad you do and I'm glad to meet you too. How is it you haven't been here in the summers?"

"Different schedules I guess, and I like a more moderate climate in summer. Here it gets too hot."

"That's for sure!"

She smiled for the first time and Mac and Simoneska melted. Herder still looked a bit sour.

AJ had been watching Lindy take charge with some amusement.

"Uh, Lindy, what do you want me to do?" A grin crossed his face but disappeared fast when she looked at him with great seriousness.

"I want you to help do the same as they do until I find Dad's papers. Then I want you to help me read through them. If something has been going wrong with the dig, he may have documented that. It will go faster if two of us do that. The others can keep going over the grounds. You're also our doctor. There should be some medical supplies for bites and stuff like that. You'll take charge of that."

AJ looked overly serious and I knew he was laughing inside.

"I'm glad my medical training will be of use here, but I don't know if I'd recognize anything out of place in your dad's papers. Maybe Matthew would be better at that."

I spoke up. "AJ, before I forget, Adelina sent medicines she prepared for us and I'll show you what they are when I get the chance. She's a curandera for Ramon's family." AJ looked a bit skeptical and I continued. "I think we'll find them very effective here. After all, she lives here. She knows what works and what doesn't."

"Sí, hermanito. Her creams to keep away insects and prevent infection are very effective." Ramon said.

Oh, yes, and they are good for much more too. It was an effort to keep my face very straight.

Watching the faces of Herder and Simoneska, I could see that they had been thinking they would be examining Ian's papers. Lindy didn't notice their expressions. She was assuming she was the person who knew her father best, who had actually worked on the dig before, who would spot anything out of place or out of the ordinary, and she clearly wanted someone she chose to do this. She had chosen AJ. That was it.

Simoneska's going to want to see those papers. He opened his mouth to speak but was stopped by a carefully unobtrusive look from Mac.

"There is the rest of the search." MacPherson said quietly.

"What rest of the search?" Lindy asked.

Herder replied, "I have men ready to send out to question the people in the villages around here, and search places to which your father might have been taken."

Lindy slowly looked at him, then at MacPherson and Herder. "Do you think my father has been kidnapped for sure, or even killed?"

Her chin was up and her shoulders back, waiting for bad news. The men looked uncomfortable.

Herder stiffly tried reassuring her.

"We can't really rule anything out at this point but of the two, kidnapping is the most likely. It's not our final conclusion," he emphasized. "Right now, we prefer to think your father has gone off on some matter having to do with the dig. That's why we want to have you go through it thoroughly. You will be able to tell, if anyone can, what is out of place or unusual. It's just that as soon as we heard the facts, we felt we ought to take some action." He only succeeded in sounding condescending to me. Lindy's reaction was similar to mine.

"I'll want to talk to the workers my father hired from around here first." Her face was adamant.

"Well, we will be doing that." Herder said quickly.

"Who is 'we'?" I asked.

Herder seemed reluctant to answer, or maybe he just thought I didn't belong in the conversation.

Not even looking at me, he said stiffly, "I have enlisted the help of the Mexican police from this district. They are waiting for my call to begin a search."

Oh, no. Dangerous. "If you begin a search now, and with police, that will shut people up. Especially since I've been informed some of the police in Mexico may be working for the drug cartel. People will be afraid to talk to them. If Dr. Stewart is alive, it could get him killed."

Even I knew that. I didn't tell him Ramon was my source of information. I knew instinctively Herder would never count him as a reliable source.

"She's right." Mac added his voice to mine. "People are afraid of police down here. Lindy is the logical one to talk to the workers. We can have Ramon and Jorge round up those who'll talk."

"I want to question them first, before anyone else does." Lindy was not to be put off. "I know them. I know their families. I played with and took care of some of their children. They'll talk to me." Determination was in her voice. The unsaid part of her sentence hung in the air. "...before they will talk to you and your men." Her jaw was set, her arms folded across her chest.

Herder's mouth drew into a thin line and I thought we'd have a not-so-polite fight break out, but he nodded.

Lindy went on.

"I'm determined to do everything I can to find my father. We may need a search like that eventually, I agree, but here is where we need to search first. Let's get started. What we need is in my father's tent, if it hasn't been looted. If it has, I've brought supplies."

She turned and left us all standing there and, with extreme care and on a narrow line, she made her way to a large tent. We got the message.

256

She called back to me, "Mrs. K, can you get the camera equipment from the car please?"

Herder seemed to want to protest, but at a sign from Simoneska, he kept quiet. Mac caught the sign. They moved closer to Herder.

"Walton, I think it's a very good idea to get this area gone over first. If it does prove to be a crime scene, then we'll know that every inch has been examined to *our* satisfaction." Mac said that very quietly. "She does know those workers well. She's a real asset, Walton. I know Ian. If something was going wrong, he left clues. He's damn clever and from what I've seen, he's got a daughter just like him. Use her."

Simoneska nodded assent. "I agree. We'll have a clear base from which to operate without wondering what we trampled on or obliterated."

Herder was displeased but outnumbered.

AJ and I were standing behind the others and he mouthed, "There's more to this" to me and then "later". I gave a small nod and went to the car for her pack with the camera equipment.

Will this be like a crime scene? I hope not. I've seen one too many of those already. Two, if Art was murdered, or if it was someone else's body. I hope Lindy never has to remember the dig that way! Ramon thinks he's dead. Where is Ramon?

I looked around to see where he was but he had disappeared. So had Jorge.

Lindy returned by following her own footsteps, with all equipment in a large carrier. She sent me to the car for her backpack which had more supplies. We were put to work.

Forty

Mac made us all walk in the dust and had me take pictures of the footprints of each of us. He then went over any other areas where he found prints and we photographed those as well. Lindy, in the meantime, had recruited Simoneska and AJ and they were laying out the grid, she starting from the other side of the camping area and Simoneska on our side. I heard Mac murmur to Simoneska, "You should hire her."

I found, to my relief, that concentrating on the task I was given eased the oppressiveness of the green wall somewhat. My mind had time to form the unasked questions piling up one after another.

Are we actually documenting a crime scene? Is this why they've so quickly acquiesced to Lindy having her way? I expected three men to put up much more of a fight to maintain control, especially from a pint-sized woman, a college student at that. Are we being kept occupied and out of his hair as Herder conducts quite another kind of investigation? Are they here to see if there's any evidence that her dad has himself been involved in illegal activities? Are Mac and Simoneska trying to keep the police out of it? Why? Do they think police are not to be trusted too? What "more" does AJ know?

I hate having no answers. Much like my son.

An unknown time later I was interrupted in my musings and camera work by a growl from my stomach so I blamed any lingering uneasiness on hunger. I should have been more attentive to it.

We arrived sometime just after noon, I think. Time seems different here. It seems like the sun is overhead longer. I can't judge the time here like I do at home.

Lindy had us at work since we came. I realized we all would have to eat soon.

"Lindy, I need a break. I'm hungry."

She looked around. We had made great progress in laying out a grid and it was nearly done and mostly photographed. There was just a corridor in the middle to be examined.

She called out to Mac. "What have we found so far?" He was on the fringes near the place where we drove in and came over to the table that AJ had set up near the tents.

"Not much, I'm afraid," he replied. "We have a few candy wrappers, bits of string, some torn pieces of paper which have writing on them, a metal hook, cigarette butts from the outer rim of the grid, and Herder found the hole which had been dug for the latrine on the edge over there." He pointed in the direction of the far edge of the jungle. I could see disappointment on everyone's faces that we hadn't found more.

"Lindy, we really have to stop for some food soon. I'm famished and I think the men are too."

I no sooner had the words out of my mouth than a call from our van made me look up. Jorge had the back open and signaled we could eat.

"OK, Mrs. K. I just want this last corridor done. We'll be able to set up our own tent outside over there where the van is parked." She had said this for all to hear and Simoneska nodded to her. "The men can set up theirs where we came in."

Simoneska looked satisfied as he observed the large rectangle of space. "Yup, we've got this part thoroughly examined. We've got a base here. If we take a break I can upload the photos from the cameras to my computer and we can check to see if we have it all. When we know they've turned out well, we won't need to preserve any part of the grid except maybe that section over at the far edge of the jungle."

Lindy nodded slowly. "Yes, that's what I've begun to think too. We can put up tables and begin bringing things from dad's tents. I'd like to go through dad's personal stuff first."

We didn't get to that. Although we ate swiftly, the sun was low in the west when we finally finished our supper.

Ramon pointed out that dark would come quickly and abruptly. We hadn't found a generator although Lindy said there should be one at the site.

Ramon set up a sturdy tent for Lindy and I. The other men set up three tents in their area.

We had accomplished a thorough search of the entire camp area up to the jungle perimeter. Most of the grid was down. Simoneska was uploading photos to his computer. Mac prowled the perimeter until the light faded. Lindy declared we would tackle the tents and sheds tomorrow. We would be able to search the dig area then too.

Abruptly sunlight went out. Tropical darkness took over. A Black Wall replaced the green.

Forty-one

Ramon has gotten us very comfortable sleeping gear. This day has been long but I am determined to get as much into my journal as possible even if it's by flashlight. I'm making detailed outlines of all that's happened the last three days and I'll be able to fill this all in from memory later.

All that sex with Ramon has caught up with me. Tonight the idea of sleeping alone, of actually sleeping, seems great. This padded mattress feels heavenly.

Lindy and I tucked our bags and cases under the cots, she on one side and I on the other, and that leaves a nice space in the center so we can move easily. These are heavier duck cloth tents, not the thin-walled kind I'm used to. They're very firmly staked into the ground. Air vents line the upper walls like netted windows.

"It's getting cooler, thank god!"

"The air temp drops quite a bit, Mrs. K, or at least it feels that way when the sun isn't up." Lindy made herself ready for sleep in light cotton slacks and a T-shirt. I had my cotton shift and robe, certainly not "jungle" gear.

"You won't need that robe here. Just keep your nightwear as light as possible and you'll be more comfortable. The mosquitoes will stay out of the tent because there's netting over the openings. They aren't that bad this time of year. It's summer that's really bad. We use lots of bug repellent in summer." She broke off as memories of working with her father flooded back. *She's on the edge of tears.*

"Lindy, I've been wondering. The equipment is still in camp. No break-ins or loss. The tents are up and seem undisturbed. Is that usual?"

"Well, if Dad had wanted to close the dig down, that all would be removed, to prevent loss of that equipment. He would also have closed up, covered over, all trenches and other open earth to prevent looting of artifacts. The men I talked to before said he didn't do that and I checked and he didn't, although he locked up the sheds. This makes me think he left intending to come back. There are still a few artifacts in one of the tents and I don't think they've been catalogued. If he left for good, they would have been packed up and sent to the University in Merida. What is unusual is that it hasn't been looted. Someone has ordered hands off. I don't know who would have done that.

"Mrs. K, I don't think my Dad is dead, like they do." She sees my surprised expression. "Oh, yes, I know they think that may be what happened! I think Dad is still alive. What do you think?"

"I don't know, Lindy, but I think if all this was left as it is, he's probably alive. Something else disturbs me though. I feel as if we're being watched. I can't decide if it's for good or bad. I'm wondering if there are men who worked here who'd like a chance to talk to you without the others around. Or, are we watched by some who don't have such good intentions."

"I feel that too. That's why I want to question the men myself. They know more about what happens in the jungle than anyone and aren't going to talk to Herder or even Simoneska. I'm pretty sure they'll talk to me. At least, some of them, those who are loyal to Dad or haven't been bought off."

"Lindy, you're a lot smarter than Herder, and even the others, are giving you credit for. I'm impressed. What have you planned tomorrow?"

She seems relieved to return to that subject. "I'll want Mac to search beyond the perimeter to be sure we don't miss anything accidentally or purposely discarded. AJ and I can begin on Dad's tents and papers. Probably Simoneska too. They have a pretty big financial investment in this. He'll want to find anything relating to what was happening here and he'll want to get at the dig itself too."

She looks very tired and dejected. "They're cooperating just to humor me."

I can see her self-doubt creeping in again. "No, I don't think so, at least not entirely. You *are* the one who worked with your father. I know they have that in mind. Mac and Simoneska backed you against Herder."

I told her what happened. "Herder is the only one who thinks he should be in charge, and I see that as his job. Being totally in control goes with the territory, in his case. I think for now he'll cooperate with the others, at least the other men. I'll help in any way I can. I feel like a fifth wheel here though. I'm certainly not an expert like the others or you. Your father taught you well. I'm impressed at what a grasp you have of what to do here. I just want to give you lots of moral support."

"Oh, Mrs. K! I'm so glad you're here. I don't think I could do this alone." She became silent for a brief time and then spoke again. "Will you have a try at piecing together that paper we found torn up today? I want to know what's on there. It's in very small bits. Someone tore it up as tiny as possible. That makes me think it was deliberate and they didn't want anyone reading it. It will be like a jigsaw puzzle."

"I'd love to. That I know I can do."

"Just a warning, Mrs. K. Never put on boots or shoes here without thoroughly shaking them out first. Scorpions, spiders, small snakes and poisonous toads are possible residents. The tent should keep them out but it's not a guarantee. Be sure you keep your flashlight right there by your bed."

"Oh! O. K. I'll be sure of that."

She turned off her flashlight and I turned off mine and gasped and I turned it back on to finish this. Without it I can see nothing, not even the glimmer of a shadow, not even through the vents to the outside. The blackness is total. And the idea of things creeping into my boots leaves me nervous.

This has been a strange day. My sense of time has changed. Everything we did today seems to have taken so much time and yet I have no sense of time passing. I feel suspended, waiting for answers to reveal themselves, and unable to make that happen.

I know when I turn light off the blackness will press down on me.

I hope I don't have to pee during the night!

Forty-two

I didn't have to pee.

I thought, when I went to bed, I'd be kept awake by the strange jungle noises but I fell asleep fast and heard nothing until Lindy's voice awakened me as she gently shook my shoulder.

"Mrs.K. Mrs. K. It's morning."

Raucous cacophonies of sound grew louder as I came out of my deep sleep. A demented early morning bird song was in full cry and their sharp calls competed with each other to dominate the jungle airwaves. They jabbered and rattled through my head and body. Lindy said monkeys were chattering as well.

How is it possible I've been sleeping through all that? No nightmares! I slept so well. Ramon. It's all that sex. I want more. I want to make love with him here in the jungle. At that thought I felt a rush of warm liquid inside me and realized I had to pee very badly.

Opening my eyes, I saw Lindy framed in the dim light already dressed for the day in her jeans and another T-shirt.

"Time for breakfast, Mrs. K. We're starting again. This will be a long day." She left. I had the wonderful task of discovering our "facilities".

Our latrine, and I use that term loosely, was a wooden box with a hole in it sitting over what I hoped was a large and deep hole in the ground. There was an old and tattered sheet tacked to some poles for a privacy curtain. I looked around. No men watching unless there's someone in the jungle. I didn't care at this point.

However badly I had to go, I had a vision of snakes down in the hole. Or spiders. Or lizards. I found a stick nearby and hit the box with it, then stuck it down in the hole and twirled it around a few times, decided it was this or wet pants, or bare ground. I sat down and did not feel sorry for creatures under me. Relief.

Inside the tent, I washed, brushed my teeth, combed and tied my hair back with a scarf, dressed in my chinos and shirt, put on my socks and new boots, very carefully shaken out, and felt ready for the day. The green was less intense. More relief.

Early morning felt cool, fresh with moisture. Some of the plants near the camp dripped dew from leaf to leaf. Drops of water hung from a huge spider web up in a tree about twenty feet away. Dappled light filtered through the canopy, growing stronger moment by moment. The jungle chorus diminished a bit as the light grew. *This is beautiful, incredible!*

A muffled groan came from the direction of the men's tents. A loud belch followed, then a low-voiced comment and male laughter. Lindy stood in the door of her father's tent across the clearing.

When I went to the other side of our van, I found Jorge and Ramon setting out food.

"Did you sleep well, Anna?" Ramon's question was full of meaning. He stood bare-chested. Memory of the touch of his skin left me breathless. I could only smile and nod. A wave of desire raced through my body. His eyes and quick move to hold something in front of him told me he was aroused. We both were breathing fast. Out of the corner of my eye I saw Jorge slowly observe each of us and heard him release a low "whhhh" of breath. He had a wide grin on his face when I finally looked at him.

"Yes, I slept very well, thank you." I emphasized 'very'.

"My brother slept very well also," Jorge said in Spanish. Ramon rolled his eyes and laughed. The sexual spell broke. Turning back to the van, he put on his shirt.

We were joined by AJ and Mac moments later.

While we ate at the truck, Lindy and Simoneska discussed the plan for the day.

Simoneska was hopeful. "So far, Lindy, we've found no signs of mayhem, nothing missing in this area, the other shed locked, all intact. I'm glad we didn't react with an all-out search. We may be able to find your dad without that. He could be out there looking at other potential sites and walk in here any moment. What's your thinking on our remaining tasks here?"

"Dad's papers and belongings, questioning the workers, then going over the dig itself for clues," she replied. She pointed out the torn papers to me and let all know I would be attempting to put them together.

"If anyone can do it, she can," AJ stated. "She's great at puzzles. I used to get mad at her because she could walk by a huge puzzle we were working on, look at it a few minutes and then pick up two or three pieces and set them right in."

Herder interjected that he had to get back and a helicopter was coming for him around noon. He would help until then.

Mac and AJ were assigned to get the generator working. "I hope you know what you're doing," AJ said to Mac, "because I sure don't."

Mac laughed. "Well, I do and I'll teach you the basics. It's easy and a good skill to have. We ought to have as many people as possible who know how to use it. Including you, too, Anna."

"Not yet. I need her here." Lindy insisted. "But maybe later. It's easy, Mrs. K."

"It sounds like I'll have a whole lot of new skills before I leave here."

"That you will. I'll teach you how to survive in the jungle if you want." Mac offered,

"I'll take you up on that. I can do that in Wisconsin forests but I think here is a whole different ball game. It would be interesting for me. Just learning the plant names would be amazing. For today, though, I'll stick to putting a small puzzle together."

AJ and Mac left to work on the generator. Lindy, Simoneska, and Ramon discussed hiring workers to help us.

"I don't know whether we'll need them on the dig yet, but maybe, and certainly I want to see them and question them." Lindy insisted again, wearing her determined face.

"We'll need some," Simoneska stated. "I'm going to want to examine the trenches and see if we can do any more this season. I can supervise that until we find your dad, Lindy. I'll have to do a report on what I find."

Ramon volunteered to search out all those who worked on the dig and round them up. Lindy gave him names that she remembered and the names of the villages they were from.

"You and Jorge round up everyone who worked here that you can find, por favor. Tell them they will be paid. Mrs. K, I'm going to need to borrow some money from you for that, I'm afraid, since I'm running low right now."

"Not necessary, Lindy. I have access to funds so I'll be responsible for that," Simoneska said.

Ramon, preparing to leave, assured Lindy. "We will try to be back by noon, mid-afternoon at the latest."

Lindy continued her plans. "It would be good if we can add the men's footprints to those we have on camera and identify any who walked here." She and Simoneska walked away discussing more details.

I followed Ramon and Jorge to the truck. They began unloading the food and putting it in the men's tent. "Jorge. Ramon. I have some concerns. First, I feel like we're being watched. So does Lindy. Have you seen anyone, sensed anyone? Second, you may need more cash for our food and supplies and I have some money in my bag that can be used for all of us. I want you to have that before you leave. And third, do you think some of the workers from this dig might be involved in Ian's disappearance?"

Jorge was attentive but once again didn't speak. Ramon answered my last concern first.

"It is probably true there are some workers who know what happened and who are involved. Some who will not want to be questioned and some who may have been bribed by the cartel. We will be watchful of how each man does or does not cooperate. I have had these thoughts also.

"As to the money, I still have some from the household account but will remember you have more if we need it. Will you let Lindy know we will be going as far as Chetumal to get more water and fresh food and any men who may be from there also, not just the men near here?

"The watchers? Oh, yes, they are here. We feel them too but have not been able to find them. Yesterday we walked around looking. Be careful, Anna. Watch Lindy carefully. If they have Dr. Stewart and he is not cooperative, they will want to have her to make him cooperate. My senses tell me she is in great danger. Warn the others."

Jorge got in the driver's seat. Ramon breathed softly, "You must be careful also, Diosa." He squeezed my hand briefly, got into the truck and they were gone up the hill.

I returned to the group where Lindy and Simoneska were talking about the dig. He was saying, "We agree with Ian it's only one small part of a huge complex site that's never been uncovered. We really want this to continue. How, and who will do it, well, we'll see what we find. I'm very eager to get going. We need to find our archaeologist, and get back to work."

Lindy stood. "Let's review the photos of the center area to be sure we have good exposures. Then we can examine the path to the dig itself and photograph that." Lindy indicated the area she meant with her arms. "That area way off to the left seems of the least interest to us. I'd like to leave markers up in case we think we might have to comb over that area again.

"We can get Mrs. K set up over there in the shade" she motioned to our tent, now standing all by itself across the clearing, "on that extra table. I want to know why someone went to the trouble of tearing that paper into such tiny bits. Right now, it's the only thing that even hints at being a clue. The rest of us can begin on Dad's tents here."

We set up the table and I was given tweezers, a small delicate brush, some firm paper on which to assemble my "puzzle", and some glue just in case I needed to stick pieces down. With no breeze, I didn't think I would need that, but later found that the pieces were very light and tended to get out of place. In the moist heat, they also stuck to me. I found a small box to hold the pieces, rather than the plastic bag they were in, then drew up a camp chair and began.

Mac came back with the announcement that the generator just needed gas, oil, and priming. He wanted to search here because those items seemed to be missing from the dig's storage building. Lindy informed him of the gas cans we'd brought and he went to get those.

Simoneska came over to me with a canteen of water. "Keep yourself hydrated. This heat can get to you." He looked at all the tiny pieces.

"Better you than me," he grinned. "I have no patience for stuff like that. I've always assigned the picky stuff to the college students who come as interns. Consider yourself an intern on a dig."

"I think that's great! It makes me feel important, like I'm really contributing."

Mac had come over to peer at what I was doing. "Better you than me," he echoed Simoneska's words and they both laughed.

"What will you be doing?" I asked him.

"The generator's taken care of. AJ took to it like a pro so he can be in charge when you need it. I'm going on jungle reconnaissance. People walking through jungle leave trails. I want to know where they walked and..." he waved his hand in the air... "stuff like that," he said in a dismissive tone.

"That takes patience, just like this." I pointed at the puzzle pieces. "Needles in haystacks, don't you think?" He grinned, shrugged and walked away. There is much more to that man than meets anyone's eye. I wonder what other skills he has.

Simoneska, Lindy and Herder set up tables they found in the shed and began on Stewart's tent first. AJ came back from the dig and joined them. I forgot about them as I became absorbed in my task.

The morning now echoed with quiet jungle sounds, pierced now and then by a distant screech. I quickly became accustomed to that, although I jumped the first time I heard a deep grating growl nearby.

"It's a howler monkey, Mrs. K." Lindy laughed as she noticed my startled look. "Wait until you hear a jaguar!"

"I wouldn't have called that a howl. Wolves howl. That's more of a roar and I happen to know jaguars cough. I think." Howler monkeys and jaguars! I'll be wishing this is just Oz before it's over.

Absorbed in my task, I lost the feeling of being watched, working for a time with moderate success. There were letters, numbers, and symbols on the paper, in faint pencil marks, but none seemed to make any words. I made progress by trying to match sides of each piece with another, not an easy task but possible. The letters proved to be always combined with

269

numbers in sets, with a small symbol now and then. Are those glyphs?

My task was complicated by the fact that all was written in the smallest possible size. I had only ever seen one person write that small. He had been an IRS agent, auditing our taxes, a humorless man, thin and pinched. It had displeased him greatly when he had found nothing wrong.

Someone went to a lot of trouble to make sure this was not easily read, like some private list for that person's eyes only.

Time went by unmeasured until I rose to rest my eyes, stretch, get more water, and see how the others were coming. I was surprised when I discovered it was only an hour later. *It's become hotter now and the Green Wall is closing in, an airless cage. Rotting vegetation smells so thick and heavy here.*

I had forgotten that Lindy would be searching her father's belongings. Now she stood amid his clothing and personal items lying in piles on the ground outside his tent. Tears were forming in her eyes.

"This is almost all his clothing! His blue plaid shirt is gone, his vest with all its pockets isn't here. He must be wearing his cargo pants. I don't see them here. His toothpaste is here, dental floss is here. He never goes anywhere without that! He hates food in his teeth. He jokes about being 'long in the tooth' now that he's older."

The tears slid silently down her cheeks. Simoneska, sitting at a nearby table, had been working his way through a pile of papers. He got up and came over. AJ, also reading a pile of papers, did the same. "Don't jump to conclusions, Lindy. Not yet." AJ put his arm around her shoulder. "He could have more of any of this with him somewhere else."

"Yes," Simoneska added. "My impression from reading these reports is that he definitely planned to explore outlying potential sites. What about you, AJ? What about his personal papers?"

"Well, I've found piles of papers under his cot. Lots of piles, actually, but in organized fashion, thank heaven. He even kept your letters in the order you sent them, Lindy. There are bills, personal and for this site. Business letters. You're going to need to go over these too, Matt. Here's a list of workers names and notes on each..." he handed that to Lindy. "That will certainly help you later. Too bad we didn't find this before Ramon and Jorge left. Don't make any decisions yet on what happened. You still have to do those interviews."

"Mac is out there. If anyone can find out what's been going on, he can." Herder added. He was re-reading the papers Simoneska set aside.

Lindy turned to Herder. "You said Mac worked at the embassy. Who does he work for? You? I'm kind of uncomfortable with his being here. My father never even mentioned him to me, not ever. I don't know why that is. I mean, he seems a nice enough man but why don't I know of him?"

"We-el-l-l, as far as working for the embassy, yes and no," Herder said, looking disgruntled. "Once I was told MacPherson is under contract to the embassy in Mexico City. But even I don't know for sure. It seems to me that he's very much his own man. My guess is he contracts his services to whoever he wants. I've tried to find out if he's CIA, or DEA, or even Interpol. He keeps very quiet about what he does and so do the other sources I've asked."

"How is your puzzle coming?" Herder asked me. *He doesn't want to stay on that topic. What does he know that he's not saying? Or is he just uncomfortable with her tears? And why didn't Stewart tell his own daughter if he knows Mac so well?*

I gave them all a summary of what I was doing and what I discovered so far. "It could be in code, and I've begun to think of it as an inventory of some sort, with items labeled by letters and numbers. I'm going to wait until I do much more before I make any conclusions."

Herder, carefully taking items out of the second tent and cataloguing them, changed the subject. "When I leave, I'll be going to Cancun and then to Merida. We could already have more accurate news there."

He's not even listening to me. We weren't talking about that. I bet he could get news if he wanted to with that cell phone that's in his pocket. Maybe we're in too remote a place for reception. Maybe. You can give him the benefit of the

271

doubt, Anna, but Herder knows more than he says. *Maybe he already knows Stewart's been kidnapped, and I bet he suspects who it is that would kidnap him. Maybe he's just humoring all of us and has an investigation in place in secret. Or is he just a slightly pompous bureaucrat who has to see himself in control of all this? Or what? What is the role of the CIA? Or the DEA? Or any authorities, for that matter? I hate being kept in the dark.*

I decided I would bring my questions up to Mac and Simoneska if we had time alone.

I haven't gotten to talk to AJ yet about what he learned in Cancun. I need time to talk to all these men. It looks to me like Ian left with only the clothes on his back. If he was scouting out other sites, that wouldn't be the case, would it? We just don't know.

I gave Lindy a hug. "Just keep going through it all. Every little thing we can find out is important now. It's early yet and only our first full day here. This day may bring us a lot more information."

She sniffled a bit but agreed and began repacking her dad's clothing.

I returned to my own work. Noon would probably bring the return of MacPherson, Ramon and Jorge. Herder would be leaving. I wanted to have the paper together, if not deciphered.

It doesn't help that the pieces are ¼-inch size. Someone really wanted to destroy this. They've been recently torn too. They're faded but the edges aren't yet deteriorating from the heat and humidity. A few more days and they would have been unreadable and the edges too soft and blurred to match. The person who tore this up was counting on the jungle heat and humidity to destroy it. We found it before that happened.

I interrupted my work again briefly to ask if there was a magnifying glass available. There was. I walked over to the tents and could see that most of the contents had been catalogued on Simoneska's computer and replaced.

"We're almost through with this, Mrs. K. How are you coming?" Lindy had finished with her father's belongings, returned them inside his tent, and was going through stacks of papers AJ had set out for her.

Judith M Kerrigan

"I have the edges mostly done and I'm working on the inside. I need some extra paper, a pencil and an eraser if you have it. I want to be able to try sketching the symbols. Some have mud over a part, or indistinct lines. It helps me to try out variations."

"Where's AJ?" He was not around.

"I sent him to the dig to begin an inventory of the stuff in the storage shed there. He's really careful about the way he works. That must be his training as a doctor."

I returned to my puzzle.

"I'm getting a good picture of what Ian did so far," I heard Simoneska say to Lindy. "His insistence on digging in this area is exciting. I know this will be a major site. And he is meticulous about details! I love that!"

Slowly I made sense of the lines, about twenty of them. It looked more and more like an inventory of something. There was nothing that gave me a key to what was written. I wanted to make copies but I knew the images would not photograph well. The writing was so faint in places I wasn't even sure I was reading letters or numbers correctly.

Simoneska found me some gel medium they used to preserve certain types of finds. I brushed it over the paper and it brought out the faint lines better. I finished by making copies by hand as accurately as I could, then gave the original and three copies to Lindy and kept two which I tucked into my duffel bag. Time for some journaling.

I feel like time is plodding along and we're getting nowhere. Is this an exercise in futility? Maybe Herder's right and we should have an all-out search of this jungle, but where would we even look? Well, this is one morning and the day is far from over.

Forty-three

It was almost noon. As Herder prepared to leave, I told him, "By the way, I gave my friends, Agathe Grimm, Caitlin Fitzgerald, and Caroline Bradley, the phone number of the consulate should there be any problem back at home. I'd appreciate being notified immediately if there is. They're caring for my other children. I do have a cell phone with international capabilities, but it may not work here." I gave him my phone number on a slip of paper.

"I'll be most happy to do that. We can get a message to you quickly. Cell phones do work here if you go to a high spot."

He headed immediately for the hill. The heli was due to land up there soon and I could hear a very distant thump-thump of an engine.

The others had taken a break and were already searching through the food, laying out what we would need.

Mac returned, stepping out of the Green Wall near the foot of the hill.

"Perfect timing." he smiled at the sight of the food. "My stomach's been growling for an hour."

He came over to me, asked about the paper and I got him a copy. Glancing at it, he put it in his pocket. There was an odd look on his face and he began to speak to me, changed his mind, shook his head and walked away.

He's found something.

Mac waited until we were all eating, seated around one of the tables. He reported he had found many signs of activity in the jungle around the site. Some of it was old, on trails not recently in use, others obviously used by locals for access to and from local places. He had found nothing of interest there.

He had, however, found trails of recent use that avoided the site by going some distance around it. These had shown considerable traffic.

"They run in more or less direct lines from village area to village area but not into the villages themselves. There are three of these, one north and one south of this site that run roughly east-west, and another some distance toward the river that's a north-south trail. They follow the old sacbes, the old Mayan roads of long ago."

"Here's what I've found."

He laid out scraps of paper, a sock, a discarded pair of very old shoes; a small square of bubble wrap which he thought had come from the packing material used at the site, and numerous cigarette butts. Whoever had used these trails had not been all that careful to hide their coming and going but had remained at least a quarter mile from our site.

MacPherson paused, looked at me, took a deep breath, and pointed with his chin toward Lindy, seeming to want to alert me for some reason.

He turned to her.

"I also found this."

From his pocket he drew a watch and laid it on the table. Lindy turned white and breathed in sharply.

"That's my father's! I bought it for him! I gave it to him! Oh god!" She laughed oddly, a semi-hysterical sound and I moved quickly to her side as she reached for it. I glared at MacPherson for bringing it up with so little warning, but he was watching her.

"It was hidden along the old east-west trail that's just north of here. I found it in the eastern direction, deliberately hidden."

AJ looked excited. "Do you think Ian hid it?"

"Yes. I also found this." He drew out a pen and laid that on the table. "This was thrown in the underbrush some miles later."

Lindy looked at it, picked it up, and pointed to the side of it, showing me. The pen was inscribed "To Dad from Lindy, Happy Christmas".

"I just sent that to him before Christmas." She was crying, tears dripping slowly down her cheeks.

"There's more. Some shards of a mug with parts of the letters D A D on some of them. A piece of soap and pieces of string and dental floss. They all were left at various places along the trail. I think either your father was searching for the outlaws and captured by them, or kidnapped outright.

Whatever, he left these as signs. He would have no reason to leave these if he was there of his own free will. I haven't followed the trail to its end. Not enough time. I'm pretty sure they took him in the eastern direction, which would lead to the Río Hondo if they didn't turn aside. I had to turn back. I left the other items on the trail to mark it for myself in case I have to follow it again, although it's pretty clear to me that, even though it's old, an original Mayan road, and goes through the thickest parts of jungle, and is very well hidden, it has definitely seen a lot of recent use.

"At first, I did think maybe Ian was after someone who might have been looting the site, but I think he would have notified authorities of that by now. It looks like he was with more than one person, a group. He was walking freely at first, but then was made captive or restrained in some way. There were five of them. The tracks are too mixed to be sure of what actually was happening but they are recent. The trail isn't all that cold. He was held a few miles from here for several days. There's evidence of eating and sleeping in one place."

Lindy jumped up. He read her mind.

"And no, we can't go after him immediately. Besides the fact that we aren't equipped, and that it would endanger his life—they're violent—and endanger our lives because they're armed, I still think there's something here that will give us more clues to what's going on. We need you to be here," he pointed at Lindy," to go over this place inch by inch. I'll call Herder on my cell and let him know about this. I can follow the trail myself and locate where he is better than a huge group of people. I don't make noise. All of you would sound like a herd of elephants, and the police would be a disaster. If this is about drugs, these men are dangerous, well-prepared for any assault by police."

"Herder suspects that." I interjected. "He told me before we ate that he thinks it's about drugs. He's going to institute an all-out search."

We had all heard the sound of the helicopter come, land briefly, and then take off and recede.

"Then I have to talk to him right away. An all-out search may be the worst thing that happens right now. It could definitely get Ian killed. We don't even know where he is, but if

I have a chance to follow that trail, I can pinpoint their camp location. I'm going up the hill for better reception." He pulled out a cell phone from one of his inner pockets and took off running.

So he won't be overheard? I thought. He's read more on that trail!

I had my arm around Lindy's shoulders and I hugged her as she broke down and began to sob. I let her cry until she subsided.

"Now is the time to find out all we can from here, to find all the pieces. Your dad is very smart. He knew just what to do and he had faith that you would follow through just as you have. His letters with their strange tone, and his terse phone calls at Christmas time, all this was part of his plan. Remember, if anyone can survive, he will."

I wish I truly believed that.

Still sniffling a bit, she nodded yes. "He did warn me. He ..." Her head came up off my shoulder. "We have to examine everything again, absolutely everything! There may be messages in his letters, words he used, clues, a code. I have to talk to the workers. Where is Ramon?"

Where indeed?

"Lindy, he told me they will be going all the way to Chetumal to pick up workers from there and more food and water. I suspect he's making the rounds of every hamlet around here. He'll be here. In the meantime, I do know this. I think your father's alive. He's counting on you to scour this site for those clues. You're the one who's known more about his habits than anyone. Can you pull yourself together and tell us what to do so we can finish the job here? There's still the dig itself, and the workers to interview. If anyone can get truth from them, I think you can. The ones who want to help will show up, and you'll be able to learn a lot from them."

Simoneska added, "You may be able to figure out from that list who *isn't* showing up. We'll need to know that too. If and when Herder returns with the federal police, you'll want to be able to tell them everything you learn."

I had drawn Lindy into a hug, but now she pulled back, eyes wide.

"Do you think they suspect my dad of running drugs?" she gasped.

I couldn't lie, remembering our detention at the airport on this trip, the suspicion I've been under since September and especially since Conrad's death.

"Who knows what they suspect? I think they'll investigate everyone until they have a clear picture of what's going on."

"But the more we find, the less we'll be part of their suspicion, Lindy," AJ reasoned. "Come on, let's eat and get back to work."

Lindy pulled herself together again.

She's learning to be brave. I and my children have learned how to be brave for many years. It's a hard and terrible lesson and it never feels brave while one does it.

My heart went out to her, knowing what a painful process this would be. I looked at AJ. He was watching her and nodding slightly to himself, remembering.

Forty-four

We had re-examined all of the belongings, papers, and finds from the tents and the shed when, under a tarp behind the shed, Lindy found a pile of shoe-box-sized containers of artifacts. She was horrified and called Simoneska over. He squatted and took more of the covers off. He swore.

"Now I know Ian didn't leave without being coerced or forced by someone. He would never leave these finds sitting around like this otherwise. In fact, I can't think why any trained workers would do this. Everyone is taught how to treat any find with great care. This is awful!"

Simoneska went from box to box, examining each. "What the hell happened here? There isn't an archeologist in the world who would do this! I didn't find any records of these in the reports either.

"Lindy, I just can't make myself leave these this way. I know you want to focus on your dad but can we take time to photograph and catalogue these? I just..." he was pacing back and forth... "I just can't leave these like this."

"No. I can't either." She stood up. "We have to take care of these. Since there are no workers here and, but for this, we're done with this area, let's get to work. With all of us, we can at least catalogue and pack them to be taken to Merida. I only hope somewhere Dad made a record of where and how these were found."

By mid-afternoon, we had photographed, labeled, catalogued, and carefully repacked all the shoeboxes of artifacts. Simoneska set up another table away from the rest and had me put them in larger boxes for removal to Merida.

Mac came over, a single box in hand. "This is the last of it. Lindy's rechecking her dad's papers to see if we somehow missed a reference to any of this stuff."

I looked over to see her reading by her dad's tent door. AJ was wandering near the perimeter of the camp.

"Mac, what do you think really happened here?"

BETRAYAL by SERPENT

"Anna, I don't know for sure but I do know Ian is in very real danger. I found spent shells from discharged guns along the trail and especially where they camped. No blood or body parts or body. He wasn't dead but he was threatened. Actually, I'm avoiding thinking he might be dead."

"I wish Ramon would come with the workers. It will give Lindy something more to do. Maybe we should go over to the dig and start on that."

"Yeah," Mac agreed. "I'd like to do that. I just can't get over the hunch that Ian left us a clue there somewhere." He went to get something to drink.

I looked for AJ. I was still hoping to talk to him about whatever he had learned in Cancun, but he had begun to carefully walk the section of the grid still marked off, then expanded his exploration into the perimeter at the far edge, searching through grasses and brush for anything he could find, creating a grid as he went and photographing everything. He had just picked up something when we heard the trucks.

There were three, our rental and two others. Held together with duct tape, ropes, and baling wire, one truck clattered slowly down the hill, a cloud of oily smoke coiling into the air behind it. The other chugged down with grinding gears, a stuttering motor and squealing brakes. Workers began jumping out even before they stopped.

Lindy immediately went to meet them. Several came toward her and greeted her with familiarity. Most were very short, stocky men, wide of shoulders, with strong wood block bodies.

Simoneska went to meet them also. There was a round of introductions and one of the men, who had been introduced first, seemed to be in charge. He immediately had the rest sit down on the ground and small campstools were found for all but me and AJ. I noticed several glances our way from the workers but they soon were attending to Lindy.

She began by greeting them in Spanish and then continued in English as she told them of her worry about her father. She asked to speak to each individually about anything they had noticed or knew about what happened. Ramon translated into Spanish and then into Mayan.

I watched faces. *There's tension in this group.* I saw some men nod and others with eyes shifting away from her. Two looked very uncomfortable. I tried to memorize their faces so I could tell her later. *Will this get us any new information or are they too afraid to speak?*

I remained where I was and finished the last of the packing. Mac had disappeared. AJ was still at his search. I took the time to add to this journal.

Sometime later, AJ came over to me, carrying a brown bag from our lunch. He laid it on a chair next to me. As he bent down, he breathed, very quietly, "Take a look but don't take it out now." He straightened immediately and left. Out of the edge of my eye, I saw one man watch him with interest and look at me, then poke an elbow at another and say something.

A private interview area had been set up by the two men in charge. I could see there was a hierarchy in the group, with one leader, an assistant, and the rest obeying commands.

Lindy interviewed each man privately, one by one, some distance away behind the trucks, out of the eyes and ears of the group. Occasionally the expression on her face let me know when she was finding information that added to her current knowledge. More often she looked disappointed.

When I was sure no one was watching me, I peeked in the bag. He had found a gun, partially wrapped in a piece of camouflage cloth. Instinctively I kept my face carefully bland and continued with my work.

Finally the interviews came to an end, most of the workers departed in their trucks and the man in charge and three others, along with Lindy, Mac, Simoneska, and AJ, left for the dig.

Ramon came over and explained that four men had been hired to help us and that they were known to Lindy. He and Jorge sat for a brief time at the table, both mostly silent, looking solemn, although Ramon asked what, if anything, we had found. I explained about the artifacts and what we had just done with them. I told him about the paper, showing him a copy. He made no comment.

Then he looked at Jorge and they nodded to each other. "Dr. Stewart has definitely stumbled on some illegal operation, has tried to do something about it, but has been taken by those who were smuggling," he said in a low voice.

"Are you sure?"

"Sí. Three of the men have told us this. They talked to us about it on the way here. They all know what goes on in the jungle. Here, most of them pretended to know nothing, even for Lindy. They are afraid. There are fellow workers who act as spies for the cartel. Villagers have been killed, including two children who were murdered when their father refused to do what the cartel wants. Local police have been bribed and can't be trusted."

His face was hard. I could see he was thinking of his cousin and his own children. I waited for him to go on but he didn't. Jorge had turned his back to us. The muscles of his back and shoulders were rigid with tension.

"What exactly happened to Ian Stewart?"

"One man said he walked off of his own free will but the men with him were armed and he was not. He believed Dr. Stewart died because he hasn't returned. Others are not so sure. They think El Doctor may still be alive."

He looked off in the distance and I thought he was thinking of his cousin.

"Have you ever heard any news of your cousin?"

"No. Nothing."

"His parents must have been devastated."

"You know his mother, Anna. She is Adelina. He was her youngest and last child."

I looked at him with shock. "Oh, my god! How has she managed? How can she...?"

He interrupted.

"The job at your house saves her sanity. When Señor Wentworth closed the house for a time, she became more and more depressed. El Señor was here briefly at Christmas but he didn't believe he would be returning anytime soon. She relied on this money to try to find out where her son is, to pay for information. She has never given up hope. When AJ called to open the house, it was just in time. It is the only place that doesn't remind her of him. Also, it is quiet, and it is a much better place than the one she lives in. Her own house is small, and crowded, and poor. It reminds her of how little she could provide for him."

I tried to imagine what it would be like if one of my children had been taken to be sold into sexual slavery. I couldn't, except to know I would feel enraged, horrified and helpless.

I wanted to know what Conrad had done while in Mexico and was about to ask when Lindy and Mac returned from the dig.

Ramon and Jorge got up abruptly and went to the truck.

She began to tell me what she had found out. "Dad had a computer here. The men saw it. It's missing. I didn't find it in these tents or in the sheds. We're going to go ahead with examining the dig. We'll work as long as we can, into the night if we have to. I just came back to eat a little something and refill the canteens."

AJ came loping into camp. "If we're going to work after sunset, I want to chow down." He headed for the truck. Jorge had heard and seen him and was already getting out food and water and bringing it to the table where I had worked earlier. Ramon and AJ got more and they set up a buffet.

"Well, we've scoured this area for anything it can produce," Lindy declared. "Tonight and tomorrow we work the dig."

I looked at AJ and he turned away. I wondered why he didn't say anything about the gun. *Where's the bag? It's gone from the chair.* I saw AJ go into the office tent. *Why hasn't he mentioned that?* I was sure he had it. I made up my mind to corner him as soon as I could and find out what was going on in his mind. In the meantime I wanted to know more about Conrad's trip to Mexico. I looked around but Ramon and Jorge were not in sight.

Frustrating! I want to know what others know!

Forty-five

The next time I saw Ramon and Jorge, we were already at the dig where I was introduced to the two Mayan workers who had appeared to be in charge, Hernan and Jaime. The other two were at the far end of a long trench that ran the entire side of the huge structure. They seemed to be searching for something.

Directly in front of me, I looked into a pit where there were gridlines up, and several levels of excavation.

I was assigned the camera again.

Mac, Simoneska, AJ and Lindy agreed they would begin to comb the site looking for signs of any burials or holes. "If he hid anything, he'd be most likely to bury it but I think it's unlikely Dad would have buried it in the site itself because he wouldn't want to disturb anything of interest." Lindy said.

The men agreed. "However, to eliminate the obvious," Simoneska said, "I think we should do the trench first, just in case. He could have decided to put it in the trench because it *is* already excavated and no one would look there."

"Ok," Lindy said. "Then we know that's done."

Mac instructed AJ and I. "Here's what I look for—signs of loose dirt, slight depressions in the dirt, or slight mounds. Beyond the trench, look for vegetation that's dead when it shouldn't be, or missing where it should have been growing, any sign that the vegetation is not as it normally would be. If you step on any dirt and it gives under your feet, freeze and call me over. You can probe the dirt with a stick too. Anna, you follow behind me. I told you I'd teach you. This will be your lesson for today."

Split into four teams, we began at the ends and in the center of the long trench, carefully probing the earth. Time edged toward evening and I wondered if we'd be able to see very well when darkness came. A string of lights had been run along the trench, propped on poles stuck in the ground, not yet turned on.

We found nothing in the trench. Mac then formed us all into a line along the trench, facing outward. He had us move out slowly, covering every inch of ground. "Again, if anyone sees anything suspicious, stop and call me."

It was interesting to watch Mac. He sometimes was down on all fours, his head close to the ground looking for minute disturbances. He kept up a running patter about what he saw. Several times someone stepped on a soft spot and called him over but they were nothing but small piles of rotting vegetation.

He and I were moving outward from the northwest corner of the structure when, abruptly, about thirty feet out, he stopped and called to us all to halt.

"Anna, bring the camera over here next to me. Photograph this from a low angle, this side. Lie down if you have to. I think that will show what I see."

He showed me the area he wanted photographed. I didn't see anything remarkable about it but did as he asked. He pulled out some dying vegetation from a 4' x 4' area of the ground. It came out of the dirt easily. No roots.

He instructed AJ to kneel across the area from him. Following his directions, they began scooping debris to the sides gently with their hands. What had looked like solid ground was in fact soft.

Mac called the others to us. Hernan brought flashlights and tools and the other workers came running with a screen, wheelbarrow and shovels. Lindy and Jaime knelt and began to help, each person carefully removing about an inch at a time.

"Jaime, did my father dig any exploratory trench here?" Lindy asked in Spanish.

"No, Señorita Lindy. I never saw him near this place."

As the dirt was removed, two workers sifted it through the screen and piled the sifted dirt in wheelbarrows, removing any tiny objects that were left on the screens, carefully bagging and labeling them after I had photographed them. Lindy had me photograph each layer also. She explained to me that normally nothing would be excavated this fast.

The light was leaving us and Hernan ran across the clearing and started up the generator. Light pooled behind us, while the jungle breathed itself into darkness. We needed flashlights to illuminate the deepening hole.

Even though this was "hasty", it was a half hour before they hit something, about four feet down. Simoneska joined them. Mac's hand, reaching several feet down into the hole, scraped across what appeared to be a board. When he brought it up with another handful of dirt, caught on his fingernail was a long piece of green string.

"What is that?" Lindy asked. "Oh! I know what that is!"

"Dental floss. Your dad was here." Mac was grinning. "This is the place."

We had questions. He ignored them.

"Well, this sure isn't Mayan," he murmured as he peered down into the hole at the boards. I shined the flashlight Hernan had given me down into the hole for a better look.

"Someone else, AJ, hold the flashlight. Anna, take pictures. Use a night setting. Here, I'll show you." He showed me the setting for low light, cautioned me to hold the camera braced firmly, and made sure the flash was working. Lying on the ground beside him, camera and elbows braced, I began to take pictures.

Simoneska had gotten a more powerful flashlight and held it high over the scene.

Slowly they pulled dirt from along the sides of what appeared to be a small crate or wood box, moving faster now that they were sure this wasn't an archaeological finding.

Finally, Mac and AJ pulled up on each side and the box came free.

"This is heavy." AJ observed as they set it on the ground beside the hole.

Mac had the workers remove all dirt from the hole in case there was something else under it. They found nothing more.

Jaime got tools to open the box. It was about two feet wide, over two feet long, and three feet deep. We all stood around it, excited, expectant. McPherson pried it open. At the top, thickly wrapped in plastic, was a leather bag and in the bag was a computer. A collective sound of approval came from the group and Lindy grabbed it, jubilant, and danced up and down, not even noticing as Mac removed packing material and uncovered another package.

He lifted a large uneven object swathed in heavy canvas, loosened the bindings on the canvas, took that off and found another wrapping of soft cloth.

Lindy stopped her dance. "What on earth is that?" she asked.

We were awed into silence when the cloth was removed.

An exquisite white marble sculpture rested on the ground, a beautiful nude woman, her arms wrapped around a tiny baby, nursing the child at her breast. Lindy slowly sank to the ground in front of the statue, her mouth open, jaw dropped.

"Well, I'll be damned!" Mac whispered.

"Wo-o-oh!" This from AJ. He looked at me. We were both thinking of the gallery. I looked at Ramon. He was nodding, as if this verified something for him.

"Madre de Dios!" Jorge exclaimed. Someone else said something in what sounded like Mayan. I remembered one of the words for woman, ix'chel, recognizing it among the other words I couldn't understand.

We all jumped when, suddenly, the generator sputtered and the string of lights flickered.

"I think we've done enough here for one day," Simoneska stated, standing up. "We need some time to absorb all this. We all need to talk, to figure out what this means and what we do next."

"I want to know what's on this computer," Lindy exclaimed. She was hugging it to her chest.

I stepped up and took photos from every angle I could. Mac rewrapped the statue, and we all headed back to the main tents.

Lindy stated she wanted us all to meet in the morning, everyone, to talk about this.

"As much as I'd like to examine this computer tonight, I need some rest."

AJ spoke up. "I agree, Lindy. We all want to know what's on there and then we'll need to sit down and talk this over and plan what next to do. This sculpture puts a new light on some things I learned while in Cancun. There's definitely been an art black market running along with the drug smuggling. Earlier today I asked Ramon and Jorge to see if they could get more information about it around here. The men didn't tell you all they know. Ramon and Jorge learned that some of the men who worked for your dad were paid by the cartel. The villagers have been threatened with death, two children killed, if they talk to anyone. There's much more to this than we've thought. Ramon and Jorge have agreed to try to find out more tonight. There are small cantinas where locals hang out, where we would not be welcome. They will see what information they can pick up."

I looked around. I hadn't even noticed when they left. I decided to speak up and tell them what Ramon told me.

"Ramon said a few of the men gave him and Jorge information about the smuggling but most of the villagers are terrified to speak, even to you, Lindy. The local police can't be trusted. We really are in danger. We're being watched just as you and I thought. Ramon said you're particularly in danger of being kidnapped, especially if your father's still alive. It looks like your father was gathering evidence against them. They'll use you to make him tell all he knows. Then they'll kill you both."

Simoneska looked grim.

"That's it then. We need to have Hernan and the men stand guard over our camp tonight. I'll set that up. I wish I'd hired more. Mac and AJ, we'll all be on watch, taking turns. We're also going to be armed. I haven't wanted to bring out weapons but I brought some just in case. I'll go up the hill and put in a call to Herder. I don't know that I'll get hold of him but he needs to be part of our plans. In the morning, we can decide what we want to do next. I'll be closing the dig trenches and arrange for removal of anything of value until we can excavate in safety. Lindy, we'll make it a priority to find your father first, of course. Politically, I can call in some favors from higher levels. We'll see what that can do."

"We have an additional weapon but no ammunition for it." AJ told them what he'd found.

"Wow! Someone got careless, to leave that out there! How did I miss that?" Mac looked disappointed in himself.

"You didn't search there. It was the other direction from where you went. I figured you wouldn't have time to search there so I thought I would."

"You didn't do too badly, for an amateur. I'll take you with me next time."

Lindy spoke up firmly. "I think the women should be part of the watch too. I do know Tae Kwan Do, even though I can't shoot. Mrs. K, you and I can share a watch."

There was a loud chorus of no from the men. Lindy got her determined look. She didn't win this time and I was very grateful. I wanted a good night's sleep. Tomorrow would likely be a very difficult day, particularly if Ian Stewart was found dead, or if we had to flee or fight.

If we make it to tomorrow. What's to prevent them from attacking us during the night?

I took Simoneska aside and told him my fear.

"I've thought that too. They haven't so far so what I'm thinking is that right now they don't want to call a lot of attention to their activities, which would happen if they attacked us, but we'll have to act fast tomorrow morning. Plan on being up early."

A short time later, in our tent, Lindy collapsed in exhaustion. "I want to keep on but I'm so tired. It's been such a long day. I really didn't want to watch or I'd have fought them. I'll watch if I wake up though. They can protest all they want. I'll go and take my turn, but I need sleep right now."

"I know. I'm beat too."

I'm outlining this day in my journal, my mind racing with questions. Even though there's no proof of connection, I can't help but think of Conrad's gallery and the sculptures there. This one would fit right in.

Could there be a connection? What could possibly have caused Dr. Stewart to hide his computer and the statue like that? Why was Conrad in Mexico? What did he find out? Did that have something to do with his death?

Would someone kill to keep these art pieces flowing to collectors? Are all Conrad's paintings and sculptures genuine? Or are they just very good fakes? Did he get them through the black market or did he buy them legitimately? Did he know about the smugglers? Did he find a connection to Wisconsin? To The Firm? To my husband?

When I finished, I turned out the flashlight and let the night surround me.

Lindy's voice cut through the blackness. "Mrs. K, I've sensed it all day. I know you're right that we're being watched."

"Yes. Ramon said he and Jorge sensed it too but they couldn't find anyone out there. Lindy, was your father armed? Was that his gun? While you were questioning the men, AJ found that gun wrapped in camouflage cloth. It looked like it had been there a while."

"I don't know, Mrs. K. I know he can shoot but he never carried one openly. He never taught me to shoot and I never would have asked."

I was changing for bed in the darkness. I decided to dress like Lindy, in light pants and a T-shirt. Getting out of my bra felt heavenly but it didn't relieve the pressure inside my chest from the creeping fear and the feeling of a presence out in the jungle.

"Where is your dad's computer, Lindy?"

I heard a soft giggle. "I'm sleeping on it." I heard her thump her mattress.

"It's my first job of the morning. I know there's information on this that Dad wanted to keep safe or it would never have been hidden. I bet this will tell us a lot! Night, Mrs. K. Get some sleep. It'll be a long day tomorrow."

"Just as soon as I finish this last bit of journaling." I had turned on my flashlight to make last notes.

When will the human snakes strike?

Forty-six

Of necessity, I've written this later, in the weeks since it happened. My memory was badly affected but as I write, some events are almost too vivid in my mind. Others I may never remember, or they are fragmented into a wild sound, a flash of movement, a sharp awareness of danger, deep immersions into the color green and sensations for which there are no words. I can't write this without feeling a strange confusion, some panic, and deep thick fear. The strangeness feels like an alien infection of my memory from some other reality.

I see this time in three segments—my time in the camp on the Rio Hondo, the time in the jungle, and the hospital afterward.

...the Rio Hondo...

I couldn't breathe. I tried to take in air and panicked. My body struggled. My chest wouldn't expand. Something pressed on me. My mouth was covered. There was a horrible taste, a gagging smell. I screamed inside, "I'm dying." My world dissolved into black and I floated in a tunnel. *I'm not supposed to be here.*

I came to consciousness lying face down on a hard surface, gulping air. I raised my head and was overwhelmed by a wave of nausea and more darkness. Dust choked me. I coughed and cringed from pain. Around me was a rotting smell, like mildew or mold. I smelled dirt, shit, sweat, a metallic smell, a blood smell.

I couldn't move my arms. My wrists were tied behind my back. With attempted movement came vicious pain. My head began throbbing, pounding at the base of my skull. A knife blade stabbed between my shoulders. My chest and lungs hurt. My breasts, crushed under me, felt bruised. My lower back had more knives in it and I felt a burning sensation in my ankles. Movement was excruciating. I started to cry and it got worse. I couldn't hang onto any thoughts. They came. They scattered and disappeared into the pain.

A forever time later, my mind suddenly switched on. Now my thoughts were racing, beating me up. My breath came faster and faster. I began screaming. Then nothing. I must have passed out.

When I came to, I was still on my stomach. My shoulders ached but my hands were untied and above my head. My legs were still bound to something. My breasts ached all around my nipples. I was naked from the waist up.

Oh god! Was I raped? What happened?

My attention went to my vagina. No pain there. I wanted to feel there but when I moved my hand to the waistband of my pants, it was gritty on my skin. Dirty. *Don't touch there.*

I slowly turned on my back, which twisted my legs. I tried to sit up. Movement brought on retching and dry heaves. Dry mouth, dry throat. Dizzy.

When that stopped, I began to hear sounds. Heavy breathing. Slow breathing like someone sleeping. An engine. A bird singing. Sound of water. A distant splash. Men's voices.

I am a captive. I am someone's captive. How? Where? Who?

There was a very sore spot on the left side of my head. I felt it. Sticky. I smelled it and tasted it. Blood. My head was bleeding. *It's clotted now.*

I was in a shack made of boards. There were very thin cracks between the boards and light showed through but inside it was so dark I couldn't see details. A grey curtain of some cloth hung down on my left. My shirt was lying about four feet away. The air was hot, close, humid, dusty, and suffocating. It stunk of urine, sweat, gasoline or some fuel and other rank odors.

It smells like someone is roasting shit in here. This place is baking in the sun. I'm baking. I'm so hot and thirsty.

From behind the curtain came the sound of heavy breathing. *It's Lindy! They got her too!* I began to shake so badly I thought I was having a seizure. What finally broke my panic was a long and very loud snore.

That's not Lindy. That's a man! Oh my god! It's AJ!

Waves of guilt and fear washed over me again and again. I lost control of my bladder. The seizures went on and on. Pain took over.

When they subsided I forced myself to move, to curl up my torso along the floor, then push myself up slowly little by little until I was sitting. I reached for my T-shirt, barely able to pull it to me, almost falling over again. When I tried to put it on, I couldn't raise my arms high enough to do it. More pain.

There was another cloth on the floor next to me and when I pulled it to me, out fell a kitchen knife. The absurdity of it sent me into giggles. I heard voices coming closer and froze. They passed by. I heard them speaking in a language I didn't understand. Not Spanish.

It was odd. I had forgotten all about the snore. I felt weak, lay down again, and a charley horse sent a cramp through my right leg. I moaned and sucked in my breath.

"Sssst! Hey! Who are you?" growled a man's rough low voice.

American! That's an American accent! That's not AJ.

"I'm Anna. Who are you?"

"I'm Ian Stewart. I'm an American, an archaeologist."

Lindy's father? That's Lindy's father!

I suddenly didn't want to speak. I knew Lindy could be here somewhere. How could I tell him that? He had tried so hard to keep her out of this.

A barrage of questions came from his side of the hut.

"You're American too. Why are you here? How did you get here? What do you have to do with this crew of thugs? You can't be on their good side or you wouldn't be in here. Shit! Wait a minute! You're a woman! What's a woman doing here?"

He had continued speaking, mumbling his words, when footsteps approached and a raspy angry voice spoke.

"Venga! Venga! Andando! Hasta arriba!"

I heard scraping sounds and a groan of pain and the door banged shut. Footsteps moved away. A voice swore in Spanish. Another in American.

Waves of self-pity washed over me. I fought them by trying again to free my legs, belted, I soon realized, to a long thick metal pipe. *I want to get loose. I have to get loose!*

That's when a terrible scream came from somewhere in the camp. Then another. My body jolted with the sound. I knew instantly whose scream it was. I lay down in tears, my arms covering my face. I could only pray for him. I had never heard someone being tortured before. Something snapped in my mind. I forgot my name, where I was, only heard more and more screams. It was eternity before they stopped.

This is the first point where my memory slams into a brick wall.

There were footsteps approaching, the door opened, and his body was thrown into our shack again.

Am I next? I heard men's voices outside, arguing. I broke out into a heavy sweat of fear when I heard the word mujer. Woman. *They'll take me now.* I began to shake violently. My mind separated from my body. My thoughts came from somewhere up at the roof of the shack, then farther into a dark place. I can't remember them.

I heard their words, many I couldn't understand. One voice, the Spanish speaker, sounded angry, disgusted. I caught his words, "...un mujer...un mujer... ¡Estupido! No la perra vieja. Su hija, no esa."

The sound of the other voice was ingratiating, whining. *He's making excuses. He's being reprimanded.*

They moved away. My body kept seizing, out of control, my mind still gone. Slowly I came back to myself.

After a very long time I realized I knew what they said. Perra, a female dog, a bitch. Vieja. Old. An old bitch. Hija. Daughter. Finally I put it together.

They want the daughter? They wanted his daughter. They got the old bitch. Me. They didn't get her. How did they not get her? She was right there in the tent with me. I'm so glad they don't have her. What do they want with her? Yes. To blackmail him. To use her to make him give up what he knows or has. It has to be. Why else? And when they failed to get her, they tortured him.

I struggled to sit up and lifted the curtain. There was more light coming through cracks on his side and I could see him fairly well in the gloom. He was definitely not Indiana Jones. Not even close. Ian Stewart was a small man, with thin ropy arms, a caved-in chest, and a balding head. He looked like a very short version of Ichabod Crane. Or a scholar. Most definitely not an intrepid explorer. He lay in front of me, his head toward me, on his back, passed out. His arms and torso were bare and there were dozens of small dots, raw and dark red, all over him. Cigarette burns!

His shirt lay to one side, slashed into ribbons. There were small dark pools in the dirt under the edges of his body. I reached out and took some of the dirt in my fingers and smelled it. Blood. He had been beaten.

Just beyond where the curtain touched the floor there was an open space at the bottom of the wall. Beyond the wall was a tin can. I reached for it but it was too tall to pull into the shack and I reached into it to turn it onto its side. Liquid! I smelled my fingers. Tinny. I took the edge of my shirt and dipped it in and tasted it. Water. Tinny, but water. Slowly I squeezed water between his lips. He sucked—a reflex. I did that again and again until there was no more in the can. Then I sucked the last of it from my shirt.

The top of the can was still attached, jagged where it had been cut. *That may be useful.* I hid the can and the knife under his shirt, thinking they would probably not pick up the torn shirt.

Exhausted by this activity, I lay down and slept.

Ian woke me up, shaking my arm. He was lying on his back next to me. The noise outside our hut was of many trucks, shouting, movement of men. I thought I heard weeping at some point but it was so brief I discounted it.

"You have to get out of here," he said.

I motioned to sssh him.

"They can't hear us above the noise. Talk in a normal but low voice. You need to escape."

"We both have to escape. I heard them torturing you. You're hurt. You need a doctor. My son is a doctor. He can help you." I heard my voice crack and shake. Fear again.

He hissed and groaned as he changed position to face me.

"Look, lady! I don't know why you're here but you won't live long if you don't get out of here. They'll keep me alive. I've got insurance and they know it. They won't kill me until they find out what I know but I heard them say they got the wrong woman, meaning you, and they aren't going to send you back to wherever they got you. Where did they get you, by the way? How the hell did you get mixed up with this crowd? You're too old to be someone's girlfriend here. They like the young chicas. And sometimes chicos too. Sick bastards!"

Oh, god. I'll have to tell him. He isn't even connecting me to the dig, to Lindy.

"I was kidnapped from your dig. I know who you are. You're Lindy's father. I'm Anna Kinnealy, the woman she lives with when she's in school."

"What the hell!! Oh, shit! Oh, my god! They got her too. Lindy's here? What the hell are either of you doing here?" This was followed by a long string of swearing.

"No, wait! I don't think they have her here. They got me instead. I'm the wrong woman. If they didn't blackmail you by using her somehow, they didn't get her. I'm the old bitch, la perra vieja. They wanted the young woman and we were in the same tent and they got me, not her."

"Mother-fucking sons of bitches! She's not here. They would have used her for sure if they have her. Killed us both, all three of us, if I had talked. Shit!"

He sat up. His back was covered with long raw welts where he had been beaten. It amazed me that he could move at all. He must have been in pain. But his energy was intense, and his mind sharp. He was definitely not any scholar stereotype.

"Who's at the dig? Who came with you? Name them, all of them," he demanded. I listed everyone and told how we came to be there, beginning with Lindy's concern over his letters and ending with the discovery of his computer and the statue.

He listened, silent, and then filled in what I didn't know.

"I've known for all the time I've been here about cartels, but their activity didn't affect our work until back in September. I found out about the art work, about the animal trade, and of course the drug trade but I thought if I minded my business, they'd mind theirs and anyway it was all up north. I found out about the trade in women and children when the family of one of my workers had a child disappear. Desaparecidos, they're called. The disappeared ones. That I couldn't ignore. I began to collect evidence. Names, dates, places, what they shipped. The statue was the first hard evidence I got of the art trade.

"I know about Conrad Wentworth but never met him, just that there was an American trying to rescue some of the art. I called Mac. He hates the trade as much as I do, hates the toll it takes on indigeños, the Mayans. Hates that they are sucked into it. He's been helping out in the north but he came south to help me.

"The cartel is vicious, incredibly well-organized, into everything they can to make money. The tlatoani is cold, unscrupulous, loves violence."

"Wait. What's that word?"

"Tlatoani. It's the old Aztec title for the ultimate ruler, the priest-king. This organization is structured like the old Aztec culture from before the Spaniards came. Only they'd never let a real Aztec take over the top. He keeps himself well protected, well hidden from the dirty work. Think of him as the Mafia Boss of Bosses. And just so you don't underestimate his role, under Aztec rule, the tlatoani was responsible for offering blood sacrifice of other humans to his gods. Anyone captured by his warriors was considered an offering to the gods. He cut out their hearts while they were alive. This is a lot more than a drug cartel. It's almost a cult, a religion. They even have ceremonies where woman and children are raped, killed.

"They call themselves Los Serpientos, the serpents. KA'AN or KAN is the Mayan word for serpent. It's related to lightning, as in striking like lightning, and to being the captors, those in control. Their modus operandi against anyone in their way is to strike hard and fast. And deadly."

"Ramon told me that. His cousin was kidnapped eight years ago. He was just nine. Ramon and his family still search for word of him. And Conrad wrote the letters K, A, N in the snow as he was dying."

"If Conrad wrote that, he was in deep, deep shit. Members of Los Serpientos have the serpent glyph tattooed on their inner thigh up near their balls and hard-core members must pass a test, rape of women and children and killing at least two before they're accepted into the cartel. I just learned that from one of the Mayans in this area who opposed them. His cousin joined and my friend killed that cousin to protect the women and children of the family He himself is an outlaw now, doing what he can to stop the cartel."

He was quiet for a while, then continued.

"So it's South America, Central America, and North America, even into Canada. That takes incredible planning and coordination, and lots of bribery. This cartel rakes in billions. I wouldn't be surprised if Herder is on the take to persuade him to look the other way. He's a toady. I don't trust a toady. Simoneska is ok. He's got a great reputation, but I don't think he can fight this. I'm glad you got those artifacts packed up. They are catalogued properly. It's on my computer. He'll get them to the right place if they got away from the site alive.

"Anna, you need to know there's a chance they might have been attacked too. But I don't think so. Whoever took you was incompetent. They sent some underlings who didn't know what they were doing. And Herder didn't order his all-out attack yet or we'd both be dead. Someone was supposed to contact me at the dig, to meet me there, but whoever he was, he missed me. There's a movement among Mayans to stop this. I wanted to connect with that person. It's a very secret group right now.

"I'm intrigued by the paper you put together. There are more like it on my computer but without a key to their codes, I couldn't make sense of them."

"It looked like an inventory to me."

"Yup. I think that's what they are. Who has my computer?"

"Lindy had it under her mattress when she went to sleep."

"Anna, you have to get out of here. Mac's out there in the jungle and he's probably pinpointed this camp's location by now or is very close. I need you to get to them to warn them, to get Lindy and that computer out of here."

"What about you? You're badly hurt. You need medical attention. They've tortured you. You're the one in the most danger. You have all that information."

"He won't kill me until he has the computer or the information on it. And he'll never get it from me."

The noises were still going full force outside. Ian sat and listened to what they were saying.

"They'll be done in a few hours. Time to teach you how to get to safety and help."

He wasted no time, drawing a map in the dirt, with all the twists and turns of the road, all the villages, the geography between the site and the camp. He drilled me over and over on it, taking my hand and tracing the map until I could repeat all the information by heart. Then he began my lesson in jungle survival. After that it was a quick verbal self-defense course in hand-to-hand combat. When I protested he gave me a lesson in why I should know that.

"Listen, honey. You'd better hope they don't come for you for their little games. This is the way it is. You are in danger of being tortured, raped, sodomized, beaten, burned and killed. Get the picture? This is not a fairy tale, which is why you must go. If, out there in the jungle, one of them gets hold of you, you will go for their eyes with the intent of blinding them, for their lower lip with the intent of ripping it off their face, for their penis and balls with the intent of destroying any chance they have of ever using them again. It will be your life or theirs.

"You will have to walk night and day, hopefully ten to fifteen miles a day. You will be barefoot, unfortunately, but natives walk barefoot in this jungle all the time. You will be hungry and thirsty. You may have to drink your own urine."

"You will know directions by where the sun and moon are in the sky. They rise in the east and set in the west. If you can't tell, you climb a tree and wait until you can. If it's pitch dark and you can't see, same.

"The lives of your kid and my kid depend on you. If you get tired and need energy, make yourself angry by thinking of what they do to children. That will get your adrenaline going. Adrenaline is a drug. Use it."

He crawled over to a rucksack at the back of the shack and took out a small plastic container.

"You'll mark your trail with this. Dental floss. Mac will look for this. It's a game we play. He'll find this easily because this is the white stuff. When I want to make him work, I use green."

"How is it you have dental floss? That's so absurd."

"When they 'politely' asked me to come with them, they were still being accommodating. They just wanted to 'chat', and would I come visit their camp? So I did what anyone would do for a walk through the jungle and took my backpack. They were armed of course. When they took me prisoner and searched my bag, no one down here knew what it was. When I showed them, they laughed and thought I was crazy. They just tossed it in here with me. Wasn't that nice of them? I have clean teeth. Use about six inches at a time. On the ends of branches or whatever sticks out."

"Go as far as you can as fast as you can tonight and tomorrow. You'll be at your strongest. After that, if you don't find water and food, you may find yourself getting weaker but I hope by that time Mac will have found you. You can do this."

All the while he was talking he had been sawing away on the thick belt around my ankles with the edge of the tin can's cover. Now I felt a snap and my ankle came free.

"Rub it. Get your circulation going."

Shortly after that my other ankle was free.

"Stand up and walk. Move."

I crawled to the wall and pulled myself up and took painful steps around the shack. Slowly my circulation got better. I thanked myself for having walked for exercise at home. My legs were in good shape.

I sat down again.

"By the way, it's been a great treat but I think you should put your shirt back on before you leave."

My arms flew across my chest. "How can you see in this dark shack."

"You have very white skin." I could see his grin. He had very white teeth.

I put my shirt on. He sighed with regret.

Much later, he said gently, "Anna, you need to examine your breasts very carefully. You've been injured."

I caught my breath. "What do you mean?"

"You're badly bruised around your nipples."

I turned away, pulled up my shirt and gently felt myself. I was still very sore. Even in the deepening gloom I could see the marks.

"What happened?"

"The men played with you, pinched you while you were unconscious. You're at their mercy here and they have no mercy. You must leave or they will do much worse. Hopefully they do think of you as la perra vieja. They're winding down now and will soon begin drinking."

I felt myself go pale at the thought of what had happened and it was that moment when I knew I would leave no matter how much I feared going alone into the jungle.

"When will I leave?"

"You'll walk out during the night, after they are very drunk. There will be a skeleton staff. They will never believe you would be so bold as to do that, so will underestimate you. Shit, I almost forgot! Can you still spit?

"What?"

"Spit. Saliva. Any in your mouth?"

"Barely. Why?"

"Pick up some dirt, put it in your mouth and make mud. Rub it on your face. You need to cover that white skin."

I did but there was little moisture to work with.

"Can you pee?

"Can I what? Pee?" I was too embarrassed to admit I had already discovered I had peed out of terror earlier. My pants were still damp.

"You've peed your pants already while you were out cold. You probably shit in them too. That happens in this kind of a situation. But if you have more, you need to use it to mix with dirt and cover your skin and light clothing."

He heard my small cry, which came from the discovery that he was right. I had pooped too. A loose, dirty mess. I was the one who smelled so bad! It was not some other something from out there. It was me.

301

BETRAYAL by SERPENT

"By the way, the worse you smell, the better. You'll be left alone by quite a few animals, human and other. Not snakes, they're attracted by heat but they'll try to avoid you, too."

"Oh, no. Not another anaconda."

"Only pythons here, no anacondas." He laughed.

I smeared.

As he predicted, they drank.

"Lie down and I'll make it look like you're feet are still bound. If they try to pick you up, go limp. Pretend you're out cold. If they take me, you count seconds for ten minutes, then use the knife to lift the latch. They are so overconfident they don't even lock this place. Go quickly across this path to the edge of the jungle and left to the road and then right. They have a fire going and will be focused on that."

I put the knife and the floss in my pocket and lay down to wait. He dropped the curtain between us and the Black Wall dropped on me.

My fear grew as I waited. I told myself I had to do this, that I had to get back to AJ and the others and back home to my children. That we are all in danger has become so obvious. Whatever Art and Jon had been doing way back then, whatever Conrad had discovered, just because AJ and I came here—we are targets. Waiting was horrible.

Finally, I heard his soft words. "It's time." I panicked at the thought of leaving, of being alone again, of going into the darkness.

"They're drunk enough now. They won't notice you. The moon will be out soon. You'll be able to see the road by the dim firelight as you walk away."

It didn't happen. Two men staggered past and stopped about fifteen yards into the camp beyond our shack. It soon became clear why. Their sexual grunts and groans came through the darkness.

"Another frequent activity here," Ian breathed softly.

We waited for them to finish. Once was not enough. It went on and on. I covered my ears.

We waited long after they were done to be sure no more would come.

"Stay in the shadows at the edge. Squint your eyes so they don't see light reflected from your pupils. Move slowly when their backs are turned, pause every few seconds in the underbrush to be sure no one is looking your way. Stealth. It's all about stealth. Imagine you're a cat, a jaguar."

I slipped out the door quietly, crossed the road and stopped in the bushes, crouching down, waiting, watching. In the firelight, I spotted the sentry posted where the road came into camp and moved slowly toward him a few feet at a time. I almost cried out when I saw him turn and come toward me. He got within six feet from me, but I saw him lift the bottle to his mouth, backlit by the fire another five yards away. He swayed slightly, then turned to the fire again. With his back to me, I slid behind a bush, eased my way under and between other bushes to the road.

Out of his line of vision, I walked quietly away.

Forty-seven

...the jungle...

My time in the jungle has holes in it where memory fails me. Except for the first day, perhaps even that day, I'm not sure of all that happened.

Beyond the fire I had seen shadows of more men and heard the drunken slurring of speech that sounds the same in every language. Grunts and a brief muffled cry came from somewhere over there. I got myself quickly away.

Too soon the time came when the sounds of the camp faded and the jungle night grew louder. Scratches, stirrings, whisperings, a distant cough or grunt, wings whirring and fading, night birds calling. And everything went black. No light.

Terror hit me then. Intensely conscious of my bare feet, every step I took became a fight, a step over the edge of fear into an unknown blackness. Fear behind me. Terror before me. Every time I lifted one foot, I had to make a forced conscious decision to set it down on the road. Reduced to the senses of sound and touch, the only connection I made to any reality was the soft dirt on the road beneath my feet. There was no time, no place, nothing except that dirt and the night sounds. And the sound and feeling of the rapid pounding of my heart.

I heard, now and then, the sounds of a scream away in the jungle. Frozen by fear, I would wait until I could make myself move again, and then take another step, and another, and another. And so I went on.

Sometime, in that blackness, my sense of smell became acute: the earth was heavy and thick with the decadence of rotting vegetation; the plants smelled of a deep green-black soup; erotic flower perfumes drifted on the air; and the scents of life and death mingled in a heady wine. I smelled awful, like poop and acrid sweat.

Sometime, in that blackness, I became conscious of a growing light. I thought it was dawn and felt blessed relief. It wasn't dawn. It was the moon. Slowly the light grew as it filtered down through the canopy. Shadows of leaves and plants became touched with a faint silvery gray. My heartbeat slowed to a normal rhythm and at that point I began to walk with purpose, setting a cadence for myself—breathe, two, three, four—breathe, two, three, four.

I remembered Ian's map and forced myself to review it in my mind over and over. And so I walked under a waxing moon and into the light of dawn and the insane cacophony of monkeys, birds, insects, and other unknown beings. Screaming, howling, roaring, caws, clacks, and chatters broadcasted their intentions for their day. My plan? Keep walking. I was sure I was not far enough away from the camp of smugglers, not even close to the dig.

Just as the sunlight broke in full, a large multi-colored bird with a long beautiful tail swooped down through the trees ahead of me, bringing with it the most amazing feeling. Suddenly, I was filled with joy. I took it as a sign of hope. I have since learned that this was a quetzal, a blessing.

I drank all the drops of dew I could find dripping from the leaves, slurping them up greedily. I found a tree with one piece of fruit on it and three on the ground being decimated by ants. I ate the one on the tree and announced to the ants "I'm bigger than you and hungrier." I shook them off and finished their meal.

The full heat and humidity came and now my mind began to cloud, to lose track of things. It was the beauty of flowers that drew me on. I would find a beautiful flower and bask in its color and then move on in search of another.

Once I had to leave the road fast. I heard trucks coming toward me and dived into the underbrush and scarcely dared to breathe as they rattled past, going to the river camp. I worried about searchers but amazingly no one seemed to be searching for me from back there. I could only hope that I would come upon Mac somewhere ahead of me.

I succeeded in cutting off a big loop in the road where it headed south and then back north again before it continued west. I found my courage and headed into the Green Wall. I thought I might have made a great mistake in doing this because the going was rough and the direction of the light became ambiguous, but I did it and was triumphant when I broke through at last.

I waited for the light to slant to the west and continued.

But twilight came and with it growing apprehension, then all-out fear of the looming darkness. In panic I found one tree leaning against another and climbed up there, splayed over it like a cat, paws hanging down. There I spent the night. Sleep was fitful. During the night I heard trucks again, motor noise growing and then fading away. Lights flashed through the trees, then disappeared.

The moon came up and I was about to slide down the trunk when I heard rustling in the brush below. I thought someone was there and waited, frozen, scarcely breathing. Finally the shadow of one small animal passed by, then more of them. A small herd of peccaries slowed, sniffed, caught my scent, but passed on. Again I was about to get down and there was another one. A straggler. "If you don't stay with your troop, you'll get eaten." I said to him softly. He moved on. Minutes later I heard a thrashing in the underbrush, a small strangled cry, and a low growl of satisfaction, a cough, dragging, and then total silence. Not a sound from anything in the jungle. I stayed in the tree, praying the peccary was enough of a meal for the jaguar. The words of Mac and Simoneska echoed in my mind. "Better you than me."

From this point on, my memory is a blur right now. Perhaps I'll remember more when I'm back home but for now there are only bits and pieces.

I remember a swamp, ripples just under the water, a snake on the edge that struck at me and missed and then slithered away. I was very thirsty at this point and took off my shirt, got it soaking wet and sucked water from it.

I became steadily weaker, lightheaded and dizzy. The line between hallucination and reality disappeared. Fragments of memory—a large dark green snake draped over tree limbs, cries of children, a strange flute-like song, pictures from the mind of a jaguar, the moon growing larger and larger, terror when I knew I was lost, an incredibly thick swarm of some insects, hunger and thirst, and walking, always walking.

Whether I would make it to the dig or not, I didn't know and after a while, I lost the will to care. I tied floss to bushes and trees until it ran out. I left the empty floss container at the foot of a tree. I tried to make marks on the trunks of trees with the kitchen knife but they were only slight scratches.

Of how I was rescued, I remember nothing.

Forty-eight

...the hospital...

I awoke in a room with a window. I was lying below it and a dim light came through it. I was on some sort of pad. No jungle. No dirt or hard ground. There were coverings over me. I was shivering, but from cold or illness, I couldn't tell. A woman was bending over me, a glass in hand. She fed me water. I felt totally astonished at the taste, it was so good. I had no strength to move.

After that began periods of consciousness which even now seem like hallucinations to me. Yet I know some of what I remember was real. I write them down here so I won't forget again. Maybe I'll remember more later.

I wake to a dim light. *Is it night? Where am I?* I see Lindy's face, scared at the disappearance of her father.

Ian. I left Ian in the camp of the smugglers. Where is he? AJ. AJ!

I can't speak. A tube is down my throat. The IV is in my right arm. I try to touch it with my left hand and can't move my arm. I panic and dissolve into tears, an emotional flood.

No one is in the room with me. I hear the calls of a monkey troop. Feel intense hunger. No one comes into the room. My foot dislodges something at the end of the bed and I hear it drop on the floor.

They'll come for me now. They'll torture me. I have no troop. I've lost my troop.

Far back in my mind, I know my thoughts are unreasonable and paranoid but I can't stop the wild swings of mood and the mental visualizations of the horrors and fears of the past days. I try to gain some control by going back to my conversations in the hut with Ian.

The map. Trace the map. Remember.

Still no one comes.

I woke again and Lindy was bending over me. Her face was swollen, her eyes red. She looked ill.

I heard her whisper, "Oh please live!" and heard her whimper small crying sounds.

I tried to talk but the tube was in my mouth. I moaned a sound. She started at the sound of my voice.

"Mrs. K, I'm so sorry! You have to live! Please live!" She began to cry.

I tried to reach out with my right arm and succeeded in moving it to the edge of the bed. She reached for my hand and stopped crying.

"Will you live? Say you'll live!"

I nodded yes but really wasn't sure. She continued speaking but I heard her voice in bits and pieces, quick phrases, a word or two.

"...jungle...fallen log...snake, ...just after helicopter ride...Dad too...crocodiles..."

She went on talking but what she said made no sense. I could feel what little energy I had leaving me and didn't want to pass out. I wanted to ask her about AJ and Ramon and the others. She seemed to read my mind. I read her lips.

"AJ's safe...AJ... here..."

I heard no more.

I'm lying down and feel a bed under me. I open my eyes and see an IV snaking its way to my arm and a bag hanging from a hook above me. Memories of nightmares return and I struggle, trying to get up.

Must walk! I have to walk!

A woman appears and gently pushes me down. I have no strength to resist.

"You have been very ill, Señora. You must rest. The doctor will be here shortly and he will tell you more."

I begin to cry.

"Where are my children? I left them in the cave. You have to find them or they'll die!" I grab her hand. "Please tell them to find my children!" I am sobbing.

"Shh-sh-sh! Your son has come and gone many times since you came here. He will be back soon.

My son? They have my son too! I feel complete despair. She has a drink for me that glows a deep orange color.

Blood! She's making me drink blood! Oh god! What happened to my blood? Is the priest making me drink the blood of the children? I must fight her.

Blood tastes good!

I came to in gloom, a small light across the room. Someone was at the foot of my bed but I had trouble focusing my eyes at first. The shadowy figure did not move. I felt a spoon touch my lips and turned my head slightly. A small old woman was dripping something into my mouth. She smiled and nodded.

I'm hallucinating again.

My mind went back to the plane in the jungle and the very old woman who had given me medicine then.

She's here again. Or I'm there again. Which is it?

She seemed to know what I was thinking. She nodded yes and faded out. The Elf Queen stood there. She put a cool hand on my forehead and the coolness spread through my body.

"You must stay." Her words hung in the air like snowflakes.

"Help me, Grandmother." I was a tiny child again, a baby.

She opened the top of her dress and took her breasts out. Milk dripped from her nipples and she leaned over my mouth. Sweet white milk trickled down my throat and a sudden intense hunger arose in me, demanding, urgent. I began to suck greedily, a baby at its first feeding. Little by little, my body filled with her milk.

Again I heard "You must live" float over me and crystals hung in the air, became snowflakes and drifted down around us.

"Love is waiting for you. I love you, Macushla."

She faded into the old woman and then they were both gone.

The shadow at the foot of my bed moved and came to my side. It was Ramon. He took my right hand and stroked it.

"Mí amor, you are recovering. Your pain will leave you and by morning you will be much better. Mí abuela, my grandmother, brought you medicine. It will counteract the poison. She likes you and knows you are ill. She said she saw your spirit trying to decide to stay here or go. She said you must stay. You have more life to live. I hope you will stay too, Diosa. Yo te amo." He smiled gently. "You are a very brave woman."

"Don't feel brave..." my mouth was puckered and I couldn't speak clearly. "Water. Agua."

He reached for a glass with a straw in it and held it to my lips but I was unable to suck very well. He took a cloth from somewhere and wet it and dripped water into my mouth. There was some kind of glow around him and I couldn't see the edges of his head or body. He became blurry. I felt his hand lift mine and there was a touch and then nothing.

...consciousness comes...

I awoke in sunlight, the head of my hospital bed higher than my feet and several pillows propped under my arms. The sides of my bed were up. I moved my head without thinking and felt no nausea at all. I took a deep breath and my chest rose and fell easily. I felt soreness, but no heaviness or difficulty breathing. I had a sore throat.

The IV was gone, my left arm still covered. I could move it. I reached over and lifted the edge of the covering and dropped it, horrified. I picked it up again and lifted it away. My left hand and forearm were an ugly gray/black/red color, streaked, swollen. The swelling was partially into my upper arm. I remembered someone telling me about a snake bite. I had a frightening picture of what it must have been like when I was brought in.

I looked to my far right and there was AJ, sprawled out in a low chair, asleep. I cried silent tears of relief, not wanting to wake him. He was safe! That alone made me feel better. There was a low cot in the corner of the room and I wondered if he had slept there.

I looked around the room and saw a table with flowers on it, big beautiful tropical flowers, red and orange and pink. Their color pulsed at me. I knew I was better. I tried pulling my legs up, bending my knees, and was happy to find they worked.

A nurse came in with a tray of food and, to my surprise, I thought I could actually eat, although I didn't feel particularly hungry. *How can I not feel hungry?*

"Señora! Es muy bién, muy buena you are! What a strong woman you must be! You have survived so much! Now we can begin to get you fat again!" She bustled to a rolling cart and set the tray down, moving it to the bed.

I heard AJ yawn. When he saw me awake he jumped up and came over. He was smiling from ear to ear. "About time, Mom!"

He bent over, kissed my forehead and took my face between both his hands. I saw him fight back tears. "God, Mom, I was so scared! I didn't think you'd make it. Yesterday the doctors said you were fading fast. I'm so relieved!"

He took a deep breath. "I..." He broke off and shook his head from side to side. "I had visions of having to tell the others you died. I had visions of never talking to you again. I thought..."

He turned to the nurse. "I'll see that she gets fed." He sent her away.

AJ sat down and took my good hand in both of his and pressed it to his forehead. He took deep breaths for several minutes, fighting for control.

"God, Mom, I was so scared!" he said again. "So scared!"

"I want to know what happened," I croaked, my voice was still rough.

"You need to eat first."

"I'm not hungry at all. I don't know why. I don't remember eating anything for a long time."

"You've been on intravenous and tube feedings. You weren't able to swallow until yesterday morning. They pulled the tube out then. Is your throat sore? It should be."

"Yes. And my chest too. Why is that?"

"We had to give you CPR. We had to keep your heart going."

I looked at him in alarm.

"Why? What happened to me?"

312

"Besides the dehydration and lack of food, you were bitten by a snake, a baby one, but very poisonous. You didn't die right away because first, we must have found you right after it happened, and then because it was a baby and you are an adult. Your size saved you. We got a tourniquet on your arm and got you into a medical helicopter. I was really worried because baby snakes have no control over the amount of venom they pump out. I thought you might have gotten too much for us to help you."

He laid his head down against my shoulder. I had a picture of him doing that when he was little, his black curly hair all tousled.

"I was so scared. All my medical training seemed useless down here. I've had some hard and fast lessons in indigenous medicine. It was Ramon who got you some real help. He has a curandera in his family. She came last night with medicine. He said you'd be ok now. I didn't believe him."

He picked up the spoon.

"Some food first. This is some sort of pudding, mushy stuff. It should slide down without too much trouble. You've been able to swallow water and other liquids."

I was remembering the grandmother and the Elf Queen. *No wonder I don't feel hungry. I've had all the mother's milk I wanted.*

I started to ask more about her but he had a spoonful of food at my mouth. I dutifully took some and swallowed. Very mushy, sweet. Fruit, I thought. I felt like a baby again as he fed me spoon after spoon.

"Stop! Too much! My stomach is cramping slightly. Maybe a few swallows of water though." He helped me drink.

"Ok." He pushed the cart away. Going to my left side he began to examine my arm and hand.

"It's really looking good compared to what it was. Here's the puncture area." He pointed to the outer side of my forearm just above my wrist, his eyes grim and serious. "We had a tourniquet on quickly but," he took a ragged breath, "when your heart stopped...it was bad. Touch and go.

"We barely found you in time, Mom. If it hadn't been for Mac, tracking the dental floss, we wouldn't have been close enough. That was really difficult. We went to the camp and

313

found Ian, who told us you were gone. Until then we didn't know you'd escaped. There were fifteen of us and we backtracked, Mac picking up your tracks in the dust of the road. At first, when you left the smugglers' camp, he found it easy to follow you, even when you went off road. You had a pattern to what you did. But after you got to a swamp, he had a hard time because you backtracked. It took him a while to pick up your trail again. Then he discovered you went in circles. Ramon figured out you doubled back and slipped through and eluded us. As you went on your tracks became more and more erratic. When Mac found the empty container, it helped. We decided to search around the tree where you left it in widening circles."

"I think I was delirious at times, hallucinating too."

"Yeah. We figured that. He found two places where it looked like you slept, but then, after a time, nothing. You wandered way off the road. We might not have been able to find you at all but you picked up some fellow travelers. You rescued five children from the smugglers and got them through some really heavy jungle to the top of an overgrown pyramid where they were hiding. We found you passed out at the foot of the place under a log. They told us what you had done."

I looked at him in astonishment.

"I don't remember any of that. How could I not remember that?"

"Because the venom has affected your memory, not to mention the trauma of the whole ordeal. Trauma like this plays havoc with short-term memory. You may have memory losses for some time.

"It was amazing what you did. There was a small truck convoy that stalled as they were heading for the river with items for smuggling, including children for sale. The men were late and trying to rush, knowing they'd be punished. One of the lead trucks broke down and the drivers were all up front arguing over what they should do. The children told us they were crying, that they didn't think they would ever get free. You sneaked into the back of the truck, untied the ropes holding them, and led them into the jungle covered by the noise of the engines and the argument.

"One thing, though. The children say you brought a jaguar to help and it led you all to the pyramid, to that room at the top. That was a little odd. When they heard and saw us rescue you, they came out. They recognized Hernan and Jaime. I think their imaginations ran away with them." He laughed.

He'd never believe it if I told him. I'm not sure I believe it myself, but I remember a jaguar, pictures from a jaguar's mind.

He stopped to shake his head and run his fingers through his hair. I noticed his hair was longer than when we had flown down. He hadn't shaved, his face thinner and shadowed by a short beard.

"How long have we been down here? How long was I out there? And in here?"

AJ looked apprehensive.

"Now don't get upset! It's been a while."

I tried to sit up higher and only succeeded in sliding down lower.

"Just how long is 'a while'?"

"You were three and a half days and nights in the jungle after you left the smuggler's camp. We found you the seventh day after you were kidnapped. I thought you were dead, Mom. I was looking for your body."

I gasped.

"If I was kidnapped the night of the second day we were there...my God! AJ! The others! Cory and Alex and Marnie! Who's been taking care of them? They must out of food. Out of money."

He held up both hands. "Stop! Stop, stop, stop! You are such a Mother." He rolled his eyes.

"Between Aunt Carrie and Marthe and Caitlin, Alex and Cory have been mothered to the point of serious protest. Marnie of course, has loved it. Money is not a problem. I called Clayton. We're OK. In fact, we're more than OK. We're doing fine. More of Conrad's stock holdings were liquidated and we're just fine."

I breathed a sigh of relief.

315

He continued. "I hope you won't get mad but now that you're getting better, I think you'll take this next news with some degree of calmness."

He looked like the proverbial cat that had eaten at least one dozen canaries.

"They'll be arriving later this afternoon."

I burst into tears.

"Well, that isn't exactly calm, but it's better than I thought."

He let me cry for a time and then said, looking serious and scared again.

"I wish I could say that it was because you were better, but I called them down, Mom, because we thought you'd die and I knew they would have to be here, would want to be here. Needless to say, they're very happy right now. I called about five this morning, when we were sure you'd make it, to let them know of your improvement. Ramon went to Cancun to prepare for them. Marthe's coming down with them to rein in the boys a bit. They're pretty high on the news of your recovery and the trip combined.

"There's more you need to know. Because of the viciousness of the cartel, I've set up guards for all of us. Ramon and Jorge will be guarding Marthe and the kids the moment they're off the plane and there's been a guard outside your door the whole time. The house is secure too. I've got Jorge in charge of our security and that of those who helped us.

"We've chartered a private plane to bring them here. There's a suite of rooms in a nearby hotel here in Merida, and a private limo to get them to the hospital. We're taking no chances on a car bomb or sniper or any kind of retaliation. Just for now. Mac says he thinks the cartel is pretty crippled but I want us all safe."

I closed my eyes and relaxed. I had been about to tell him I had seen Ramon, and the old woman. I stopped.

Later. I can tell him later. I'm living in more than one reality. I'm sliding between them. It's easy. I thought only shamans did this. How strange!

There was so much more I wanted to know.

"How is Ian? And Lindy? She was really frightened and shaky when she visited me."

"She visited you? No. She's been with her father the whole time."

"No, AJ. She came to see me. She talked a lot but I couldn't hear most of what she said. Just bits and pieces. It made no sense. I think it was before they left. She was so upset!"

"Mom, he's not here." AJ's expression was worried, a frown creasing his forehead. "You really must have hallucinated this. He was flown back to the states as soon as they stabilized him. He has a lot of information on the cartel that has been running this. Lindy went with him."

"He was beaten very badly, burned a lot, whipped." He shook his head. "It was gruesome! The next day the men in camp didn't discover you were gone until very late afternoon. There had been a lot of drinking.

"Whoever is at the head of this was occupied with seeing the 'shipments' got to their destinations in Mexico and the Caribbean. When he got back, he finally decided to deal with you, probably to find out what you knew and then kill you, and when he found you gone, he took his anger out on Ian. But Ian created even more of a diversion, telling a tale he made up, supposedly in response to the torture, and the head guy sent his men to the coast instead of into the jungle looking for you.

"At the dig, Mac and Simoneska and I and the workers loyal to Ian began not only looking for you, after we discovered you'd been kidnapped, but we also badgered Herder into facilitating a national and international operation to take down the smuggling group. It took precious days of time as the agencies either dragged their feet or resisted cooperation and then haggled over jurisdiction. While they bickered, Mac and Ramon, who organized the Mayans into a search party, found the camp.

"I became furious at their bickering and finally I had information sent to every law enforcement agency I could think of. I called the FBI, Interpol, the DEA, etc. I really made a nuisance of myself. I took a page from Big John's book and even phoned our senators and congressman and called the State Department. I bugged Mexican federal authorities too.

"No stone unturned, as Simoneska said. CCAI leaned on all their contacts too. The result has been raids all along the coast, operations at the US/Mexican border, on the American side in four border states, and in Belize and Guatemala. By the way, the cartel's name is Los Serpientos, The Snakes."

"Yes, I know. That's why Conrad wrote KAN in the snow."

"What? How did you know that? KAN means serpent—one of the meanings."

"Ian and Ramon told me."

I was slumped way down the bed and tried to sit up higher and somehow hit my left arm.

"Sssssssssss!" I sucked in my breath in pain, my body arching, which made it worse.

"Mom!" AJ yelled for a nurse. Seconds later she came running. "She bumped her left arm."

"It's time for her shot. It will help with the pain. This pain is good. It means she won't lose her arm."

Lose my arm? I could lose my arm? I was panting, shaking again. She gave me the shot. I had an eternity of pain before it took effect. By that time I was wrung out.

Worried, I still had to ask, "What's going to happen to my arm? Why would I lose it?"

"You won't lose it now, Señora" the nurse answered, "but the nerves are coming back to life and that is why you feel the pain. This is very, very good. You rest now, Señora."

"Mom, she's right. Rest. I'm going to Cancun this afternoon to be there when the plane arrives. Now that I know you're better, I feel I can leave you. I can fill you in on everything that happened when you've recovered. You know the highlights now."

He was right. I was slowly sinking into the painkiller and just wanted to sleep.

When I awoke I found Mac standing over me. I thought maybe I was dreaming. When he moved closer I knew I wasn't. He had one arm in a sling. With his other hand he took my hand.

"Hey, woman! It's good to see you alive!" He was grinning from ear to ear. "It's good that both of us are alive!"

"What happened to you? Why is your arm in a sling? How did you find me?"

I was grinning too.

"Last question first. With great difficulty! You sure gave me a workout trying to follow you! Ian never made me work that hard. To answer the first two questions, I was shot when we went after Ian in the smugglers' camp. Just a flesh wound. In and out. Bloody but not lethal. Sure hurts now though. The jungle really got to you, didn't it? The human snakes got me and the baby snake got you. We make a good pair!"

"I'm glad you're ok."

He lifted my hand to his lips.

"I'm glad you're ok, too," he said softly. "Don't stop me. I have something to say to you. If I were the marrying kind, I'd ask you to marry me. You're only the second woman in my life I have wanted to be with and the other one, well, she left this lifetime a long time ago. I have to go. We're still tracking some of the human snakes, and their captives. I love you, lady. You have courage. You take care of yourself and those kids of yours. I hope we meet again."

That was it. He was gone.

A dream comes. There are children in a procession in the jungle. It is dusk. They are carrying candles and the light of the candles shines through them. I see that they are dead, spirits dressed in strange clothing, from a different time and place, yet they are Mayan. A large heavyset man appears some way in front of me, his back to me, and he is directing their moves. He looks familiar, somewhat like Art but I can't tell. He is much heavier than Art. I see Ramon in the distance on the other side of the procession. He has on a jaguar skin and is very angry, fierce, watching the children. He begins to chant a strange song and the large man melts away and the dream melts away.

I awoke again to find my children around my bed.

Forty-nine

...journal...recovering in Mexico...

We had two weeks together before I sent them home.

A beautiful and touching highlight was our visit to the scene of the plane crash. With Adelina helping us we made our own ceremony. Not quite an official Mexican Day of the Dead, but close, with flowers, candles, food to eat and presents for the curandera and her family. Ramon helped us find the gifts. AJ and I told again what we had found, we all told stories of Art, good memories, and we sang all the Irish songs. We cried, but it wasn't the horror I thought it would be. Ghosts were put to rest for all of us.

In spite of my injuries I grew stronger and felt better quickly, except for my left arm. With Ramon as our guide, we visited Tulum, Xelha, and ChiChen Itza, where I made it up and back down the Pyramid of the Feathered Serpent on my butt. We dived off Cozumel and swam with turtles off Isla Mujeres.

Finally I ordered them home. The boys had missed a week of school and loved that far too much. Cory and Alex tried their best to find reasons not to go. I left them at the airport with dire warnings of permanent grounding until age fifty if they didn't make up what they missed of school.

Lying in that hospital bed left me time to review all that had happened. From AJ, I learned the fine details of the raid and the aftermath of our kidnapping episode. Yes, police had gotten some of the men involved in the operation of the cartel. No, they hadn't gotten the top man. He was free to continue, perhaps inconvenienced, but still in operation.

Yes, they had freed some enslaved women and children. No, they had not stopped the trade. They had slowed it for the moment, but it would spring up elsewhere because all the big players were still out there.

Yes, apparently, the paintings in the gallery were bought from the black market. Conrad's love of art had overtaken his good sense. He saw a chance to acquire great beauty and could not resist. No, they're not fakes. They are the real thing. That is the bit of good news. The bad news is that there is no way I can keep them. So I'll have to face returning most if not all of them to their original owners. I am so disappointed about that. Curiously, Interpol has been the only police force that has been interested so far.

Politically, I am deeply disappointed in the role of the American consulate, in the wishy-washy behavior of Herder. After I got stronger, I went to the consulate and gave him a piece of my mind. I don't believe in meekness anymore.

Another ominous realization is that we are all in danger still, even more than before. We have thwarted more than one person's greed and that has made us implacable enemies. Coming to Mexico to see me put our whole family in danger. Los Serpientos goes on. KAN sends his lightning to strike wherever he chooses, even to the shores of the Fox River. Our appearance in the Yucatan made us visible players in this vicious game—targets.

We were followed, watched whenever we left the house in Mexico. I would not have known this but for a very silly observation. One day while we were shopping and in a café eating lunch, I saw a man with a mustache of hair both red and black. I was amused by the colors, thinking he fit right into Mexico. It was not even due to my usual color sensitivity. That had quieted down completely and I was just noticing the normal riot of color that is Cancun. Then I saw him again, in the market later. Again, at supper in the same restaurant we went to, and again while we watched the street performers in the square. Alerted, I saw others. There were at least three others, taking shifts. At ChiChen Itza, at Tulum, at all the sites we visited, even diving off Isla Mujeres.

I don't know if they followed Marthe and the children when I wasn't with them. They were certainly there when I was. I've warned everyone to be alert. We're still in danger. If I weren't recuperating, I'd be back in Green Bay. I'm worried about everyone there.

Jorge is looking into this matter for me.

I have questions now about the role of everyone involved. How I wish I could question Lindy and Ian. Why was

BETRAYAL by SERPENT

it that I was kidnapped and not Lindy? Did the smugglers really make a mistake? Was it really about her and her father only? Could I accept Ian's explanation for his not being tied up as I was? Could I accept Lindy's explanation of his activities? Could I accept anyone's explanation of their activities in this? What was on his computer? Why and how is Mac so involved in this? What about Simoneska? He seemed to be easily out of it all, on the periphery of anything illegal. Was he really? I know AJ would attribute this seeming paranoia to my trauma. It is! A person doesn't go through all this and come out of it with trust intact. Sometimes paranoia is because there is real danger. We must choose carefully who to trust.

Ramon hovered in the background, helpful, unobtrusive, expressing concern for me but backing away while I was with the others. There was the visit in the hospital to bring the curandera and only one more time we were alone until they left.

After we were back in Cancun, on a day everyone else had gone diving the reef off Cozumel, that was the day I chose to inventory the artwork in the gallery.

I had called Sotheby's in Chicago. As luck would have it, they maintain an office in Mexico City and agreed to send an appraiser. I wanted to make my own inventory first. I went down, unlocked the door and turned on the lights. I hoped for a long last time alone with their beauty.

After a while, I heard steps and Ramon walked in as I was on the final few. He came up to me, took me by the shoulders, turned me to face him, and looked at me for a long time. His face was sad. His eyes looked tired and old with too much painful knowledge.

"Diosa! I am so sorry I was unable to prevent this terrible ordeal you have had to endure. I did not know all this could happen. I thought Lindy was one who was truly in danger."

He pulled me to him and kissed me on my forehead and my eyes.

"How is your arm?"

He took my left hand and moved my arm so he could see the place where I had been bitten. It was still somewhat red but receding with each passing day.

"I still have some nerve pain at times but I'm getting better. It's better."

He kissed the bite.

"There! That is how to make it better, yes?"

I laughed. "Yes."

"I would kiss much more. Soon there will be no time. You will be leaving soon, and I must work for my family. Besides this house, we have many others we care for and I am kept very busy at the hotel, but today this I will do."

He pulled me to him, put his arms around me and kissed my lips, running his own lips and tongue back and forth, around and around mine. All boundaries between us dissolved and I melted into him. He filled my mouth with his tongue and I sucked him, hungry for more.

After all the harshness of the past few weeks, his energy felt incredibly warm, sensuous, intense. When his hands began to move up and down my back, I could barely breathe with the intensity of my desire. He slid his hands to my hips and held me to him. I felt him hard against me and I couldn't bear the thought of not having him inside me.

"Te quiero! I want you!" I rubbed my body against his.

"Querida! Wait!" He moved to the door, closed and locked it and returned to me. "If you are bruised, sore anywhere, tell me. I don't want to injure you any more than you are."

"Don't stop!"

He led me over to a long couch and undressed me. Kneeling in front of me, he pressed his face and lips into my stomach. Moving downward, his tongue found more of me and I opened my body to his mouth. We spent the next hours exploring every inch of each other, making love in the gallery, on the roof, in my room, in his room, in the room of mirrors. Even now as I write this I can feel him inside me. We had long hours of erotic and emotional lovemaking. When he left, it triggered more days of pain, of grief at what may be the end.

Through sheer force of will I'd held myself together until Marthe and the others were gone. When they left, I fell apart for four days, in shivering bouts of fear, or teeth-baring rage, or sobbing grief, my moods unpredictable and intense. Adelina nursed me with indigenous medicines: AJ monitored my physical signs. Between bouts, I couldn't even think. I just let it all flood out of me. Adelina understood. She knows pain. She called Ramon to return to me. He knows pain too.

So with Adelina's care and Ramon's lovemaking, and AJ's love, I've made some progress in this recovery. I've almost succeeded in pushing the words "It's not over" into the back of my mind. Sometimes I almost succeed in believing we're not in danger any more.

Sometimes I love denial.

Fifty

...journal, the last days at Cancun...

AJ chartered a sailboat for the two of us in Cozumel and we sailed out onto the Caribbean and scattered Conrad's ashes into the clear turquoise waters. Dolphins surfaced as the last ashes fell and splashed in the water around the boat for a time. I slipped into the sea and swam with them for hours.

When we got back, AJ left Cancun to rescue his medical career. He didn't want to leave me but I insisted I wanted quiet time in my house. I can think of it as my house now. Conrad's ghost might still be enjoying the ether around it, but I am the one who has to close it up.

I finished the inventory of the art. Sotheby's man came, supervised the crating of the pieces, and gave me a list and an estimate of their cost. Interpol came with him. Their man said some of the pieces were property of Jewish victims of the Holocaust, pieces that have been on their list for years.

"Mr. Wentworth was helping to find those pieces and return them to the owners. He's been working with us for a long time," the man said.

I felt wonderful about that. Conrad was exonerated. They've already found some of the rightful owners and in time will auction off any that remain. If there is enough from those sales, I will create a foundation for a school in Puerto Juarez.

If no one claims the beautiful statue of the Nursing Madonna, I'll keep her, my reminder of the Elf Queen's healing.

Between us, Adelina and I disposed of the extra food to her family, and she gave every room a thorough cleaning with the help of Tomi and Juanita. She wouldn't let me do that. I've gone through everything Conrad left there, giving away any clothing I found, and reading the household files he had there. There wasn't much.

AJ found an inventory of the upper floors of the house on Conrad's computer and I have it now. I have it all insured.

BETRAYAL by SERPENT

Ramon helped with the paperwork for the transfer of the lease to my name. I gave Power of Attorney to him so he could deal with Sotheby's if necessary. That business won't be settled for some time yet.

Today he is gone too. We have not made any promises to each other. Our lives are so different. I am immensely grateful we had this time. I would have stayed closed off emotionally and sexually but for him.

When Adelina left last night, it was with a contract making her the official custodian of the house permanently. I gave her a generous bonus for caring for six additional people and set up an account in her name at a local bank for the household expenses and her pay. I closed the old account Conrad had left for her and added the money to hers. She will supervise a skeleton crew of caretakers as needed. She informed me she was sending four children to school because of this job.

Just before she left, she came to my office where I was still occupied in updating this journal. She handed me a small package. I have enough Spanish now to understand most of what she says.

"This is for you. It is for good fortune."

I opened the box and there was an amulet, a beautiful carving of an amber-colored stone. It was of a woman who looked like the Virgin of Guadelupe. I said it looked like that to me, and she nodded.

"Sí. That is who it looks like, La Virgen, but it is not. It is of one of our Mayan goddesses, who we knew thousands of years before the Spanish told us of Virgen. She is La Madre, the mother. She is the La Patrocinadora de Las Mujeres. We made our ceremonies to her on Isla Mujeres. You remind me of her. She suffered much also. She will protect you now."

I thanked her sincerely. I knew in my head and heart that our problems were not over yet, that these matters were unfinished. I would need a guardian. All I knew of the smugglers lay like dark water covering unknown depths and dangers where crocodiles awaited prey. I thought it the best gift I could have and told her so.

As she went through the door, she turned.

"She is also called La Diosa!"

I stared at her. Her face showed no sign she knew who called me that. She left.

I spent the last of my time in Conrad's bedroom, where I removed all my clothing and stood looking at my body in the mirrors. I have traces of bruises on my back near my shoulder blades, on my hips and thighs, and one ankle is a bit yellowish. My breasts still have bruises but they too are healing. My emotional reaction to what the men did to me has been much healed by the respect, the tender touch and gentle kisses of Ramon when he holds them. There are pink spots where insect bites have been, but not as many as I expected to see. I have lost some weight but strangely, not much, or I've gained most of it back. All in all, I don't look bad. In fact, I love how I look.

I can't help thinking how incredibly lucky I've been. I could have been dead. La Patrocinadora and the Elf Queen are guarding me.

I gazed for a long time into my face, seeing a different person behind the eyes.

How is it I grew stronger through all that pain and fear and struggle? I certainly didn't feel like that's what was happening to me! But I did get stronger. I am stronger.

Longing for the touch of Ramon, I packed my belongings and sat on the bed on the roof a long time into the night, watching the stars.

The next day Jorge sent a car that took me to the airport. I flew into what was left of February winter, below zero, frozen tundra, frozen everything.

A warm welcome from children and friends though.

As I was preparing to leave, I found the copies of the paper I put together for Lindy and set it with other papers on my desk. One of those papers was the inventory from Sotheby's and I suddenly saw something that brought me up short. The paper was the same as the inventory, only in much abbreviated form.

Adelina told me Ramon had gone down to the site before we arrived. He was the only one who had access to the gallery. He was the only one who could have brought it to the site. He tore it up, knew I pieced it together, and never told me. Was he the contact Ian was waiting for? If he was, why didn't he say something?

Once again, who can I really trust?

Part Three

Green Bay Wisconsin

Fifty-one

Dream...

Moonlight ripples around me, pale white gold, sliding across my skin with the light touch of a lover. I stand thigh deep in the dark green-black leaf-covered coolness of the water. Smells of the swamp are thick, filling my nostrils with deep rich ebony air. I am one with all of nature and my body vibrates with the thousand energies I know and love. A thought drifts through my mind...tonight all is well.

Suddenly, lightning strikes! My spirit reaches for peace but a merciless evil shreds my serenity, rips into my spirit, slashes at my heart! Far across the lake a ripple disturbs the stillness of the surface. Very slowly Ka'an emerges. His hungry vibration precedes him seeking food for his belly, seeking a sacrifice to Chac, God of Rain. I see his eyes glowing golden yellow around dark slits. I smell the blood he craves.

Behind me, crouched in the tangled grasses on the shore, I hear Bala'am, Jaguar, my guardian, growling softly, encouraging me to stand, to face this threat. Ka'an moves nearer and my body fills with the cold dark blue of dread.

The desperate calls of the little ones rend the night. I sense their fear clawing the air, seeking me, unseen hands reaching, begging. Tiny cries echo over the lake. Whimpers and soft sobs disturb the lightless air around me, growing louder as the ripple moves toward me, becoming pleadings, accusations, cries of despair and hopelessness. I can't see them, reach them. I must find them! Help them! They are children gathered for sacrifice.

The greedy insatiable One demands more and more blood and flesh. They are my children and I can't remember their names. If I remember their names I can stop him. Why can't I remember their names?

BETRAYAL by SERPENT

I know this Ka'an, this golden anaconda rising from the depths of the lake, coming faster and faster, jaws open wide now. He loves blood. He delights in hatred. He bathes in greed.

Now he towers over me. The jungle reverberates with their cries, their screams. A child rises with him, floating in the air. He offers the child to me, a girl, her naked limbs dragging the surface of the lake. I take her but I am too late. Her heart is gone, a gaping hole in her chest, a sacrifice to keep his empire growing. Blood pours from his mouth and drips from his jaws. He has eaten her heart.

The lake is deep dark red. I smell the putrid reek of her decay. Too late I remember her name is Daughter. My Daughter.

"You have given your daughter," he hisses. "Now the other children will be saved. Your name is Betrayer!" He gloats as I bow with despair.

Bala'am screams her rage as the golden snake wraps itself around my legs, slithers up my body, squeezes my chest. I am choking, unable to breathe, gasping for breath, struggling. The air is thick, drowning me. My chest won't rise. My throat won't open. I am dragged into the black water. I feel myself strangling, gasping, trapped...

I wake up struggling for breath, on the floor next to my bed, on hands and knees, bedclothes twisted around me. Cory is kneeling next to me, his eyes wide with fear and concern.

"Mom, you had another nightmare. You screamed and called for Marnie. What's wrong? Why are you having so many nightmares?"

I grab the hand he offers and slowly stand up.

"It's the aftermath of being lost in the jungle, honey. It's OK. I'll be OK. It's just a dream. Go back to bed. Did I wake anyone else?"

"No, Alex is dead to the world. You know how he sleeps. Marnie hasn't come out of her room and Marthe is sleeping at the house in Allouez. And AJ too. Are you sure you're all right?"

"Yeah, I'm fine now that I see I'm not wandering in the jungle anymore. Waking up here is very reassuring, even with nightmares."

"But you're sick. Can I get you something?"

"Honey, it's really OK. I'll be well soon. You'll see. I'm never sick for long. You know that."

I could see he didn't quite believe that but he went back to bed.

I remain awake. I am not reassured. I dread returning to sleep. Even when I'm awake, I'm having flashes of memories that, visually, seem harmless enough but carry the emotional burden of terror, of feelings of abandonment. My paranoia is high with a sense of impending threat I can't shake.

It seems impossible to explain post-traumatic stress to anyone who hasn't experienced it.

I need to find a counselor who knows how to deal with this. Grace has retired. And I'm ill.

Fifty-two

...journal...

I've been home for four days. Flu invaded my body three days ago. So has a tropical parasite...

"...from walking barefoot in infested soil or drinking contaminated water, not uncommon in the tropics," my doctor informed me. "The nearest specialist in tropical medicine is in Milwaukee. I'll make an appointment for you." I went home from her office and dragged myself up the stairs to bed. The appointment is for next week.

At least I can write today. I've been too sick to journal much of anything.

Flu is not my greatest problem, nor the parasite. My problem is the growing intensity of impending threat. I can feel it. I can almost taste it. It's never been this strong before. The closest I came to this was the feeling at the dig when I knew someone watched us. More than the sense of someone watching, it's a feeling of malevolence almost pounding to get into this house. It comes and goes. I can't pinpoint any person or source either. I want to cower in my bed.

And, of course, there is so much more. Ramon is constantly in my thoughts. I feel him and taste him and the hunger that was awakened in me is more than I know how to handle and made harder to bear because I can't think how we would ever fit into each other's lives. Back here, without him, Loss, Guilt and even Shame haunt the space in my head, ghosts refusing to leave.

Another ghost, Grief, sits here in my bedroom awaiting her turn. Conrad's loss is overwhelming me again now that I'm so close to where he was murdered.

Worst of all, my memories are being stripped of all their previous meanings because underneath lies the threat of complete disillusionment. Who was Art really? If he wasn't who I thought he was, then who was I to have been unable to see the real person?

334

...two days later...

Today the flu is dying a death by drowning brought on by the gallons of herbal tea Marthe is pouring into me. She brought me the accumulated mail to read. I almost threw out the following letter, my address typed on it, no return address. I thought it was junk mail.

January 25
Dear Anna,

I'm writing this in a hurry so I'm sorry if it seems a little disjointed. I'm not even supposed to be writing to you at all. We're in protective custody on our way to a new place and someone is with us most of the time. If they know I'm writing to you they'll stop me. I hope you're safe. I want to warn you. You are in great danger! Please don't minimize what I tell you. I did that for so long and look where we are now. I heard of Conrad's death and realize you need to know these things. This is our story.

When Sam joined The Firm (Sam and I called it that too) he was very happy. Although it seemed there was such great potential for all the lawyers there and everything seemed on the up and up, his happiness didn't last very long. First, Jon O'Keeffe was very hard to work with. He had such strange mood swings. He put on a good face when in public, but that's not how he was at work. Sam looked on it as just temperamental for a while, eccentric even. Then something happened and we stopped having Jon to our house.

This is hard to write because I'm still so angry about it. Sam caught Jon being sexually seductive to our oldest daughter Rebecca. Sam confronted him and threatened to expose him.

He would have too, except Big John intervened, covering it all up. Long story short, Big John told Sam that he would create a major scene and Rebecca would have to go through hell if we wanted to prove it in court. So we didn't. We couldn't put an eight-year-old through that.

That alerted Sam though. He stayed there but over the years, he became more and more suspicious of other things, like the amount of money Jonny was bringing in. It was huge, more than any lawyer in The Firm was earning on cases.

335

BETRAYAL by SERPENT

Against all the partners' wishes, even Art's, Jon defended some of the Mafia from Milwaukee and Chicago. His criminal defense cases always seemed to get resolved in his favor too, far more than any criminal defense lawyer usually wins.

Sam went to Art with his suspicions and Art told Sam that he'd been suspicious too and that he was watching Jon's cases to see if he could find anything illegal. He told Sam to keep out of it so he wouldn't get hurt by it. This was about two years before Art died.

For a while it seemed all right. Sam worked in the corporate field so their work didn't really overlap. About a year before the plane crash, however, Sam became really worried again. He noticed that Art was bringing in a lot more money than seemed right, given the number of his cases. Sam thought that Art was doing whatever Jon was doing.

Sam began secretly to check all the cases, all the books, and he found serious discrepancies, which he documented. He told no one, not even me, at first. He tried to get into another firm and found out that in Green Bay legal circles The Firm, and by extension, he himself, was tainted by the reputation that Jon had.

We needed the money because our daughter Rachel needed extreme medical help so he stayed with The Firm. When he told me, I wanted him out but I didn't know how we'd pay the medical bills either. Rachel required intense home care and I couldn't work. To my regret, I didn't insist on it.

He tried to build solid evidence that would hold up in court but never could get to the source of what was going on.

One night, quite a while after Art was killed, Jon walked in while Sam was at work and became suspicious. He threw a huge fit, a terrible scene in which he spewed out racial and religious slurs. That's when we knew we had to leave. We thought that if Sam left it would all die down and we'd be safe. It didn't. Jon continued to threaten, but the really dangerous one was Big John. He made our lives miserable, even down in Madison.

Now I believe that if there has been anything going on, Big John was behind it all. I was so relieved when I heard he died. The harassment died with him, but Sam kept certain connections and documented all he heard.

I don't know who is behind it now but Sam told me just before he died that it's a group of men and if one dies, they have another take his place. He wouldn't tell me any more than that. I do know that over this past year he was feeding Conrad information every chance he could.

Sam believed Andy's death was a murder. He thought Jon O did it. Yes, there was talk of suicide because he was gay, but that was an attempt to smear Andy and muddy the waters. We believed Jon was one of the men who took over from Big John as the leader.

Last month Sam went to the FBI and told them all he knew because he thought the money was drug-related. He was killed three days later, execution-style, a bullet through his forehead. Please, please, Anna, trust no one. No one! I won't be writing you again. Just please take care of your family. Please destroy the envelope. The postmark is not where we'll be but I don't want to take any chances.

Jane

There were two more letters. One detailed every move we made while we were in Mexico. The second contained a threat to my life. These were postmarked Green Bay.

Menace is inside my life now, inside my door.

Fifty-three

...Saturday...

Today Mexico's influence on everyone around me almost overrides the threat I feel here. It's been a long day.

Like chameleons, we all changed our colors there. My now-so-adult children—they won't let me use the word children at all—are fired up with plans for their future. While I lie here in bed, they have made me their captive audience. Change is the order of the day.

AJ, while monitoring my temperature and blood pressure, announced his plans to study tropical and indigenous medicine and to begin a clinic in Guatemala after a year or so with Doctors without Borders. I received a long dissertation on world poverty and the lack of medical care along with a lecture on what I should do with our new wealth and his immense gratitude to Conrad for making us wealthy. I was mute during all this, trying not to vomit all over him.

He looked at me apprehensively. "I hope you're ok with this. I'll be traveling a lot and not just for medicine. I'm going to help Ramon. He's changed, Mom. He's looking for ways to help more than his family. We're going to search the world for others who have made effective changes and fit those to Mayan culture."

AJ paused, an uncomfortable-but-determined look on his face. "Mom, I know about you and Ramon. He talked to me about that."

I felt embarrassed. "AJ, that's very private for me. I have such a strong prohibition against discussing this with a son, even a daughter. I wrote about it in my journal but I just can't share that with you yet. Maybe when you're older."

"I know. I'm not asking you to. I just want you to know, Mom, he loves you. He never before loved anyone other than his wife. He still loves her and won't stop loving her. Ramon is a very extraordinary man and has great self-control. He's had to give up a lot in his life to make it to where he is. Love from a woman was one of those sacrifices. Now, he's allowed himself to feel love for you. I just want you to know I'm happy with that. I also will tell you that I don't think he'll allow his side of your relationship to develop if you don't let him know you want it to continue. He'll sacrifice again. That's what he does."

"Thanks for telling me that. He didn't say that to me. We both have such different lives and so I never even thought of taking it farther. I didn't think he did either."

I gazed out the window at the frozen world, so far from Ramon in time and place and temperature.

"I think of him every day. I saw his dedication to his family. I don't know if I can ever be part of that." I grew silent, aware of the hopelessness of our worlds coming together.

We both were silent for a while. I broke it. "Did you know that Mac made me a proposal of sorts? He said he'd ask me to marry him if he was the marrying kind...his exact words. Seven years without any man and now two of them. I'm not used to that. I don't quite know what to do with men who are attracted to me."

I turned back to AJ. He was grinning. "Way to go, Mom! I like them both but if I had a voice in this, Ramon would be my choice. And I think you knew exactly what to do with Ramon."

"AJ! Oh! Well! I did, didn't I?" Embarrassment colored my cheeks. AJ's grin got wider, obviously much amused by that.

"I'll let him know how I feel. I'll call, and write to him too."

That was my brave voice speaking. Inside I've yet to discover who I am without children. Inside an unknown threat insinuates itself into my thoughts constantly. Inside I want to know why Ramon didn't tell me he visited the site. Inside I'm confused and scared to find out the answer to that.

"I have to leave, Mom. Do it soon." He got up to go, kissed me on my cheek, was at the door, and turned around, grinning. "I really don't want to discuss your love life with you either, or mine, but I just want you to know I'm already 'older'. Celibacy isn't my thing. I discovered sex is fun a long time ago." He winked and waved.

His voice echoed up the stairs. "And no, there's no special someone and no prospect of grandchildren from me for quite a while."

Oh.

AJ left before I got the letters. He doesn't know about them yet. I have to call him, so he can be on guard.

...still Saturday. A mother of young adults doesn't get undisturbed bed rest. Marnie appeared at my bedside.

"Mom, I have to talk to you. I know you're sick but can you just lie there and listen?" As if I had a choice. She didn't wait for an answer, uncharacteristically pouring out what was on her mind.

"Mom, I know this sounds crazy but I want to travel and have a career as a model." She was sitting on the edge of the chair in her eagerness to tell me. I had seen that look in Mexico, where she blossomed into excitement and openness. Marthe said that, since Mexico, she's been moping around the house listlessly between her hours on the phone with friends.

Now she pulled out professional photos and laid them all out on my bed. I was almost speechless at the beauty she projects from those photos. But not quite. This scared me. She's under threat just as we all are. I tried to get her to see it but she is determined to do this and wouldn't hear any words of caution. I got her to agree to call Aunt Carrie and enlist her help. I'll get to Carrie too. I'll have to tell her about the letters and threats. Oh dear! I wish I knew who Conrad had watching Marnie. I'd call him now.

I've called AJ to tell him about the letters and to ask him to check Conrad's files and email me anything on security he finds. I amended that to open all files and email them to me. I may not be able to get into the attic but at least that will be available when I'm ready to work.

...still Saturday, next visitor...

Alex paced the room.

I wanted to believe Alex and Cory were just back to being high school kids. It wasn't true. They changed too.

Alex announced, "I want a gap year, Mom."

"You what? What's a gap year?"

In a long and carefully detailed explanation, he told me. He wants to leave and travel for a year before he goes to college. He had his sales pitch all ready. "It will really broaden my horizons, Mom. Think of what we saw in Mexico. There's stuff like that all over the world. See here?" He handed me a thick catalogue of possible places he could live and learn for the next year.

Unlike Marnie's modeling, with its potential for exploitation, I'm ok with Alex going away to work and study. I can get him away from here, away from whatever impending embarrassment and threat that I feel growing into our lives. He was surprised I agreed so easily.

Still Saturday, and Cory decided he's writing a screenplay about the whole adventure. He's nagged me to get my journal done so I have. Except, his version is censored. I will not discuss Ramon with him. Or Jane's letter. Or the threat to me.

He came to the door with the script in hand. "It's only missing one thing, Mom. Some spicy romance! Do you think I could add an affair between you and Ramon?"

He went back to The Dorm with my firm NO. "You'll have quite enough with the story of the jaguar." I called after him. "That's very mysterious. Make that the central idea."

Then he came back and told me he wants to become an actor, screenwriter and producer, that he wants to study acting in England and New York, and that he wants to begin learning dancing and have voice lessons.

"But I'll finish out senior year here, Mom, because I have so many friends and don't want to miss that."

Whatever. I just threw up again.

Aunt Carrie called. MomKat's Alzheimer's is worse. It's progressing too fast. What do I have to do to care for her? That's another concern I have to resolve. How will I take care of her? Aunt Carrie moved in with her for now and we have a visiting nurse but if Carrie goes with Marnie, I'll have to take over.

...and still Saturday...endless...

Caroline and Caitlin showed up at the door of my bedroom right after Cory. I almost didn't want to tell them all that happened. Now I'm so glad I did. I told them everything, even about Ramon.

They were pleased. "It's about time you got laid,' Caroline blurted. "I thought you'd announce you're becoming a nun!"

"Hah! No convent would have her!" Cait hooted. They discussed my sex life for a while and then got to the real reason they came.

"We're starting a business and we want you to be part of it. It's one you'll love. Here's our idea. We buy up the small older homes on the West Side that are in poor shape, fix them up to look like Irish cottages, complete with garden in front and maybe thatch or grass roofs, then we rent or sell them outright." Cait glowed at the prospect.

I am intrigued. They agreed to take me to Milwaukee to the doctor and we would discuss it more when I'm well. I sent them home. At the moment I feel like I'm dying.

Fifty-four

...journal...mid-March...

The strangeness of what I experienced in Mexico completely overwhelmed me even as I began to feel healthier. Who was I there? What possessed me to have an affair with a man I hardly knew? Affair? Not even that. How could I have been so different from what I am here? I've become two people: the practical, down-to-earth woman who lives in this cold northern climate and the intensely sensuous and impulsive female who spent hours having sex with a man and who lived inside a jaguar's mind.

Back to this reality, Anna!

It's one week after our Milwaukee trip, at the end of a three-day blizzard. "The Troubles", as Aunt Carrie refers to the whole thing, have bubbled to the surface. I had come to think of them as snakes sinuously slithering out of my dreams, where they live continuously, but I killed that metaphor for the time being, bubbles being less threatening.

I don't want to face what's here again. I'm still having emotional and sexual aftereffects. Ramon never leaves my thoughts. One side of me wants to return to Mexico. Instead, I have to be here. This is Bubble Number One. After AJ's revelation, I knew I had to talk with Ramon, to ask him directly about the paper I put together and what he had to do with it instead of stewing about it. More than that, I want to tell him how I feel about being with him.

I phoned him after AJ left and got voice mail. I left him a message saying I want to be closer to him and hope he feels the same. He hasn't replied. Is he just busy or has he changed his mind about loving me? Was AJ wrong? Is Ramon in danger too? I feel like a teenager again. This is ridiculous.

Second Bubble, my health. Nightmares are a constant. Sleep is elusive. My left arm aches if I do too much. I feel physically tired very quickly if I try to do anything. I make myself walk in the cold air and swim in the heated YW pool. Everything is such an effort.

More worrisome than the physical symptoms are the mental ones. I forget what I'm thinking, lose focus, have small memory lapses, am startled by every small sudden noise, have sudden fits of shaking. I've phoned counseling agencies and can't find a counselor who's trained in both EMDR and hypnosis, as Grace was. I'll keep looking. Meantime, I have to make lists of everything. Hence this catalogue of things that I have to do.

Bubble Three came with this morning's call from Clayton.

"We have to talk. I've found some old files in Conrad's office. They concern The Firm. I can't imagine why they're even here. You need to know about these right now. Can you see me at one p.m. today? I'll have lunch brought in for us."

He sounds like he's ordering me in, somewhat imperious of him, but I'd be concerned too if I was the surviving partner in a law firm where the other partner was murdered, an unsolved murder at that.

"Not a problem, Clayton. I'll see you then."

Number Four. Right after that the police called. Klarkowski was polite but firm.

"We want to know more about what happened to you in Mexico. We're searching for any connection between what happened down there and our investigation up here. Can you come at one?"

I let him know I had a meeting with my lawyer at one and would see him after. "Lawyer" is a magic word. He easily accepted a 2:30 time.

Good. He's sounding less hostile than before. This is a good thing. We have to talk. I still haven't shown him the letters.

Number Five. I haven't heard from Lindy and she isn't enrolled at UWGB for the second semester. Where is she? Her things are still in her room.

Caitlin had a host of question about just what her role had been and I began to wonder why she chose to live with us. Is there more to this than I've seen so far? It doesn't seem like this could have been a setup, but it's not impossible. I hate to think someone might have been manipulating us all along. No. That's too paranoid. I just hope she's safe. Still, I plan to bring this up to police. Can they find out if anyone is in a witness protection program? Is that even where they are?

Bubble Number Six, the Big Bubble.

I've done nothing with any of Conrad's papers or his computers, or the files upstairs, knowing that once I begin it will mean long days at it. In the meantime, Marthe and I went to Conrad's house yesterday and the last of his things are cleared out, but the house is Bubble Number Seven.

The insurance money is available and the place needs redecorating. Cait and Caroline are helping with that, the plan to build a decorating business hatched among us on the Milwaukee trip. We'll use Conrad's house as our showplace, with Marthe as the hostess. Once the place looks decent again, I plan on using the masks as the main decorating theme. C&C love decorating as much as I do and will do most of the work. Cait is a natural at dealing with the tradespeople needed. Her three oldest boys will work into the business. Caroline will research and travel for the decorating side and I'm the money, which limits my involvement but still, I have to spend time consulting with them. Rob is our accountant.

They also want a trip to Ireland to gather authentic ideas, crafts, furniture and décor.

"Aim for September to do this," Caitlin said.

Clayton still hasn't sent the masks to me. Remind him again.

Bubble Number Eight will take longer. Rob took a look at Conrad's will and let me know I'll need a big-time accounting firm, specialized legal help and investment advice. I haven't even opened the envelope with the list of holdings yet. I don't have any idea how to go about finding these firms. Rob said he'd research top-level firms. It's a decision that will take time. We set a business meeting for 4:30 today.

And last but most immediate—security. At the least, let the boys get a dog. Ask Clayton what he recommends for something further.

All these decisions and plans are highlighting another symptom. My decision-making ability is impaired. I don't seem to be able to think ahead and know what to do. I feel so very frustrated. And scared. Will this confusion and indecision be permanent? I feel so much more responsibility now. I have to pull myself together.

You're going to have to pop these bubbles yourself, Anna. Get on with it! You'll get three done today.

I have a headache and my arm aches.

Fifty-five

I went to the YWCA, had a gentle workout, swam for a time, came home, showered, dressed warmly, and drove through the snowy not-yet-plowed streets to Clayton's office amid soft flakes slowly descending from gray skies.

When I walked in I was expecting Ardith. Instead there was a young girl at the receptionist's desk. Clayton was in the waiting room.

He showed me into what had been Conrad's office and I was plunged into disappointment. All the elegance was gone. There were piles of files on the long table, no flower bouquet, the gray silk drapes had been taken down and replaced by lime green (lime green? Eeewww!) and all the masks were gone.

It's like his memory is being erased. I resent this. It's too soon. I felt like crying.

"Where are the masks? What happened to them?"

"Oh, I had the office girl pack them up. I guess they're yours. They were listed in the inventory of his art and you are the heiress. Didn't someone call you about them? Someone was supposed to do that. Now that you're back, I'll have them sent to your house right away."

He had taken off his rumpled jacket and thrown it on the table on top of the files and was tucking in his shirttails.

"Where is Ardith? I want to see her, or at least to call her and see how she's doing."

"She retired. You know what a lot of money she got from Conrad. She said she was going to travel. I think she had Italy in mind. I'm not sure. I'm still looking for a good legal secretary. I have a temp for now."

I was shocked. No party? No goodbyes?

Pointing to the files on the table, Clayton went right on talking. "I have these laid out in sequence, in order by date. Seems to make better sense that way, although I can't make any other sense out of them."

347

He picked up the phone to let the receptionist know he didn't want us to be disturbed.

"It seems that Conrad began investigating The Firm even before he became your lawyer. In fact, he might not even have taken your case if he hadn't already been suspicious about them. He hated divorce negotiations. He never even mentioned these files to me back then."

A slight note of annoyance or resentment crept into his voice. I could imagine if they were partners, Clayton would not feel good about being left out, or about Conrad's surreptitious investigations.

"He liked you. He thought you were being shafted. Conrad had a finely developed sense of justice. He couldn't see you and your children lose what was rightfully yours.

"But, as I said, he was digging even before you came in. It appears the trigger" he held up one file "was a loss the D.A. had in court over a case Conrad apparently felt should have been won. The Firm was the defense team, and it was a team, not just one lawyer. Art and Jonny O were acting in defense of a local doctor accused of supplying drugs to adolescents. Maybe you remember because it made the Press-Gazette and television for weeks. The evidence was not just circumstantial, it was strong. Do you remember Art discussing this at all?"

"I remember the case from the papers but, I'm sorry, Clayton, Art rarely discussed cases with me. He made a real effort to leave work at work. That's not to say he didn't have legal books and such at our house. He had an office in what is now my office, and there are still files in our attic."

"You have files? Really?" He leaned forward eagerly. "From when Art was alive?"

I nodded and was about to explain more. He didn't notice.

Looking surprised, concerned, and very interested, he went on, "Anna, I think those might be very important. We really must look at those."

Then he stopped himself abruptly and leaned back, as if coming to a decision. I waited while he was silent, brows furrowed. I watched the mesmerizing swirl of snowflakes out the window twisting and fluttering in the wind.

348

I wish I was meeting Conrad. I wish he was alive. Why did Ardith leave like that?

Clayton's voice broke in. "No. One thing at a time. Let's go over what's in front of us."

So I said nothing more.

We examined each file case by case. The Firm was the only legal firm that was involved. Conrad had collected fourteen cases where the defendant was acquitted in spite of hard and fast evidence of guilt. Not all were drug cases per se but most had drug involvement, that is, drug offenders, as defendants. Three involved robberies, two more were burglaries, three included assaults, though not involving weapons. Six were outright drug cases.

"Of those, only one other became a prominent case, a vice principal at a local high school who was accused of providing drugs for students. You might remember that. It was in the news too."

Clayton put the last file on the pile and dropped into the chair at the end of the table where Conrad had often sat. I felt my heart tug inside, missing Conrad's calm confident way.

"I do remember Art mentioning that. He assisted Jon O'Keeffe but I don't know how involved he was."

Clayton continued. "I've reviewed these several times and find no real connection among them other than Art and O'Keeffe. There were different judges involved, many police officers investigating, and different police departments in some cases. Of course there were some of the same persons involved in some cases, but I haven't found any reason to think that Conrad was on to something for sure."

I was puzzled. Why would Conrad have done this so long ago? I looked through each file at the names involved and, other than some lawyers and judges I knew, the names meant nothing. I looked at the dates. The cases began years before Art was killed and ended about three years after.

Why did Conrad begin and then stop investigating these? Did Ardith know of these? Are some of these cases the same ones Sam found? How did Conrad get copies of these? From Sam?

I thought of his computers, one in this office, the one AJ had found, and the one from Mexico. *I've got to see what's on those computers.*

"Clayton, do you have his computer from here in the office or did the police take that when they were gathering evidence?"

"We gave them all access to it but they didn't get the computer itself. It belongs to us and is here at our firm. We of course wanted to cooperate in every way we could to find his murderer. Ardith is the one who helped police gather information after his death. I don't know why he did this. I found nothing that explains this. Ardith mentioned nothing either. I just found these in the back of one of Conrad's file cabinets."

"Perhaps he was suspicious that someone was taking bribes, that someone was paying off or threatening people. Would this have anything to do with his being on the ethics board?" It was the only thing that I could think of.

"He wasn't on the board back then. If he had suspicions, he didn't leave any inkling he found something to substantiate them. He left nothing indicating what he thought."

I was thinking about my next meeting with police.

I am definitely going to ask for copies of Conrad's papers. Why haven't they even asked me about those? Well, I've been gone for weeks but...maybe that's what Klarkowski wants today.

"There was nothing on his computer that relates to these? I find that curious."

"Nary a thing. Very frustrating it's been! I've been wondering why he went to all this trouble and not one note on this in the computer. Some of these files are from our pre-computer era. Maybe they never made it onto any computer at all. That's why I'm so interested in the files you have. I bet there's more to this." He leaned forward again, looking much like a spaniel ready to hunt. "How soon can we do that? I can help, you know."

I felt uneasy. I didn't want Clayton or anyone rooting through Art's papers.

Not before I do. I want to know what's in there before anyone else seizes them or sees them.

"Clayton, you know what? I'm almost well from my adventure in the Yucatan. I'll make it my priority to go through the files I have to see if there's anything related to what you have here. I frankly don't think there is. What I think is in there aren't legal files from the firm but stuff left from his schooling and copies of journal readings, research, things like that. I'll begin tomorrow to sort through drawer by drawer. Whatever isn't relevant I can get rid of and then give the rest to you."

I could see he was not quite satisfied with that and he offered to have someone come and move all the files, but I refused outright.

"It's the last of what Art left behind that was his and I want to go through it first. It's a personal thing."

"Oh, right. I can understand that, Anna. Of course, and they're not going anywhere. I just hope something can be found that relates to all these."

He asked for details about what went on in Mexico and I gave him an overview.

"That was exciting! And frightening! You don't know where Lindy and her dad are now?"

"Not a clue." I looked at the clock. "I have to go now. I'm off to meet with Klarkowski."

"You don't know what he wants either?"

"Not really, except he's interested in making a connection between the drug smuggling down in Mexico and drug selling up here. I don't see how my experiences can help with that but I'm willing to do what I can."

I've just been censoring what I said to my own lawyer! Why am I doing that?

Jane's words echoed. Trust no one!

That, and the feeling of malevolence is still ebbing and flowing around us.

351

Fifty-six

I decided to walk through slush and snowflakes down Adams Street to the police station, past legal offices and the city and county buildings, and old St. Willebrord's Church, a favorite walk. There were few cars on the street. Ordinarily this scene would have calmed my mind, but not today. I talked to myself along the way.

My sense of foreboding is every bit as strong, stronger even that it was at the dig in Mexico. Even without the letters I'd feel it. Conrad must have suspected some kind of collusion between lawyers and judges to let these people off. Are police officers involved as Ben suspects? If so, which ones? How could any collusion happen when evidence was strong for conviction? Bribery? Blackmail? Who did Conrad trust? I'll cooperate with Klarkowski but I'm not turning anything over to anyone until I figure this out.

I expected to be shown into Klarkowski's office. I was not. I was taken instead to a room with the proverbial one-way mirror.

Oh god, I'm in some cop story on TV and no lawyer this time.

I sat, my hands together on the table, feeling myself in the edgy heightened awareness I had in the jungle.

After a seventeen-minute wait, Klarkowski came in.

"I apologize for being late. I've been on the phone. I'll get right to the point. The call was from the FBI. We're coordinating all law enforcement efforts, including international. It's about time, past time. This will get bigger. What I want and need from you is the full story of what happened in Mexico. Whatever you did, it's set off repercussions all over."

"What I 'did'? I only played a role because I went down there to support Lindy and to settle Conrad's affairs there. I had nothing to do with what eventually happened."

"Well, Anna, *anything* that might be a connection I am now making my concern."

Wary as I was, and still remembering my confrontation with him, I felt this man was honest. Although dog-like in pursuit of what he wants, he is not arrogant, not out to impress. His suit was old and worn, his face tired-looking, his body sagging, his eyes earnest. It may have all been a very practiced act but I didn't think so. I wondered who was watching behind the mirror and said so.

He apologized for seeing me in this room but said he shared his office with another detective and the man was seeing someone in there right now.

"Well then, I guess this story begins shortly after Conrad's home was trashed, when our boarder, Lindy Stewart..." I gave him a full narration of what led up to our trip to Mexico, what we did and saw at the dig, and what happened while I was captive and after. He didn't interrupt.

"I learned that the smuggling involved drugs, humans, and gems and artwork and animals. I was told that it was a highly organized operation, and a big one. I was told that the cartel was crippled but they didn't get the top man. The name of the cartel is apparently Los Serpientos. This does relate to the letters in the snow, K, A and N, which you showed me. KA'AN in Mayan is snake, a meaning also related to lightning, especially lightning strikes. Maybe Conrad was trying to write some kind of clue as he died."

He stopped me. "All you've told me isn't a great help but it's something. Can you tell me any more about the people you met? What was this Herder like? Simoneska? And Mac? All of them. I want any impressions you may have had of them."

I began with Ramon and went on to explain about the Aguilar family business, their loss of a child to the cartel, that Conrad had an art collection in Mexico bought on the black market and that Ramon now has Power of Attorney to administer Sotheby's disposal of it. I told him Interpol was involved in that, that I hired Sotheby's to return the art to owners if they could be found and to sell the pieces if not. I included that Conrad was working for Interpol to recover works of art stolen from the Jews. I described my impressions of all the others, ending with my concern about Lindy and her father and their whereabouts.

Klarkowski was particularly interested in Mac and asked several questions about the role he had taken and his skills. He had no information about Ian or Lindy.

"I wouldn't be able to find them if they're in witness protection. Only the agency involved, and then only those with a need to know would have that information."

"Regarding Mac," I said, "several people speculated he might be DEA or CIA or something like that" and then I had a sudden flash of memory. "But when he visited me in the hospital the second time he said that he worked for himself. He said he's originally Canadian and part Native American from the Cree tribe. He's a bit mysterious. He was certainly well trained and at ease in the jungle."

"Anna, can you think of anything or anyone who seemed to be connected with Wisconsin?"

"Well, me, AJ, Conrad, and Lindy. And long ago Art and Jonny O."

"Yes." He leaned forward, put his elbow on the table, his chin on his hand, and looked directly at me. "Yes."

Suddenly he did not seem so rumpled and tired.

"Surely you don't think we're running a drug ring! I don't have the desire, the time, or knowledge! That's absurd!"

"Yes. It is absurd, but stranger things have happened. As it is, I believe you, but someone you know," he rapped the tips of three fingers on the table top, "is involved, maybe several someones. How well did you know Conrad?"

"Beyond being my lawyer and my long time employer, I don't know much at all. He occasionally came to our parties over the years Art was practicing law, but not all the time. He was pleasant, even fun, but never spoke about his home life. He was a connoisseur of very fine art, didn't drink that I ever saw, and was a brilliant lawyer. I know he was a painter with much talent, and Clayton Foster told me he was a superb pianist. Clayton told me he was gay but I never saw him with any man. He escorted women to cultural events like the symphony. Maybe he was bisexual. I don't really think I knew him well. He kept himself to himself, as they say."

"And yet he left you a substantial inheritance. Why is that?"

"I was more surprised by that than anyone. You were there. You know that."

I leaned forward. "Look. What I know for sure is that there was something he wanted to show me the day he was murdered. I told you and your officers then of the call he made to me. I think it actually had to do with The Firm, my husband's firm I mean. But of course I never got to know. Those papers you picked up when he was murdered—there was something he wanted me to see in those, something important, and I still haven't seen them. I'd like to see what was there, to have copies of them. Maybe I could make some connection that would help you."

He didn't respond. I went on.

"But to stay on topic, when I was called to be at the reading of his will, I couldn't imagine why. I thought maybe he might leave me one of the masks from his office because I'd admired them so often over the years. Instead, I got all that money and the houses.

"The only thing I can think of was that years ago, when he agreed to take my case against The Firm, he was very incensed at what Jonny O was doing and gleeful at the thought of opposing him. I was in deep grief then, as I am now, and was only too glad to let him handle it all. You remember that even then he felt something was wrong with The Firm. He told me before he died that he was sure their books were off and expressed deep regret he'd not fought them harder for what we were owed, but he thought we'd never have gotten any money at all then, that Jonny O would have delayed any settlement interminably.

I was having an internal debate about telling Klarkowski about the files Clayton had shown me.

I'd better mention them. I don't want Klarkowski suspicious because I've withheld that information from him.

"There is something that I just learned which might be relevant, although it's old information."

I told him briefly about my meeting with Clayton and the content of the files, and that the files had stopped being compiled years ago.

"I don't know if that has any relation at all to the papers in the briefcase or what's happening now. You'd have to see Clayton about those. They belong to his firm.

"Detective Klarkowski, I've cooperated fully with you and I'd like that reciprocated. I want to know what is in the papers Conrad was bringing to me."

I handed him the letters I'd received. "I'm very worried. My life is threatened, my family watched. I think Conrad was trying to find out why and who. This has been going on since September. Conrad had Marnie watched because of the letters we've received. She left both job and school and came home in January because she was frightened at being followed. I deserve more cooperation from you."

He read the letters from Jane and the anonymous writers and set them aside, looking more and more concerned as he went through them.

"Well, I'll certainly see what I can do. This letter from Jane Soderberg—we were told about the threats to that family. We'll take these letters very seriously. I'll get the file on Conrad's death and copies of his papers for you. I'll call you when I have that done. I do want to know if you can make any sense of them.

"About security, we don't have the personnel to assign constant watchers to you but I'll give you the names and numbers of some firms we use. Retired officers often will take on something like this too. I'd advise you to hire someone as soon as possible. Have there been direct threats to your children?"

I shook my head no. "Just me, but I know someone is watching them."

He had only a few more questions about AJ's role and whether he would be available for questioning. I told him where AJ was and gave his cell number.

He politely walked me out. I had the feeling I was being watched but didn't see anyone except the officer behind the front desk. I wondered if Klarkowski had someone record our conversation. If he did, and I found out, he would be in trouble. I had been schooled in my rights by Art.

He had made no firm commitment about when he would get me copies of Conrad's papers.

It's "don't call me, I'll call you". He'll stall. I can feel it. I won't push this yet. I'll wait to see what I can find on Conrad's computers. It could all be there.

I was grateful for the walk back through the snow to my car.

I still have the meeting with Rob. I have to put that off. I'm tired, hungry and feeling too stressed. I need a break.

I got out my cell phone and was going to dial his number when it rang. It was Rob.

"I need a rain check, Anna, or we can meet at our house tonight. I'm running late."

"Great. I've just finished at the police station. I'm tired and hungry. I was just calling you to ask the same thing. Let's do it tonight if you want. Call me when you get home. I have the file ready for you to go over."

We agreed on 7:30.

It was becoming winter dark, I was hungry, and I drove to Panera in Ashwaubenon, picked up soup and sandwich to go, found they had a few of their mouth-watering cinnamon bagels left, bought some of those, and drove home.

Fifty-seven

Marthe left a note she was at the Allouez house writing. Marnie left a voice mail telling me not to worry because all her Girls were on the lookout for followers.

If the follower is male, those girls will spot him.

Tired, I showered again, trying to wash the taint of suspicion and mistrust away. It didn't work. I made myself tea and settled on the couch in the living room after feeding the boys and sending them off to a basketball game. How can I have them watched while they're at school? At games? Out having fun? Do I have to hire bodyguards? That seems so extreme. The boys will never agree to that.

I reviewed all I had not told either Clayton or Klarkowski: the meeting with Jenny, my intimacy with Ramon, the paper I had deciphered at the dig, the paper from my coat pocket I had found on the night of Conrad's death, and the computers.

OK, Jane. I'm listening to you. They'll have to earn my trust. Even Klarkowski.

I sent her a wave of love and kindness and said prayers for her safety and ours.

At 7:15 Caroline called. "My stallions are fed and watered. Come on over."

I grabbed the file Clayton had given me, made sure everything was there, threw on my coat and hurried over, buffeted by March winds.

"Whew! I almost got blown down river. It's wild out there." I said as I hung my coat on a peg in her back hall.

"I've got hot chocolate going for us. Rob's in the den. I'll bring it in when it's ready."

Rob was blowing his nose when I entered. He apologized. "I've got a rotten cold so sit far away. I don't think you want any more, given what you've already had to endure this winter. This won't take long so just kick back while I look these over."

He took the file I handed him and settled himself in his big leather chair. Caroline brought in the hot chocolate, but didn't stay.

"I have a meeting at the boys' school. See you later."

I was grateful for the silence, for one meeting where I could let someone else do the talking.

Robinson is originally from Georgia, with long years spent up north which took most of his southern drawl out of his speech, but when he's intensely involved in something, it comes back.

I heard him mutter softly, "Mah god! Unbahlivabul! Mah god!" He didn't look up, just kept reading, his eyes wide open and travelling swiftly over the paper, jaw dropped, sitting straight up in the chair. I watched as he opened the envelope, read it and gasped.

Finally he stopped and looked at me. "Anna, did you read all this yet?"

"No, I left it until now because there was so much happening. What's wrong?"

He just stared at me.

"What?"

"Anna, you are probably one of the wealthiest women in this town, maybe in this state. Didn't Clayton tell you this?"

"No, he didn't. I can't be. How could I be? What is it? What was in the envelope?"

"Well, first, you have over thirty million dollars in investments. Stocks, bonds, funds, in addition to the cash you already know about."

I blinked rapidly. It took me several seconds to breathe again. My skin crawled. I felt sheer panic.

"Clayton told me there were funds but not which ones and how much was in them. Of course I knew about the cash in the Green Bay account, and some of the stocks were sold to provide us with more cash because we had to see that there was money for Marnie and Marthe and the boys."

"Anna, that was very small potatoes. You also have the houses and the one in Cancun is valued at almost $1,000,000 while the property in Allouez is worth $335,000. But that's not even the start. Some of the masks are priceless, one of a kind and rare. Then there's the art in the house in Cancun, two of them are by Vermeer, a Kahlo that's nearly priceless, others of lesser value but still worth a great deal. We're not even talking the gallery there, just the upstairs. Sadly the art in the house here was so badly damaged it may not be reparable but I think you should consider having some of those pieces restored if possible because if they're rare, they're still worth a lot of money.

"Anna, it's a good thing you're sitting down because there's more. Besides a key to a safety deposit box here in Green Bay, you have a Swiss account. He put that in your name months before he was killed. It's yours free and clear. The value he put down here is over nine million in cash, artworks, precious stones and gold. There are keys here and papers proving your ownership. One of the keys is for a chalet in Switzerland on Lake Como."

I couldn't speak. I opened my mouth but nothing came out.

"Are you sure Clayton Foster didn't know more about the Swiss thing?" He pronounced it "thang". His Georgia drawl was so pronounced I had to translate it in my head before it registered. I shook my head no.

Finally I whispered, "There's a Swiss chalet? How could Conrad have a Swiss chalet too?"

Rob looked grim. "Anna, I'm concerned. Clayton was withholding information from you. I can't understand why he'd do such a thing. He should have told you all of this. You need to confront him on this."

Before I could comment, he continued.

"Anna, I have to tell you, our firm, as it is now, can't handle all this for you. You'll definitely have to have a big-time firm, one that has lawyers and financial advisors and a team of accountants and tax advisors. We can't do this. We can help you find that kind of firm, and we can oversee things pretty much as they are for now. You're going to owe a lot of taxes on your inheritance here. The fed and the state will want their share. We are able look into that right away for you."

I was completely unable to fathom it at all.

"There's one thing more. Conrad left you a letter. It's sealed."

He handed it to me. "Maybe there's an explanation in there of why he chose you for this. I can see you look pretty shocked at this news."

"I can't get my head around this, Rob. Why am I his heir at all? There was nothing I ever did for him that was out of the ordinary. He did more for me than I ever could have expected, offering me the job, paying me out of his own pocket, fighting with Jon O'Keeffe for my money, just being a friend. I owe him!"

"Well, woman, it looks like he didn't see it that way."

"Rob, this is too much. I don't know how to be rich, no—not rich, wealthy. I'm already rich in children and friends and people I love and who love me. What will I do with all this?"

"Whah, ya'll'll pay mah bill! Ah don't mind charging you at all, given the circumstances."

"I should hope so."

He laughed. "I reckon you ought to go home and read that letter. I'll get in touch when I have information for you. If it's ok with you, I'll contact the Swiss bank. Let me know when you can clear some time to go there. You'll have to meet them face to face. And you need to tell Clayton I've taken over the finances. I'm going to do an audit as soon as possible."

Caroline was gone when I left. That was just as well. I was unable to speak, to comprehend it. The wind blew me to my back door. I never felt the cold.

Where is Lake Como? A chalet? Gold?

I read the letter but it is so personal I can't bring myself to write about it. Conrad had fallen in love with me, yet he felt he could never tell me because of his sexual preferences for both men and women. He believed I would never accept that. He wrote that I must go to Switzerland to see someone who knows his story and gave me a name and address.

He knew he would be killed.

I am sick with sadness. Just terribly, terribly sad.

Fifty-eight

Life is so strange. The out-of-the-ordinary and the mundane meld into one. I always thought of them as polarities. I can feel only embarrassment at all that wealth and can't bring myself to tell anyone how much it is, even my own children. And I now feel a great weight on me, an obligation to find out who murdered Conrad. I can't put off the files any longer.

I called AJ again and asked him to open everything he can on Conrad's computer and the external drive and send all the files to me.

Today, Saturday, I got Cory and Alex to bring down everything in the file cabinets from the attic.

Whining, grumbling and groaning is a special skill of teenage boys, as well as working as slowly as possible. It took all morning and the threat of a late noon meal to get them to finish it. There were four file cabinets of legal size with four drawers each and twelve boxes of varying sizes filled with books and some loose-leaf notebooks.

I was unable to help them. I tire quickly if I do anything heavy, although I've gotten my walks up to a mile, even in snow. Going up and down stairs repeatedly leaves me weak. My left arm still aches and gets sharp pains every so often.

While I was waiting for them to finish, my mind drifted back to Cancun and even further.

Questions. Always questions. What was going on back then? Why are these files here at the house? Was the office not safe? What was he hiding? Cancun has something to do with this. What? Why did he go to Cancun really? What went on down there? What have we gotten into?

While in Cancun, AJ and I had agreed to be on watch. We knew we might be targets of the cartel and wondered how long their reach was. I had another good reason to be cautious. I received a warning I didn't tell to anyone. I forgot it in the excitement of leaving the hospital to be with my family, then forgot it completely. Now it had spontaneously come back to me while I spoke to Klarkowski. I write it down here so I won't forget it again.

I had a second visit from Mac at the hospital in Cancun. He came to warn me about what could happen, to be sure I remained on guard.

"Anna, I can't, no, won't, discuss everything I know with you, to protect both you and your children. The past few days have been bloody. The cartel is retaliating on those opposed who have families here.

"We didn't get the top dog, the mastermind, if you will. Someone spent a lot of time developing this smuggling and has made a TON of money! We're talking billions here. A market half a world wide and more. North, Central and South America, with trafficking in children to Far Eastern countries, and the art market involves Europe. Whoever heads this cartel is an extremely wealthy man. He can and does buy anything and anyone.

"He's also vicious. He ordered his army of men on a killing spree, with armored vehicles no less. Twenty-three Mexican police have been killed, four with their entire families. Six American border police were either killed or injured. Worse, two cartels are at war, using beheadings, executions, fire, torture, whatever they can use for intimidation and retaliation."

His face was red with anger, his eyes bitter and icy and he paced as he spoke. "We've cut major supply lines to the cartel and from them. The person at the core may be extremely angry and vicious but he'll have a hell of a job rebuilding. For now, up north as far as you live, your children will be safe, I hope. We've taken measures to shield you and them from association with us, spread the word kidnapping you was a stupid mistake, that you're just a mother hen with Lindy as your chick.

"You need to know that your last name was familiar to some of the men we caught, not because of your kidnapping, not because they knew about the plane crash years ago. I think for other unknown reasons as well. I can't help wondering if Art was in it, how much and what kind of involvement."

He paused, his face knotted in a frown.

"Anna, have you ever thought your husband might be alive?"

I struggled to sit up in bed, still weak. He came over and helped me up higher in the bed, then sat next to me, his arm around my shoulders.

"No and yes. Not after he was gone. I felt he was really dead. I never even questioned it back then. It's bothering me now though. What if he didn't die? What if he just deserted us?"

I could feel my tears starting.

"I haven't wanted to think about it. It hurts too much and then I get too angry. Why do you ask?"

"We're still hearing rumors there's a gringo running a cartel. However, we're also still hearing there's a former Mexican police officer running one too. I have to keep my mind open to any possibility. My own hunch is that if Art was involved in any way, he was a long-ago victim. I don't put much credence in rumors among drug runners."

"Ramon told me he heard those rumors too. I don't feel like Art's alive. However he was involved, he loved our kids and would want to see them."

"Did he love you enough to come back to you?" Mac said this very softly.

"I thought so once. Now, I don't know. I don't want to talk about that now."

I changed the subject.

"Where's Lindy and her father? Are they OK?"

"They are, although I don't know where they are now. Ian was a great help in observing and documenting what he saw. Just the information I heard was great and there was much more. They flew him out because he was in bad shape, probably to Washington, D.C., for medical care and for debriefing. He had a lot to tell them I didn't get to hear. They're safe."

"She has things at my house in Green Bay. Can I send them to her? No, of course not. Tell her I'll just keep them for her if you see her."

"I won't be seeing her. Put them away. This all may lighten up and she may be able to resume her life up there someday. When I last saw her she just wanted to remain with her father."

"Mac, I heard children whimpering, crying when I was in that camp. I thought it was my imagination. I was disoriented. Was I hearing things?"

The pit of my stomach was churning as I waited for his answer.

He stood and walked to the window. When he turned back he looked so deeply sad and I felt my heart break.

He took a deep breath.

"You weren't hearing things. You did hear children. We found twelve children. There were some we didn't find in time. Three were dead. Young boys. They had all been raped. Repeatedly."

His voice was a hoarse whisper. He was silent for a long time.

I was remembering what I saw just beyond the fire as I left the camp.

Was that a man raping a child? Oh, no! I walked away. I walked away! What a terrible thing to do! I should have done something! What could I have done? Those children died of sexual brutality. And what could you have done, Anna? Anything? Something!

Mac continued, "You know, some are sold by their own parents. Extreme poverty does bad things to people. Some of them" he looked distressed and angry, "some of them are actually sold by parents who aren't poor, especially girls. Some are orphans. Some are kidnapped off streets in the cities, or from towns in the mountains."

His voice broke. He turned away from the window, his face hardened into anger and rage.

"There's a big US connection..." his voice went on but I wasn't hearing him.

I lay back in bed as his angry words vibrated in the air. I knew enough about history to know he was telling the truth, but it was hard to take it in because behind his words the sounds of the weeping children filled the room.

I escaped while they were being raped. I felt tears running down my face.

Finally, I began hearing him again...

BETRAYAL by SERPENT

"I get so upset about this. I'm part Native American from Canada. Cree. I was 'given', meaning kidnapped, and 'adopted', meaning sold, to a white family, raised white so I could be 'civilized'. It wasn't until college when I took Native Studies as a fill-in class one semester that I found out my real history. Other natives recognized what I was never taught to see. Now, I've read everything I can on our history, visited many tribes in Canada, the US, and down in Mexico. I learned my survival skills from the tribes."

He turned around, saw my tears, came to me and took my face between his hands.

"I'm sorry, Anna. I'm so sorry. I don't often get on my soapbox. Soapboxes don't get anything done in my book. Waste of time and energy. I shouldn't have come here and dumped this on you in your condition either. I'm so sorry."

He sat on the bed and took me in his arms.

"I'll tell you this. I don't work for any government. I do what I do on my own. Yes, there were children. Those we found alive are safe now, for the moment. It was incredible the way you rescued the children you found in that truck. That's five more who lived. You keep telling yourself that. I admire you. You have sheer guts!

"I'll say it again. If I was the marrying kind, I'd camp on your doorstep hoping you'd notice me. But my work doesn't allow for relationships. You get well, you hear. Go back and be a mom to your children. You love them and they love you. It's a ray of light in my life to have seen that. I have to go now. You take care."

He kissed me, then stood and turned abruptly, as if he was fleeing something, and left. I didn't see him again.

Running through my head are the unanswered questions, the ones I don't want to ask.

Did Art desert us to become involved in all this? Was I married to a man who betrayed us all?

Worst of all, did I leave the children in the camp to be raped while I fled? Did I really want to know what was going on beyond the firelight?

Truth? No. I just wanted to get out of there with my own life intact.

I have not told this memory to anyone, not AJ, not Cait or Caroline, no one. I feel so ashamed, so lacking in courage. I know I blocked it out because I didn't want to see my own act of self-preservation at the expense of the children being raped and abused just beyond the fire.

Now I clearly remember hearing their strangled whimpering cries.

Fifty-nine

"Earth to Mom. Where are you?" Cory was waving his hand in front of my eyes. "We're done. Can we go? Us and the twins are ordering pizza at their house. Caroline's coming over here."

He held up his cell phone. Texting. I still haven't gotten the hang of it. In fact, I think it's a dull way to communicate. I'd much rather speak face-to-face and hear a voice.

I looked at the table. *What a job this is going to be!*

"We and the twins," I corrected automatically.

"I thought you're staying here!" He looked appalled.

"I'm correcting your English and you know it. Yes, go off with you. Don't forget that after the game tomorrow our family is coming over for supper, so don't make any plans with Jekyll and Hyde."

"They're not Jekyll and Hyde anymore. Now they're Stan and Ollie." The twins have made it their current goal in life to re-create character pairs.

Alex lumbered in with a large box.

"The last one" he panted, setting it down with a thump on the floor. "You should see the attic. There's a lot of space up there. We could fix it up for a room for me, by myself, all by myself!"

He glanced at Cory with one of their conspiratorial looks.

They've already been planning this. I'd better stop it right now.

"Nope, nada, never, not. Not at this time. No. N. O. I hope you have this message firmly implanted in your brains. Now go eat pizza. If you stay, I'll have you take the furniture in Lindy's room up to the attic and store it."

That threat helped them make up their minds. They looked disappointed but shrugged and left.

Marthe was standing, hands on hips, in the door to the long hall, shaking her head. "They never stop! You know, sometimes I envy you having children but other times I'm glad I missed having to rear teens."

Caroline walked in hearing the last.

"Oh, yeah! Loads of fun! Do you want to know what they really want, or should I wait and let them tell you?" She was smirking, her "better you than me" look.

"Now what?" I couldn't imagine.

"They want to turn the attic into a seventies disco as a hangout for their whole group of friends, only with rap music and hip-hop. I heard them discussing it, imagining how they would fix it up, talking about break-dancing up there."

"No way. I hate rap. The beat is so repetitive, so aggressive and the obscene words! Besides, I can't deal with a large group of teens right now no matter how fun they might be. I have my limits."

"Speaking of limits," Caroline was looking at the mass of stuff in the dining room, "haven't you bitten off more than you can chew here?"

Caitlin walked in just in time to hear that.

"Geez, Annie! Where did all that come from? Wait! I need coffee first," she gasped, and headed for the kitchen.

I answered Caroline. "Yeah. Probably. I don't even know what to look for. I just know I have to find out what's in these files."

I gave them all a summary of my meetings with Clayton and Klarkowski. Then I took it farther.

"I have a growing feeling of impending threat I can't shake. It began as soon as I was back here. It's hard to explain. It's like I felt at the site when we were being watched but much more. Malevolence is the only word I can think of that comes close."

"Yup! Definitely coffee. This will take more than a minute." Caroline interrupted, moving into the kitchen.

Caitlin dropped into a dining room chair and propped her feet on the table.

Marthe made herself some tea. They settled themselves after Caroline put a cup of tea in front of me.

"All the questions are driving me crazy. I have to get them out of my head." I went over everything again, from the suspicions of both Conrad and Sam Soderberg prior to their deaths through all the meetings, the papers, what Mac had said, everything. I showed them the recent letters.

"I can barely sleep."

Cait took her feet off the table and leaned toward me.

"Then, honey, you have to go way back to before Art's death and face the possibility he was involved in this in ways he hid from you. Annie, the man *lied* to you. Look what we have here." She spread her arms across the piles. "He didn't keep business out of here at all. He kept it from you, but not at the office. Why? What? Was? He? Doing?"

My chest felt heavy. *She's right, Anna. You have to face this.*

"Yes, I know. I'm trying to face facts. Like...Fact: yes, he hid all of this from me, lied about all these files being here. I took a quick look at these. They're not research. They're individual cases. Confidential files.

"Fact: If I'm honest with myself, I have to admit our marriage was not in a good place even without this. He had grown distant, indifferent or colder or, I don't know, something. He was letting something pull him away from me.

"Fact: he wasn't there emotionally or physically for the kids either. Fact: he was making more money than any lawyer would, even the best of lawyers. Fact: the number of trips he took on business was increasing. Fact: he was more involved with Jonny O than ever. That about covers it I think."

"That's only part of it." Cait looked her toughest self, the street kid from the neighborhood. "Now take a hard look at the plane trip, Annie."

"The plane trip. Ok, what I think of, what stands out first, is all the planning they did. I just figured then that the prospect of flying so far was exciting and they both were enjoying the anticipation. Fact: planning took them weeks, almost a month. Why? Does it really take that long to plan a plane trip, even one to Mexico? I wonder. Why did they research every place they could land? Well, I figured pilots have to do that but was it for the trip down or, big OR, did they plan to bring contraband back and need other places to land? Fact: Art gave me almost no information on where they were to stop. He said I didn't need to know, that he'd call me whenever they landed and let me know he was ok. Fact: he didn't call until he was in Miami, then again in Cancun. I didn't question it. I was used to his being so independent. Now maybe it wasn't independence; maybe it was more than that."

"Now the crash, Annie."

"OK. Question: did he die or was that someone else? If someone else, is he still alive? An open question now. No. Back up. Were Art and Jon fishing? If not, what were they doing? Why was the plane so far from Cozumel? Why did it crash inland and not near the coast? Why was Jon found wandering so far from the plane? If he was in the cockpit, why was he not burned? Did he really lose his memory? Why was the body so charred? Why didn't it have any identifiable remains with it like teeth and bones? If it wasn't Art, how did the ring get on the finger? Who was it if not Art? What was the role of Arispe Sandoval? How did Arispe Sandoval get my name and phone number? He wasn't the person in charge of the investigation of the crash. That man was killed by one of his own men not long after. I never met that investigator. Was it all staged as I felt it was? If Art is still alive, where is he?"

I ran out of breath.

Caroline had been quiet, listening, her arms crossed over a pile of books on the table. Now she sat back.

"You forgot a part, Anna. Go back to the phone calls and Big John's role here."

"His role here? Well, OK." I dredged up that memory. "One thing does stand out. Why did Big John rush over to manage everything? I didn't think anything of it back then. I was so worried and I was grateful for the help."

"I noticed," Caroline said. "He was in total control here. He ordered Jenny to stay with you here and to record everyone who came. Now, that's a nice thing to do and very helpful but given what we know now, you have to ask why? Was he ever that attentive before? Not that I saw."

"No. He wasn't." I paused, thinking. "I don't think I have to go over all the questions I'd have regarding Jon's behavior."

"No," Cait said. "That's pretty damn clear. He's always been his asshole self. Please don't sugarcoat his behavior."

"No. I don't, but then a big question for me is how much control did Big John have over Jonny O?"

371

BETRAYAL by SERPENT

I went on and on, unloading all the doubts, inconsistencies, fears, and possibilities which had been creating my mental whiplash.

Finally, I'd had enough. I wanted to stop. "I think that's all the questions I have for now."

"Annie, you're forgetting someone."

I looked at Cait's face, sympathetic but adamant, daring me to face it.

"Ramon." I sighed. "He hasn't told me the full truth either. He was at the dig before we went down there. He never mentioned that to me. Why? I've called him and he isn't answering my calls. Why?"

Marthe had remained silent the whole time I'd been talking. Now she looked at me with a very kind, but sad face.

"There are two more questions you haven't faced, my dear. If your husband was involved in such nefarious dealings, you must also ask the questions...did my husband have a mistress and did my husband also kill others?"

Cait, Caroline and I looked at her with horror. Then I realized that if he was involved with men like drug runners, he had the potential and the opportunity to do anything else. Anything at all.

Was he unfaithful? Now I know what it feels like to think that about my husband. *And you, Anna, knowingly went to bed with a man who is married. How does that feel? Chickens home to roost, Anna!*

I thought of the things Art had done while still a child, the cruelty to animals, the indifference to others' pain. Was he a sociopath? A man with no conscience? Did he even love me? Was he able to love anyone?

What do you do when there are no more fairy tales?

I put my head down and cried.

And after a while, there was nothing else to do but stop crying. I felt empty. No hope for a happy ending. Strangely, I felt relief in that. Why does the loss of hope bring relief ? I don't know.

Set the questions aside, Anna. There are no answers now. There's only one thing to do. Go forward. Get this mess out of your life.

"Thanks for letting me cry. I needed that. I'm ready to get on with this."

Caroline and Marthe nodded. Cait got up, came around the table and gave me a big hug.

"Annie, I love you and I'll support you any way I can. I can't believe you've stayed so strong with all you're facing. I'll help you with this mess today but I regret that I can't next week. I've got extra hours at work and I have to take them. Five boys eat a hell of a lot. One question I have before we start is who do you want us to trust here? I know Marthe and Caroline and Rob, and you can count on me and my boys, but who else?"

"I hadn't thought of that."

"Do you trust Klarkowski?" Caroline asked.

"Yes. Yes I do. I know he's been just doing his job as a police officer. Actually, next to Rudmann, he's been pretty patient. He reminds me of a hunting dog though, sniffing out everything he can.

"There's AJ, of course, and my other kids, and then Clayton, and Ben. There could be someone at The Firm who leaked information but I wouldn't know who that would be and it's probably someone long gone. I guess that's it."

"Well, then. Let's get started on this stuff," Cait declared. "What do we do first here?"

With that, we began. I set up a database to list the books and, in spite of our late morning start, we made easy headway for a time. We would have been through the books faster except for a discovery Marthe made when she was flipping pages in one of them. Some had underlining in them, others had notes stuck in them. Most were notation free, but we wondered if some notations might be related to cases in the files, so we ended up going through each book page by page, adding post-it notes.

Hours later we boxed up the unmarked books to be given away and set the others on the window seat. Cait left to feed her boys.

Caroline and Marthe stood in the arch to the living room with hands on hips, surveying the files and a pile of notebooks. I walked between the piles.

"I think we can eliminate those notebooks. I'm pretty sure they're from Art's college days. I'll page through them tomorrow."

Caroline ran her hands through her hair. "I'm glad Rob is at March Madness with the boys." The state basketball tournament had begun and they were in Madison.

"He's dying to pick his way through stuff like this. One less we have to swear to secrecy. I'm assuming all this is confidential. This is a lot and, Anna, I can't help tomorrow either. I'm supposed to drive down to Mad City and meet them."

"Secrecy. That adds another dimension to this. Even though the files are old, is there a confidentiality issue here? Does lawyer-client privilege exist all these years later? Just in case, I'm swearing you to secrecy. But confidentiality or not, I have to know what's here, and I need your help.

"Tomorrow afternoon and evening are out for me too. I'm supposed to have my family over for dinner tomorrow night after a basketball game with the boys at school."

I called Aunt Carrie and told her I was taking them out for dinner because I didn't feel up to having everyone over yet. I told her to meet me at the Wellington. Then I called the Wellington and made reservations.

"Now there's a benefit to being kidnapped and wandering in a jungle I never expected. They think I'm horribly ill still, that I'm too exhausted to cook."

Caroline and Marthe laughed.

"We've got a good start. Let's plan on Monday a.m. bright and early, if that works for both of you."

Sunday, after mass, I went through the notebooks. I was right. They held notes from Art's long ago classes.

At dinner, I carefully censored my account of what happened in Mexico. Aunt Carrie was not fooled and attempted to grill me. I ignored her or changed the subject. She got the hint. She assumed I didn't want to talk with the boys there. I assumed she would assume that and I was right. I also assumed she would not forget. I'll be grilled until well done the next time she gets me alone.

In the end, Cory held court, with his dramatization of his tour of Mexico. Alex held an audience with talk of his gap year. They both dramatized my journey up and down the pyramid at ChiChen Itza on my butt. That fulfilled everyone's curiosity and then some.

Marthe spent Sunday writing.

Sixty

...journal...Monday night...

This morning we put the three extra leaves into the table, sorted the files by year and began.

"One hundred fifty-seven files. One from twenty years ago. We'll be at this for days."

We've had to read page by page, checking the books for any notations related to the files. Some are. Some files are thin, but others are anywhere from a half-inch to three inches thick. I found Art's dictionary of legal terms and we needed it many times. It was slow and incredibly boring. As time went on, however, I became angrier with each file I read.

He kept this all from me! How much more did he keep hidden, lie about?

The files became more numerous in the two years before Art died. We slogged on.

Five p.m. We looked at each other and knew we'd had it. We compared our lists, Marthe summarized our findings on the computer and made copies for each of us. Caroline went home. Not one thing stood out.

...journal...Tuesday...

Began at 8am, and by noon we had made great headway into the piles. Our notes have gotten longer and more detailed. We ate lunch and had just begun on the files again when I got a call on our house phone from Klarkowski. I put him on speaker.

"I need to ask you about a young man associated with Lindy. What can you tell me about Richard Attenborough?"

"Pretty much nothing. I never met him and Lindy only just began going out with him about mid-semester last fall, I think. She stayed overnight at his apartment sometimes. In December she went to his home in Milwaukee and when I saw her in Cancun, she had broken it off. She said she didn't like his partying. I know they were having sex. He plays basketball. That's it. Why do you ask?"

"We're going down a long list of who she had contact with at school. I thought she might have brought him to your house. We're also looking at him for some possible drug activity."

"You know, she never even brought other girls home, now that I think of it. I just assumed she was immersed in school and that whatever she did with friends, she did there."

I added that to my list of questions. *Why had she never brought anyone home?*

"I did go with her to Walker's Tae Kwan Do studio. You might check with them."

"We are. Have you had time to check out those files?"

"We're through the legal books, which we tackled first. I plan to turn most of them over to Clayton's firm. We're doing the files now. It's a huge task. The dates go back twenty years. We're doing a summary of our findings as we go. I'll keep you posted."

I assured him he could have someone get them when we're done.

...journal...Wednesday night...

Today our days of boring and dull and sometimes incomprehensible reading began to make sense to me. Patterns emerged. I knew that each member of the firm had tried cases on their own. I also knew that some cases were handled by a team. The teams that handled all these cases were headed by Jonny O. In fact, these cases were all handled with Jonny O as lead. Art sat in on two. None of the cases were those handled by Soderberg and Moss, alone or together.

Caroline stretched and leaned back. "It looks to me like Art was definitely monitoring what Jonny O did, just as he told Sam Soderberg. He didn't trust him. The question is why? If Jon had mood swings, maybe he had to be watched, supervised. Or, was Jon into something illegal and Art trying to catch him at it? Or were they both?"

"As far as I knew, Jonny O was a competent lawyer. Art never even hinted he wasn't and I don't see him keeping that to himself if Jon wasn't pulling his weight. If his behavior was unstable and it was hurting The Firm, I think Art would have said something."

We sorted the cases into subject matter, still retaining the timeline from earliest to latest. Thirty-five were burglary, two were arson, and four were assault. We hadn't gotten to them all yet.

"But here's a pattern. All are drug related somehow and every single case in defense of the perpetrator! Curiouser and curiouser. I'm positive these are related to the files Clayton showed me."

I had forgotten the names on the cases in Clayton's office. I called him and he was out. Put through to voice mail, I asked him to call with a list of the names of the defendants, their lawyers, the dates, and particularly the judges who had heard the cases. I knew I wouldn't be surprised if there were connections.

Later, I sat upright suddenly, a light dawning. "Not one of these files contains the outcome of the case after it went to court. Why not? Why not a final ruling, a decision in a person's file? Of course there must be a ruling, a decision, a verdict. Were they never concluded? Were papers removed from these files? Why no documentation for those?"

"Wow! You're right!" Caroline said. "Let me go online and see if I can find anything about that. There must be a record of decisions."

She tried the Clerk of Courts office, the Register of Deeds, the morgue of the Press Gazette.

Not much. If we wanted to find out more, we'd have to go to those places and dig for hours, maybe days. Those she found, a few, had verdicts where there was acquittal, or they were thrown out of court.

"Who was getting these cases thrown out and why? Did Art become suspicious because there was a pattern of no convictions? Did he remove the papers showing the outcome of these cases? Were these files tampered with somehow? Was that possible?" My patience was growing short. "If Art was here right now, I'd throw a fit the like of which he never saw."

We went back and checked every book for notations that might pertain to any case. We found nothing that made any sense to us. I looked for references of previous relevant court decisions pertaining to the cases.

"This is so weird. I know Art always included research into court precedents in files. He would have everything he needed written out so he could easily refer to it. How come none of these files contain anything like that?"

Caroline had just finished reading another file. "I can tell you this. I'm glad I didn't even think of studying law. This stuff is incredibly boring. I hate the jargon. Give me plain old English anytime."

We now knew who the judges were.

"Just two judges in all these cases. That's significant. I'm actually pretty sure they're the same judges mentioned in the files at Clayton's office. I'll wait for his verification though. No. Wait. There was one more in those case files. Still, not totally surprising. We're not looking at a huge court system for this area. What if these judges aren't on the up and up? What if the system was manipulated to make sure these two got the drug-related cases? What if the system was manipulated to keep them in place because they made decisions in favor of drug dealers? Another possible pattern?"

Today ended with no further discoveries and more questions than answers.

...journal...Thursday...

This afternoon we finished the files. Marthe updated all our notes and made copies for all of us. Caroline has a fund-raiser tonight.

"There's supposed to be members of The Firm attending. I'll see if I can probe a little. Maybe the whistleblower is still there. A long shot but why not try?"

She'll report back to us in the morning.

...journal...Friday evening...

We all have to admit we're frazzled. Caroline came up with nothing about The Firm. The two employees at the gathering had not known Art. They were hired three years ago.

"So! Here's what we've got. Art was reviewing Jonny O's work. The patterns we see raise some serious questions about Jon's role in The Firm, Art's too for that matter. I'm now suspicious about some court proceedings in Green Bay and Brown County, about the ethics of two judges, and about the extent of influence of those involved in the drug trade on that system. This is serious enough that I'm calling Klarkowski. He needs to get these now. I feel nervous about even having them in the house. We can't do any more. I'll be relieved to have this gone."

I got Klarkowski's voice mail and asked him to call as soon as possible.

I put what was left in my office. Just some loose notes we found which seemed unrelated to anything. We left everything we had done in piles in the dining room, took our now lengthy and carefully notated lists with us, Caroline to her home, Marthe to her room, and I tucked mine in a book in the library.

Neither Clayton nor Klarkowski returned my calls.

Reviewing the work in my mind, I felt it was worth it just to get it done and out of the way. But I couldn't help feeling disappointed that we hadn't learned more.

There's one more source I want to talk to. Ardith. I bet she knows more than she let on. I have to get her address and phone number. I called Clayton's office again but the receptionist didn't recognize me and of course wouldn't give out Ardith's address or phone. She said she'd ask Clayton but "he's out". I asked her to call Ardith and request that she call me. She refused, saying again she would ask Clayton about it.

Later, I tried to watch TV but couldn't concentrate. The boys did their homework in the kitchen, then went up to play computer games. I decided to go all the way up to the attic to see what would need to be done to bring down the filing cabinets, and what else I might get rid of.

I made it to the Dorm, but I had to stop and rest on the way to the attic and I noticed that the boys had left a stack of what looked like ledgers on the attic stairs.

Ledgers? Did Art do bookwork for the Firm here too?

Shivering in the cold attic, I checked each drawer and found some loose papers the boys missed. They had numbers on them and I thought maybe they belonged with the ledgers. On top of one of the files was an old metal box, locked when I tried it. I searched for a key in the files. Nothing. I called down to Cory, asking if they had seen a key to a locked box. He came bounding up.

"Yeah, the box was in this file cabinet, but there wasn't any key we could find. Sorry, Mom. We forgot to bring it down."

I pointed to the ledgers.

"Oh, yeah. Those too." He scooped up all of them and headed down as Alex came up the stairs.

"Alex, no disco. It's out of the question." Disappointment on his face. "But I think this would make a nice place for you." Grin from ear to ear. "It will take me a bit before I can decide what to do with this stuff but we don't need this extra furniture any more. Think about what you might want to have up here. I'll look into having heating installed. A bathroom too."

He let out a whoop and bounded back down to the Dorm.

I tucked the ledgers, the box, and the odd papers on a library shelf behind the door. I'd had my fill of legal everything.

AJ had called and left a message. "Mom, I'm emailing you the rest of the files from Conrad's computer. You have to see these! He suspected some serious problems in Green Bay and Brown County judicial circles, and there are some files scanned in that don't make any sense at all. I'm in a hurry. Call me when you've had time to go over them. Love you."

Brain freeze! Can't do that now! One less thing for me though if he has all that done.

We had a quiet night. I wrote today's notes in this journal and hope for undisturbed sleep. The feeling of impending threat had eased during my preoccupation with the files but it's intense right now.

Sixty-one

... Friday night-Saturday...

My body arched up off the bed to the sound of shattering glass. I didn't stop to put on a robe or slippers, but grabbed my cell phone and dialed 911 as I ran out of my room. I almost collided with Marthe as she shuffled into the hall, still sleepy.

Cory and Alex came bounding down the stairs.

"It came from downstairs, Mom." Alex would have dashed down the front stairs but I caught him.

"Get the flashlight from the cupboard there." I pointed to the linen closet where I kept one for emergencies.

Cory held up a flashlight in his hand. "I've got one too."

The dispatcher answered. I didn't wait for any questions. Knowing I was recorded, I gave our address first, then brief details.

"We've had a break-in. We need the Green Bay police now. We heard glass breaking. We don't know what or how. This is Anna Kinnealy and there are four of us in the house."

Her calm voice assured me she had the details and asked me to remain on the phone. I left it on and told everyone, "The police are on their way. Marthe, you and Alex take the back stairs. Go slowly and cautiously. Don't challenge anyone. Keep safe, but try to see what that was. Cory, come with me down the front stairs."

I spoke into the phone as we crept down the stairs.

"I'm not hearing any more disturbance, no running feet, no sound at all."

That didn't mean it was safe but my intuition told me someone or something had left the house.

We got all the way down the front stairs seeing nothing, hearing nothing. I saw a light go on in the kitchen. I clicked on the lights in the hall and the living room. The door to the library was closed. I moved to the pocket doors to the dining room. They were slightly open and the kitchen light shone in from the back.

Moving the doors slowly apart, I felt a cold draft. I saw at once all the files were scattered, the books out of their boxes, everything had been completely torn up. It was a mess. I felt sick. Someone had been searching. Where was he? No one in sight.

"Mom. Look." Cory pointed to the window. Both the storm window and inner glass pane were out. Freezing wind blew into the large opening.

"Stop! Don't move." I said in a low voice as I grabbed him. "Someone could still be in the library."

I heard sirens coming close.

"Wait for police. Alex, go unlock the front door and turn on the porch light. Cory, get the back door. No. Wait! Someone could be in the back hall or down the basement."

The sirens were outside and they stopped. Red and blue lights flashed through all the windows.

Alex got the front door open as the officers came running up the steps. I heard him tell them someone had broken into the house. They came in with guns drawn, moving carefully, keeping him in the front hall. One of them was Ben.

"Ben, we've had a break-in."

I indicated the mess in the dining room. "Someone has been searching for something. We all woke up to a crashing sound. We came down with flashlights to see what it was and found this."

"Mrs. K, I want you to stay right where you are until another officer can escort you out safely. We'll do a thorough search of the house. There are officers searching the grounds also. Where can you go until we know this place is safe?"

Cory flashed his cell at me. My opinion of texting got a little better. "Mom, we can go to Caroline's. I just got a text from Jake wanting to know what's happening. They're awake."

"Ben, that's right across the street, the Bradley's."

"Works for me," he nodded to an officer who was just behind me. She touched my arm and motioned to the boys and Marthe.

"Ben, be careful. I think whoever it was left in a hurry but the library door is still shut. We haven't gone in there yet. I don't think you'll find anyone on the upper floors. We came down both front and back stairs and didn't find anyone. Still..." my voice trailed off.

"We got it covered, Mrs. K."

Officers began moving into and through the house. "Are the back door and the cellar locked?"

"I checked the back door when I went to bed. It was locked. The cellar's supposed to be locked at all times. It's winter. There isn't any reason for us to use it."

He nodded.

"We'll get you all out first and then tackle the library."

Another officer stationed himself to the side of the library door. Ben headed through the kitchen and turned into the hall to the back door.

The officer with us introduced herself as Sally. She moved us all into the front hall. Noticing we had bare feet, she asked if there was something we could wear. I told her about the boots in the back hall and another officer went for them. We put them on and she escorted us to Caroline's house. The front porch light was on and Rob was waiting.

It was a half hour before Sally came and got me. She asked Marthe and the boys to wait.

Lights were still flashing from two police cars. A third was parked with them, with no identification on it. I walked in to find Greg Klarkowski standing in the pocket doors surveying the mess in the dining room. He turned as we walked in.

"I'll take it from here, Sally."

He remained at the door of the library.

"The house is clear, Anna. Can we use your office to go over what happened with you and the others? It's undisturbed. Except for the dining room, so is the rest. It appears the prowler was looking for something here in the dining room. There are a couple of books lying in the snow. Looks like they were thrown out in frustration, as if whoever did this was angry. Or crazy."

He was about to have us both sit down when we heard a shout, then several shouts and some turmoil from under us.

"Now what? Anna, stay right here. They found someone. Do not move from here!"

384

Sally came running in.

"Sir, you need to see this! There's snakes in the basement!"

"Again?" Both Klarkowski and I exclaimed at the same time. Sally looked a bit puzzled but continued.

"Ben and Xavier were nearly bitten. We think they're poisonous. They're very aggressive. They were behind a wall and came out of a small hole at the bottom. There are three at least. I've radioed for animal control but I don't think anyone there has ever dealt with this."

"Tell the men to get out of there. I don't want them bitten. Close it up! Oh shit!"

He looked at me. "Sorry about the language. Will they stay there? Can they climb up through the passages in the house?"

"I don't know but I don't think so. We shut and blocked everything we knew about after last fall. I don't think the boys have opened anything up but I'll have to check with them to be sure. How could they have even gotten in?"

"Ma'am, there's a basement window broken."

As Sally said this, Ben and another officer, who I assumed was Xavier, came in from the kitchen.

"This is serious, sir," Ben said. "The snakes are Black Mambas. Very poisonous, very aggressive when cornered. Just saw a National Geographic on them. They're an African snake. I recognized them right away. They move too fast to shoot and it's dangerous to shoot down there anyway because the bullets might ricochet. We'll have to wait for animal control. Mrs. K, I think someone was trying to kill you."

Klarkowski fired orders at his crew.

"Check the rest of the house thoroughly and be very careful. Go very slowly. Let's start with the library here. I'll want to use that for interviewing and as a base. Anna, we'll need to leave the boys and Marthe at the Bradley's. You, too, later. I'm going to treat this as a potential crime scene. I do need you to answer some questions first."

"Yes, we can use the library. You'll need me for more than questions." I answered. "I want to show you all the possible places a snake can hide in the house. I really think they came in by the basement but if this is a deliberate murder attempt, I'll want you and me to go over this house with a fine tooth comb. Black Mambas are serious business."

Klarkowski nodded. "But not you, Anna. We'll do that."

"You won't know where to look, where the Hidey Holes are."

"We'll find them. I don't want anyone bitten."

He looked over my shoulder.

"Sally, when they clear Anna's bedroom, can you get some clothing for her?"

I was wearing Caroline's jacket over my nightgown.

"I'll need some for the boys too, and Marthe since they can't come back here for a while."

She nodded and bounded very incautiously up the stairs. I thought she might have felt like a babysitter.

"Detective, thank you. The boys will need clothing for school. And I will have to help you in finding the Hidey Holes, or the boys will. I don't want the walls all torn out."

"They'll likely have to miss some school. It depends on how long it takes to interview all of you. Can we get started? I got your voice mail but had no time to answer it. Until animal control arrives, you can fill me in on what you've found. I'll consider whether or not to have you help find the secret places."

"Fine. I think our library is safe enough. There's one small place in there. I can show that to you right now. Do you want coffee? I can make some before we start. My coffeemaker is fast."

He began to say no and then realized they could be occupied for the rest of the night.

"OK, yeah, good idea. Everyone here will need it."

He followed me to the kitchen and I directed him to where I kept the coffee as I filled the pot and set it to brewing, got out cups, spoons, cream, milk, and sugar, and left it all on the shelf.

We left it to perk and started for the library. Sally came with my clothes and I ducked into the bathroom to change. When I came out he was standing in the door of the dining room.

"Are these the files you talked about? The ones from your attic?"

"Yes." I sighed. "I could just cry seeing this! You have no idea how much work we've done this week."

I gave him a summary of what we had found.

"We read through every single file. Now, it will take days to straighten this out again."

"Anna, doing that is out of your hands. I'm taking everything in as part of a crime scene. This room was the target. I'll have officers box this up. We'll sort it out. Can you tell me just how you went about it? I want to know every detail. Who worked with you on this? You didn't do this all alone, did you?"

"Oh, no, not alone. It took three of us five days, six days really. Caroline and Marthe helped. We started with the books." I gave him a detailed account of our procedure.

"Where are the file drawers, the cabinets? In your office?"

"No. They're still in the attic. I had the boys empty them, just bring down the files. I planned to have them moved down and sold when we were finished. There's no reason for us to keep them."

"Do you mind if we take them to the station? They'll be returned to you later but space is limited for us and we can use them while we examine the files."

"Go ahead. I'll have one of the boys show your people where they are when you're ready, although they're easy to recognize."

"Later. I need to question you now about what's in them."

I smelled the coffee as the machine finished brewing. We got our drinks and returned to the library.

"I use this as my office as well as our library. Take the desk so you can write."

I moved my laptop to a shelf.

"Did you use that laptop to record what you found?"

"Yes and I can print out that file for you."

"How were these files acquired? When did your husband first begin to bring them home? Just start at the beginning and tell me all you can."

387

BETRAYAL by SERPENT

So I got out my copy of our findings, printed him a copy, and began. I was sufficiently scared. No more question whether or not to trust Klarkowski. I have to. We could all be dead.

I was very conscious that there were at least three poisonous snakes in the basement, perhaps more in other hidden places. Any nagging doubt that the previous snake "incident" had been meant as a threat to us was gone, so all the questions I'd vented to Caroline, Marthe, and Caitlin, I now listed for him. He asked clarifying questions of his own.

"You're welcome to all the files. I hope you can make some sense of this. I think you ought to talk to Clayton too, and get those files I told you about before. I think there's a definite connection."

"What has been Foster's role in this?"

"He's been supportive. When Conrad was murdered, Clayton offered to take his place as our lawyer. I hired him after the reading of the will to help me through that time. Now I think he's very interested in what Conrad was finding. He'd like to see the papers you found the night Conrad was murdered. He said he would subpoena them. Did he?"

Klarkowski didn't answer. He sat back and was silent while he drank his now-cold coffee. I offered to get him more but he declined. He looked at me speculatively, and seemed to be trying to make a decision. When he spoke, he leaned his elbows on his knees, his face worried. He looked tired and rubbed his face with both hands.

"Look. There's much more going on than I can tell you about. I believe what you've been experiencing is very definitely related to our investigation. We can't consider what we've uncovered as hard evidence yet but we do know there are some powerful people around here who may be, no, *are* involved. What you've found here supports what we're finding. It's a mess. We've got literally dozens of cold cases reopened now. We're up to our ears in work."

He kept on rubbing his eyes and ran his hands over the stubble on his face.

"For years, we thought each case was separate. We didn't begin to look at them together until last year when another detective began pulling cold cases and realized they were all related to drugs, to some of the same people on both sides of the law, and certain legal firms, or rather to certain *lawyers* in certain firms. That's why I want these files."

"Yes. I know what we've discovered here will fit with that."

"But then there were the cat and snake incidents, which were just bizarre things, not seeming to have anything to do with anything, except they happened here in this house, to you and your family. It was Conrad's death which made us really sit up and take notice. The papers he was bringing to you still don't make a case for us. In fact, some of the files make no sense to us at all, but clearly he was onto something, and he related it to your husband's death. There was a note to that effect in his handwriting in the papers..."

At that point there was noise in the hall and Ben stuck his head in the door.

"Sir, the officers searching the neighborhood found someone. Can you come? Do you want him in here?"

Klarkowski stood up slowly, with a weary groan.

"No. I want him at the station for questioning. I'm through with Anna for now but I still have to question the others. What about animal control? I don't want anyone here until those snakes are gone and this place is searched for more of them. I want officers posted here 24/7 until we can clear this scene up.

"Sir," Ben interrupted, "there's more. The guy is stoned out of his mind. We have an ID. He's Richard Attenborough, the boyfriend of the archaeologist's daughter, Lindy Stewart."

My jaw dropped. All the tiredness left Klarkowski's face. He looked elated.

"Excellent! Another connection! Take him to the ER and have them find out what's in his system before you take him to the station. Let's hope it's something illegal. We'll need a warrant to search his place. Let's see if we can get something on him. I particularly hope we have to wake up a judge who let some of our pushers go in the past. Serve him right."

Ben was grinning. "Sir, we have something on him. He has pills and powder on him."

Klarkowski smiled. "Oh, how wonderful!" He turned to me.

"I'll have you escorted to the Bradley's. I'll speak to Cory, then Alex, then Marthe. I'll be over to see Mrs. Bradley later since she helped sort through this mess."

He stood looking at that mess through the door and sighed.

"It'll take a lot of work hours to pull those files together."

He looked at me.

"Do you think you and Marthe and Mrs. Bradley would be able to help reconstruct this stuff?"

"Yes, of course. We'd all be willing to help. If you could assign just one officer, that would help it go faster. We can do it right here instead of downtown."

He grinned.

"Done! You know, I think we're finally getting somewhere."

I thought that too but it wasn't a good feeling. The knowledge of evil erodes my spirit, my soul. There is no getting innocence back. I thought I could protect us. Those snakes could have killed us, killed us all.

Sally took me upstairs to get clothing for the boys and Marthe. I grabbed my purse and our heavy jackets.

As we made our way across the street, I got my one and only glimpse of Richard Attenborough. A tall lanky young man was being loaded into the rear seat of a black-and-white just down the hill past our garage.

Sixty-two

...journal...Saturday...

Morning came. Interviews with the boys and Marthe were done. I had to be present for Cory's because he's still a minor. Alex, now eighteen, could have been questioned without me but I was with him anyway. Only the prospect of getting some of her clothing got Marthe back here. I made a hotel reservation for her in a suite with a hot tub and she left mid-morning in a cab to go and get some sleep.

I asked Klarkowski to contact Allouez police to check the house there. He arranged it but I'll have to go over to be there.

The boys, "delighted to be of service" as Cory put it, never made it to school. They were employed by police, Ben prompting them, to show animal control all possible places snakes could travel in the house. As before, we had to wait for the Snake Rescue team from Milwaukee. They showed up much faster for police than they had for our previous episode. Klarkowski too was very interested in the hidden spaces of the house and took a "guided tour" from Alex, thanked us for our cooperation and left.

Police had cars and a cordon around the house but it didn't stop small groups of people gathering on the other side of the street and morning traffic moving slower than it ever had before. Aunt Carrie drove by "quite by accident". Or not. Caitlin called asking what trouble I managed to get into this time.

"After you've had some sleep call me and we'll talk. There's neighborhood gossip you want to know." She hung up to go to work.

Caroline turned the house phone off and let everything go to voice mail. She kept her cell on to fill in Rob, now at work.

I was in a fog. "I'm so tired I feel nauseated. I wish this was over, Caroline. It's crazy but I feel like I've forgotten

391

something. I can't think straight anymore. I've got to get some rest." We were waiting for Klarkowski to come back and interview her. "This is triggering memories of my exhaustion in the jungle and in some crazy way it feels like it's piling this huge weight on me."

"What is it you think you forgot? Oh, forget I said that. Dumb question."

"I don't know and at this point I don't care. I have to get some sleep. They're going to want to get started on that mess in the dining room right away and I'll need to be there."

"Go up and lie down on our bed. I can handle that. Rob called. He says he can't concentrate at work, that he wants to help too. Yeah, right! He's dying of curiosity. It's bringing excitement to his accountant's mundane life. He'll fend off Klarkowski and I think Klarkowski will go for at least a day's delay. We know what to look for better than anyone and they only have to pay one officer by the hour instead of several. If he buys it, then I'm going to collapse too."

I slept until late afternoon. After their interviews, the boys sacked out in Caroline's family room for a few hours, awakened to "help" the snake team, and were now revved up with energy, but kept a respectful noise level until we old ones revived. Ah, Youth! No, make that Bah, Youth.

Caroline reported the day's happenings to me. She said they took three snakes away and found no evidence of any more. Police vehicles had taken the file cabinets to use for the sorted files. Rob had succeeded in getting the file sorting postponed for two days. She'd gotten sleep too. We were discussing supper and feeding husband and boys when Klarkowski came to the door.

"Good evening, one and all. I have some good news for you. The house is clear. You can return home. No more snakes. And, we have a confession from Mr. Attenborough. Drug-addicted though he is, he was persuaded to give us a full story. It seems he has been addicted for some time, also dealing for some time. His 'handler' or supplier, whom he can't name because the person never identified himself, but we have a good description, who arranged all drug and money interchanges anonymously...I won't go into detail how that was done...that person somehow knew of the hiding places in your house. He apparently found that out from Richard, who heard that from Lindy who found that out when she heard the boys talking. Attenborough and the other dealer decided to try using them for hiding contraband. Lindy may or may not have been party to this. We can't be sure. We've forwarded all facts in the case to the Feds, with a request to advise us about where she is. I'm not holding my breath on that one.

"Last night, Attenborough was sent by someone, we don't know who yet, to see if he could find one special paper which holds the key to something important in the drug trade. He said he was told it's a code using Mayan glyphs. Anna, this may be our first real connection to the source of drugs coming up here. We want that key! Attenborough didn't find it. He threw the books out the window in frustration.

"I took the liberty of having the window boarded up. An officer will pick you up in about an hour to go over the Allouez house. Their police report no footprints in snow and no sign of a break-in.

"In view of the fact that Lindy isn't here, and is an adult, we had to go to court to get a warrant to search her room but I'd like your permission to do that too. It won't take us long. We'll have it done right away. I also have a warrant to search the hiding spots in the house for stash. Attenborough says they never succeeded in doing that but I must do it." He gave me copies of the warrants.

"We also had to get a warrant to get the files from Clayton. Being a lawyer, he was not about to just give them up. Wanted all i's dotted and t's crossed. He's definitely going to subpoena ours. I will give you access to those as well. How soon do you think we can have the files in the dining room reorganized?"

He's more excited than I've ever seen him. Now he's got all the access he needed to our house and to Lindy's things. He's loving this.

"I'm estimating one day at the most. We have myself, Carrie, Rob, and Marthe. If we also have an officer, using our notes, and organizing by names and dates, we should get it together really fast."

"Hey, Mom, us too!"

BETRAYAL by SERPENT

The boys were in their most "we're adult" adolescent stance.

I looked at Klarkowski.

"Ok by me. The sooner the better. I'll have an officer remain with the papers tonight to be sure you and they aren't disturbed again. When the shift changes tomorrow morning, another officer will be at the house to assist you. You'll need the extra help."

He continued. "Attenborough is small fry, Anna. This doesn't get us the leaders but we now have much more to investigate, such as suspected bribery of certain members of the judiciary, and that long pattern of cases undermining our attempts to break up any drug traffic here. We also think we have promising evidence of connections to Mexico. Some of the cases, as you saw, involved fraud and arson. We think those crimes may be part of the pattern too.

"Oh, and it was Attenborough who brought in the snakes. He'd been told to frighten all of you, to somehow get you out of the house, and he tried, but he's addicted and not professional, therefore incompetent, and you don't seem to frighten that easily. It was a deadly, but relatively clumsy attempt on his part. It seems he has an acquaintance who keeps dangerous pets—illegal imports no less—another case we have to investigate."

Later he popped in to report on the search. "We didn't find a thing in the holes. We tested for marijuana, cocaine, anything else. Your house is clean of any illegal substances, except for some traces of baby powder in one place. About the cat, we're still wondering how that fit in. Attenborough denies it. If we find out, we'll let you know.

"I want to thank both of you women for what you've done so far. I am also cautioning you to leave the rest to us." His stern glance took in four teenage boys as he continued.

"If Attenborough really had been a professional killer, you'd be dead. That goes for you boys too. We do thank you for your help in finding all the hiding places in the house. You can return home but, as I said, I'll have an officer stay with you overnight and until the files are done. Then I'll have the house and neighborhood checked by mobile units for about a week or so."

The boys advanced into the room and would have peppered him with questions but I spoke first.

"Did he kill Conrad? Who killed Conrad? What was his role in this?'

Klarkowski looked solemn and was very brief. "No, he didn't. We don't know yet just what Conrad's role in this was or who killed him. We're still investigating that. We have to wait for more from Mexico. That's all I want to say at this time."

He left.

Caroline and I looked at each other and shook our heads. "Who would have thought, back in summer, that all this would happen?" I said.

I called Marthe and told her she could come back. She elected to remain at the hotel, citing the comforts of the hot tub. I called Aunt Carrie and Mom and Caitlin and gave them abbreviated versions, then called AJ and Marnie. That took more time. They wanted to rush home. I asked them not to do that, citing all the extra people already in and out of the house.

I wanted rest and quiet. Caroline offered her house for us all for the night. The boys stayed there. Snakes or not, I wanted my own bed.

I trucked my things back across the street, Alex helping me.

"Watch out for snakes, Mom. There might be more."

"If they didn't get to us before they were discovered, they won't be problems now. Those poor snakes were so out of their habitat in that cold basement I'm surprised they didn't freeze. It's still human ones I worry about, but it appears our particular snake-drug dealer is finally off the streets."

"Mom, do you think Lindy's involved in drugs? Or any of this stuff ? I mean, she seemed ok." He looked hurt, as if she had wounded him somehow.

"Honey, it's hard to know. I really hope not. If not, she's certainly been naïve, but then, so are a lot of us, especially about drugs, and the uglier side of life."

"Are you sure you'll be ok here alone? I could stay if you want."

BETRAYAL by SERPENT

"No, I'm ok. I'll be fine but it's sure cold in here. Will you turn up the thermostat? I'm going to clean up the remains of the coffee and the meals the police brought in."

Alex left. I kept all the lights on for a while. In spite of my bravado in front of my son, I didn't like the picture in my mind of the Black Mambas. I had seen the National Geographic special too.

I finally settled in the library with some chamomile tea, turning out all the other house lights except the dining room, where the mess still lay all over.

Chamomile tea. That's what Peter Rabbit's mother made for him when he got sick and he got better. Will I get better too? Well, at least I have Peace and Quiet.

The phone rang. It was Ben. "I'm assigned to guard your house tonight, Mrs. K. I'm heading over."

"Ok. Come to the back door. You can park in the driveway by the garage." He arrived ten minutes later. I made him coffee, gave him bedding for the living room couch, and went to bed.

I wrote most of this journal account that night, but, in light of what happened next, everything else was written later.

Sixty-three

Dream...

Black and gold pour along the dry, tan riverbed, slowly filling it with liquid, smelling of rot, oozing around rocks and stumps of trees at the edges. I stand, watching it creep toward me. I have been walking through a desert, mouth dry, becoming thirstier and thirstier, and now I am near collapse, seeing there is no water in the riverbed.

As both colors come nearer they become snakes, first the black one, it's mouth open and fangs dripping, then the gold one, long and thick. Rooted by fear, I am unable to move as they reach me and wind themselves around my ankles and slide up my legs.

I try to scream and can't. No sound comes out of my parched throat. They reach my hips, waist, imprison my arms and squeeze my throat, choke my breath away. I begin to twist and struggle, fall to the ground rolling around and around.

The snakes turn into a dark shadow, then become human, become Jonny O, on top of me, a pillow in his hands. I succeed in fending him off briefly but he is kneeling over me, coming down on me again, using his weight to pin me, trying to cover my mouth. I grab his wrists and dig my fingernails into him.

I hear him growl a low curse, I dig harder, and he pulls back. I thrust against him, toppling him over onto the floor, falling on top of him, still digging into his wrists, rage flooding me.

Bastard. He's trying to get me to have sex with him again! He'll be sorry! I can smell the alcohol! He's drunk!

I push my body up and bring my right knee up and forward, grinding it into his groin, then lower my face to his and bite into his lower lip, dragging it down and out. His hands let go of the pillow that he holds between us and he screams loudly. His scream echoes in my room.

BETRAYAL by SERPENT

Blood. I taste blood. This isn't a dream! Fight! Fight! I let go of one of his wrists and dig my fingers into his eyes, releasing his lip. Suddenly I feel he isn't fighting back and I roll away. Scrambling to my feet, I reach for a vase to hit him. As I turn toward the table near the door where the vase stands, I see a silhouette in the doorway. I think help has come.

Oh my god! It is a dream! That's Big John. He's a ghost! He's dead! He's not alive!

I feel dizzy, caught between dream and reality, and waver in indecision.

Big John stands there, a gun in his hand. I turn back to Jonny O, who is attempting to get up from the floor. I begin to tell Big John what Jonny O has tried to do when the gun flashes. The sound hits my ears and head and jerks me backward. I hear the vase crash and break.

Shocked, I hear a thump and turn again to see Jonny O writhing on the floor. Another shot. He stops moving.

"Bastard! Sorry piece of shit! Not the son I wanted, damn him! No balls! No guts! A fuckin' fairy!" Big John's face is contorted with hate and fury, his voice loud, rough, grating. The gun smokes briefly in his hand. I smell gunpowder. Time stops and freezes that moment in my brain.

Where's Ben? Can't he hear us?

Eyes cold, Big John turns to me. "And another stupid bitch! Not enough I married one, now I got to deal with another."

He walks farther into the room, kicks his son with the pointed toe of his black boot.

"Time he's gone! Made excuses for 'im all my life. Nearly brought it all down, he did! Incompetent fag! Too stupid!"

I look toward the door, draw a breath and scream for Ben. Big John laughs, an ugly gravel sound.

"No use, girlie girl. He can't hear you. He went down first, then that fag of a son of mine. Now you."

My body begins to shake as my mind labels what just happened. *Big John...has murdered...this is murder. Jonny O...trying to murder me. What is going...on...here?*

398

My thoughts become very slow, hard to complete, plodding through my mind word by word.

Ben...dreamland...permanent...oh...no....Ben...dead.

"So, here's the bitch who's fuckin' nosiness has made a mess of things. Couldn't just go back to the Irish Patch and be a common housewife. Had to have money! Had to have Your Share! Had to make everyone suspicious! Had to have that bastard Wentworth dig into the books."

Big John is pacing slowly as he speaks.

Alcohol. The air reeks of alcohol.

I can't get any sense of direction. I feel suspended in space and time, disoriented. I watch as blood oozes over the carpet.

Big John's voice echoes as if he is far away.

"Well, an' it's comin' to a stop. I'm puttin' a stop to it. Be better off if the whole litter is drowned. Kill 'm all. Two down, how many more to go? Nits make lice. They'll have a nice big reward for me for this. Spend the last of my days in luxury, I will."

I come slowly out of time and space to feel cold, very cold. Somewhere a draft is blowing on me through the door. Big John's words, seemingly the gibberish of an old drunk, begin to trickle into my mind, to take on meaning.

He wants to kill more. I spoiled something for him. What did I spoil? Is Big John connected to all that's happened? Nits make lice. Kill the young. No! No!

That thought brings me back to fight mode, to total awareness, clearing my mind. I think Big John is too busy ranting and pacing to notice me stiffen. I'm near the door and just about to turn and run when he brings the gun up, aiming it at me.

"Yer goin' nowhere until I say, my girl." He's tuned into my energy somehow. "I suppose yer wonderin' what it's about. Ya can't have figured it out all by yer lonesome. Yer not that bright. No woman is that bright."

He snickers. "All stupid bitches, ya are. Only good for one thing and not always so good at that either. Frigid wife, frigid daughter. I heard you wasn't so frigid. Maybe I'll have some use for you before this is over. Right now, you'll do as I say." As he speaks, spit sprays from his lips, dribbles down his chin.

He brings the gun higher, pointing directly at my heart.

"You go out that door easy. We're goin' down to the kitchen slowly. I'm right behind you with this gun and I'll use it on you if you don't do as I say. You got big black garbage bags?"

I nod yes.

"Good. We'll need four."

I move slowly through the door down the back stairs to the kitchen door and he follows, the gun trained on me all the time. When I reach for the light switch next to the kitchen door, he jumps forward and jabs the gun in my spine.

"I need a light."

My voice shakes as I speak. Alcohol fumes surround me.

"All right. Turn it on. Where are the bags?"

I point to the cupboard under the sink.

"Get them now. No unnecessary moves."

We cross the floor slowly and I get out the box and pull two from it. "Open them up all the way and put one inside the other. So they're double strength."

I do as I am told.

"Ok, now do it again. Make another one like that."

I do. I'm shaking inside. It hasn't reached my hands yet. I fight to keep them steady.

"Now come back upstairs, slowly, no sudden moves, no tricks."

I edge up the stairs to my bedroom. He is right behind me with the gun in my back.

"Now, yer goin' to put that boyo's body in one of those sacks."

"I can't lift him. He's far too heavy for me."

Blood has spread further across the carpet.

"Ya damn well can! Yer a big strapping girl! Ya can slide 'im in, one part at a time. We'll cut 'im up if we have to!"

I realize with horror that Big John is coldly willing to cut up his only son's body to get what he wants, or order me to do it. My stomach turns at the thought of that grisly task.

Oh god no! I'll never be able to do that!

400

"Maybe I can slide him in." I move toward the body.

"You do that."

What happened to Ben? Where is he?

I kneel down at Jonny's feet and pull the bag up over them, then up his legs, folding them into the bag. When I get to his hips I have to roll the corpse and slide the double bag around his torso. Getting the rest of him in seems impossible. Big John is pacing behind me, closer and closer to me. I look up to find the gun pointing between my eyes.

"Get him all in!" he orders.

My hands are slippery with blood. Dizziness hits me. My left arm is aching intensely.

I get him in by slowly pushing the corpse into fetal position, finally shoving Jonny's head into the bag.

"Stand up!"

I stand, holding onto a nearby chair, trying not to throw up.

He points to the remaining doubled bag.

"Put it in that one."

I do that.

"Now, yer goin' to slowly drag that bag down the stairs an' into the kitchen an' down the back stairs an' outside. That piece of garbage is going out!"

He snickers at his joke.

"Don't ya think that's funny, taking a piece of garbage out? A big piece!"

"I don't think I have the strength." He ignores me.

He's crazy drunk. He's mad.

My mind begins to work better even through my nausea. I begin to hope for a break, a way to save myself and get to some help. I know he has to be stopped. I move slowly, stalling for time. I try not to think of Ben.

"I'll need a jacket, a coat. It's cold out."

"Oh no, you won't. Not where yer goin'. Now pull! And no tricks!"

"We'll have to take the front stairs. The back ones are too narrow and not as slippery." I want to get a glimpse of Ben.

"Just do it!"

He waves the gun toward the front stairs.

401

BETRAYAL by SERPENT

I drag. Jon's body is very heavy and the plastic doesn't slide all that well on the carpet. When we hit the wood of the stairs I have to struggle to keep it from sliding down too fast. I sit on the stairs under it and hold it up with my body as I edge down one stair after another. It rolls down the last three stairs before I can stop it.

Again, I must tug and pull hard to haul it over the carpet.

Ben's body is on the floor of the living room next to the sofa where he'd been sitting. He must have been asleep when Big John came in. He isn't moving and I hope he's only out cold but I feel more fear as I realize there will be no help from him. Then a wave of sickness comes as I realize he's probably dead.

When we hit the smooth kitchen floor the bag slides easily but I fake struggling with heavy weight and stall as much as I can, sending prayers to anyone higher up anywhere in the nearby universe begging for interference of any kind.

I know Big John is drunk but he's not unsteady. He holds the gun firmly pointed at me. We move slowly through the back hall and down the back stairs, and he directs me to pull the sack outside. I get the outer door open and the cold hits me. A biting cold wind and sleety mist. I feel needles on my skin.

March weather. Will I ever see the end of March? Will my children live? Is Ben really dead?

"Down the hill. To the river."

Oh my god. I get tears in my eyes and they freeze as they slip onto my cheeks. I am shivering violently. The blood has frozen on my arms and hands.

It's dark out here. I'm going to try to get away. There's brush down below. If I stumble and roll maybe I can hide in the dark. Maybe I can hide behind the body. He'll make me go in the river. He'll send us onto the ice. How long before we hit a weak spot on the ice and drop in?

I know I have to try before we get to the river.

We'd had a February thaw that had opened the river in the center. Now it had re-frozen a good way out but how far and how hard I couldn't know.

I back slowly past our garage entrance down the hillside, down past the bushes. I can't see a way to dive into the bushes without getting shot because Big John is following so close, just above me on the hill. Over my shoulder, I can see the river path coming up, and my mind is seeing Conrad's body on the path, seeing my own body on the path.

"Stop!"

I am at the edge of the path, shaking badly from cold and fear.

"Take out the other sack!"

I do that. He holds out his hand for it and grabs it from me.

He laughs again. "That's the bag yer goin' in!"

He's going to shoot me now.

"Now drag that bag." His gun hand comes up and he gestures to Jonny's body. "Take it down the rest of the way to the river!"

My bare feet, cold and numb, slip on ice trying to get it over the path but it sticks on something. Before I can decide when to make my move, I tug too hard, losing my balance and falling backward, rolling down the hill to the river, the bag following me.

Hope of escape! *Keep rolling into the mist, into the dark!*

I hear Big John shout, shots fired, and then it seems the whole sky lights up, crackling, exploding.

Firecrackers! Firecrackers? I need darkness!

I try to roll to one side but Jonny O's body bag is on top of me.

I hear a shout, "Mom, Mom, where are you?"

"Cory, watch out! He's got a gun!"

Then shots, pain searing through one arm. I don't lose consciousness, to my surprise. I am desperate. I think he's shot Cory. I try to push the bag off me with my other hand. It's a struggle. Jonny's body is pinning me down. My right arm is useless.

I begin to shout, "I'm here. I'm here."

I am shaking so violently from fear and cold that I feel like I'm being violently slapped around.

403

BETRAYAL by SERPENT

Big John yells as he comes toward me. He grabs the bag off me and I think he'll shoot me again but he seems not to see me under it. He stumbles the rest of the way down the bank, dragging the bag after him.

I hear very distant sirens, see shadows running along the path, finally another shadow above me on the path, looking back and forth, then down.

"Here! I found her!" I hear Alex shout to someone.

The sirens scream closer and red and blue flashes pierce the night from the top of the hill. I hear a volley of shots.

Shadows come down the bank, two of them. Bending over me, they pull, lift and yank, standing me up and moving me quickly up the embankment to the path. My legs are still holding me up somehow. Not anything I will. They seem to move without me.

"I'm shot, I think. There's a body in that bag."

"Mom. You'll be all right! We've got you now."

I slump against someone who, I learn later, is Rob. I am picked up and carried up the hill toward flashing lights that have just arrived, a waiting ambulance. Other flashing lights are behind it. The lights hit my eyes like lightning strikes. I'm still shaking violently.

The pain in my arm comes through the cold and I dissolve into tears and groans. I think they give me a sedative. I remember them laying me down. I remember telling them I was shot in my arm. I don't remember the ride to the hospital.

I do remember Alex's words.

"We got you, Mom!"

Sixty-four

I woke to a gray light floating through the window, knowing where I was. I didn't have to ask. An IV in my left arm dripped blood into me. My right arm was in pain.

Oh shit, my dominant hand! I grew up forbidden to say shit but this deserved a shit.

Aunt Carrie was snoring in the chair, her head back and mouth open. *Shit! Shit! Shit! Shit! Shit!*

She jerked awake.

"And more shit!" I muttered.

"Anna Kinnealy, is that any way to talk? So, you're finally awake! I almost shook you awake. I want to know what happened. What the heck was Big John up to? How come he's alive again? Why were you helping him get rid of Jonny's body? Who would have thought he wasn't really dead?"

She would have gone on and on but a nurse came in and, with stern looks, shooed her out.

"I'm going to get some breakfast. I'll be back soon," she declared, backing out the door, having the last word.

"Now we need our rest, don't we? We can't be having talk, talk, talk," the nurse cooed at me. I almost called Carrie back.

Ah! The royal 'we'. Why must nurses speak like that?

I felt intense irritation snap through me.

"Why must you speak like that? There is no 'we' in this bed. You are not in need of rest unless, perhaps, you worked two shifts in a row. Are any of my children here? I want to see them right away. They need to be warned. I want to know they're all right."

She looked down at me, literally and figuratively.

"WE have some procedures which have to be done first. The doctor is on her rounds and will be here in six minutes. I'LL take your vitals now, remove the bandage from your arm—she wants to see what's happening there—and when she's done and you are bandaged again, there are *numerous*

405

people waiting to see you. WE will be very happy to get them out from under OUR feet."

She did as she said and finished just in time.

Watching her remove the bandage from my arm, I was surprised and disappointed to see how little bandaging there was. Somehow I thought a gunshot wound ought to be treated much more seriously, more bandages, padding, a large wrapping. I felt slighted somehow.

My doctor was feeling too cheerful for my taste. She came in humming an unrecognizable tune, off-key. "Well, Anna! You are the hero of the hour from what I understand. You lured a murderer into the river, saved a policeman's life and only a flesh wound to show for it.

Only a flesh wound? Saved a policeman's life? Whose? Who did I lure into a river? Where's Ben? Is he dead?

She glanced at my arm. "Looking good. You can bandage that back up, Nurse. Anna, your vitals are good today. We only want to finish this drip," she flicked the bag a bit "and set you up with a follow-up office visit. I'll prescribe an antibiotic and some pain meds. Are you allergic to anything? No? Great! See you in a week."

She was gone.

A few minutes later they all swarmed in. All ten. Marnie and Marthe sniffling tearfully, Caitlin and Caroline holding flowers, Alex swaggering, Cory grinning, the twins looking uncomfortable, and AJ looking somber. Klarkowski brought up the rear.

They approached the bed as if I was fragile.

Good. Let them think that! Maybe I'll be pampered for a while.

It was a very short while, less than three seconds.

"Mom! How could you go back to that house alone?" AJ and Marnie demanded, in synchronized outrage. Then they all broke into questions.

I held up my left hand with its IV trailing and kept it there until I had silence from all of them.

"First, I thought it was all over with the arrest of Attenborough. Second, I sleep best in my own house. Third, the snakes were gone. Fourth, I was exhausted. Fifth, I wasn't alone. Ben was there, and I want to know what happened to him before I answer any more questions."

Alex looked slightly chastened, which didn't last long. "Ben's ok, Mom. He's got a concussion. We think Jonny O somehow had a key to the house from when he was our friend and he sneaked in and hit Ben on the head and knocked him out. Ben came to as we were rescuing you. Klarkowski is really steamed about that." He glanced behind him. "We think he chewed Ben out, but Ben's ok."

"Good! Now if you're all quiet I'll tell you just what happened." They were. I did.

"So here's the short version. Jonny O was murdered by his father and it seems Big John set it up so everyone thought he himself was dead but he was apparently still running the drug group behind the scenes. He talked about being rewarded because he was planning to get rid of all of us."

Cait stepped up and jostled the bed and I winced. She didn't notice. She leaned over me eagerly.

"That's what I wanted to tell you. There were rumors that his ghost had been seen at their house. The neighborhood knew something was up. There've been rumors for months that Big John was alive, but people didn't believe it."

My arm was in pain. I had so wanted them to be there and now I wanted them gone.

"Detective Klarkowski, I'll be happy to answer your questions as soon as I can. I'm pretty sure from what Big John said that he's the person behind the drug smuggling and selling. I think you'll find in the coming days that more will come out.

"Now, I want to know just what you two were up to last night." I looked at Alex and Cory.

Cory looked smug. "Mom, you've lost a day. This all came down the night before last. If I must say so myself, WE," he pointed to himself, "and Jake and Jim, are the real heroes." He and Alex preened. All four stood in a row, arms around each other's shoulders, looking smug.

"What happened to Big John? Do the police have him in custody?"

All of them became very quiet. Alex and Cory looked down.

Klarkowski stepped closer and spoke.

"He grabbed Jonny O's body and ran out onto the ice, firing until he had no more bullets. We fired back but didn't hit him in the dark. The ice got thin and broke. By the time we got there he had sunk beneath the water twice. He didn't come back up. We haven't found his body yet. We're dragging the river and have divers there, but no luck."

Cory spoke. "Mom, we didn't go after Big John. Do you think we should have? Were we bad to let him go out there?" I saw the guilt on his face and Alex's too.

"Boys, look at me! You are not responsible for the choice Big John made. You would not have been able to rescue him. His size alone would have prevented that and he was very drunk. He would not have allowed your interference in what he wanted to do. Drunks don't. They don't listen. Do you understand?"

"Yeah," Alex said, "but it sucks anyway!"

"I know. It does."

"Mom, Jenny O called." Marnie interjected. "Her mom is in Winnebago again. Mrs. O'Keeffe tried to commit suicide and was so violent no other mental hospital could take her without endangering their staff."

AJ joined in.

"Aunt Carrie said Jenny O was here in town so we went to their house. She wouldn't say much to us but she asked me to tell you she feels relieved. She said to thank you."

I nodded. I saw their expectant faces watching me.

"I can't tell you all about that right now. I gave her my promise. A promise is a promise. She has very good reason to be relieved."

What horrors must Jenny and Jonny have suffered at the hand of their father! I'll have to see her again, let her know we support her.

But first...

I smiled at them all. "I want out of here and, a big AND...

"I want ice cream, hot chocolate fudge sauce, honey-roasted nuts and whipped cream for dessert. AJ, you will have to stay. I need a ride home."

Alex shook his head. "Not at home, Mom. The house is still a crime scene. How about we rent a hotel suite and hold your party..."

Klarkowski intervened, a slight grin on his face. "You can go home. Our CSI people are finished."

With some regret, they kissed me and left. "And balloons! I want balloons!" I called after them.

"AJ," I gasped. "Get me some pain meds. My arm is killing me."

He did and waited until it took effect.

"Thank you. It hurt so much."

"Mom, are we still in danger?"

Klarkowski was still in the room, waiting. I motioned him closer with my good hand.

I looked out the window, thinking.

"I don't really know. Big John talked as if he was behind something, probably profiting from drugs, but I don't entirely buy it. He was a drunk. Drunks don't run things well for long. My guess is there's someone waiting, eager to take his place, if that person or persons haven't already.

"AJ, I'm convinced Art was definitely part of the problem although I haven't been able to figure out his role in this yet, but he was deeply involved."

I brought him up to date on the files.

"Mom, I agree with you. I'm reserving my opinion until there's definite proof, but my hunch is that he was making money right along with the Big John and Jonny O."

He got up and began to pace. "I get so angry when I think he might have been involved!"

He stopped to gaze out the window. "How many kids out there have they hurt by bringing drugs to this area? How much of what we lived on was from dirty money? I get sick at those thoughts."

He turned back to me.

"I'm not afraid to find out, Mom. Are you?"

"No. I'm determined to find out all I can. You realize this may cost us a lot?"

"Oh, yeah! I've already been shut out of the lives of some of my former classmates just because of what has become public so far. Alex said there's talk behind his back at school, stuff on Facebook too. Marnie, I don't know. Damn, she always seems so far away! It's like she's living in some other world sometimes, but I think her Girls haven't deserted her. Alex and Cory will get it worst. They're still in town and high school kids can be really mean. I let them know they can call me anytime."

"I'm so glad I have you!" I looked hard at the man who was my son. "How are you doing this and your practice too? What about your training?"

"Mom, let's finish this later. Detective Klarkowski wants to question you."

Klarkowski brought a chair to the bedside and took out his notebook.

"First, Anna, call me Greg. I've begun to think of you as part of my team. We might as well be on first name basis."

It took over half an hour but Klarkowski was satisfied when we finished.

"By the way, I agree someone else is running this." He stood up. "I have to go now. I'll be in touch if I find out anything."

I looked at AJ. "I'd like to think it's over for now but I won't bet on it. Greed is such a powerful motivator. Someone, several someones, have been making a lot of money and they won't want it to stop."

He nodded. "I think there's more to it too. I agree. They'll rear their ugly heads again. You can bet on it. I'm going to get to work on your discharge and warm up the car. Don't go anywhere and don't get shot again before I come back."

"By the way, there's someone else here to see you."

He grinned as he walked out.

Sixty-five

A few minutes later Mac walked in, smiling broadly. "We've got to stop meeting like this. I know that's a dumb old line but I had to use it. It really fits the occasion. You smell a lot better this time."

I had to laugh. "So true, and I'm the one shot this time. At least I didn't spend five plus days in a jungle smeared in shit."

"Better you than me" he said.

He sat down, looked at me solemnly for several minutes, then nodded. *I must look like hell right now.*

"You're so changed, lady. You're not who you were when you stepped off that plane years ago in Cancun."

"How do you know what I was like that day? You weren't there."

"Actually I was. I remember you well. You would not have known me."

I looked surprised, couldn't hide it. He wasn't smiling.

Suddenly the hotel lobby flashed back into my mind, and the man in the bar.

"The man in the chinos and sunglasses in the bar. Was that you?"

"Good eye! Great memory! I'm always suspicious of everyone until they prove to be trustworthy. It's one of the problems with what I do. No trust unless it's warranted, earned, and even then I know too much about the human psyche to think the best of us can't also be the worst of us given sufficiently trying conditions. I was there because I had to vet you out. I was just beginning to make a connection regarding smuggling to Canada. The crash was just one of the avenues I was pursuing.

"Ian had called me down. Besides being old friends, he had already run into problems. He didn't have a lot of support then for his explorations and wanted help. I went down to help him make safe connections.

BETRAYAL *by* SERPENT

"I don't have much time. I want to warn you again. You're in deeper than you know. *Don't* relax your vigilance just because you're up here in Green Bay. I don't know if Klarkowski shares much information with you but..."

"He doesn't. Not so far. Only what he has to."

"...I will. The O'Keeffes became loose cannons in the group who runs it up here and were cut out. They're not the big guns any more, and haven't been for some time. They became dangerous to you because they wanted to know what your husband knew. Maybe they thought that would allow them to take control again. The murder of Soderberg was done or ordered by someone already in control with a lot of influence in the organization. The attacks on Moss and Wentworth were done by someone else, someone with a huge, almost psychotic rage. Whoever he is, he's the most dangerous person now. He may not be running it but he thinks he should, that he has the right to do it, and I believe he's from here. Please take extreme care.

"I told you supply lines in Mexico are broken down enough so that they'll have to take a long time to fix it, to make the connections they need, but I've underestimated them before. I can't stop any of you from being hurt. I wish I could. I just don't want you to walk into anything as naïve as you were years ago."

He looked long at me, face grim, eyes tough and shrewd. I held his gaze without blinking.

"Your eyes tell me you're not like that anymore. Sad. I hate seeing people become suspicious, watchful, aware of those who poison lives. I hate watching the loss of innocence. However, that awareness can save your life and the lives of those around you. Don't go back into denial."

"No, don't talk," he said as I took a breath to speak. "I really don't have much time. I've made my connections with Klarkowski, another good man, by the way, and I have a plane to catch. Trust him. If there's any more, the least little thing, tell him."

He got up and came to my bed and stood there, looking uncharacteristically hesitant. Suddenly he bent and kissed me on my cheek and then on my lips. He took my face between his hands.

412

"I'm semi-proposing to you again," he whispered, taking a ragged breath and shaking his head, "but I can't do that to you. I walk too close to death. I'd only bring you more grief."

He walked quickly out.

Another good man. He always leaves me feeling warm in my heart.

The nurse came with a wheelchair and I went home with AJ and had my welcome home party, complete with banner, flowers, ice cream with chocolate fudge and nuts, balloons, and four teenage boys who are my heroes.

Alex filled in more of their story.

"We couldn't sleep, Mom, and took the dogs for a run on the river path. We heard muffled shots but thought it was a distant tire blowout or something. I saw someone walk by a window in the house and thought maybe Ben was walking around in the dark. When the lights went on, I saw Big John and knew something was really wrong. We watched the windows from outside and saw you in the kitchen. Then you went up the back stairs with him. We knew that wasn't right. You'd never have done that. We didn't see his gun at that point but decided to set up a trap and were still planning when you came down the front stairs with the bag. We saw his gun then.

"Jake and Jim had some old fireworks stashed away and got them out, setting them up ready to light for a diversion. They went in to wake up Rob.

"In the meantime, Mom," Cory continued, "I called and got hold of someone who knew what Klarkowski was working on and the officer said not to try to go in at all, that they would sneak up and surround the house. I stayed on the phone but we know this area better than the police do so Alex and I were down by the path while you were being forced to drag that bag down. You fell backwards because we had put snags on the path. We wanted you to fall back because you would fall into a hole and out of his line of fire and you did. It worked. Well, it almost worked. You weren't quite out of the line of fire. Sorry."

Alex added, "Big John began to fire really wildly all along the edge of the path when you fell." He demonstrated.

413

BETRAYAL by SERPENT

"When he got to the ice, his gun was out of bullets. I heard it click a couple times. I knew he couldn't shoot you then."

He was glowing as he told it, but his face got worried as he came to this part.

"We were really taking a chance and we didn't have any other plan to back it up and we could have been shot and we knew it so don't yell at us, OK? We didn't have time to do more."

I got up and gave all of them a hug with my good arm. "If I survive your teen years, I'll be amazed."

Marnie made a face. She looked at the mess still littering the dining room.

"First we have to survive your strange life."

Sixty-six

...home again...Wednesday...

I had everyone put off reorganizing the files for two more days. Two more days of mess. Two days of headache, an aching right arm, antibiotics, and attempts at rest. Even two days didn't feel like enough but I wanted the mess gone. I had to get my bearings. I thought with Big John and Jonny O dead I'd feel relief from the threat. When that didn't happen I needed time to think. When I tried to think it through I ran into my own emotional aftermath.

Marthe played nurse to me. In front of her, I pretended to sleep a lot.

When she left my room, the whole messy picture became a movie in my head. My life, my husband's life, my children's lives. I cried myself in and out of sleep for the first day. Then I stopped. No more self-pity, which is what this has become.

I know three facts. The questions don't flog my brain incessantly anymore, I now have intimate acquaintance with feeling betrayed, and there is still a tangible presence of hate and rage looming.

Klarkowski has an officer here 24/7. He's taking no chances. He wants those files. Ben, Sally, and another named Kelly take shifts.

This is the morning of the third day. I made myself get up and into action again.

"I can't use my right arm. All of you will have to do the work." I said to Caroline, who came to see how I am and puttered through the piles looking for a pattern in the chaos.

"So, tell me something. How involved in this do you think Art was?"

"Truth?" I hated admitting this truth to anyone, not even my best friend. *Face it! Face it now! No maybe. No thinking he might still be the Good Guy!*

"I think he..." I didn't even want to say his name "...was making a lot of money from whatever he was doing. I think he bought the plane with that money. I think now that he was killed by someone in a drug cartel in Mexico because of his involvement with them. What I can't figure out is why Jonny O was let off, unless he ratted on Art or unless he was still useful to them in some way.

"I went online and Googled 'Mexican drug cartels'. My former husband"...I was hearing the anger and bitterness in my voice... "bit off a whole lot more than he could chew."

"Your belief in him is shattered."

"Oh yes."

Rob, Caroline, Marthe, Cory, Alex, Jake and Jim, and Sally. Eight people. Less than one day. 157 files. Eight sheets left we couldn't account for. Klarkowski said we saved the taxpayers lots of work hours.

After my house was in order, I went to the West Side and persuaded Aunt Carrie to host Caitlin, Jenny O and myself to an old-fashioned Irish tea, i.e., gossip session. I didn't have to persuade her very hard. The conversation in this one held more truth than most of the gossip had for the last thirty years.

Jenny O gave us chapter and verse of Big John's abuse of her brother and her mother as well as herself. Cait revealed three episodes of abuse she'd had to endure from Jonny when she was young. I told Aunt Carrie of his attempt to rape me. She cried and then scolded me for not telling her back then.

Caitlin told me how hurt she had been when I had married Art. He had been a secret tormentor of hers when we were children, until she had beaten the tar out of him in a fit of rage. She felt I had betrayed her, even though she had never told me. I told her I was sorry I didn't have her back at the time. I could have beaten the tar out of him much more easily. I was bigger.

Caitlin then surprised all of us, especially me, by revealing she knew a secret about The House that we didn't know. She called her boys, we got in her van, and she drove us back to the East Side and parked at the foot of Emilie Street near the path behind The House.

"Show them," she said to Liam. He jumped into the snow on the banks of the river just below the path. Pulling out a large pile of brush and snow, he dropped down to hands and knees and crawled into a hole out of sight. Leaving Patrick to wait there, she had us go into my basement.

Presently we heard a noise behind the walls of the cistern. A dirty face peeked up over the top of the wall just a few inches below the ceiling beams.

"There's a passage into your house," Cait said, "a tunnel from the river bank. The boys were over here the other day because they were curious about all the happenings. Just by chance they found this. Liam fell into the hole and while they were digging him out, the boys pulled out brush and debris and there was the entrance."

I was astonished, then worried. I wondered out loud if someone had used the passage to gain access to the house before.

"My god, Cait, what if there had been more snakes in passage? Liam could have been bitten."

Sean's deeper voice broke our horrified silence. "We cleared it out, Mrs. K. We made sure it was OK. We think it was something someone did a long time ago. There's some old wood in there that looks like it was used to shore up the sides and top. It's in pretty good condition. It widens out some as it goes along...roomy actually. I don't fit but Liam had plenty of room. I think a small or skinny man could get through if he tried."

"Well, it's going to get closed up permanently now."

Cait told Liam to crawl back and then come into the house. We examined the walls of the bin but there seemed to be no cracks, no way over it but the narrow opening between the top of the wall and the wood beams of the basement ceiling. I made a mental note to call Klarkowski and have them check it.

Upstairs, I sent a dirt-encrusted Liam to the shower and put his clothing in the washer. We continued our tea at my house.

For Carrie's benefit, I told again the whole story about the Yucatan, Conrad's suspicions, and the files. If she had an

417

opinion, she didn't tell us. Strangely quiet she was. She's hiding something.

They left after supper and I went to the library and set out what I had forgotten about in all the excitement, what I finally remembered—the ledgers, the odd files, the miscellaneous papers, the locked box, and Conrad's computer from Cancun. I downloaded the files AJ had sent me from the computer we'd found at the house on the river. Then I copied everything and hid it all. I don't want them damaged or stolen by any prowler. My arm was aching again and I put off further probing.

The House seems to have had a long secret life of its own. What more will I find? Caitlin's right. I can't put off additional security any more, but what kind? We've already got cameras, alarms and new keys, none of which worked. Wait! Wait! How did Jonny O and Big John get in? They didn't have the new keys. They couldn't have come through the passage. Too large, both of them.

I went to the back door. Scratches around the lock. Front door, the same. Someone's tampered with them.

The malevolent presence still persists. Why?

Sixty-seven

...three days later...

I've gone through all of it, the ledgers, the odd papers and Conrad's computer files and as I write this, I am going through an untamed storm of rage and disgust. Art betrayed me long ago, betrayed us all, everyone. Lived a monumental lie.

It has taken me three days to discover that my former husband knew about the traffic in women and children. He recorded it in the ledgers, along with purchases and sales of drugs, black market art, and animals. He created the codes because he got the idea from books I had purchased on Mayan art, on Mayan glyphs. He took over the local branch of this cartel from someone whose control was sloppy. He reorganized it and expanded it.

I know because I remember rescuing the children. What triggered my memory were two glyphs in the ledgers that read in Mayan "child of woman" (girl) and "child of man" (boy). I knew the translations from that book I bought long ago.

It happened when I opened one of the last ledgers to a random page. There on the page were the glyphs and suddenly my mind slipped into another reality. I saw those signs! I remember...branding. Branded. The foreheads of the children! I thought they were branded.

I am dizzy with hunger, sick, and beyond exhaustion, but I have to get the children away from here, out of the truck and to some safe place. I loosen their bonds and drop each one to the ground in the swiftly coming dark, while the men are up ahead, arguing. We hold hands and I hurry them into the jungle. It becomes very dark as we walk deeper and deeper into the brush. Soon night covers us totally. We stumble but keep walking, stopping only to listen for sounds of pursuit.

BETRAYAL by SERPENT

My senses are acute, my eyes seeing in the total dark, like a cat. I don't know what direction we're moving in but we are going up a rise, a long slow grade. The children are eerily quiet, frightened into silence. After walking a long time, I see slivers of light through the trees. The moon has come out. From the top of a hill I see a very large shape, like the pyramid at the dig. I head toward that. When we arrive I am impelled to climb to the top by night pictures from the mind of the jaguar. She slinks through the thick vegetation with us as we struggle up the slope.

The children scramble ahead of me. I drag myself slowly after them. At the top, there is a stone room, with openings on each side. The moon, shining through one side, shows a hole deep enough to hide them. Perfect! They'll be safe here. I try to show them what I want. They understand and jump down inside and turn to look up at me. In the light of the moon I see their foreheads. They are branded. Black ink. Signs. Why do they have those signs on their faces? I see the signs. The three girls match. The two boys match...

Some of these are records of the sale of children! Years! This has gone on for years! Someone knows about these and...Art knew about these! He knew. He could read them. My god! Right here in the house. Right under my nose. Right where his children were living. He knew about the trade in women and children. Sick. Sickening.

I swore. I used every word I had ever heard that described a man who would, without scruples, participate in the trade of women and children, put the lives of his own children in danger, betray his own wife. I ranted and raved at his ghost until I was empty of the hot anger, until a cold icy rage filled the void. For the first time in my life, I was glad someone was dead and that man had been my husband.

I couldn't even cry. With teeth clenched and jaw tight with furious determination, I deciphered the earlier simpler coding, based on numbers and letters, and then found that Conrad had done the same. I didn't need to get the papers from Klarkowski because I found them in the files AJ had sent to me.

420

I found a record of every piece of art Conrad had bought and sold and a record of his contacts with Interpol. I found the record he kept of his negotiations and the investigations he did when he was trying to get a settlement for me. He suspected The Firm of money-laundering. He tried to find out if there were Swiss or other offshore bank accounts for Art and Jon. He found out that Big John had a home in Ireland. He even somehow got copies of the Mexican papers investigating the plane crash. He found names, phone numbers, addresses.

I copied everything onto flash drives. Years ago a woman I knew had done an investigation into absentee landlords and the neglect of their properties and turned her findings over to the Press-Gazette. The file got "lost". One of those landlords was a state senator. I vowed this would not happen now. I made copies for everyone and every agency I could think of.

As I was finishing that I happened to notice the old box that had been in the files. I got a screwdriver and pried it open. And it was there I found the key to all the codes in the ledgers, in Art's handwriting, dated from fifteen years ago.

I loved a man who betrayed everyone who loved him.

And I knew another man who loved enough to give his life for me and for my children.

Yesterday the locksmith came. He found scratches around our front and back door locks and they had been tampered with. He drilled out the cores and gave me new keys.

I want to make one more copy but I'm out of jump drives. I want to tell AJ about this too. After I got it all put away, and while I was eating a quick snack, I called AJ on his cell. He answered immediately.

"Hi Mom." He sounded tense.

"Why do you sound so tense? Marnie's the one who's having problems. My intuition was humming this morning when I thought of her."

"Great radar, Mom. We've got a serious family problem. Can you come up for air from the books for a day or two? We need to have a family meeting tonight."

BETRAYAL by SERPENT

"I'm up for air from the books. I just need one more jump drive. I was calling to tell you what I found. It's stunning, but your news first. What's this about? What's happening? Where are you?"

"I'm on my way home, coming up from Chicago. I'll wait until I get home to tell you. Plan on all of us for supper. Sammi and Alicia too. They're with me. I'll pick up a jump drive for you."

He ended the call. Chicago? Now what? My radar reviewed each of them. Marnie, really not ok. Cory and Alex, ok. Get ready. It's the next crisis. My quiet one is not doing well.

I called Klarkowski. He wasn't in. Is that man ever in? I left a long and detailed message and asked him if he could meet with me tomorrow. I called Clayton too. Same.

Everything is put away in one of the Hidey Holes. I feel empty now.

While I waited for AJ and the girls, I went to the florist and bought a bouquet of golden roses. I walked south along the path to St. Francis Park and left it where Conrad died.

Two questions remain...
Who killed him?
Who runs the group now?

Sixty-eight

AJ was home in two hours. He'd been north of Milwaukee when I called and flew low the rest of the way. Before he'd tell me what was happening, he asked me for a quick summary of what I had found. I got out all the papers and walked him through it.

"I thought you had gotten through more of Conrad's files when you had the computer." I said.

He shook his head. "Nothing like this. I got into some of it but I didn't have the rest of the papers and certainly not the ledgers or the Mayan book. Not enough time either. It sure makes a lot more sense now that I see all this. I'm not surprised, Mom, that he was in such a dirty business. It makes me sick."

I gave him his copy on the flash drive.

"I don't believe I know the whole story yet. I do know I can't take this much farther. I've called Klarkowski and asked for an appointment tomorrow."

I looked at his worried face. "Now tell me what's going on."

"Mom, I just spent time in Chicago looking for Marnie. She's going to need our help. She's having nightmares. She's drinking, using pot, maybe harder drugs, hiding it from everyone or trying to. Sammi and Alicia called me. They confronted her before Christmas but she wouldn't listen to them. I went to Chicago to find her. She wasn't there. They told me she's here in Green Bay. She's been here in town, hiding from all of us."

"But, AJ, she seemed all right before Cancun, and when she was there, and even since then. I haven't noticed a thing. She's been where? I thought she was in Madison, not in Chicago and now she's here? We have to go to her."

He stopped me when I jumped up.

"I know where she is and she's in a safe place. I asked her if she wants help and she does. So I took the bull by the horns. I'm sorry for not consulting you but you've been busy and so have I. This all came up really fast. As far as seeing symptoms, she's probably still very good at hiding them, disguising them. It would take a professional to recognize her symptoms. Hopefully, she won't be too far into addiction yet."

He was watching my expression closely.

"Mom, I know paying attention to these books is something you had to do. Please don't feel guilty. Marnie's a grown woman. She's responsible for herself. She could have asked for help but, true to form, she chose to withdraw."

I knew he was right but I did feel guilty. And very, very angry at Art. His own daughter. His little girl. Daddy's girl. Using the drugs he helped bring to this area. The colors I see now are a deep dirty red mixed with acid green.

AJ updated me on what he'd done.

"I have a counselor coming over tonight. She's very experienced in both the alcohol and drug field and the mental health field. I want her to do an intervention. I sat in on several in Minnesota and these can really work. Because I'm a doctor, I can also get help for her at a good treatment center. I've got a call in to Hazelden. It's expensive but they're the best. The biggest hurdle will be that she'll have to go through a detox program at a regular hospital first and she might balk at that. I have some places alerted. The key is to get her in and follow through with it all right away."

He continued. "I hate to tell you this but you look like death warmed over. You're still recovering from being shot, from being kidnapped and roaming a jungle for days. Mom, this is one situation where you have to let the pros take over."

I sagged into a chair. "You know what? My emotions for the last weeks have been so intense I'm wrung out. I won't argue with you. I'm very tired. I need a long rest. Marnie won't open up to me anyway. She retreated years ago when her father died and I think she's retreating now because she doesn't want to even think her father is involved in anything bad. Modeling seemed like it might be a good thing, a way for her to come out of herself. She won't be able to do that on drugs. I'll back anything you and the counselor decide, but I'm a little nervous at this 'intervention'.

"Good. The backing, I mean, not the nervousness. Although, when I think about it, it might do Marnie good to see you nervous and scared. We've all expected you to be strong for us and you expect that of yourself. We could use a lesson in seeing you as human.

"She's really had Sammi and Alicia worried. They didn't have my phone number. They were afraid to tell you. Sammi finally was in town a few weeks ago, saw Cory and he gave her my number. Part of me would like to tell Marnie just to knock it off and get her act together but if I do that, she'll just push me away and retreat more. She doesn't have your guts, Mom."

He went to get her and bring her home. I sat down with Sammi and Alicia and they filled me in on what they'd seen.

We had the intervention. The counselor, whose name was Sandra, took the lead. I broke down and cried. Cory got really mad, which he usually never does. Alex got silent, frightened. Marnie agreed to treatment when she saw the reactions from us all. AJ and Marnie left immediately afterward for Minnesota to detox at a hospital and she will be in Hazelden soon.

My rage at Art has not lessened with the knowledge that drugs my husband helped introduce into this town could kill our daughter.

If Art were here, if he were alive, would he care that his own daughter had been hurt by his greed? I don't think so.

Mental inventory: Tomorrow, make that final copy to the flash drive. Get that stuff out of the way and out of the house. Hug my boys. Call Sammi and Alicia and tell them I love them too. REST! Tell AJ how proud I am of him. Write Marnie a letter telling her I love her. She's safe for now. Two safe in Minnesota. Away from here.

Here, something vicious still looms. It's still not over. Well, I'm going to get it over with. Show it all to Clayton and then send it to Klarkowski.

Get it out of your life, Anna.

Sixty-nine

It's early morning. I had a hard time sleeping. Guilt marched in and planted himself at the end of my bed, smirking. Helplessness, sagging woefully, stood next to him. I feel as if I've neglected Marnie somehow. Yes, she's grown up. Yes, she's responsible for her own behavior. but I know she's facing a painful part of her life. She was a scared little girl last night. Yet, she'll grow from this if she chooses. If I have learned anything in my life, it's that pain brings choice...go backward, stay stuck, or grow.

Everyone is still asleep.

Embarrassment stood at my shoulder, mocking me. I was going to give police papers that proved my husband was in the drug trade, even worse, the human trade.

Rudmann will be so happy.

I hear stirrings upstairs. They will all be down in minutes, the boys to school, Marthe to wherever she plans to go.

Just get them all off somewhere and then put your own ducks in a row, Anna. I'll need a lawyer, in case I become a suspect again. Will we need police protection? Will there be threats to us still?

I called and left yet another message for Klarkowski, briefly explaining what I discovered and asking him to come for the ledgers and miscellaneous papers as soon as possible. Then I called Clayton, again getting voice mail, and left him a summary of what I found. Anxiety made me restless.

I put it all into a large box in the library and closed the door.

By 8:30, everyone was gone and I had just gotten the dishes in the dishwasher and turned it on when the phone rang.

Clayton sounded shocked.

"Oh my god! Geez, Anna! I just learned that you got shot! I didn't know. I've been out of town on a cruise. I gotta hear about this. I got your voice mails too. I'm coming over right away. You said there were papers and ledgers. I want to hear the whole story, see what you've done, have a look at those ledgers and papers before Klarkowski gets them in his hot little hands and I have to get a court order to see them."

"Not a problem, Clayton. Come on over."

I put on coffee and got out cream and sugar and put the large box on the dining room table.

He was over in less than ten minutes, looking impossibly tan, excited at the prospect of learning more about the papers.

"Wow, Anna, you've been busy lady! So, I want the whole story. Where can I put my coat? Here on this pew? This is a pew, isn't it? Where in the world did you get this?"

I explained about the pew as I was getting his coffee. I poured more coffee into a thermos pot and brought all to the dining room on a tray. Clayton was eyeing the box.

I set the tray down on the buffet. "You should have seen the other piles of files and books we went through. It was huge. If Caroline and Marthe hadn't helped me, we'd never have gotten as far as we did. I have a copy of our findings for you."

"Are you talking about the files that Art had in the attic? Where are they now?"

"Yes, those files. The police took them."

He listened closely as I told him all we had done and what we had found.

"I'm amazed you made as much sense as you did, got as far as you did. You say Caroline and Marthe helped you? How much do they know?"

"All of it, except for what I found yesterday. Rob, and Cory and Alex and Sally, the police officer, helped to re-assemble the files after they were torn apart, but they didn't get very far into knowing what we found. Now, with what I've just discovered, I know it's a huge smuggling operation. Very organized. At least it was."

Clayton had finished his coffee.

"Can I use the bathroom, get myself some water? Can you get out what you have? This will take a while. If there's any

427

reason you might need a lawyer, I want a thorough look at this stuff before you turn it over to police."

I pointed out the bathroom and busied myself taking out the ledgers and papers again. I laid out the key to the codes and opened significant pages so I could demonstrate to him how I thought it worked.

When he returned he headed toward the front hall.

"I just need my glasses from my coat. Be right there."

I directed him to the paper with the codes first, then had him walk around to see how they were used and had changed over the years.

"I think Conrad had some original papers but I found no hard copies, just scanned copies of those."

"Can you show me again, in detail? I really need to get a grasp of this."

I took him through the ledgers step by step. As we went along he kept a running tally of the columns we thought were money taken in. When we finished he looked completely stunned.

"This amounts to hundreds of millions! Much more than I thought it did! Who got all this money? Art did, certainly. Jonny O? Very likely. Big John? Absolutely. And Conrad. Yes indeed, Conrad!"

A strange sound crept into his voice, a meanness when he said 'Conrad'. He saw my face, my look of protest. I felt a quick flash of some kind of threat.

"Now wait, Annie! Think about it! He was certainly born rich, that we know, but he got richer than I ever thought he was. That may not have been just good investments. The question is, why did he want to expose it? We'll never know that now, will we? So! The next question is, what to do with this? What to do? Have you called police?"

"Of course, and I left a summary of what I've done on Klarkowski's voice mail."

Clayton had seated himself across from me at the table, and was gazing out the window. Suddenly, my stomach tightened. The ominous malevolence was right here, present in full force. The way he looked and sat, still and seething at the same time, hit me in my gut. Before I could even put it into thoughts or words, he turned his head and stared at me and I

428

knew the source of danger. He slowly took off his glasses, carefully folded them and set them on the table.

"Well, Annie," he said very gently. "You know the old saying, curiosity kills the cat. You'll be joining Marthe's cat soon."

His voice turned very soft, an eerie parody of kindness.

"You won't be turning this over to the police. You'll be turning this over to me."

His right hand came up over the tabletop. In it was a gun with a silencer on it.

I was standing and involuntarily backed up against the hutch behind me. Surprise and fear plastered me to it.

"You can't possibly get away with this. Klarkowski will know." I started to tell him that everyone will know, that I had made many copies. I stopped myself just in time.

"Oh. I will. I'll get away with it all. I'll get my share of this if it kills you."

He gave small laugh at his joke.

"There is so much money hidden somewhere, that Swiss account, a Cayman Islands account maybe, and it's mine! I earned it. I should have had a larger share long ago, but I was kept in the dark by the grand Sir Arthur Kinnealy Sr., by Bon Vivant Jonny O'Keeffe, by Big Shot John O'Keeffe, even by my own partner Conrad. Conrad the Count! Conrad the Perfect! Conrad the Fairy! *You* have Conrad's money and that is money *I* was supposed to get. Did you think I didn't know?" he hissed, leaning forward.

He gestured with the gun. "Sit down!" he ordered. "I'm going to tell you a long story. Since you'll be dead soon I suppose you should know why." He laughed again, a giggle this time. "Don't you think that's fair of me? Especially since I let you do all the work for me?"

I watched Clayton, the man I had thought harmless, slowly letting some inner demon take over—his eyes dark blue pools where madness swam with hate—his face where furor appeared and faded, uncontrolled. I knew I was in great danger.

"Now let's see." He tilted his head to one side. "This story should begin 'Once upon a time' because it goes back a long way to when Art and company were just starting out. See,

429

they needed startup money, which they certainly didn't have. They hit up Conrad and he hit up me for some of that money. Imagine! He was heir to so much money but he hit me up! Well, I was from a wealthy family too. I could afford it I suppose. He didn't want to use all his money though. He wanted to buy art. A collector of fine art—that's what he wanted *his* money for.

"Well, they paid us back with interest, didn't they? The Bowery Boys from the West side, the Jew, and flitty fairy Moss, an old classmate of mine. Did you know we went to school together, Andy Moss and I? Oversensitive little creep! Couldn't take any teasing at all.

"They made money! Imagine, those four from the wrong side of the tracks making all that money! More than any court cases would have, could have, brought in. I knew what our firm brought in. The rumors were that they were doubling it, tripling it."

He stopped talking briefly. I waited. I thought he'd lost track of his train of thought. He began muttering, "No. Blackmail doesn't bring in enough money. Not for the tastes I have! I wanted it back, I did." His head jerked oddly.

"Conrad now, he had all the money he wanted to indulge his tastes. Like the house in Cancun. That's a beautiful house! I just visited there. Told them I was your lawyer in the US. Just passing through. Thought you might be still there. Hadn't kept up to date on where you were. Shocked! I told them. Shocked that you had suffered so much. Left them to hurry back to you. But I learned a lot. Oh yes! They seem like good people. Too bad they have to die too. Left a message with another of my contacts to kill them."

I paled at the thought of Adelina, Ramon and the others dead. It took all my self-control to keep from interrupting him.

I held myself quiet, determined to learn all I could. What had he done? Had he harmed them already? I knew he wasn't lying. Wasn't bluffing. He wanted to brag.

"What's the matter, Anna? Don't like that idea? Why should you care if some spics die? They're already murdering each other right and left. Besides, the servants at the house are Indians. They don't really count down there. Here either. An inferior race, just like Jews."

430

I could feel the hate energy pouring off him uncontrolled, uncontrollable. He was lost in it.

"Where was I? Oh, yes. Persuasion got me what I wanted. I found out what they, Art and company, were into. Very lucrative! Very lucrative indeed! I persuaded them, Art and company, to let me join them. Expenses are huge in an operation like this. You wouldn't believe the expenses! Investigations of those judges backgrounds so we could 'persuade' them to throw out cases on technicalities. Augmentation of certain judicial and police salaries. They really aren't paid much you know. Here or in Mexico. In fact, in Mexico, they pay us to hire them. Did you know that? The 'gifts' they receive are so generous that they pay us up to $400 a month to work for us. Some police down there make up to $100,000 US dollars per year! Amazing!

"Yes, these past few weeks I paid a great deal to investigate what you did down in the Yucatan. Over $5000 US to police and certain members of the Aguilar family. You know, some of them really want a higher income. They have serious needs. Don't like being told what to do by Ramon and company. They sold out the others. I knew it was possible. There are always those who will sell out for money."

He was watching my face with satisfaction. I couldn't keep the fear and disappointment from showing.

He gloated. "Anyone can be bought, Anna. Anyone."

"So let me tell you, when I read that will of Conrad's, I was very, very angry. I knew he had kept money from me. He had me investigated. Me! His partner! I was supposed to get that money. I was supposed to get more money from The Firm all these years. They held out on me. Multiple sets of books. That doesn't even cover it. They had a set of books just for the drug money. We were supposed to be partners. Art and Jonny and Big John and me. Me, who helped them get a start! They held out on me, and on the others. Oh, yes. There are others who like the good life.

"My first clue was Art buying that plane. But then he pointed out that we could use it for importing our merchandise, and we did, so I kept quiet. Then I found Conrad's list of the art he was buying in Mexico. 'Rescuing it,' he said. That's how I found out art had been added to the trade and how much money that was bringing in. They didn't tell me about that."

He had been working up more and more anger as he spoke, gesturing with the hand that held the gun, rocking forward and back. His voice alternated between high and intense and an intimate whisper. I shivered with fear and disgust.

"I found out about the young boys and girls myself. Personal experience, you might say. Monterrey is a wonderful place for little boys. I like a little on the side now and then. Oh, you needn't look so horrified! Even you must know that some of us prefer the young ones. I was discreet about that. Went out of the country for them. So much freer in other countries like Mexico, Bahrain, Thailand. Mexico is closer. That's where I learned what else our little group was doing. Was I getting any profit from it? Of course not! I had to pay for mine!"

He snarled with resentment and slammed his free hand on the table. I thought he would shoot me right then, but he seemed to have an obsessive need to talk and I wanted him to keep talking until I could figure some move to make. He began railing against Conrad.

"Conrad! Mr. Self-Righteous! Mr. Greedy for his precious works of art! Mr. Elegance and Class! Mr. Born With The Silver Spoon! I knew he had found out everything. I was not about to let him get away with that! Bastard! Fucking fairy bastard! I loved hitting him! I loved killing him as much as I'm going to love killing you! And your children! Yes, Anna, your children and everyone involved who knows anything about this! Why do you look so shocked? Did you think I'd let you all ruin what I've waited so long for? I've planned this completely.

"You'll all be dead. I'll be long gone! If I can't take over right away, my escape is all set up. My partner has the whole structure of this group under control.

"Everyone will be shocked. You, of all people, involved in the drug trade. Your whole family killed by a drug cartel because of what you did, what Art did. A West side slut who got above herself, true to her roots. Green Bay will gossip for years on your murders." He looked inordinately pleased at the thought.

432

He gazed around the dining room, waving the gun in the air. "This was my house, you know, and I'll have it again. You and your Catholic brood have fouled it up. Did you know you bought it from my family? Did you know that? I lived here before you bought it, when I was a boy. I know this place like the back of my hand. It's mine. I've been here when you were all gone. I've come in and out for years, had you watched so you didn't harm this house. I came from money. You didn't. You didn't deserve something like this. You've changed it! You had no right to do that!"

He's crazy. Jealousy and revenge and greed and madness combined. How did he keep it together all this time?

I was slumped down in the chair across from him, looking as meek as I could but hyper-alert, hoping for a phone call from Klarkowski to distract him, or for some idea of how to end this without being shot. That's when I heard what Clayton did not—a faint sound that was not part of the usual house sounds.

Is someone here? I need to keep Clayton's attention until I figure out what that is. I hope that's help. Who?

"Clayton, I don't understand some of this. How did you keep this secret in Green Bay? This is a big small town. How could you keep this from even being a rumor?"

"My dear! In this town, as in any town, money rules. How did we keep it a secret? We didn't brag. We weren't showy about the money. We agreed on that until Art bought that plane. I was glad when he went down with that plane. That was a coup on Jonny's part! Take out a partner. More money for the rest of us. Or there should have been. *I* didn't get more. Big John did though! He and Jonny made out great. There's a home in Ireland, another on the Riviera. Jenny don't know about that. She'll never know. Little bitch. That crazy woman Big John was married to didn't know about that. Smart man, Big John. Too smart for his own good. I thought I killed him up there in the mountains. Thought I got him but he got away."

I had heard sounds twice more while he spoke, a click, and soft scrapings. I couldn't imagine what that was nor could I pinpoint the direction. I cautiously glanced around, looking for some way out of this. *Don't wait for rescue by someone*

BETRAYAL *by* SERPENT

else. Form a plan and decide what you can do. Keep him talking for now. Feed his ego.

"Were you the one who had someone put the snakes in our house?"

"Oh, my god! That petty little stuff! The anaconda was that Attenborough boy's silly idea. I kinda put him up to it, knew he liked his drugs and would do whatever he could to get them, so it was easy to promise him a great high. Now, I liked the mambas better. That scared everyone! I have an underling who has a bond with deadly snakes. I use him sometimes when I want to persuade someone to obey. He enjoyed 'persuading' Attenborough to do that too. A little continuation of the theme, as it were. Just a little fun!"

"And the cat?"

"I did the cat. I have a way with animals, don't I? Pussy thought I was going to play with her. I taped her mouth shut and worked fast. Ripped the tape off when I was done and just strolled away.

"Now, the letters I sent to you. That took a little more doing. Actually a lot more. I've had you and your children watched for ages, know every move you make. I have five men on that. Hired the entire firm. Expensive but worth every penny to keep you all in my sights."

Pretend naiveté, I told myself but I was shuddering inside at the coldness of his mind, his enjoyment of cruelty, at the violation I felt from his secret intrusion into our lives.

"It took four of you to run this before. How can you do this all on your own now?"

"My dear, I don't do this on my own. I have gathered a few like minds, my kind, who like to make money, who like to make people do what they want, who like to do what I like to do. It's done in many towns and cities. We find each other. We have a fine tolerance for each other's eccentricities."

"I don't understand."

He looked at me with contempt and yet some interest.

"No. I suppose you wouldn't understand. You don't seem to have much interest in sex. You haven't had a man for years. I call you the Virgin Anna, except you aren't really a virgin, are you? Five pregnancies do not a virgin make!"

434

He smirked at me, enjoying my discomfort as he spoke about my sex life.

"Men with my tastes in sex, for example, can find each other easily these days. The internet you see. We have our own 'gentlemen's club'. Not that strip joint over on Main Street that pretends to be a fancy place. We have our own group and our own little 'sweet ones', our own meeting place. You would be quite surprised to learn who we are. A doctor. A priest. A photographer. Professional men only. We don't allow riffraff."

"You have sex with children?" I could not disguise my horror.

"Of course! You really are quite dim-witted. That's what I've been talking about. You needn't look so disgusted! They want it! They love it!"

The look on his face, the desire in his eyes, made me decide it was time to make a move. I couldn't listen to any more of this.

Even if he succeeds in killing me, he can't get away with it now. The evidence will be all over this room, the house. What if...?

He banged his free hand on the table, rage in his eyes, and I jumped. And at that moment I realized there was someone else in the house and they were near. I can't describe how I knew. I just knew. But rescuing me was up to me.

"You stupid, naïve woman! This all has to do with my livelihood. That million plus you saw on one of those papers is just one part of what we make. And it is we. It is men you can't stop, men who prefer to live above and beyond anything your little life and Conrad's little life are worth. You've been lucky so far, but your luck has run out. I got rid of Conrad and you will be gone today. Today." He slammed his fist down again.

"I know you've called Klarkowski and told him what you found. He won't believe you. I have an impeccable reputation. I have already told them you knew about your husband's illegal activities, were his accomplice. I will give them proof, quite convincing, the ledgers, the key written in Art's hand and in your possession. Lying to police all this time. Withholding evidence. And after I kill you, I will see that your children have accidents, one by one. You won't be here to stop me."

He stood up abruptly, the gun wavered to the side a bit.

BETRAYAL by SERPENT

Now! I dove headfirst under the table, slid across the floor, grabbed for his legs and pulled. The gun went off. I saw a large rock on the floor in the kitchen door and two small hands pulling away from it. *Liam!*

I had hoped that Clayton would fall backward but instead he only stumbled and caught himself and a shot whistled by my shoulder under the table.

Letting go of him, I rolled to my right. As he bent over to look under the table, I was up and crawling toward the kitchen door. I grabbed the rock and rolled myself around into the back hall. He shot again and hit the door jamb. I flattened myself against the wall just around the corner and stood.

No one is here. Where are they?

As Clayton, enraged, charged around the corner, I brought the rock down on his shoulder, then up to his jaw. He staggered slightly. His gun hand was swinging toward me and I caught it with my other hand and pushed up and forward with all my might. My momentum slammed us into the far cupboards. The gun went off again. I pulled him toward me, backing up a few steps so I could yank him farther forward off balance, then quickly slammed him into the cupboard again. His free arm came up and he knocked the rock out of my hand. He kept holding the gun and wouldn't let go.

I heard Caitlin's voice yell "Girl's fight!" I knew exactly what she meant. I drew his gun hand down to my mouth and bit his wrist to the bone, grabbed his lower lip with my free hand and yanked down on it. He screamed and dropped the gun. I pulled him forward again by his lip and slammed him back again. His body sagged and, adrenaline racing through me, I picked him up and threw him across the kitchen. Then Caitlin was standing next to me and handed me the gun.

"The police are outside. We heard everything he said." She turned. "You can come up now, boys." They all crowded up from the back hall. I heard Klarkowski's voice telling the boys to get out of his way.

Clayton was back on his feet ready to attack again. Klarkowski looked uncertain as Clayton began to talk.

"These women have been attacking me. I want them charged with assault! I was just here to find out what she's..." he indicated me with a nod "...been up to. I've suspected her of involvement in selling drugs for a long time. Her husband was doing just that and the proof is on the table in the dining room. I tricked her into showing me what was there. She knew all about it."

He straightened into a proper lawyerly position, expecting to be taken seriously.

Caitlin laughed. "Boys! Show the police what you have." Sean stepped forward. In his hand was a small tape recorder. He explained that he recorded most of what Clayton had said. He looked directly at Clayton and told him, "I heard you. I recorded you. I'll be a witness that you said you're the one running the drug ring.

"Absurd!" Clayton spluttered, but his arrogant stance slumped down a notch.

"There's more." Caitlin said that softly, but she was rigid with anger, her hands in fists. She turned to Sean. "Get Liam."

He went down the back steps, took his little brother's hand and brought him up to the kitchen.

"Is this the man? You can tell us. We won't let him hurt you."

Liam nodded and started crying and turned into Caitlin's waiting arms.

Sean stood as rigid as his mother had been.

"This is the man who's been sexually abusing my little brother. We have proof. We have a hospital test and this recording. He admitted he sexually abuses boys."

I was also rigid with anger. "He's one of the men who have been running the drug operation around here. I have more proof of what the others' did. The papers I have here will fit with what you have at the station. He admitted to me he was in on it, although he didn't know everything. I'll be happy to testify."

Klarkowski turned and handcuffed Clayton. "You have the right to remain silent..." and so on.

As he was being taken to the front door Clayton spoke, looking at me, his face a cold mask.

"You are a dead woman!"

When he was out the door, I slumped against the wall. "What the hell took you so long? I thought someone would never come. He's crazy! I've got to get to a phone."

My fear is destroying me. I've tried to call Ramon again and again and only get voice mail. I'm so worried he and Adelina and other family members may be dead.

AJ is on a plane to Mexico to find out what happened.

Seventy

...next day, Thursday...

Greg Klarkowski called this morning.

"Clayton has confessed to the murders of Conrad and Andy, the attempted murder of Big John, as well as given up the names of the men in the group of pedophiles. He also trashed Conrad's house. He denies Sam's murder. He says that was ordered by someone he doesn't know. I think he's telling the truth there.

"There's more. Can I come over later and use your office again? Meet and question everyone involved? I also want any more details if there are any to be gotten."

"I'll call them all. Everyone will want to know what you've found out. Give me a half hour to connect with everyone to set a time and I'll call you back.

"Greg, I'm terribly worried about the Aguilar family. AJ's in Mexico but hasn't connected with them yet. Can you call there? Find out something through police?"

"I'll try but can't promise anything."

We all met late this afternoon.

When Klarkowski arrived, Ben was with him, both of them dripping from the cold rain March skies were shedding on us.

I had hot drinks and juices for everyone and we all crowded around our dining room table, which I'd had the boys extend to its full length of ten feet. Marthe helped me serve.

Caroline and Rob brought the twins. They, Alex and Cory, and Aunt Carrie were in high spirits. Cait and her boys were subdued. Surrounded by his brothers, who kept reassuring him he'd be ok, Liam looked like an angry cornered badger, which is a very dangerous animal.

Woe to anyone who tries to harm him now. He's got his own private army. And they'll all fight.

Klarkowski, looking fresh, rested, suit pressed, was also in high spirits...

...well, as high as he gets. Not quite the level of adolescent boys or Aunt Carrie. If I didn't know better, I'd actually think she's flirting with him. Damn. She is flirting with him.

Under the pretext of serving her more coffee, I pressed my hand firmly into her shoulder, brought my mouth down to her ear level and quietly murmured, "Knock it off!" through my toothy smile. She rolled her eyes and murmured back, "It's my life". I murmured, "It's my house."

That's all we had time for. Klarkowski began to speak.

"First, I want to thank you all for coming. I know this was short notice. Second, this is still part of our investigation and I'm here to enlist your continued cooperation with us. Third, I'll ask you to hold questions for later. Now, as I told Anna on the phone this morning, Clayton Foster has confessed to the murders of Conrad Wentworth and Andrew Moss, whose death he ineptly tried to set up to look like a suicide. He has also given us the names of all the men in the group of pedophiles..."

"What's that?" asked Liam.

There was a long moment of silence as we realized that he wouldn't know that term.

Cait put her arm around him. When she spoke I heard the anger in her voice. "That's what they call men who do to children what Mr. Foster did to you. It's another name for a..."

"Mom." Sean gave her a warning look. "Not now. Not here."

She jerked her face away, hard lines breaking into hurt as she fought not to cry.

"What Mom said, dude. A grown-up name for the kind of man who does creepy stuff to kids."

"Oh. Is that a bad thing to call someone like him?"

"Yeah, dude. A real bad thing."

"Good. Then I'll call him a pedophile too."

Klarkowski took a deep breath and continued. "We also know now that Clayton Foster is the source of the letters that you and your family received, Anna, even before Conrad was your lawyer. He has an obsession with this house, believes it is his by right since he grew up here. His father lost it many years ago, declaring bankruptcy. Later, he became jealous of Conrad's attention to you and angry at his employment of you. Clayton did have five men watching you. He hoped to keep you intimidated, especially you, Anna.

"After Conrad's murder, he wanted to be sure you kept him as your lawyer so he could know what you were up to. It seems he's always been envious of Conrad Wentworth, envious of his sophistication, his..."

"What's envious and saw-fist-whatever that word is?"

"Hush! I'll explain later." Cait looked embarrassed.

Cait embarrassed? That's a first!

To his credit, Klarkowski seemed to realize he wasn't going to get anywhere with Liam or a roomful of boys by limiting questions. He patiently explained to Liam what he meant, then took up his narrative where he left off.

"Clayton's envy extended to Mr. Wentworth's looks, his good taste, his money, everything. He was sure that Conrad was making money on the drug trade, or, if not, that they both should be. Clayton shows only contempt for Conrad's ethics. His envy goes far back before Art bought the plane, when Jonny O was making so much money and when Big John O'Keeffe's construction company was doing so well, even to his childhood contempt for Moss. He was and is furious that he'd not made money the other men were bringing in and he's been attempting to take over the drug trade up here. That's why he went to Mexico, under the guise of being on a cruise. I don't know yet who he spoke to there or if he was successful at making contact with a cartel. I also don't have any news yet on the Aguilar family."

Klarkowski had seen my face cloud up at the mention of Mexico.

"Mr. Wentworth, for his part, began his search many years ago on the suspicion that something was not right in the legal and judicial systems in Green Bay. With the death of Art, he became even more suspicious."

Klarkowski had to stop to define "contempt", "ethics", and "suspicious". Caitlin finally told Liam to write down the words he didn't understand and she'd explain later. He told her he couldn't write words he didn't know because he

441

couldn't spell them. Sean said he'd do that. Klarkowski smiled at them both in gratitude.

That look was more than gratitude! He's interested in her!

He continued. "Because Mr. Wentworth already had a home in Cancun, he spent time down there carefully questioning police, consulate and embassy personnel, and others. He had already become involved in the illegal art trade due to his love of art and his horror at what might happen to all of it. Interpol will be filling us in on that.

"Anna, we know Conrad had found information on the illegal trade in children and had begun to do something about ending it. He went to senators and representatives in Washington, D.C., and to the Mexican government. I'm sorry we withheld his papers from you but the leads he left law enforcement are being followed and we couldn't and still can't discuss the details. I just want you to know that those papers have been very helpful to international law enforcement."

"I want to know if you know anything that will help the Aguilar family and help Adelina find her son."

"I'm afraid we don't. I wish I could promise you we would know that but I'm only party to the cases up here, not in Mexico. And I'll talk to you later about those computers."

He didn't look pleased. Too bad. He'll get an earful from me about withholding information.

"The main reason I'm here now is our local investigations into these murders and into drug trafficking here in northern Wisconsin. I've asked you all to be here because we need your help. We want to go over all you know again. I know you've been questioned before but we're looking for any clues, even the slightest bits of information you might remember, rumors you've heard..." he looked at Cait's boys "...on the streets, anything.

"Anna, I know it's not easy for you, but I'd like to ask you to go over with us again your entire memory of all you experienced prior to and after your husband's death. We want the whole picture in the clearest detail possible. We're going to have you come down to the station and walk us through the connections you made from the papers you just processed. By us, I mean several police departments, the FBI, possibly

Mexican national law enforcement and Interpol. There are some honest men in Mexico who want to stop this. You will want to have a lawyer with you."

"Am I under suspicion of participating in that, of aiding the men who were involved years ago? I want the truth out in the open now. I want to know I'm clear of any suspicion."

I shushed the protest from Alex and Cory and waited. Klarkowski looked a bit embarrassed. "I don't quite know how to put this without offending you somewhat so I'll just say it. We strongly considered that but we've come to the conclusion that you were unbelievably naïve back then and couldn't have run a drug ring if someone tried to teach you. We see your husband as a skillful manipulator who nevertheless got himself in over his head when he tried to play with the big boys of the cartels in Mexico. That he was relying on backing from Jon O'Keeffe was another great mistake. Jon O'Keeffe was his father's pawn. When Big John learned that Art had tried to deal with the cartels on his own, your husband was murdered. We think Big John ordered his murder, and Jon O'Keeffe helped set it up. I'm sorry. For the sake of you and your children, I wish I could say that isn't so, but it is. No sugar-coating that, I'm afraid."

He was looking at the boys with deep regret in his eyes. I moved behind Alex and Cory and stood with my hands on their shoulders.

"Just so you boys know too, we know you're nothing like your father. From what we've learned, your dad had a bad hand dealt him as a kid and it left him with big flaws, although it appears he really loved you. People we've talked to say he bragged about you, was proud of how you were turning out."

"So his flaws got him killed, didn't they now." The bitterness in Cory's voice ripped at my heart.

"And left us without him." Alex breathed out the words as if he had a great weight inside pushing them out. I could only hold their hands. Innocence and trust and belief destroyed.

The malevolence was gone: the terrible sadness will remain for always.

BETRAYAL by SERPENT

Klarkowski questioned each person involved. Liam will be interviewed by an expert in sexual abuse, with Cait, Sean, a counselor and social worker present.

He took me aside before he left.

"Anna, we think there's still someone out there who's keeping a very low profile, but who knows how to reorganize this. Clayton clammed up when we tried to find out if there were others under deeper cover. He won't talk about that at all. He keeps insisting he's the one but he doesn't have the personality, the control, or the skills to run something like we're seeing. I think you and your family and friends are safe for now but just be warned.

"I'm ignoring that you withheld information from us."

At that, I blew. "You stop right there. If you'd been forthcoming with me about the papers you found the night Conrad was killed, maybe this would have been out in the open weeks ago. Also I had no clue these things were related to any files Art kept. You got those files with my full cooperation and I'm the one who got shot, not you. Would you like to discuss this further?"

He was silent, looking at me sharply.

"I mean that about getting a new lawyer, a good one. I don't believe you've been involved but there are those who aren't convinced you're quite so innocent. I'm sure you know who I mean."

"Yes. It may take me a while to find someone."

"Call me as soon as you do."

They will strip my memories from me again.

How often does a person have to do this to have the memories leave? I suspect the answer is never. Ghosts. Always ghosts.

The phone rang and I grabbed it, Alex, Cory and Marthe right next to me. I put it on speaker.

"Mom," AJ sounded calm, no tenseness in his voice.

"Everyone's all right. Jorge Aguilar's security team became suspicious of Clayton when he was here and stepped up guards. There was an attempt on their lives but Jorge succeeded in getting police to cooperate and two men are in jail.

After the others' questions were answered, he had me turn the speaker off and he continued.

"It's tense here, Mom, but they're all safe. Right after you left, Ramon had to go to the mountains and move his kids because someone found out where they lived and they were under threat too. We have them all safe now. I'll be home soon, but right now, he'd like to talk with you."

We spoke for an hour. He will come up when I am questioned by law enforcement, and I will be going to Mexico when the boys are safe in their summer activities.

Danger has brought us closer.

Seventy-one

...journal...May...excerpts from the aftermath...

I've been so busy this journal has been written in bits and pieces.

It took me two weeks to find a new lawyer. Several firms declined. I have a woman, Abigail Woodman, from an Appleton firm, thirty years of experience, including international law and a stint as a district attorney. She likes high profile cases and mine is certainly that. She's handling the media for our family, thank god. It's been fierce.

Abigail was with me as I went through my journals one more time. Klarkowski, a representative from the FBI, police from Mexico, and numerous other law enforcement officials then had me go over all the ledgers and computer files again. This time there were no holds barred by law enforcement.

Ramon was there as a witness, with AJ and Mac, to what happened in Mexico. Cory and Alex were witness to what happened in Green Bay. Grace was there. She came out of retirement to be there, knowing I might fall apart. She used EMDR to help me remember, then hypnosis to help release the trauma. It took five days. It was grueling but I held up pretty well, and lost it only once, when I had to describe what I heard beyond the fire the night I escaped.

I was ordered to have a psychiatric exam. I passed with flying colors. The psychologist noted I was "remarkably skilled at coping with trauma." Surprise, surprise.

Hoping to find out about Adelina's son, I kept asking for lists of children by name, or even by city, or anything. Those they kidnapped, bought, and abused remain nameless.

There is a grand jury investigation into the involvement of certain law enforcement and judicial individuals in a long list of drug and other cases. Klarkowski tells me the drug trade in this area has slowed for now.

The picture of Art that emerged was not pretty. I was able to pinpoint the change in his attitude toward me. There is no denying he chose to distance himself from me, from us. I would not be surprised to learn he had a mistress somewhere. Or several. Maybe Greed was his mistress.

Clayton is in jail awaiting trial on numerous charges. His lawyer is trying to plead insanity. That's not going to happen. The prosecution has his successful work history to point to. On the pedophilia charges, Liam and Sean's testimony will be a start. The publicity brought others who were harmed to the police. Seven so far. We learned Sean discovered Liam right after Clayton had ended a 'session' with him and got him to a hospital.

Caitlin and other parents are raising hell with social services. It seems others had reported him as suspicious and nothing had been done. I added my testimony about what Clayton had said to me but their testimony will be what convicts him.

Liam has a good therapist. Caitlin and I went looking for someone who is an expert in trauma. Jenny O has been a great help to him, sharing what happened to her and letting him know he can feel better about himself. She explained that it's like a deep cut or wound, that he would have to clean all the infection out and then it will heal. He will have a scar and the scar will hurt from time to time but he won't be wounded like that again.

I hope.

The priest Clayton mentioned was first moved to another diocese. Others came forward to say he'd abused them. They're still trying to bring him to trial. I have left the church. I am so angry, not at God, but at the men in the church who cover this up.

The photographer was found to have a large collection of porn on his computer, most of which he created using young children. He was selling it on the internet. He'll go to prison.

BETRAYAL by SERPENT

No one besides Clayton and Attenborough have been charged yet with any drug-related offenses.

...journal...April, May and June notes...

Aunt Carrie, Marthe, my kids, Caroline and Rob and their boys, Mac and Ramon were much entertained with the story of my "knock-down, drag-out fight" with Clayton, as told by Caitlin and her boys.

Ramon and I had almost no time together here in Green Bay.

We don't expose MomKat to anything distressing anymore. Her dementia has progressed to mid-stage. She's in a very private residential home where they have her sing a lot. She loves that. As soon as they play the old songs, she stands up and starts singing. I love it. I go when I can and sing right along with her.

Ramon enjoyed one of our sing-a-longs before he flew back.

Interpol called me and I had to fly back to Cancun, then immediately to Sotheby's in Mexico City. By the time we were done I was well acquainted with police of several nations because they came from Italy, France, and England looking for their lost art.

Ramon was with me but again we were rarely alone and I had to fly north right away.

AJ is with Doctors without Borders in Guatemala. He and Ramon began working on plans for the clinic in the southern area of the Yucatan. He's learning and preserving medicine from the last of the direct descendants of the Maya, the Lacandon tribe. They've recorded the medicinal knowledge of the curanderas in Ramon's family too. One of AJ's classmates from medical school, a very pretty girl, has joined him. I'm eager to meet her.

They are lovers.

Alex graduated and we had a great party for him. He has a summer job as a camp counselor and will leave for Belize

448

Judith M Kerrigan

in late August for the first part of his gap year and goes to China for the rest. I was worried about the danger from a cartel in Belize. He decided to use my maiden name for now. The publicity is still fierce. He has his own guard who is there as his 'fellow student'.

Marnie's career will take her to Paris for fall fashion week. She remains straight and sober and seems much happier, if distant. She completed treatment. We all took the family treatment workshop at Hazelden. I even took her Girls along. We have a much greater understanding of what addiction is and what it does. She attends NA in Chicago, where she met a model, a longtime member, who is her sponsor. She has not chosen to confide in me. That hurts a little. I'm learning to let go. I attend Alanon with fair regularity. I should have done it years ago. It would have helped me deal with the drinking members of our family and the west side neighborhood.

Aunt Carrie confessed to me she is the woman in the painting with Conrad. She refused to say any more except "We had very interesting younger days." She then took off to Chicago where she can assist Marnie in her modeling career. I want details! I'll corner her when I get to Paris.

Marthe now lives in Conrad's Green Bay house, showing it when we need to have a show house for the business. Her book is selling moderately well. She has a beautiful white longhaired cat she calls Princess. Madame Queen would be a better name. She also has a guard dog who was already named Prince, after the rock star. There is a slight resemblance.

Caitlin and her boys live in The House while their house is being renovated as one of the model Irish cottages of the west side and she and Caroline run the decorating business from the library. Cory lives with them and is singing with a rock band so is off on his gigs whenever they're booked. In September he begins his senior year and then he'll take his gap year in England learning acting and stagecraft. I maintain a

449

small room in The House but I don't belong there anymore. I don't quite know where I belong anymore.

We employ a security firm and there are discreet bodyguards wherever anyone goes. Mine, Melissa, travels as my "personal assistant". She's teaching me hand-to-hand combat.

The House is guarded by three dogs, which is where Caitlin drew the line. Sort of. All five of her boys wanted their own pets. The iguana adds panache. Supposedly the tarantula never leaves its cage. Same for the gerbils.

Her boys are all learning Tae Kwan Do.

I researched the history of The House. Clayton did grow up there. It had been owned first by his grandparents. His grandfather was the one who dug out the long passage in the hillside, apparently for use during prohibition, which seems to have augmented the family fortune quite a bit. It's now filled in.

I'm writing all of this in Mexico. For now, Ramon and I are together in my Cancun house. We make no plans for our future, loving each other day by day.

Adelina has gathered a group of women from Puerto Juarez and we're getting input from them on what they want to have taught in the new school. I've leased the land for them in the hopes that no politician or wealthy landowner will take it away from a rich American woman, whereas they might from Mayan people. The men are working on the building already. I'm looking at starting a bank modeled on the Grameen bank in India.

The search goes on for Adelina's son. She doesn't want to give up, although once she said she knows he could be dead. She said she doesn't really feel that's true though.

Ramon took me to see his wife. She is still in a mental institution. He still loves her deeply. She didn't recognize him when we went there. A nurse said her paranoia is much worse and she isn't responding to meds anymore. She's tried suicide several times in the past year and attacked staff too. It is so sad.

His mother still rears his children, Angel and Juanita. She doesn't approve of me. They're very close to her and I know she'd feel terrible if anything happened to them. She thinks if I'm around the cartel will target them. I hired guardians for them and that eased her mind somewhat. They are a joy. We've taken them swimming and diving at the sea turtle farm at the southern end of Isla Mujeres and to other entertainments and family gatherings. They find my Spanish amusing and are on a campaign to improve it.

Ramon did tear up the paper found at the site. He had found it in the gallery at the house. When he opened the house, he was astounded by the art there.

"I became suspicious that something was not right about it but I could not find out anything. When I learned about Lindy, I went down to the dig to find out more about what was going on from men I knew. I discovered the art was gotten illegally. Even before you arrived I was trying to decide what to do about it. Reporting it to police would only result in its return to the illegal trade. I did not have time or a secure way to contact Interpol.

"I am much relieved that you will send the beautiful art back to the owners, Anna. I did not want you to be in trouble for something Señor Wentworth had done. I did not know the significance of the writings on the paper at the time but I was worried, very worried that you and AJ would be considered part of the cartel, or that someone in the cartel would attack you trying to get the works of art back. AJ is my friend, my brother. You are my love. I wanted you both to be safe."

I invited friends and relatives down to Cancun for two weeks. Ramon took us to every site he could and was a fund of information for us all. Aunt Carrie flirted outrageously with Mexican men and almost got herself into trouble one night. I rescued her and she owes me.

The Fitz boys learned a whole new world of cultures and will learn more. I've scheduled an Ireland trip for us all prior to the Paris shows. Afterward I travel to Switzerland. Rob got in touch with the bank and with the man Conrad named in his letter. I negotiated with Rob and his partners and they will be expanding their firm and hiring experts who can help me manage my holdings. I want someone I trust to help me.

451

I have not taken Jane's and Mac's warnings or Clayton's threat lightly. I know too much. The cartels are viciously busy. Drug wars on the US-Mexican border are horrible. Total casualties number in the tens of thousands. There's evidence, not just rumor, of a yet another cartel using the Yucatan for its base to transport its merchandise. Activity in southern Yucatan on the coast is increasing. Rumors still persist that one cartel is headed by a gringo or a former Mexican policeman. We are told there is war between them for control. Ramon and I are followed. We've reinforced the security of the house in Cancun and the homes of anyone associated with us, especially the Aguilar family, who have moved into their own family compound, a former hacienda west of Cancun. Jorge is expanding the family's security business. He has many clients. Everyone is nervous. The city of Monterrey is now the scene of brutal murders, in addition to the border wars.

I haven't heard from Lindy or Ian. Ramon and I went down to the dig. It's going strong and there is another archaeologist in charge. He doesn't know where they are. Simoneska was reassigned to a dig in the Middle East. From the frying pan into the fire!

Cait called. She is furious. Somehow, Clayton is out on bond awaiting trial, although he is on a bracelet. I listened to her vent for a full half hour. She takes solace in the fact that she's in charge of The House and by devious ways made sure he knows it.

She's dating Greg Klarkowski. Well, actually, they've gone beyond the dating stage. He's close to retirement and including her in his plans for that. He has *no* idea what he's getting into. She wants to visit us and have the roof for their bedroom.

Seventy-two

I called Klarkowski before I left for Mexico.

"Greg, I can't get one thing out of my mind. It's what Clayton said about someone who can reconstruct the whole northern drug scene. There's only one other person who had the complete trust of Conrad and Clayton, who had access to everything and everyone they both knew and did. You know who I mean."

"Yes, and we can't find her. No daughter in Arizona. No Seacrest at all. She's disappeared without a trace. We have no leads on her. She's not in any system.

"We think she's been collecting information for years from both law firms, and that she might be that someone Clayton Foster talked about to you, but his hatred of women is fierce and his ego won't let him even think a woman could take control. He's given us nothing more. And he may not really know who it is. If she is the one who can reorganize it, she kept a very low profile and might not ever have let him know. It appears she fooled even Conrad.

"Watch your back, Anna."

Epilogue

Dream...

I see the eyes of the jaguar just before she leaps at me. Expecting raking teeth, I lift my arms in front of me to defend myself. To my surprise, I feel the thump of the jaguar as she lands inside me. I feel her heightened senses, her prowling spirit, her desire to hunt.

This desire to prowl is intense. Restless! On guard! I hear leaves brush against us, insects in the grasses, birds in the trees, and humans, smell the humans, a sick smell, reeking of some poison! They sit around a fire and make their noises.

A scream comes from the far side of the fire. A human is on the ground moving up and down over something. I hear groans, moaning, heavy breathing. He gets up and staggers away. Another takes his place. Another scream splits the air.

A human gets up and picks up a small bundle and throws it away, into the night. Jaguar and I move through the jungle and around the fire, silently, stealthily, to see what is there. I feel a growing horror, a screaming pain, a deep terror.

I see the child. Jaguar is leaving me, repelled by the smells of poison and sickness. I am crying.

The moon comes out from behind clouds. A sign is stamped on the child's forehead, the sign of cold and frozen Death.

I look into the jungle and it dissolves. There are bodies of children as far as my eyes can see. They rise, one by one, moving slowly and sadly through piles of papers scattered on the ground. When they reach the Pyramid of the Feathered Serpent, they climb up the steps on hands and knees.

I feel an Eagle soar into me and I am raised up over the pyramid, hovering in the air, waiting for food.

The tlatoani stands at the top, obsidian knife raised. He brings it down and raises his other hand. Blood drips from it.

BETRAYAL by SERPENT

The heart on the plate is still beating, spraying more blood. Priests toss the body down the steps of the pyramid and the sacrifice is done.

More are coming. Hundreds of men, women and children form a long procession up the steps, stretching across the courtyard below, and out along the sacbe.

Eagle and I soar down over them. All are branded. I read the glyphs on their foreheads. Child of man. Man. Child of woman. Woman. We reach the end of the line and I am dropped from the talons of the Eagle to the edge of a lake below. On my hands and knees, I see my face in the water. I am branded. My brand is different. It is the glyph for Bala'am, jaguar.

The waters of the lake become deep and total blackness. Someone is waiting for me in the depths. I hear the words, "She is the sacrifice." Terror freezes me. I can't breathe.

I wake gasping for breath. Another nightmare. The pictures of the glyphs branding the children hang in the dark night surrounding me. I let myself cry silently, knowing, now and always, that children and women are being kidnapped, sold, raped, and killed.

Will it ever end?

Ramon slides his body along mine, one arm wrapping over me, his breath mingling with mine, his lips on my eyes, drinking my tears.

"Querida, soy aquí. Te amo." His whispers open my heart. I pull him onto me, wrapping my arms around his body, my legs around his legs, inviting him inside me. For now, there is love.

For now, Ramon and I have had a whole month to ourselves. The colors of my world are brilliant and warm. We touch with love and respect and adoration and passion, with our minds and hearts and spirits. Even without touch, our minds and spirits mesh. Healing! Amazing!

Pure grace!

ABOUT THE AUTHOR

Judith M. Kerrigan is the nom de plume of Judith Kerrigan Ribbens, a visual artist, amateur photographer and writer. She holds a Bachelor's Degree in Human Development, University of Wisconsin-Green Bay; a Master's Degree in Expressive Arts Therapies, Lesley University, Cambridge, MA and is a Licensed Professional Counselor in Wisconsin. She has been a counselor for over twenty years, including thirteen years as a crisis counselor.

A mother, grandmother and great-grandmother, *Betrayal by Serpent* is her first novel and was begun at the age of seventy-four and completed two years later.

Born in Green Bay, she was a longtime resident and has an extensive family background there. She now resides in the Wisconsin countryside.

A second book in this series of three, *Revenge of the Crocodile*, is in its beginning stages. The third book will be titled *The Jaguar Hunts*. Tentative publishing dates are 2014 and 2016 respectively.

Judy holds a limited number of expressive arts playshops each year for groups who wish to arrange these.
Contact 920-471-8500
Please arrange six months in advance. Thank you.

Book signings may be scheduled at least one month ahead.
Contact information:
Email: jkerriganwriter@yahoo.com

Websites and Blog:
For much more on the writing of this book,
its characters, settings, events and illustrations of The House
and Mayan art, go to
www.judithkerriganribbens.com

For online galleries of visual works:
www.artid.com/judyribbens

To purchase prints and canvases of selected works:
www.fineartamerica.com/judyribbens

"Writing this book has been much more fun than all the
reports, assessments, papers, etc., I've ever done. I hope all
readers enjoy it as much as I have."

10209536R10262